GODS IN THE RUINS

A Vatican Archives Thriller

E.R. BARR

TELEMACHUS PRESS

The publisher does not have any control over and does not assume any responsibility for author or third-party websites or their content.

Cover and title page art by Howard David Johnson

Published by Telemachus Press, LLC
7652 Sawmill Road
Suite 304
Dublin, Ohio 43016
http://www.telemachuspress.com

Visit the author website:
www.talesofconorarcher.com

Categories: Fiction / Thrillers / Historical

ISBN: 978-1-951744-53-3 (eBook)
ISBN: 978-1-951744-54-0 (Paperback)

Version 2021.04.21

PRAISE FOR E.R. BARR'S
THE TALES OF CONOR ARCHER

Barr excels at world-building, using existing Native American and Celtic lore to create a rich mythic heritage all his own ... Barr also shines at characterization, making Conor and those around him well-rounded and easy to empathize with ... The use of lyrical refrains combined with the author's own Celtic-inspired verses throughout the book gives the story a larger-than-life, legendary quality similar to Homeric epics. This beautiful stylistic choice lends a certain gravitas and suspense to the story ... This book is strongly recommended for lovers of Tolkien, Pratchett, and George R. R. Martin.
—*Forward/Clarion Reviews*

From debut author Barr comes an urban-fantasy novel about an adolescent boy on the cusp of mysterious change and the strange town within which he seeks refuge ... Full of folklore and charm, the story is an inviting mix of the fantastic, the innocent, and the altogether sinister ... The book avoids the clichés of the genre while providing a swift, spiraling journey. A novel entry into the world of teenage fantasy that ultimately unfolds into a truly epic saga.
—*KirkusReviews*

This tale is epic in scope, destined to become a saga. Despite the story's magnitude, however, it takes the life of a classic campfire story. Barr's writing style is at once fast-paced, richly complex, and intensely engaging … The world of Conor Archer is carefully crafted to include real history and incorporate cross-cultural legends and lore in a manner that allows the book to be complex and multi-faceted yet easy to follow … Finally, the story itself is original and compelling … This is a book you need to read.

—*OnlineBookClub.org*

From the fantastical to the emotional, this is one book that hits on all cylinders. In fact, not since Potter has there been such a large story with so many intricate characters; except this one also gives the Celtic twist that all lovers of Irish knowledge, history and beauty will absolutely adore.

—*Feathered Quill Book Reviews*

One of the more interesting things about this book is Barr's unique blending of Celtic and Native American mythology with Christian, and especially Catholic, theology. Like in the works of C. S. Lewis … there is an underlying acknowledgment in Conor's story that God is ultimately in control of the universe and that all other magical creatures and powers are secondary in nature. Billed as a fantasy, Barr's book is darker than some and has many elements that will appeal more to the followers of horror novels than to those of the standard fantasy genre. But the author's good characterizations and intriguing mythological backdrop will undoubtedly have his fans clamoring for the sequel.

—*The U. S. Review of Books*

ROAN: THE TALES OF CONOR ARCHER by E.R. Barr is a well-written story with supernatural undertones. I am reviewing the audio version of this story, which is wonderfully delivered. The reading is clear and is delivered in a tone that respects the voice of the narrator. The pace is just right for any listener and the alternating tones will help the listener to understand and note the changes in points of view, the punctuation, dialogues, and stay engaged with the characters as the story spirals into a climax. E.R. Barr's writing is smooth and the prose sounds excellent. I loved the diction, which many readers will find familiar. The story is fast-paced and gripping. I had a lot of fun listening while driving through the rush hour traffic. *ROAN: THE TALES OF CONOR ARCHER* is a compelling story that will delight readers and have them wanting more. It was a pleasurable listening experience for me.

—Ruffino Oserio for *Readers Favorite*

I cannot say enough good things about this series. Just as *ROAN* immersed the reader in Native American folklore, *SKELLIG* sends the reader headlong into the deep-rooted Irish and Celtic mythos that have seeped into so much of our modern stories and traditions … *SKELLIG: THE TALES OF CONOR ARCHER*, Vol. 2, has easily earned 4 out of 4 Stars. The novel is fast-paced and compelling, and even at 400-plus pages, it contains no filler. Mr. Barr is able to educate the reader on Irish culture while never taking his foot off the gas. If Rick Riordan were to craft a series for adults, it would be THE TALES OF CONOR ARCHER; that being said, I'd put my money on Conor over Percy Jackson any day. If you are a fan of epic or urban fantasy, pick up a copy of *ROAN* today and know that when you are finished *SKELLIG* is waiting.

—*OnlineBookClub.org*

SKELLIG is an engrossing read with believable characters. The protagonist is a compelling character thrust into the middle of a conflict that involves magic and I loved that the author creates an enemy stronger than the protagonist. Conor is a character that is genuinely human, flawed, and who still has to hone his magical skills. His growth through the story is well-written. I loved the worldbuilding and the exquisite, magical world the author creates. The descriptions are terrific and real. E. R. Barr creates a strong conflict and then allows the characters to evolve through it, discovering themselves as the story progresses, finding strength in friendship, and exploring an existence where the natural and the supernatural meet. This is a gorgeous narrative that explores the conflict between good and evil; a story that will excite readers who enjoy tales of magic.

—*Readers' Favorite*

ACKNOWLEDGEMENTS

To William, who talked me into writing a novel in the thriller genre. He said I might be good at it. Here's hoping he's right.

TABLE OF CONTENTS

Gods In The Ruins

A Vatican Archives Thriller

CAST OF CHARACTERS

THE AMERICANS

Greg Bowman: Student archeologist in Babylon

Alfred Brummel: Student archeologist in Babylon

Fred Brummel: Student archeologist in Babylon

Bart Finch: Techno Geek for Antiquities Division CIA

Brian Jeffries: Archeologist in Babylon

Leslie Richardson: Director of the CIA

Lacy Michels: Student archeologist in Babylon

John Nance: Wealthy philanthropist to the Vatican

Rebecca Perez: Mossad trained agent transferred to CIA, naturalized U. S. citizen

Oliver Sebastian Putnam: President of the United States

Harriet Putnam: First Lady of the United States

Roger Trake: Student archeologist in Babylon

Isaac Weiss: Mossad trained agent transferred to CIA, naturalized U. S. citizen

THE IRAQIS

Dr. Frances Azar: Archeologist wife of Dr. Markoz Azar, mother of Daniel Azar

Dr. Markoz Azar: Chief Archeologist of Babylon, husband of Dr. Frances Azar, father of Daniel Azar

Tariq Aziz: Iraqi Minister of Foreign Affairs under President Saddam Hussein, only Christian in the Cabinet

Walid Badawi: Middle brother of three siblings, auto mechanic and engineer for the Babylon site

King Faisal II: Last king of Iraq, succeed by Saddam Hussein

General Farouk: Iraqi general in military oversight of Babylon and friend of Fr. Daniel Azar

General Habib: Iraqi general

Bashir Hakani: Prime Minister of Iraq

Saddam Hussein: President of Iraq (1979-2003)

THE SYRIANS

Dr. Nabil Kasser: Islamic scholar and imam, founder and head of the 'Islamic Studies Worlwide Initiative' (ISWI), based in Washington, D.C.

Anwar Sharif: Secretary of Dr. Kasser

THE ISRAELIS

Moshe Finder: Director of MOSSAD

ISIS

Hasan Naziri: Head of ISIS

Abu Shadid: Right hand man of Farid Tahan

Farid Tahan: ISIS overlord of Fallujah/Babylon region

THE VATICAN/ITALIANS

Fr. Daniel Azar: Son of Drs. Azar, Roman Catholic Chaldean priest, stationed at the Vatican

Antonio Bigetti: Pilot, Vatican Air Fleet

Nicky Farrell: Clerk at Irish College, Vatican/Rome

Maria Franco: Girlfriend of young Daniel Azar

Grigio: Mysterious dog companion of Fr. Azar

Colonel Mario Minitti: Head of the Vatican Swiss Guard

Liam Murphy/Pope Patrick: First Irish pope

Luca Rohner: Member of the Vatican Swiss Guard, best friend of Daniel Azar

Franco Salamone: Pilot, Vatican Air Fleet

THE ANCIENTS

Marduk: Chief pagan god of ancient Fertile Crescent (Babylon, et. al.)

Nebuchadnezzar II: Greatest king of Babylon (605-562 B.C.E.)

Xerxes I: King of Persia (518-465 B.C.E.)

THE AVATAR

Ranbir Singh: CIA Antiquities Division advanced computer hologram also capable of interacting physically with solid matter

PROLOGUE

TWILIGHT WAS FALLING when eight-year-old Daniel Azar skateboarded onto a sidewalk as a decrepit car swooshed by, almost hitting him. The streetlights of Baghdad were off again. Saddam Hussein had ordered the blackout in fear of a possible American attack. The day had been hot but the cool March night of Iraq was settling in with just a little bit of fog to dull the sight.

Daniel was breathing heavily from his narrow escape when he saw someone turn the corner and walk toward him. A portly man stopped in front of him and said, "Child."

"Sir," said Daniel who had always been taught by his Jewish mother to be respectful of elders, particularly in this emotion laden, religiously divided city.

"Are you Daniel Azar?" asked the man.

"Yes," he said in a small voice.

"You must come with me. Someone wishes to see you. No need to be afraid."

"A lie," thought Daniel, who had a young child's nose for the truth. Maybe someone did want to see him, but he knew to be afraid. These were dangerous days.

The man was alone; no thugs present. Good thing, neither his mother and father were home, and the housekeeper would be useless in a struggle. Besides, the man looked important. One step at a time, he thought. Picking up his skateboard, the boy followed the man to a large government limousine around the corner.

The man opened the door and ushered Daniel inside. "Do not worry," he said. "You shall ride alone back here, and I and my driver in front."

The man seemed kind, and Daniel did as he was told for now. Once in the back, he hugged the door like a lifeline as the limo sped off on the dusty Baghdad streets.

They didn't have far to go. The vehicle pulled up to the *Chaldean Catholic Cathedral of St. Joseph*, in Baghdad where Daniel had been baptized. The man motioned the driver to get the child and bring him to the side door of the church. The man and boy slipped inside the darkened holy place. Someone else was there. Only a few shrines and icons were lit by candles, but Daniel knew the archbishop immediately. After all, he went to Mass here every Sunday with the housemaid, Fatima. It was a mandate from his father who was seldom home, and his mother who was scarcely more present.

The old archbishop smiled as Daniel and the stranger came closer. "Thank you for bringing him, Tariq. This night is full of evil, and Daniel, I think, is important to all of us." Tariq Aziz, Minister of Foreign Affairs for the government of Saddam Hussein, and the only Christian in the president's cabinet, nodded and pushed the boy forward.

"Do you know why I have asked you to come?" said the archbishop.

The boy kissed the archbishop's ring and said in a small voice, "No, your Excellency."

"Good manners," smiled the archbishop.

"My father taught me," said Daniel proudly.

"Ah, yes, your father. Exactly why we are here. He wrote me a note the other day. Do you know what it said? He wrote to me these words: 'It is time for Daniel to receive his destiny.' Would you know what he meant by that?"

"No," said the boy. "Why isn't he here to tell me?"

"Because it is no longer safe for him to be in this city. Your father may be the most famous archeologist in the Middle East, but his Catholic faith will make him an object of reprisal in days and months to come. No need for you to worry about that now. His letter means I am to send you to someone who has a gift for you, something that you must hold onto no matter what happens in the dark times to come."

The child was confused. Why was the archbishop so vague and secretive? But the cleric only smiled and said, "Go with Mr. Aziz now. He will take you to your special meeting. It is what your father wants." The archbishop blessed the boy and led him back to Aziz. He whispered, "Watch over this child well in the next few hours. No harm must come to him."

Haifa Avenue, housing the best shops and restaurants Baghdad had to offer, was mostly deserted as the government limousine sped down the street. Even Daniel felt the nervous calm of approaching doom. He looked ahead and gasped, for he now knew where the strange man was taking him: The Republican Palace, the Baghdad home of President Saddam Hussein.

The limo went around to the back of the palace, which was only slightly less threatening than the side seen by diplomats and world leaders. Two Republican Guards walked down the steps to greet the limousine. It was obvious, even to Daniel, that the strange man was expected.

"This way, sir," said one of the guards. The man waited for his driver to extricate Daniel from the back seat. As the boy walked around the car, the man called Tariq extended his hand. Daniel noted to himself that he wouldn't do this normally, but he was a little scared. He took the man's hand feeling less alone. They walked together up the steps into the palace.

Later, he remembered little of that architectural wonder. Instead, his memory was of the room where the man took him. It was large, but had soft carpets. No electric lights, obviously, because of the blackout, but candles shed glimmering shadows on gold-adorned pictures and precious antiquities, no doubt looted from nearby Babylon. A replica of the famous Ishtar Gate in Babylon framed an immense picture window. The lions, aurochs, and dragons shone gold on the vibrantly blue lapis lazuli tiles.

"Thank you, Tariq," said a voice. Daniel's eyes glanced over the room and fell on a figure he had first thought a statue standing by the huge bullet proof window. He was dressed in a tribal outfit of orange and black, looking like a lion in the candlelight.

"Mr. President," said Tariq Aziz, the Minister of Foreign Affairs. "I have brought you Daniel Azar as you have requested."

"My most faithful minister for all these years," said Saddam Hussein. "You may be Christian, but there is no one else I could trust with this sensitive issue."

"Thank you, Mr. President," said Aziz, and he drifted back into the shadows in the room.

"So, you are Daniel," said Saddam kindly to the child. Daniel couldn't speak, so awed was he by the presence of the president. He knew that people seldom saw Hussein in person, and he couldn't understand why such a lowly kid as him was meeting such a grand personage.

Saddam bent down to look into Daniel's face. The boy's smooth face and black eyes contrasted with the bloated visage of Hussein. The president's eyes were also black, but Daniel only saw how puffed up and red-rimmed they were. The president wasn't having a good day. Stress lined his features like cracks in concrete.

Taking the boy's hand, Saddam said, "I know your father. He is a great friend of mine."

That surprised Daniel. He didn't see his father often, but of the many names the famous archeologist dropped, Saddam Hussein's was not one of them.

"Markos Azar," continued the president, "has been doing me a great service. Did you know that I gave him his present job to excavate the ruins in Babylon?"

Daniel said, "I knew that is where he worked, but I did not know you sent him."

"That's why I like your father," said Saddam. "Even with his family, he is discreet. And, of course, I like him because he always finds what he is looking for." Saddam laughed as if he had made some kind of play on his words. He let his orange and black robes billow as he turned and pointed out the window. "Out there, even on this night, he continues to search for the secrets of my ancestor, King Nebuchadnezzar. Did you know that my line can be traced directly back to the great king?"

The president's puffy red eyes crackled crimson in the candlelight, giving him a feral look, his hands reaching out towards the desert like the claws of a scorpion.

Daniel shook his head and simply said, "I did not know, but everyone says you do not need a famous ancestor to be great. They say there is no one greater than you in all the world."

"My people say that?" Saddam looked inordinately pleased. "They should, of course. I am about to lead them to the pinnacle of world power. My great ancestor whispers to me in the night and tells me so."

From the shadows, Tariq Aziz spoke, "Mr. President, time grows short."

A look of annoyance briefly crossed the ruler's face, but then he smiled. "Of course, my friend, of course. I forget myself." Smiling at Daniel, ruffling the child's black hair, he said, "I forget the attention span of a little boy. Daniel, I brought you here this evening to give you a gift. Would you like to see it?"

Daniel's face lit up, but then he remembered who he was talking to. "Sir, I do not deserve anything from someone so exalted as you."

"So polite. It is I who am honored that the future of our country respects his elders so much. Your father was tasked to find a small trinket that once belonged to my great ancestor. The ancient tablets speak of a talisman that he often wore in public whenever he exercised his kingly power. It was a ring called the 'Star Sapphire'. The records said it was beautiful. A sapphire surrounded by six diamonds connected to the greater jewel by what seem to be lines of platinum, unknown to artisans of that time. Set in precious gold, it was one of the most beautiful of Babylon's treasures. It disappeared from history, but legend says it was passed down from Nebuchadnezzar to his heirs. For centuries it was lost. In fact, your father thought the great pretender, King Faisal II, had found it. When I began my reign, I dug up his tomb thinking to snatch it from his dead, bone-white hands." Saddam began to giggle at the memory, but then turned solemn.

"Do you want to know something, little man? He did have it! So, I took it from him. It is mine by right, my son. Your father, my friend, established its provenance. Do you know what that means? Of course not. It means he authenticated it as the original Star

Sapphire of Nebuchadnezzar. And it found its way to me, as it was destined to do.

"The doctors and geneticists say it cannot be possible, but I know that I am the legitimate descendent of the Great King. Do you know what I did with those physicians who falsely tested me?" Here Saddam looked sternly at the boy, bent down and whispered slowly, "I got new ones."

The president stood and laughed loudly, but then he looked at Daniel again and spoke solemnly, "He speaks to me at night, the Great King ... and assures me what my doctors doubted. His blood runs in my veins. If you must know, we are so close that I believe he and I are one, that King Nebuchadnezzar rules once again through me."

Missing the sudden change in coherence, Daniel looked mystified. "Then you should keep the ring. It will protect you."

"Not necessarily. It is a fickle thing. It protects until it doesn't. It eventually tires of the bearer and moves on. The whispers tell me I should put it in safekeeping, that it need not be in my presence to protect me. And that is why you are here. I've known your father many years, and the Azar family is related to me, not so directly that people would automatically know you are my relative, but still close enough for the genetic markers to be virtually the same. When your father discovered a tablet describing this very ring several years ago in the Esagila—the Temple of Marduk in the ruins of Babylon—I was overjoyed. I have worn it publicly since, and look where we are, at the pinnacle of shaming the Great Satan and his allies! They seek to attack me, the Great King *redivivus,* and grind Babylon into the dust again. Your father wrote me, as I said, and suggested that you would be a great keeper of the ring. No one would suspect a child like you. The days to come shall be brutal, and I have no doubt we shall prevail, but we must be prudent." Saddam bent down again and whispered into Daniel's ear. "We must be prudent."

Suddenly, the dictator's hand was in front of Daniel's face, his fingers holding the Star Sapphire. Daniel could not believe how beautiful it was. Saddam smiled. "Put it on, little one, and watch how ancient jewelry works."

Daniel put the ring on his right ring finger, and it looked ridiculous. It was massive, and on his small hand it appeared like a rock had been attached to his digit. But then something happened. He thought he heard a faint buzz and felt a vibration in the ring. Looking, he saw the ring shrink to a proper size, and, like an octopus from the Persian Gulf, it changed color and shape. Daniel blinked his eyes and was amazed at what he saw, or didn't see. The ring was now a simple band of dark blue, barely noticeable on the finger.

"See!" said Saddam. "It accepts you, and on you it shall stay till I need it again."

"But how will you be safe?" asked Daniel, knowing that the president had often been the recipient of assassination attempts. Iraq was hardly peaceful, even for the latest incarnation of King Nebuchadnezzar.

Saddam laughed. "Do you hear that Tariq? The boy fears for me. Such loyalty. I knew I chose rightly. To show Daniel that he has nothing to fear, come here Tariq and let us demonstrate."

Tariq Aziz moved forward and from his robes, Saddam took out a long thin blade. "Your father also found this in the ruins of Babylon, but it is from a later time when the Persians ruled. It is beautiful, eh? Sharp as anything made today. Tariq, I want you to stab me with it—right here, in my heart."

Tariq gasped. The president truly had lost his mind, and yet Tariq was reminded that the days of destruction to come might be halted if he simply gave way to Saddam's fantasies. Tariq took the knife, and Daniel grabbed his arm, "Don't hurt him!" cried the child.

Saddam pulled Daniel's hands away from Tariq, smiled and said, "There is nothing to fear, little one. Simply hold my hand, and the Star Sapphire, which you now wear, will extend its protection over me. Let Tariq demonstrate."

For a somewhat elderly government minister, Tariq Aziz moved like a desert lion. He snatched the knife and plunged it into Saddam's chest. He knew he hit the heart; he could feel its beat through the blade. Saddam's eyes went wide and his hands came up to the knife as he began to gasp and fall. He pitched into the divan onto his side, and both Daniel and Tariq looked on in horror.

Then Saddam began to laugh. He sat up and pulled the knife from his chest. There was no blood, and it was obvious he was in no pain.

"See, my friends, Nebuchadnezzar's ring has true power. In the trial to come, I will defeat my enemies just as swiftly."

Daniel walked up to the president, and, in awe, touched the robes that clearly showed the knife had pierced the fabric. Saddam rose and approached the huge window, looking out in silence. He turned to his audience of two, raising his hands and speaking, "Babylon the Great shall rise again, and the world shall kneel at my feet."

Daniel remembered later that, at that precise moment, it seemed the world ended in fire and death. Actually, it was shock and awe, as a cruise missile plunged into the palace great room just down the hall. Tariq and Daniel were thrown to the ground as the window exploded from the blast. Daniel saw huge splinters of crystal blow past Saddam as he stood laughing in the chaos.

"They can never kill me," shouted the president unharmed by the flying shards.

"Insane!" whispered Tariq Aziz. "He's gone absolutely insane. Come, Daniel, we must leave now." Fire from the great room was sending smoke under the doors into the chamber where Saddam still raised his hands, as he twirled around in his orange and black robes, laughing at the destruction he could now see was raining down on Baghdad. The Americans had struck, and the bombs fell like hail.

Tariq pulled Daniel along with remarkable speed and burst outside to smell the fire and smoke and see the pieces of building that fell around them. Miracle of miracles, the limousine was still there, engine running, driver waiting, guards at attention. Quickly saluting, Tariq Aziz shoved Daniel into the car and sent the vehicle scurrying from the burning palace.

Daniel could hear the driver and Tariq talking in the front of the limo. Tariq said, "Change of plan. The president has lost his mind. He wanted to keep the child with Fatima, the boy's nanny. Look in the rearview mirror. Baghdad burns. Saddam might not even live through this night's barrage let alone what shall come after."

"What are your orders?" asked the driver. He always liked Tariq, one of the few cabinet ministers that had lasted decades in power. Tariq rode the waves of political power like a California surfer. Nothing brought him down.

"Plan B of course. A soldier will meet us outside the city and take him to his parents in Babylon."

"I want Fatima," said Daniel. "Why aren't we going back to my house?"

"Little one," said Aziz. "It's no longer safe here in the city. Look around you." And as he spoke, several cruise missiles flew just above them slamming into government buildings on the banks of the river. The noise was deafening, but the car never slowed. The cacophony of sound and fire were enough for Daniel though. He cowered in his seat, hands over his ears, eyes tightly shut. Shock and awe at the end of the world.

AN ANTIQUITIES PROBLEM

Friday Afternoon, 2/5, Present Day, The White House

HER FOOT GENTLY tapped the wood of the *Resolute*, POTUS's Oval Office desk, so beloved by many presidents. Leslie Richardson, Director of the CIA, was not easily intimidated, but President Oliver Sebastian Putnam made her nervous. He stared at her over the vast gulf between himself and the newly appointed Director.

"Our first official meeting," he stated.

"Indeed," said Leslie. Two could play the laconic statement game.

"You're probably wondering why I asked for you on a late Friday afternoon."

"No sir," she said. Leslie brushed a blonde lock of hair away from her face. She was a tall woman, and people thought her attractive. She supposed it might be true. "If I didn't know, I'd have to resign. I'm the Director, and I'm supposed to know past, present and future knowledge." She smiled thinly.

"Indeed," said Oliver, matching her mood, terse lip for terse lip.

Then, they burst out laughing. "I'm glad you're here, Leslie. Washington is full of pits and trolls, and I can't trust anyone.

That's what made me so pleased when you agreed to join my administration. That and the fact that Harriet is as suspicious as I am of the Washington elite and she needs a good friend."

"I haven't seen the First Lady since the campaign, but I'll be sure to touch base with her next week. You know I'm happy to help you out Oliver."

"Your FBI experience has proved priceless to you and to me. I knew you had kept up your contacts, and I thought you could handle the pressure of the CIA, politics and all."

"It's been a swamp and is still a swamp, but it's our swamp and I intend to make it my marshy bailiwick for some time. I've been brought up to speed on all important matters, so I can't help but wonder what's come up on a Friday afternoon."

The president twirled his pen in his left hand and sighed. "Ever hear of an archeologist named Markoz Azar?"

"Of course. Renowned scholar, a regular Middle Eastern Indiana Jones, responsible for several significant discoveries in the past two decades. Though it's funny you bring him up. I know more about him today than I did last week."

"How so?" The president believed he was giving the briefing but maybe she did know more than he thought.

"The Agency has an interdepartmental group called the Antiquities Division."

"Never heard of it," snorted the President.

"I didn't think you would have," she said, "though the House Committee on Intelligence, which you chaired, funded the Agency fully for all the years you headed it. Didn't check the fine print much?" She loved it when she had him on the ropes.

His face turned red, and he chuckled, "What is it? A Mulder and Scully team assisted by disaffected millennials who couldn't make it as assets?"

She turned serious. "I thought so too at first, but actually, small as it is, the Antiquities Division, AD for short, is destined to be an important part of our actions throughout the world, but particularly in the Middle East. I don't have all of our operatives chosen yet, and some may look tweedy and professorial, but they will be the best we have, as will be their backup tech support. Top notch, Mr. President. And we are just getting started."

"Good to hear," said Oliver. "This morning, I got a call from Bashir Hakani. The prime minister of Iraq called me on my private line. Said he had not talked to anyone else in his government or ours. What he told me was extraordinary, if true."

"You know he's a piece of worthless, duplicitous shit," said a scornful Richardson. "We've had more trouble keeping him in line than all his predecessors put together. I still think he is an Iranian stooge, just another one of their puppets on the world stage."

"You might be right, Leslie. But even though someone else may pull his strings, I don't think he even told his puppet master about this."

The president stood and walked over to the window overlooking the desolate winter Rose Garden. "He wanted to talk about Babylon."

"Babylon?" said Leslie in surprise. "It's been a forsaken ruin for over two thousand years."

"Well not Babylon, per se," said the president, "but one of the Temples that once was there. He said the Temple was the Esagila, the Temple of Marduk, the Babylonians' chief god. Markoz Azar has been excavating it and found something not so long ago. He found a tomb."

"But Mr. President," said Leslie. "I'm sure that's world shaking and wonderful for the archaeological world, but finding a tomb in the Middle East is hardly rare. And if it was such an important find, the CIA would have known about it."

"Maybe the Company needs bigger ears, but, make no mistake, finding this tomb is extraordinary. First of all, the tomb is very large and very old. It is set in the midst of a another, heretofore unknown, subterranean Temple of Marduk. Second, the tomb is made of an unknown compound that has defied analysis. Granted, our scientists haven't looked closely at it yet, but give the prime minister the benefit of the doubt for the moment. Third, there are inscriptions on the sarcophagus lid, a whole text actually, and Azar does not exactly know what it says because much of it is in a dialect that even Professor Azar doesn't know very well. What adds to its extra-ordinary nature is the fact that a date appears on the text, a date that is known to us."

"Again," Mr. President, "finding future dates on past antiquities is not unusual."

"It is when the sentence that contains it is in Akkadian but the date is in English and says November 1 of this year, written in our concept of time. Says it right there on the lid. In English, Leslie! It says other things as well."

"You're kidding me," said Richardson.

"Or the Iraqi prime minister is," said Putnam. "He doesn't know what to do. He knows about it because Professor Azar told him and no one else. Both are afraid that, if news leaks out, it will destabilize the already chaotic situation in the larger Middle East. Then, there is always the Mahdi."

"We don't know a lot about him," said Leslie and offered the president a frustrated grimace. "The supposed savior of the Islamic world could be a voice of reason. Could be a nut. Could even be a terrorist. There are several candidates for the position. Nothing worse than apocalyptic stuff to light the fuse of sectarian war again."

"And draw us into it, I'm afraid," said the president.

"We can't do that again," said Richardson.

"Nope," said Putnam. "That we cannot do, but these things tend to get out of hand. The prime minister has agreed to say nothing for one month. Professor Azar has agreed to do the same. Business will go on as usual, but I need your team to go there and quietly figure out what that tomb is and what is in it. And, if its contents are a danger to world stability, destroy it completely."

"Won't that cause the war we want to avoid?"

"Not if we blame it on what is left of ISIS," smiled the president.

"I'll get my team together, Mr. President. See you here this time next week."

"That'll do Leslie," said the president.

She smiled at her friend. "How about something a little stronger than tea next time. I think we're going to need it."

A SECRET IN THE OPEN

Friday Evening, 2/5, The Lincoln Memorial, Washington D. C.

LESLIE LEFT THE White House and had her driver drop her off at the Lincoln Memorial. After a brief argument, she convinced her Secret Service Protection to wait outside on the steps. In the first few weeks of the Putnam Administration, she already had a reputation for visiting the monuments as a stress reducer, making her somewhat eccentric to the agents tasked to protect her.

Just as she wished. In her nearly three decades of public service, she had learned to cultivate an Einsteinesque personality; namely, flashes of amazing brilliance masked with lovable unconventionality. The brilliance came naturally; the eccentric mannerisms, however, were tailored to deceive. Such a deception served her well in public life. As an FBI agent just out of college, she climbed the ranks by being startlingly intuitive in solving cases. She was the one that finally put the Mexican drug cartels in the grave by adopting a scorched earth policy on their hideaways and a take no prisoners approach toward their finances. Interdicting drug shipments combined with the time-honored tax evasion prosecutions served to impoverish the cartels while making them homeless as well.

Oliver Putnam had followed her career, first when he was governor of Texas, and then senator of the same state. The night he was elected president, she was the first one he called.

"I need you to run the CIA, Leslie," he said.

"I'm not nor ever have been trained in spy craft," she answered.

"Good," he said, "I'm tired of the 'old boys' network over there. They've gotten too partisan in their views. We need a fresh look at how we gather info on our foreign enemies. Your work against the cartels has been stunning. You put the fear of the ever-living God in those folks, and I don't mind telling you that you have men in the vast halls of D.C. power shaking in their boots, afraid you might turn your corruption investigating eyes inward on improprieties within the U.S. government. Controversial as this appointment will be, you will sail through confirmation as a sigh of relief wafts through the halls of Congress. Better your foresight is focused on our international front. And that's just the smarmy Washington hacks' views. My opinion is the one that counts.

"We're losing influence on the international stage. My predecessor still has a few months to screw things up more than he has already done, and I think by the time I take office we will know less about our foreign enemies than we do now. What an inept statesman! That's why I need you to help me do better. What say you?"

She said yes on the spot and never could quite figure out why. She knew she was tired of the FBI. The people were great, but she wearied of the Bureau's rules and regs which had tied her up more than once in her pursuit of the cartels. She needed a freer hand, and Director of the CIA was the breath of fresh air that gave her imagination a new spurt of creativity.

Easily confirmed by the Senate, Leslie found the Agency to her liking. Already, she had drawn up plans to confront the bureaucratic mess the CIA had become, and some of the old stalwarts were going to find themselves out on their asses because of their reluctance to change. But she felt she wasn't moving fast enough. The previous director had taken her out to lunch his last day on the job and informed her of a new initiative he had personally taken years earlier to do an end run around the president and gather the needed info to protect the United States against foreign enemies.

Years before, he had come up with a novel idea; namely, to create a department within the Agency that would be independent of controls except for the director. It would be small and elite, primarily research oriented, but empowered by a large, off the books, budget and the best talent money could hire. He called it AD—the Antiquities Division. Its role would be to ferret information out of foreign countries by infiltrating their science and research/development programs.

Leslie lifted an eyebrow as she spooned sorbet into her mouth and thought how useless that outreach would be. The outgoing director saw her skepticism, laughed and said, "Of course you think me a fool, but you haven't spent a day as Director of the CIA yet. We're not all just about spies. We come across the strangest things, but in the past few decades, we have ignored the danger they have brought us to our own peril. I've left you files on the most pertinent matters."

"The Agency's version of the X-Files, I take it," said Leslie with a ghost of smile touching her lips.

"I guess you could call it that," said her host. "It's taken me these past few years to make my plan operable. The furthest I got with the AD is its headquarters. It certainly couldn't be based in this hotbed building of top-secret gossip. So, for the last several years, I've built its headquarters somewhere else, and you will be one of the few in this agency to know its location."

That's why Leslie stood looking up at the statue of Abraham Lincoln on an early Friday evening. Dressed in a casual parka, jeans and boots, Leslie was unrecognizable. She sighed contentedly. The Memorial was a peaceful, august, and moving place. She always had loved it. Lincoln stared down wisely at her, seemingly to approve her presence. She casually walked off to the left of the statue to a doorway where a policeman stood guard.

"You're not allowed to enter here," said the officer politely.

She showed him her identification, and he blanched, profusely apologizing and let her pass. The door shut behind her, and she found herself in a newly constructed hallway with an elevator at the end of the corridor. The project to renovate the basement of the Memorial had been going on for three years. It was to be a museum of Lincoln memorabilia where the public could view and study the man and the myth. It was everything a Lincoln Library would have been had such a thing existed in the nineteenth century.

The basement museum fit the Memorial footprint perfectly. It was a massive undertaking still at least a year away from completion and served as the perfect cover for the previous director's plans for running the center for the AD outside of the Agency's bevy of buildings it owned and operated.

Leslie was speechless when she learned that the Lincoln Museum was only the first level of an even more stunning basement complex. Her predecessor had conceived of two levels lower than that, one of offices and meeting rooms with state-of-the-art technology and another lower level for research and development. These levels, far beneath the museum, spread out much farther from the museum's floor plan. The construction workers thought them part of the museum, but once the basic floor plans were excavated and formed up, he concluded their contract and hired others to finish the job. Confusion and obfuscation were the previous director's gifts, and he used them well to make the two lowest levels disappear in the minds of workers and inspectors.

This was Leslie's first visit by herself. A month earlier, she had been given a brief tour of the office, but in the intervening time, her predecessor had been busy. She even allowed him to stay involved until yesterday when he informed her that the AD was finished and ready for occupancy. She wanted to see it herself, alone.

The elevator did not descend that far. Its destination was the Lincoln Museum, but there was an access door to an equipment room, and a secret panel that led to a stairway. All too cloak and dagger, thought Leslie, but the former director was like a little child with a new toy. He enjoyed the deception and had created an excellent emergency entrance and exit.

Of course, this was not the real entrance to the AD. That was several blocks away in a building owned by the Agency but leased to a restaurant and several other clients who had offices there. The law firm of Douglas Stevens and John Anderson was the front for the AD, and on entering, any of the employees of the AD Central Command would find themselves whisked away by a newly built underground tram, taking them the one thousand feet to the real entrance of the AD.

Leslie intellectually understood all of this, but even she was stunned when she unlocked the metal doorway and stepped into the Offices of the Antiquities Division of the CIA.

"Good evening, Miss Richardson," said a neutral male voice, "and welcome to the AD. As director, you have access to all technology and files, and I will assist you in any way necessary. My programming is totally at your service. You may keep me in verbal mode or you may access my holographic image for your convenience."

"Let me see what you look like," said Leslie, not sure if she liked the whole artificial technology emphasis. A little too 'Terminator' for her, or was it 'Star Trek', she thought. But then she reassessed her opinion.

Before her, suddenly, stood a dark-skinned, handsome man of thirty with a Sikh headdress. He was about to speak when the image froze.

"You like?" said another voice.

"Who is here?" said Leslie, a Ruger LC9s suddenly appearing in her hand. Always carried it, tucked in the inside pocket of her blazer.

"Whoa, Director, I didn't mean to startle you." Around the corner came a twenty-something rather scrawny character with a man bun and a ratty beard.

O my God, thought Leslie, the stereotypical computer geek. He should have been the hologram.

"I'm Bart Finch, the tech guy for this whole place. We haven't had the chance to connect yet. The former director said you might be by today, so I thought I'd wait and see if you showed up. Besides I wanted you to meet Ranbir. Ranbir Singh, please say hello to Leslie Richardson, your new boss."

The hologram, remarkably three dimensional, spoke, "Most pleased to meet you, and again, let me say I am at your service."

"Ah, thank you, I think," said Leslie, looking back and forth at the creation and its creator.

"A lot to process, I know," said Bart sympathetically. "The former director had most everything finished last week, but Ranbir wasn't quite ready. That's also why I'm here tonight; just putting in the final touches."

"No problem," she smiled, tucking the small gun back inside her blazer. "Just wasn't expecting anyone."

It was just a faint scrape on the steps, but the sound galvanized Leslie into action. "Down, now!" she shouted to Bart. Officer Krupke, or whoever the imposter security policeman had been upstairs, popped out of the stairwell firing his weapon. With Leslie and Bart on the floor, the first thing he saw was Ranbir, the hologram, staring at him. As the assassin shot at the image, Bart shouted, "Ranbir, defend." Like someone out of the Arabian nights, the hologram raised its palms and tiny lasers, shaped in the form of daggers, fired at the man. Jerking, he fell to his knees, but he was only slightly handicapped. They had the effect of a taser. Seeing Bart and Leslie, he lifted up a shaking arm. The distance was such that he wasn't likely to miss. Leslie was faster. She fired three times, putting a bullet into the attacker's head and two in his chest.

"Threat eliminated," said Ranbir, dusting his hands together.

Leslie cocked an eyebrow at Bart. "Better upgrade the lasers, Bart. I've gotten static electric shocks more powerful than Ranbir's energy beams appear to be."

Bart just stared at the dead man, but Ranbir walked over smiling. "I told him I couldn't electrocute a mouse with the charge he programmed. Good thing you are an excellent shot."

Leslie helped Bart up and said, "Your avatar is amazing. Daggers, too, just like a regular Sikh. So lifelike it's uncanny."

"Thanks," said the shaken geek. "I'll upgrade his weapons capability but, seriously, Ms. Richardson, that guy shouldn't have been able to get in here. Who was he?"

Leslie looked at the dead man. "I doubt we will be able to find out, but it's clear we have enemies and we're not even open for business yet."

THE TOWER OF WINDS

Wednesday Afternoon, 2/23, Vatican City

DANIEL AZAR HURRIED up the *Via della Conciliazione* into St. Peter's Square, heading through the columns on the right toward the entry into the Vatican. Stopping by the Swiss Guard, he showed his ID. Going through the *Portone di Bronzo*—the Bronze Door Gate, entry into the interior of the Vatican—he was halted again by another guard who saluted him and then said, "Good to see you again, Fr. Daniel."

"Luca," said Daniel, "are you my escort to the Holy Father?"

"Indeed," said the Swiss Guard with a smile. The two had been friends for several years. Luca was taller and built more heavily than Daniel. Had his helmet been off, his cropped blond hair would easily point to his Swiss origins. "I'm to take you to the Tower of Winds," he said.

"But nobody has meetings there," said Daniel, surprised.

"Tell that to the Holy Father when you see him," said Luca.

As they walked, they exchanged small talk, but then Daniel asked, "How is he? I haven't seen him for a couple of weeks since his trip to the United States. You went with him. How did he do? The press was pretty good to him."

"The people were very receptive. Everybody likes a visit from the pope, even in America—even the atheists. He and President Putnam seemed to get along famously. As you know, we spent a lot of time in California, Texas, and Florida—not bad places to be in February."

"Glad it went well," said Daniel. "These are difficult times."

Luca sighed, "Only two bomb threats and one hostile protestor. Could have been worse. Frankly, I don't know how he does it. After the visit was over, he jumped on the plane, held a two-hour press conference over the ocean, copped a nap, and started right back to work again as soon as he came home."

Daniel laughed, "The Vatican isn't used to a young pope since the early days of St. John Paul II. My uncle just turned 50, and he can still beat me in a 4K run. Kind of nice to have that kind of youth at the head of the Church for a change."

Luca laughed ruefully, "Unless you are one of the old cardinals who always wanted to sit on that throne. This pope's bound to be there a while."

"I hope so, Luca," said Daniel. "There's a reason he was chosen, I think. And it wasn't just to walk the halls of the Vatican saying prayers."

"Yeah, I know," agreed the guard. "Here we are, the Tower of Winds." Taking out a key, he unlocked the door. "I'm sure he's up there by now. Look for him in Meridian Hall."

The Tower of Winds was once the Vatican Observatory, but Meridian Hall was the place the Julian Calendar was cast away and the Gregorian or modern calendar was proven to be more accurate. Painters had successfully frescoed and decorated the walls with religious themes involving winds such as St. Paul's Shipwreck and the Calming of the Sea by Christ. Daniel found the pope staring at the wreckage of the ship where St. Paul had barely escaped with his life.

Pope Patricius, or Pope Patrick, as the English-speaking world knew him, was a tall, athletically built man with an Irish face seemingly carved out of the cliffs that faced the Northern Atlantic. His curly black hair showed no grey, and his blue eyes could change from ice cold to welcome warmth in seconds. His powerful voice and physique made him a presence, and the press had lauded the new energy he brought to the Church.

"Uncle Liam," said Daniel, greeting the pontiff. He wasn't his real uncle, but rather his godfather. Since childhood, however, Daniel had always referred to him in that way.

"Dani, you are here at last!" He always called him Dah-nee, accent on the last syllable, ever since Azar was a little boy. The pope turned from the painting and strode across the hall giving him a bear hug for a welcome.

Daniel began laughing at the boisterous hello and said, "But why here? Nobody has meetings here, Uncle Liam." The pope grew immediately solemn and looked around. Before his election, he had been Liam Murphy, the Cardinal Archbishop of Armagh in Ireland. When he was elected pope on the second ballot, he took the name Patrick and said so for two reasons. First, he wanted to recapture the energy of the Apostle to Ireland and show the world that the Vatican would place preaching the Gospel as the first of its priorities. Second, he chose the name, he said, because it was clear the world needed to be convinced that the Church was not simply some otherworldly organization but was intimately involved in the progress of civilization.

In his opening address as pope, he had criticized the Church for being mute in the face of evil in the world and almost embarrassed to proclaim the truth of the Gospel to all peoples. He pointedly said the original Patrick convinced by example, kindness and clarity. He intended to do the same. The combination of mercy and truth puzzled the press, and the commentators could not figure out whether he would be conservative or progressive. Daniel thought his uncle took great glee from confounding his critics. He noticed the pope's concerned look as he gazed around the hall.

"What's wrong?" said Daniel.

"Everything," said the pope. "It's why we are meeting here. No listening devices in the Tower of Winds. Only a few Swiss Guard know we are even here. For the moment, it is safe for us to talk."

"Safe?" said Daniel, not understanding. "Are we in danger? Are you all right?"

The pope gave a rueful smile. "I've been pope for one year, and the only thing I know for sure is that, in this world, no one is ever safe. I have watched pontiffs age before my eyes, and now I know why. We stand on the edge of a pin with disasters and possible catastrophes all around. Only by the grace of God do we survive, and I don't mean that as a pious phrase. Nor am I referring to just the Church. I feel God every day, guiding us and guarding us, because there is a darkness all around the world, grasping for the good, waiting to destroy the innocent."

"Okay," said Daniel, "now you have me worried. What's going on?"

"I met with the President of the United States just a few days ago. He told me some unsettling news. It concerns your father."

"My father?" said Daniel.

"He doesn't seem to be in any danger, but word of his work has found its way not only into U. S. intelligence sources but also into Iranian and Iraqi government channels. They all think he has discovered something momentous, and, apparently, so does the president."

"Why would the President of the United States even care what my father finds in the desert? He has enough dead men's bones in the Middle East to worry about."

"President Putnam cares enough to break every security protocol of his country and share with me the existence of a secret agency in his government dedicated to the discovery and use of antiquities in defense of the nation and world freedom. It's just getting off the ground and already someone has tried to kill the Director of the CIA as she was touring their new facility."

"You're kidding me," said Daniel. "I mean not about the assassination attempt, though I'm glad she's okay, but is it really true that the United States has some kind of inordinate interest in relics and stuff?"

"You have your own interest," said the pope with a smile.

"Well, yes, but I have yet to discover anything that will change the world."

"As of yet," laughed the pope. "You know well, before I became Cardinal-Archbishop of Armagh, I was the Vatican Archivist. Vatican insiders use to laugh at me, saying I stayed in shape running the corridors of the archives counting the volumes as fast as possible. But I used my time in a better way. With the acquiescence of my predecessor, I modernized the archives, and instead of simply continuing its legacy of passively acquiring knowledge, I turned it into a more active institution, quietly yet purposefully seeking out buried knowledge throughout the world. No longer does the Church wait for some government to bequeath us an ancient text or artifact. The intelligentsia often thinks of the Church as opposed to science, but after the fall of the Roman Empire, we were the first to collect knowledge, document it, use it and distribute it to the world, not always perfectly, but that was our intent. For knowledge reveals God, Dani, never forget that. The more knowledge we have, the better we understand the universe and God's purpose for us."

"Sounds like you were developing something similar to what the CIA is now doing."

"Yes, but without the weapons and skullduggery," smiled the pope. "Yet, it is close enough that I shared what I was doing, indeed what I have continued to do, with the president. He had invited

Leslie Richardson, the Director of the CIA, to our meeting. How he did that without the press knowing is beyond me, but she shared her concerns. Someone does not want the United States knowing what your father is doing. With the Iranians involved, well, it could very well mean your father is in danger. Who knows what he has actually discovered?"

"I've got to talk to him," said Daniel, preoccupied with concern.

"Of course, you do, but that is not the only reason I've told you all this. Since your youth, I have trained you to be a scholar, to be an athlete and to be a Renaissance man, capable of many things. The fact that you wanted to enter the priesthood made my heart soar in admiration of you and convinced me that God has a destiny for you. The moment I was elected pope, I began to seek out what your role should be."

"Nepotism has been the downfall of many pontiffs," said Daniel cautiously.

"Yes, but I trust few people, and you I have trained. What is becoming clear to me is that you are uniquely qualified to head up a division within the Vatican that continues what I started in the Vatican Archives. You must seek out new knowledge. We have to reclaim our place in the world as a source of discovery and morality in art, sciences and culture. And I fear, it might be a dangerous undertaking."

"I don't see how," said Daniel. "I mean, I will of course do whatever you ask. I owe you so much, Uncle Liam, but how can knowledge be so perilous?"

"We shall see," said the pope. "But I think you shall find out quickly. I want you to go to your father, make sure he is safe, and find out what he is doing that has got the heads of governments twittering. He's talked of finding a huge tablet covering the top of a newly discovered tomb. President Putnam is very worried about it. It may have political ramifications. A personal visit is necessary; we cannot trust the privacy of even the sat phones. Here, in the Tower of Winds, the rumors are growing about Babylon. You are just the person to find out what's going on."

The pope paused for a moment, and then took Dani's right hand. "Still there, I see," said the pope touching the dark sapphire band round the young priest's ring finger.

"Couldn't get it off if I tried, Uncle," said Dani. "At least it's not fused to my skin. I can rotate it."

"Remember what I said about it when you were younger?"

"How could I forget?" said Daniel. "You told me what a great gift Saddam had given me. He was a monster."

"Yes, he was, a ruthless and pathological one at that," said the pope. "But I also told you what the ring really looked like. I've seen its real appearance twice, as you have. The first time was when I went to Baghdad to collect an ancient copy of the *Epic of Gilgamesh*, written on clay tablets. I received it in the name of the Vatican, and Saddam presented it to me. That's when I saw the Star Sapphire ring on his hand. Saddam had taken it off the dead body of King Faisal II, but it was your father who discovered its provenance as something that once belonged to the ancient Babylonian King Nebuchadnezzar. It was beautiful. But only Saddam and your parents knew its power. Both they and I were amazed he wanted to gift it to you, but when you told us that it had molded itself to your finger, and hidden its true identity, we knew that Saddam's possession of it was only temporary. It was meant for higher things. It was meant for you."

"Yeah, right," smiled Daniel. "I know when you saw it the second time. It has power, that's for sure. But even its resting appearance is cool enough, so I don't mind wearing it. I've tried to take it off many times but it's an impossible task."

"Don't do that anymore," said the pope sternly. "It was meant for you, I believe, and on you it must stay. You must tell me if there are any changes in it. The focus that the governments I mentioned have on Babylon and your father has me concerned, and not just for him. The United States and Iran/Iraq are opposite sides of the globe with the Vatican in between. Fate or divine Providence make it so—I don't know which, but I fear we shall find out soon. And you are in the mix with all of us. I'm sending you to Iraq to check on your father and the tomb. I'll contact you this evening with further instructions. You'll travel with a Vatican passport. Go pack. I'll have you on a plane early tomorrow."

DUST MOTES OF MEMORIES

Wednesday Afternoon, 2/23, Rome

LUCA STAYED BEHIND to escort the Holy Father back to his office, and that was just fine with Daniel. He was so preoccupied with what the pope had said to him that one of Italy's government limos almost ran him down outside St. Peter's Square. The squealing of tires got him reminiscing of a long-ago memory.

After Tariq Aziz put him in a Range Rover driven by one of the Iraqi Republican Guards, eight-year-old Daniel Azar began to cry. Embarrassed, he uttered not a sound, but he knew the soldier in the driver's seat could see through the rearview mirror the tears coming down his face. The flashes of falling bombs continuously illuminated the inside of the vehicle.

He got control of himself and asked, "Where are we going?"

Cold black eyes stared back at him through the reflection in the mirror, but the soldier said nothing.

For hours it was like that. They had outrun the bombing sorties and in the new darkness, Daniel fell asleep. He woke at once when the vehicle stopped. Ahead of him he saw a torchlit camp with a few small tents, window flaps rustling in the night breeze. The temperature had fallen markedly.

The back door opened and the soldier rather gently lifted the boy out of the back seat, set him on the ground and took his hand. A tall, young, wiry man stepped out of the first tent and began to run toward them.

"Dani, are you alright?" Markoz Azar hugged his son fiercely.

"Yes, Father. Minister Aziz asked this man to take me to you."

"Sergeant Farouk," said Markoz, "I am so grateful you brought him safely to us. I hear the attack has begun."

"Yes," said the soldier, "and I must get back. His Excellency is expecting me. We must repel the Americans for the good of our nation."

"Indeed," said Markoz. "Let me not keep you then. Again, thank you for bringing my son to me."

Without another word, the soldier nodded, got into his vehicle and drove away.

"Fool," whispered Markoz, "we are already conquered this very night."

"What do you mean, Father?" asked Dani. "I saw the president and he told me we would be victorious. You should have seen him. He was in orange and black robes. He said he was King Nebuchadnezzar, the ancient ruler of Babylon. Isn't that the same person you are looking for?"

"Yes, yes, Dani," said Markoz absent-mindedly. "Let's get you into the tent. Your mother is in there lying down. She isn't feeling well. Be quiet as you go in."

The boy found his mother sleeping, a small candle guttering on a night stand next to her bed. He had always found his mother beautiful, but even he could see she was wan and pale, a fever eating at her.

"What's wrong with her?" asked Dani.

"Just a small virus, I think," said his father. "You must help her get well. That's why I have brought you here."

Dani straightened his shoulders. "Do not worry, Father. I will take care of her like she does me when I am sick."

"I know you will, son," smiled Markoz. "You're a good boy. Always have been. Tell me, did the president give you anything this evening?"

"Oh, yes," said the boy. "It was a beautiful ring. At least it was when he first put it on my finger, and then it changed. Look, it's just a dark band now."

Markoz Azar sighed deeply. The fool had actually parted with it. He didn't believe Saddam could ever let it go, but his constantly expanding ego seemed to think the boy could be a caretaker for the relic with it still protecting Hussein. Markoz stared at the dark band surrounding the boy's ring finger.

"Oh," he said, taking Daniel's right hand, "His Excellency, the president, has given you such a precious gift. He made it look this way so no one will suspect its value or importance, and you must never tell anyone. Let's keep it our secret." And, thought, Markoz, after tonight, it won't matter if Tariq and the president ever see it again.

Daniel's mother moaned softly and opened her eyes. "Dani, my dear, you have come. Now we are a family again."

He touched her feverish forehead and felt the ring vibrate softly on his finger as it made contact with her sweat-drenched skin. She took a sudden deep breath and asked for water. Dani could swear the color was seeping back into her face.

Daniel blinked away tears as he walked through the streets of Rome. He'd get a cab soon to get back to the Irish College where he lived, but he found the streets of the ancient city eliciting more memories.

They really weren't much of a family. His mother recovered and decided that the ruins of Babylon were no place for a boy, so she and his father sent him to Rome to live with his godparent, Monsignor Liam Murphy, an old friend of the family who happened to be the Vatican Archivist. At first, it sounded like exile to the young Daniel, but the minute he met his godfather, he knew that his life would change forever.

His parents were loving and interesting in their own way, always exploring ancient tombs and cities. Daniel was proud of them. But Uncle Liam, for that is how he was known to the family, was just plain fun. Always laughing, always challenging, he settled the boy into the Irish College in Rome with rooms of his own and an Italian matriarch named Rita who watched over him by day and kept him warm and well fed.

Uncle Liam saw to his education and took him everywhere. Daniel soaked up everything like a sponge. Quick with languages, he was soon fluent not only in Arabic and Chaldean, but in English and Italian as well. The years went by. Uncle Liam insisted he try his skill in athletics, and he excelled in soccer, but his secret love was martial arts. Even there, Uncle Liam was pleased and found him the best instructors.

Though he missed his parents, Daniel saw them at least once a year. In fact, once he reached his teens, he spent his summers with them as they excavated ancient Babylon. Uncle Liam would join them occasionally, infusing the digs with an enthusiasm for ancient knowledge that even Daniel's mother and father couldn't emulate. When the three adults were together, Daniel found life was wonderful. He had a childhood and adolescence that others could only envy.

Until Maria Franco came along. She was his first and only girlfriend. He met her when he was sixteen. She was a year older than he was and already at university. Daniel was smitten with her the first time he met the lovely girl at the trattoria where she worked after class, helping to run the family business.

She was dark-haired but had beautiful blue eyes which made her face pick up the light reflected off the ancient monuments and buildings of the Eternal City. She could be hilariously funny or subtly charming, and Daniel was as in love with her as only a sixteen-year-old could be.

When he was done with classes, either from Uncle Liam or from one of his professor friends, he'd take a late lunch at the trattoria served with the relaxed informality of the Franco family. The two would eat at a table in the corner with eyes only for each other, talking about the day or concerns that could only trouble youth. He got to know her, and she, him. Her family would smile knowing smiles between each other as they gazed at the happy couple. Even in jaded Rome, there was room for youthful love.

Maria found him delightful as well and a little naïve, but he was so full of life and stories that her life bloomed with even more happiness. He was so polite and kind and always wanted to please that she quite fell under his spell. And he knew it. But he never took advantage of her. Uncle Liam had taught him well. How the cleric knew how to deal with girls was a mystery to Daniel, but somehow his advice was always right. He was actually amazed that his uncle let him date her. Things were wonderful for a year.

But there came a day when he was in a hurry. It was the spring of the year, and the Coliseum Marathon, an annual 15K run, was approaching. He was participating and wanted her to watch, but on the day of the race, she was late getting ready. That was not unusual, but it was unfortunate. It made Daniel anxious, and he hurried her. Finally ready, she held out her hand. He grasped it, saying, "Let's run and catch that cab." Pulling her across the street, he didn't see the on-coming Fiat.

It was just a tiny thing of a car. But people in Rome drove like terrorists pursued by the authorities. Daniel just missed the bumper, but Maria was behind him and took the full force of the impact. She died instantly, and Daniel was left weeping on the street as the crowd gathered. As if from far away, he heard the cries of Maria's shocked and stunned family. He stroked her hair, waiting for the useless ambulance, her broken body splayed on the cobbled stones.

Then, suddenly, Uncle Liam was there in all his priestly finery, and he lifted him up from the ground, saying as the ambulance arrived, "There is nothing more you can do here, my son. Come with me, and tell me what happened." Before they left, the priest anointed the girl, just in case a spark of life still remained, and they both prayed a prayer that sent her on the way to God.

There wasn't much for Daniel to tell Uncle Liam or explain to his friends, but there was much guilt to get through. He fell into a deep depression, blaming himself for the accident, though Maria's family desperately tried to change his mind, for they loved him like a son as well. He knew the tragedy was his fault and, for a while, Liam Murphy was truly worried for Daniel's mental health. He called his parents, who were concerned, but they said they were at a crucial point in their research and excavation. Now was just not the time to come to Rome. Could Liam handle it? There was a bit of a row, with Liam yelling. Daniel heard him but was too forlorn to take much interest.

Memories. Daniel wiped another tear from his eye, as thunder boomed above him. The storm had come up suddenly, so he ducked into a café for an *espresso*, ready to outwait the deluge. And he remembered more. The death of Maria caused a downward spiral in his life. He became cold to Uncle Liam, who was at a loss at how to help him. He spent long hours away from the Irish College, just walking the neighborhoods of Rome.

One evening, he was slogging through a rather unsavory section of the Trastevere, one of the oldest neighborhoods of the city. The area wasn't very well lit, but he found a bench next to an ancient church and sat himself down. The night moved on, but he stayed still. The evening sounds of the neighborhood rang with the clatter of pots and the yelling of Italian mamas telling the kids to get off the streets. Still, he remained there, lost in his thoughts. Without the girl, his life was empty, his future meaningless. He wished he would die.

It was a desire almost granted. He felt a blow to his shoulder and looked up to see a group of young men leering at him. Mocking his tear-streaked face, they slapped his cheek, and lightly punched his arm. The Trastevere was plagued with informal gangs like this one. He should have reacted. It probably would have saved him so much pain. But he just looked up at them bleakly. They took it for arrogance.

The blows became sharper. A punch cut his lip. A slap to his head caused motes of light to flash in his eyes. He was becoming disoriented. And then came the knife. One of the young thugs had it. Thin and deadly, and it was almost touching the tear duct of his right eye. Daniel didn't care. He looked up at all of them, sneered and said, "Fuck you."

Bad mistake. Fortunately, he turned his head, and the knife struck a glancing blow next to his eye. Blood spattered over his face. One of the men held back the arm of the knife wielder, but that didn't stop the others from raining heavy blows upon the head and torso of Daniel. The pain was intense, but he just tried to find a deep place within himself to retreat. He didn't care. They could kill him if they wanted.

It was the growl that caused them to pause. Deep and heavy, coming from the shadows. Louder, it began to roar, and suddenly, a grey shape leapt into the crowd, teeth flashing. Eyes swelling shut, Daniel only saw something huge, blurring midst the men, but he did see the flash of white teeth. And the screams—he heard the screams. Blood was everywhere, but the men were gone.

Daniel felt himself passing out, but a wet tongue, licking his battered face, made him open his eyes again. It was a huge grey wolf-dog, looking at him calmly. Fading fast, Daniel touched the canine's head and said, "Grigio, you're back."

Taking a sip from his *espresso*, Daniel smiled at the memory. For some reason, he had called the dog by the name of a famous saint's animal companion. Grigio was St. John Bosco's protector back in the nineteenth century in the Italian city of Turin. The saint was the patron of youth, and back in the day he struggled with the authorities to get the homeless children adequate housing and education. He made many enemies, and his life was often in danger. Grigio, the grey wolf dog, would appear whenever the saint was in trouble. Then the massive beast would disappear until the next time danger threatened. For many years this happened, and when the saint died, the dog still appeared to protect the orphans he had fostered and the religious men and women who guided them. He was like a guardian angel from heaven. Finally, he disappeared for good. People waited to see if the dog would ever return.

> *The battered young man came to a few minutes later, the dog still by his side. "I'm hoping you can walk me home. I'm a pretty beat-up dude here, and who knows when they might come back." The dog yipped in seeming agreement. Daniel took the beast's head in his hands and said, "I think I'll keep the name I called you before. Is Grigio an okay name for you? It means 'The Grey One'."*
>
> *The dog looked at him and seemed to smile as it panted. Then it said the word, "Gree-jo". At least that's what Daniel heard. He laughed and said, "You got it right." The dog yipped and licked his bleeding face and growled again, "Gree-jo". "All right," laughed Daniel, "The name 'Grigio' is all yours."*

Sipping the *espresso* again, he smiled.

> *The dog had helped him the long way home that night. When he got back to the Irish college, he found Uncle Liam waiting worriedly for him. He stumbled forward and hugged the man and pointed out the*

dog, but when he turned, Grigio was gone. Just like his namesake from a century and a half before. It wasn't the last time he saw the dog. The beast had this uncanny ability to show up on the streets of Rome whenever Daniel walked alone. People began to associate him with his dog, but frankly, Daniel only saw him on the streets. Sometimes at night, he would sneak food and water out of the college and place it under the trees. In the morning they would be gone with no pawprints around the bowls. Mysterious. Just like in the Bosco legends.

The dog lifted his spirits just enough that he wanted to get better. So, Uncle Liam took over, got him a good counselor, and set about reassembling Daniel's life. It took a year, but by the next spring, Daniel seemed to have regained his health and found God. Well, not really. He'd always been close to God, but now he found a purpose in his life in which God played a big part. He felt that he was being called to the priesthood. Liam was both happy and suspicious, thinking this was just another way to escape the reality of Maria's death, but Daniel assured him such was not the case. He really wanted to pursue the possibility. He was Chaldean, and there was a need for priests for that community. Iraq was his home. How could Liam not want him to at least pursue the possibility?

For once, Liam Murphy was without words. Everything that Daniel said made sense, but Liam watched him closely. He'd seen too many young men choose the priesthood to escape the complexities of life, and he was not about to let his godson make the same mistake.

Secretly, he was pleased, and he needn't have worried. Daniel took to seminary life immediately. Studies were no problem for him, and his spirituality deepened. He grew into a handsome man and as was customary on the streets of Rome, attracted the attention of the girls. Of course, he was seen as forbidden fruit, but he was genuinely engaging and interesting, never afraid to befriend people, spend time with them, and share their joys and sorrows. He just knew that he would never love another woman like he cared for Maria, and he was helped along in that thought by Maria's family who treated him like a son and stayed close to him. With Maria gone, they were happy enough to share him with God.

Liam was harder to convince, until the day of Daniel's twenty-fifth birthday. There was a chapel in the Irish College. The students and seminarians who attended there would often stop by to pray, but Daniel was a night owl and always seemed to be the only one in the chapel after midnight. This particular night was no different. Liam had taken him out to dinner for his birthday and brought him back late. He went to his room, but then thought a little stop in the chapel for prayer would not be a bad idea. Daniel knelt down in the first pew before the Blessed Sacrament. He was passionately attached to his dream of being a priest, but the loneliness he first felt after Maria died never really went away. Except for the times he knelt here, and he felt the Presence in the Tabernacle. The burning sanctuary lamp assured him that he was not alone and so he prayed.

He had always felt at peace before the Tabernacle, but this time things were different. Light seemed to expand in his body. Looking down, he saw something was happening with his right hand. The dark blue ring he wore was pulsating. For a moment, he looked up at the Tabernacle, but remembered only glancing at it. He was suddenly wracked with intense pain, and he found himself collapsed behind the pew, writhing in agony. Looking again at the ring, he saw it morph into the Star Sapphire that once graced Saddam Hussein's murderous hand. Once it had attained its original shape, the pain lessened, and Daniel could think again.

That's when he heard the chapel door bang open. He thought it was Uncle Liam, come to see what was wrong with him. He was sure he had cried out, but all he heard was panting and the sound of paws on the marble floor, nails clicking. Looking behind him, he saw Grigio approaching. The dog didn't even look at him, just stood by the pew. Its gaze was focused on the exit doors to either side of the sanctuary.

They led directly outside. It was as if the dog was waiting for something to happen.

All through the past years, Grigio had watched over him. Though the beast was not always present, Daniel knew that the dog showed up whenever there was a possibility of trouble or even danger from the activities Daniel participated in. After Maria's death he found he liked extreme sports, whether it was parasailing on the beach, sky diving, or hiking some of the tougher mountains. It was his way of flipping off death in its face. It came calling once, early. He wasn't going to be blindsided again. No matter how far from Rome he traveled, the dog always showed up if there was a hint of a problem. Both Liam and Daniel were beginning to wonder whether St. John Bosco's hound had returned as a miraculous, but reliable, bodyguard for the young man.

"But you are here tonight," whispered Daniel staring at the same doors, "and that means you expect a problem. But here? In the chapel?" He was about to ruffle the dog's fur when the left exit door was suddenly pulled open. Five black clad figures rushed in. Their faces were covered with balaclavas, and in their hands, they held automatic rifles, sound suppressors attached. It happened in a moment. Later, Daniel thought his arm had a brain of its own, for his right hand snapped forward, and he found himself pointing the Star Sapphire at the commandoes who obviously sought to wipe him off the face of the earth. Before they could fire, the ring sent out a blue light which smashed the five like a hammer. They hit the wall of the chapel, losing their guns.

He heard their dazed grunts, but their momentary inaction was all that Grigio needed. He leapt over the pew and rushed the prone thugs, ripping into the throat of first one and then another of the assassins. Daniel found himself running after the dog, his right arm pointing forward with the ring luminous on his hand. The blue ray exploded from him again and crumpled the remaining three against the wall. This time, he heard bones crunch and snap.

Over in a moment, the dog and man looked at the dead attackers. Grigio went forward and sniffed each of the three the ring had dispatched and growled in satisfaction. Not a bullet had been fired.

But some noise must have been heard, because Uncle Liam came pounding through the main door of the chapel. He stopped by Daniel's side and took in the scene, amazed by what he saw.

Not much ever shook his uncle. He glanced over at Daniel and said, "Are you hurt?"

"No sir," he said.

"Well, you certainly left a mess."

"It was Grigio. He ripped the throats out of two of them. My ring," and here he held up the now placid band of blue around his finger, "It changed and broke the bodies of the others."

"Mmm," murmured Liam.

"You don't seem very surprised." Daniel felt his legs begin to shake and his body tremble.

"Here, Dani," said Liam. "Sit yourself down. Come beast, make yourself useful here."

Grigio allowed Daniel to put his arm around him as they went back to the pew. Liam sat Daniel down, looked at him carefully and said, "I'm not surprised, except at the fact that I expected something like this to happen sooner."

"What, me get murdered?" It would have come out more challenging and authoritative, but Daniel's voice broke as he spoke.

"The ring is obviously not secret anymore. Many have sought Saddam's treasure, and I am sure whispers of that long-ago night in Baghdad have circulated through the years. Someone got enough information to act on what they know."

"You could have warned me," said Daniel, face twitching with anger.

"Why? I know something of the ring and that it would probably protect you. I couldn't let you live your youth in fear. And when this beast showed up years ago, even I thought it was a sign from heaven." Here the dog yipped and panted, tongue out, jaws open in what passed for a smile. "I just thought we had more time, fool that I was."

For a moment, Daniel was silent. "My father knows more about this, doesn't he?"

"Most likely, but we're not going to tell him about ... tonight's activities. At least not yet. It would only bring danger upon him."

In the days to come, Daniel found out little about those who tried to kill him. No identification, no known linkage to any of the regular terrorist groups, the dead attackers, all male, were ghosts before they died.

Uncle Liam made one major change in Daniel's life. He introduced him to the Swiss Guard who allowed the young man to train with them in their private gym and training courtyard. That's how he got to be best friends with Luca, and Luca got to be the only person in Rome besides Uncle Liam and Daniel who knew about the ring.

Daniel drained the last of the *espresso* and got up to leave. It was that twilight time in Rome, just when siesta was ending, for those who still did that, and the beginning of the dinner hour, so traffic, both pedestrian and vehicular, was light.

Good thing too. When the bullets shattered the café's windows, they hit nothing but did manage to shower the *barista* and Daniel with shards of glass. Daniel immediately rolled on the floor, yelling to the *barista* to take cover, questioning if there was a way out. She pointed at the back, and he grabbed her shaking hand as they crab walked toward the exit. It opened out to a back alley. Such luck, thought Daniel. Luck stayed with them because the *barista* had a head on her shoulders. She led Daniel to another door, took out a key, unlocked it and led him into the back of another shop.

"First time I've ever had to rescue a priest," she smiled, glancing at his Roman collar.

"Best time for me," said Daniel giving a little grin. A young man she was dating owned the shop. Full of athletic shoes, Daniel could see. The boyfriend wasn't there, and the store hadn't opened for the evening hours yet, so Daniel went to the front to peek out the blinds. Lights were flashing and *carabinieri*, the Italian police, were already on the scene.

Suddenly, there was a pounding on the back door. "Let me in!" said a muffled voice.

Daniel looked at the girl, and both paled in fright, especially when the pounding turned into the clear sound of a shoulder bashing the door. A man wearing a long coat lurched through the sprung door and nearly fell. He was carrying an HK MP7 submachine pistol—a vicious weapon capable of piercing Kevlar armor. He slammed the door shut and looked down the hall at the two frightened people.

"Anybody hurt?" said the man.

"Luca?" said Daniel. "What are you doing here?"

"Saving you and your new girlfriend it seems. I've been following you. I'll explain later, so put your eyebrows back down. But we've got to go now!"

Not really getting Luca's angst, Daniel peered out the blinds again. "I think it's okay. The police are here now."

"It was one of the *carabinieri* that shot at you! Somebody wants you dead! Look, we've got to go. Miss," he said to the woman, "you'll be safe when we're gone. Stay here till the police come investigating, and then just tell them you took shelter here after the windows were shot out of the coffee shop. Play stupid about us, if you would." Then Luca gave her a brilliant white smile that lit up his face.

"Oh, for crying out loud," said Daniel, "don't fall for that look."

The girl laughed. "I'll be okay. Now get out of here like he said."

Daniel and Luca hurried out the back door, Daniel saying, "You should get her number. She's pretty, calm and smart, and she didn't shriek in fear when you gave her your charming smile."

Luca didn't even answer. He just grabbed the scruff of Daniel's coat and hauled him out into the alley. "C'mon," he said, "let's get you back home to the College. And where's that dog of yours that's always around when you're in trouble? Taking the day off?"

Daniel didn't even answer as Luca pushed him into a side street, always looking, looking for anything or anyone strange or threatening. Daniel was shocked that there was another attempt on his life—it had been three years after all—but his mind was racing. Someone knew he had spoken to the Holy Father. Someone knew something about their plans.

FAST TRIP TO BABYLON

Wednesday Evening to Thursday Morning, 2/23-2/24, Rome to Babylon

NOTHING ELSE HAPPENED as they hustled their way through Rome's evening street traffic. The college wasn't that far, and rather than risk exposure, they went around back to the rear entrance where they found Grigio patiently waiting for them.

"Ah," said Luca, "the faithful sidekick. Wasn't much use to you today, Dani. Day off, faithful friend?"

The dog growled low.

"No offense," said Luca. "It's just that you could have been some help."

Luca pushed past the dog, but Daniel stopped to briefly pet him. The reception clerk met them both at the door.

"Thank God you're here, Daniel." Nicky Farrell, the clerk, was a small man from County Galway and always spoke as if the rushing winds from the Connemara mountains had blown his breath away. "Some thuggish looking people were looking for you. Two of them, I think. Went to push their way right past me. That's when your dog appeared. You shouldn't let him stay in your room, you know, but this time I'm glad you did. Chased them away, after giving one of them a good bite. I think they were going to ransack the place to find you."

Daniel cocked an eyebrow at Luca who sighed, "All right."

Luca went back to the door and looked out at the dog. "Apologies."

The dog woofed and actually smiled at him.

"I tell you, Dani, that beast is just too full of himself."

"I didn't let him sleep in my room," said Daniel to Luca. "I'm just as surprised as you that he was here. And speaking of surprises, what caused you to follow me?"

"After you left the Holy Father, he took me to his office where his secretary gave me documents and a ton of paperwork. The pontiff told me to catch up with you and keep an eye out for trouble. He really didn't think there would be any."

"He's hardly ever wrong," said Daniel, "but someone wants me dead pretty badly, and I've got a hunch they know where I'm going tomorrow."

"That may be, and is probably why your uncle also asked me to come along and keep you safe, or, more specifically, out of trouble. So, what I'm going to do is go back to the barracks, pack, and get my ass back here to pick you up at 6:30 am for the ride to Fiumicino Airport. We take off at 7:30 for Baghdad and then a couple of hours of desert driving to Babylon. Busy day."

"I'm glad you're coming," said Daniel. "It's great that my best friend has my back, but I didn't think Uncle Liam was really that worried about what we might encounter in Babylon."

"Better worry, bro," said Luca.

Daniel broke in with a laugh. Obviously, since Luca's trip with the pope to America, he'd picked up some speech patterns peculiar to the U.S.A. Luca Rohner was a home-grown Swiss boy, German speaking like most of the Swiss Guard, but he loved America and swallowed hook, line and sinker anything he could consume about the country and its people.

"Don't take it lightly," said Luca. "I won't be traveling with just my bare hands. You'll be protected."

"Sorry," said Daniel, "I really wasn't laughing about that. It's just that, suddenly, you are all Jason Bourne and stuff."

"Actually, I'm Jack Ryan and stuff." He lightly slapped Daniel on the cheek. "Tomorrow then. Nice to see you again, Nicky." The clerk waved from his desk as Luca left. Daniel went to bring the dog in, but as he looked at the receding figure of his friend, the dog was nowhere to be found.

Daniel spent the evening packing the same stuff he always packed for his summer trips to Babylon, only he added a few sweaters and a coat, just in case the weather got nasty. After a phone call from his uncle and assuring the pontiff he was no worse for the experience earlier in the afternoon, he went to bed early, expecting to be haunted by the afternoon's excitement, but he fell asleep immediately into a dreamless slumber.

Luca was as good as his word and picked him up for the airport in the morning right on time. Neither said much on the drive, except when the Swiss Guard steered clear of the main terminal and drove towards the private jets. Daniel questioned but received no answer except an enigmatic smile from his friend. It was amazing what a Vatican diplomatic passport could do. No inspection, no questions, just a guard to lead them to a plane that took Daniel's breath away. It was a Dassault 900-LX, one of the finest business jets in the world, able to travel non-stop at 650 mph just about everywhere.

"What is this, Luca?" said Daniel as he looked at the beautiful plane.

"The first of a small fleet of jets given to the pontiff," said Luca. "Your uncle has to take Alitalia when he does his globe-trotting, but he has plans for his underlings—like you for instance. He wants the Church more involved in the world, and he needs a fleet of planes that will allow his diplomats, and those doing other things for him, to fly discreetly and safely. The problem for the pope is that he doesn't want the Church to turn into some big conglomerate like every other corporation. It's got to keep its spiritual focus primary. John Nance—you know, the trillionaire—saw the need as well and bought the starter fleet and maintains them with a trust fund that won't run out until after the Apocalypse."

"Fleet?" swallowed Daniel.

"Yes, indeed," laughed Luca. "You should have heard your uncle in America. There he was with that prima donna, the Rev. Joel Osteen, who made the mistake of bragging to the pontiff about his private jet that let him travel the world spreading the good news. Pope Patrick just said, 'Joel, that's marvelous, but I don't know how you do it with only one. I find that having four is barely enough.'"

"Four?" said Daniel.

"Well, three actually. The fourth isn't built yet."

"My uncle lied?"

"Confabulated would be a better word," said Luca. "C'mon, Dani, Osteen deserved to be humbled a bit."

"Well, that's not going to go over well if they ever want to make Pope Patrick a saint."

"Look, your uncle is cut from a different cloth than other pontiffs. While he may be a very orthodox guy, he is going to bring the papacy into the 21st century. Over a billion and a half people claim to be Catholic. That's a huge force for good in the world. He wants to marshal that and give that force a focus."

"Awfully political," said Daniel. "That hasn't helped us in the past."

"You are right of course," said Luca. "But it's that or vanishing into obscurity. The Church is in danger of appearing irrelevant. Pope St. John Paul II lifted its visibility and clout by force of personality, but that vanished when he died. This Pope wants to make some institutional changes that will make other nations take the Church more seriously.

"But already, the knives are out. Moving too fast; too big of ideals; becoming more secular at the expense of the spiritual. Those are the complaints, and not one of them is worth a bucket of spit. The one thing that might blunt the criticism he will face is his reform of the Vatican. Other pontiffs tried but failed. Pope Patrick is like Christ descending into hell to bind Satan when it comes to the fiscal pilferers of the Vatican. Nobody is going to get personally rich under his reign and stay in power. He won't have it."

Daniel sighed. "It's going to make him a lot of enemies."

"Indeed," said Luca. "But it's inspired people like John Nance to help the Pope modernize without looking like some corrupt American evangelical empire."

Luca laughed again, and said, "Enough of the problems. You're going to be even more amazed at what we're flying when you see the inside. I just first saw it yesterday evening. Took a drive out here and stowed my gear and, of course, all my security goodies. The plane is called *Sky Pontiff*. Cool, huh? Kind of based on that old American show 'Sky King.' You know—'Out of the clear blue of the western sky comes, *Sky Pontiff*! You're going to like it."

They were met at the foot of the stairs to the plane by both pilots. Antonio Bigetti and Franco Salamone were ex-military and former fighter pilots.

"This thing doesn't have missiles does it?" joked Daniel nervously.

"No," said Franco, "but terrorism being what it is these days, we are a major target, so the pontiff got Israel to install its state-of-the-art missile defense system. Lasers too. We can't really go on offense, but we might as well have a force field around us. Nothing is getting through to this plane, and we might even be able to bite back."

Daniel and Luca took their seats and made ready to take off. While the jet warmed up its three engines, Daniel looked over at his friend. "I don't know what else my uncle told you, but he really must be worried about my father. This is awfully high priority for simple concern and a fast trip to check on a friend. I think something very bad, really important, or both is happening in Babylon."

"Your dad has found something more than just a tomb, hasn't he?" said Luca.

"I think so. Last I talked to him was a month ago, and he and Mom were ecstatic at the rapid rate the excavation was going. They really believe they found something historic underneath the Esagila, the famous Temple of Marduk. There are several levels, but they were able to dig down a hundred feet and broke into a chamber. That's where the newly discovered tomb was. He said it was made of something he had never encountered before. He sent a sample back to the Smithsonian to see if they could identify it. Then, of course, there was the inscription on the tablet that was affixed to the tomb."

"Didn't hear about that until last night," said Luca.

Daniel said, "Well, Uncle Liam—the pontiff, I mean—said they just got it partially translated, but the important part was already in English! Can you believe it? It's a date—November 1 of this year, written in our concept of time. How weird is that? Dad never said anything about that. It was the pontiff who told me yesterday. That's tripped the trigger inside a few governments and got the CIA interested."

"You remember what my major was in university?" asked Luca.

"Yeah, anthropology. Totally useless. No wonder you went into the Swiss Guard."

"Asshat," said Luca with a grimace. "I mean 'Father Asshat'."

"No offense," said Daniel, "but what the hell did you plan to do with that degree?"

"Says the archeologist," smirked Luca.

"Hey, I like archeology, but I wasn't going to earn my living doing it. I already knew I was going to be a priest. Besides, archs always know more than anthros."

"Well, the Pope has decided that it's not your personal hobby anymore, and, since we're historical investigators, I'm going to be Dr. Watson to your Sherlock Holmes."

"I'm glad of it, too," said Daniel, as the plane accelerated. The jet was noted for its swift take-off ability and was soon thousands of feet above the Italian peninsula.

"It's a four-hour trip to Baghdad," said Luca. "Get a nap in. After we land, we take a Land Rover to Babylon. That will be a hell of a trip."

Surprisingly, Daniel was able to fall asleep almost immediately. There was nothing he could do to prepare for what was coming. Not until he saw his mother and father and the tomb. Not for the first time, he said a silent prayer of thanks for Luca being attached to this mission. A great friend, but a superb warrior as well. If trouble came with the trip, Daniel was confident Luca could handle it.

A WAR-RAVAGED WRECK

Thursday, Early Afternoon, 2/24, Baghdad

DANIEL AWOKE ABOUT a half hour before landing, and so was able to see all of Baghdad from the air. He spotted the huge American embassy, but was greatly shocked again by the wreck and ruin he saw beneath him. Babylon may be a more ancient site, he thought, but at least the sand and wind did the courtesy of smoothing the empty streets and crumbling buildings away under tons of dirt. Baghdad, on the other hand, looked like an urban nightmare with bombed buildings appearing like decaying skulls, empty windows like brooding eye sockets.

It wasn't much different once they entered the Land Rover that was taking them to Baghdad. It was 85 degrees out, and Daniel loosened his Roman collar. Rebecca Perez was driving. She was the new security chief of the site and assistant to the Azars. She had brought along Isaac Weis, who was her right-hand man in security, to ride shotgun in case there was any trouble on the way.

"Rebecca and Isaac?" said Daniel. "You've got to be kidding. No doubt you get a lot of grief for that."

Rebecca laughed and said, "Few Christians tease us because few know their Bible well—the biblical Isaac and Rebecca being married and all, but we got pranked often in Israel."

That's how Daniel and Luca learned that both were Israeli immigrants to America and newly sworn in citizens since last year. So, they said. To Daniel, there seemed more to it than that. They were no nonsense, all business, mostly, except when humor would deflect attention away from them. Luca seemed fine with that and hit it off well with Isaac. Rebecca didn't seem to want to talk that much, so Daniel took in the ravaged neighborhoods they drove through, amazed that no one ever seemed to really clean up from the terrorist bombings that took place on a regular basis.

Rebecca noticed him looking aghast at the damage and said, "You get used to it after a while. Even the terrorist car bombs are seen as just another deadly nuisance. They go off; the dead and wounded are carted away, and the day goes on. This is a city in despair."

"I spent my childhood here," said Daniel, "and I don't recognize a thing. This was once a beautiful city. Can't you Americans get a handle on the unrest?"

"No," said Rebecca. "There aren't enough of us here anymore, so for us it's a holding action. And the government doesn't get along well with them."

"We were taught to love Saddam," said Daniel, "not Iraq. As a country, Iraq has no soul. The British carved it out of the old Ottoman Empire, but we're all just a bunch of tribes always at war with ourselves. Iran would move in and annex us if the world would let it."

"It's a land of war, indeed," agreed Rebecca.

"But it didn't used to be. It once was great," said Daniel. "My summers in university were spent with my parents at the excavation site. We seldom came back to Baghdad. In Babylon, even the dirt exudes greatness. What we once were. No wonder my father gets so excited about what he does."

"Wait till you see the tomb," said Rebecca. "It is truly marvelous and none of us can make any sense out of the inscription on the sarcophagus. The English date has us freaked out."

"Daniel can figure it out. He's an expert in ancient languages, especially Akkadian. Even better than his father," said Luca.

"Don't know about that," smiled an embarrassed Daniel. Then he smirked, "I have an achin' for Akkadian."

Without missing a beat, Luca said, "You have an achy, breaky, Akkadian heart."

"How can you joke in a language that isn't even your own?" said Daniel laughing.

"Country western music is my secret love, so if I'm going to walk the walk, I've got to talk the talk—otherwise my line dancing will look like a crippled Swiss polka."

Even Isaac laughed at that.

"You guys get done comparing weapons?" said Daniel. "You saw the duffle bags that Luca brought?"

"Impressive," agreed Isaac. "We'll be able to hold off a small army if we have to."

"Have you had much trouble?" asked Luca.

"Not really," said Rebecca. "Curious Bedouins come by, but they lust after our electronics. Your dad brought a lot of I-pads and synced them with the regional wi-fi satellites. He gives them out regularly to our 'visitors'. The Bedouin already think they are in Islamic heaven."

"Actually," said Isaac, "it's good politics and our relationship with them is strong. We're not expecting any trouble."

"Except for the Mahdi," said Daniel.

"He's not even in our area," said Isaac, "so no worries there."

"I'm not so sure," said Luca. "If the Doctors Azar have really found something monumental, the locals might get word to the Mahdi, if he exists, and he might become a problem."

Rebecca said, "Look, the Mahdi is just like every other Islamic savior that comes along every few years, makes a splash, overreaches, and then gets himself killed. This one is no different."

"Maybe," said Daniel, "but if my father has really found something sensational, the Mahdi might be able to use it as a rallying cry, one that is far more convincing and powerful than his predecessors have had. Besides, no one knows who he really is. A few claim the title. From what I've heard, he's not the usual fanatic that rises up out of the desert."

"I have to tell you," he continued, "the English date on that tablet will be problematic if word of it gets out. My uncle, the pope, thinks it will kick off an apocalyptic fervor among the Shiite Muslims and even the Sunnis. And, of course, the Mahdi, if he has any smarts, will use it to his own advantage. American Evangelicals will sink their teeth into it, already imagining the four horsemen of the Apocalypse riding towards Armageddon, and conservative Catholics will believe it heralds the end times. It's February and the date on the inscription is November 1 of this year. We don't have much time to figure out what it means."

"That's why we have you," said Luca, punching him in the shoulder. "Our priest and archeologist, *extraordinaire*. Figure it out; tamp down expectations; let the Mahdi down gently, and life will get back to normal."

"What if it is something even more unusual than we think?" asked Rebecca. "Fr. Daniel, what if your mom and dad have a King Tut phenomenon here? What if this find changes history?"

"Then the Mahdi and all others who see the end of the world coming soon will definitely be a problem, and Babylon will rise again as the greatest and most important city on earth."

THE MAHDI

Thursday Morning, 2/24, Washington D. C.

NOT FAR FROM the Smithsonian Institution, on one of the many smaller side streets, and consequently not that far from the Lincoln Memorial and the secret underground meta-building built for the Antiquities Division of the CIA, there was a modest office labeled, 'The Islamic Studies Worldwide Initiative'. One secretary served one professor who acted as the president and staff of the Initiative.

The professor's name was Nabil Kasser, a noted Syrian scholar of all things Islamic. He had teaching rights at Yale, Harvard, and several other universities. Much in demand, he traveled frequently, leaving the daily business of the Initiative to his trusted secretary, Anwar Sharif. Though Professor Nabil Kasser traveled from presentation to presentation around the world, he traveled most often to cement his position as the long-awaited Mahdi.

Whether Sunni or Shiite, all Moslems longed for the coming of the Mahdi—the 'guided one' who with Issa (Jesus) would usher in the apocalyptic age. The legend of the Mahdi was one of the few ecumenical areas of Islam where a cooperative relationship could theoretically exist among the rulers of the ancient religions.

The ambassadors of the Middle East often joked about how Christians and Moslems could work together as long as they were bringing about the end of the world.

Kasser was nominally a 'Twelver', a believer in the Twelfth Iman, the Mahdi, who as a little child, in 864 A.D., had simply disappeared one day. No one believed this was an accident. Allah had plans. The Twelfth Imam's return was eagerly awaited down through the centuries. As a Shiite Moslem, the more conservative branch of Islam, Kasser was supposed to believe that the Mahdi occulted, or went into hiding in the ninth century and remained alive and hidden since then, only to reappear when the last days are upon humanity.

But Kasser secretly took the Sunni Moslem view, which was much more vague and consequently adaptable to modern trends. After all, he didn't believe he, himself, was the Mahdi only now come out of hiding. But he did believe that Allah had called him to be such a leader. On this particular February day, he smiled at such an idea. So many of his brothers, who had claimed the title down through the years, had felt the same and fell to martyrdom, either at the hands of the infidel, or by one of the many sects that continuously troubled Islam.

He, however, possessed one thing that the previous pseudo-saviors would never countenance. He possessed the willingness to work with Christians and even the Jews to establish his bona fides to be the one, true Mahdi. He could preach well and was charismatic, his black eyes shining as he spoke. What he needed were a few signs and wonders; what he needed was to work a few miracles.

The miracles would have to wait, but he was well on his way towards establishing his credentials with Christians and Jews. He did not hate them as so many of his brethren did. He knew that in the end, they would come to see Allah as the One, but they would come of their own free will. He did not need their acquiescence or forced conversion to claim the title of Mahdi.

Not only a professor, he was an imam and knew the Koran better than any other imam alive. In fact, he often ended any scholarly presentation he did around the world with a visit to the local mosque to talk to the grass-roots believers. Already at the age of forty, he was seen as a famous preacher. Great things were expected of him. Soon, he would be able to reveal himself.

His father had been an arms dealer for the elder Assad in the good old days of the Syrian dictatorship and had made a fortune supplying the dictator with all the weapons he needed to keep his fragile domain intact. Nabil was the only heir to the millions made off these terrible weapons including poison gas. At university, he grew a conscience and vowed to use his inheritance for good, not evil. His quest to be the one, true Mahdi was seen by him as a noble cause. He endowed the Initiative with the funds necessary to give him a base of operations to further his world-wide ambitions.

Already, some of his followers were whispering the word, 'Mahdi', amongst themselves. It would not take much for the man, Nabil Kasser, to be able to proclaim himself the expected Islamic savior. But first, he needed the ring. After all, what was the Mahdi without miracles?

The Star Sapphire Ring. Nabil had researched it extensively. That ancient ring once held by Nebuchadnezzar, King of Babylon, fell into the hands of the Persians after the destruction of the kingdom and then into the hands of holy or important men for centuries, until King Faisal II of Iraq appropriated it from one of them, and Saddam Hussein took it from his dead, decaying body. That's where Nabil lost track of it. All through those centuries, it had seldom been used until Saddam somehow found a way to access its properties. It had to have power to keep that dictator in charge of Iraq for so long. Strange stories were sometimes told about what Saddam could do with that ring. But it disappeared with him, and when he was found, like a rat in a sewer pipe, the ring was not with him and he said not a word about it. Nor was he asked. Few knew he had it.

In some of the notes left by Tariq Aziz, the Foreign Minister of the Iraqi State, there were vague references to the talisman possessed by Saddam, but Aziz only mentioned that it had been given to one of his trusted associates the night the Americans descended upon Baghdad.

Nabil suspected the talisman was the ring he sought, and for years he looked for more clues. Every lead led to a dead end, except for one. Nabil discovered that one of the friends of Saddam was a famous archeologist who was excavating Babylon. From Aziz's notes, he knew that Dr. Markoz Azar had been in Babylon the night Saddam lost power, so he couldn't have been given the ring. But the same notes indicated he might very well know where it was. And he would probably have insights into who might possess such a thing.

Moderate though he was, Nabil was not immune from either ambition or a longing for power. People always seek signs, and the Islamic faith on the popular level, like most religions, put great faith in wonder workers. If the ring was real and its powers potent, then it might serve his quest to be the true Mahdi. He was humble enough to realize that if he possessed the ring and it worked, that might be just the sign to him that Allah wished him to be the savior of his people.

That was why, on this particular Thursday morning in February, he had booked a flight to Baghdad for the next day. He needed to have a talk with this archeologist and see what clues he could pry from him.

CAMP BABYLON

Thursday Afternoon, 2/24, Babylon

SEVERAL HOURS AFTER boarding the Land Rover, Rebecca drove into Camp Babylon. The February sun was beginning to set, but it was still pleasantly warm.

"They've made some changes since last summer," said Daniel.

"That's what they told me when I got here a few weeks ago," said Rebecca. "Seems like they've hi-teched it up a little. And we have flushable toilets now and hot-water showers. How can a girl not be happy?" She batted her eyes at Luca who turned a bright red.

Snorting, Daniel grinned at his friend. "You should have seen it last summer. I spent two months out here and never could get the dust out of my mouth. It takes more faith to believe this was once the center of the world then it does to believe in Jesus Christ. Cool as it is, noble as it is, it's still a godforsaken place!"

"Yet, your father keeps finding things here that makes the Smithsonian Trust Fund keep underwriting his activity."

Daniel grimaced and said, "Can't fault Dad for knowing how to market his research. Seriously though, these are some great upgrades. No tents even!"

"The 'tiny house' phenomenon, so popular in America, gave your mother an idea," said Rebecca. "She convinced your father to buy a bunch of them, make them culturally appropriate, and had them set up, each on its own concrete pad so the staff can have private housing. Hooked up to plumbing and our own generator for electricity. Wi-fi as well." Rebecca couldn't keep the awe out of her voice.

"This is the best evidence yet that he thinks he's on to something," said Daniel. "He and Mom have spent years in tents—me too—dredging fine objects out of the mud and clay here. Things that museums really value. But we weren't that different from other archeological sites. Now it seems we are. At least the pope thinks so."

Luca glanced over at Rebecca, "You have many problems with the Iraqi authorities?"

Isaac spoke up. "Every other week, a puffed-up general comes out here, supposedly in the name of the prime minister, to see what we're doing. We give tea and honey biscuits; show him the latest gold trinket we've found; and send him on his way. It's usually General Farouk, and fortunately he gets along well with your father."

"I've known him for years," said Daniel. "He's a real survivor in Iraqi politics. Five car bombs he's walked away from. He won't give us any trouble. Any looters?"

Rebecca said, "We have to keep our eyes open. The Bedouin are no problem, but we do have other locals that sometimes steal. And then, there are the spies."

"What?" said Daniel. "That would be news to me."

"Just started a few months ago, according to your father. They seem to come from southwest of Baghdad, near Fallujah, but we're not sure. ISIS maybe. I'm worried about them. They infiltrate the worker camp. We catch a few and then let them go. Your Father prefers to find out what they are up to rather than punish them.

He doesn't want an incident. It just shows that word of your parent's discoveries is beginning to be spread around."

They were talking as they walked through the camp and finally found themselves at a larger structure that was obviously the headquarters for the excavation.

"Babylon Center," said Daniel reading the sign. "This wasn't here before either."

Isaac looked approvingly at it. "Mess hall, offices, and workrooms for models of the excavations. Not Fifth Avenue stuff but still pretty nice."

"For here," said Daniel, "it's like the Taj Mahal. I wonder how Dad did it, convincing the Smithsonian Board to finance this?"

"I'm quite a convincer," said a voice behind them. Turning, they saw Dr. Markoz Azar smiling at them. He had just walked around the building and was dressed in crisp and clean khakis. Obviously, the showers were working. He was a man in his early fifties, black hair streaked with silver and a handsome face, mustache, and dark eyes that looked chiseled out of the same land as his dig.

"Dad!" said Daniel and rushed to embrace his father. Luca smiled at his friend, glad to see that Daniel's stories about his father seemed to be true. Dr. Azar and his wife had raised Daniel pretty much from a distance because of their work, but it didn't seem to diminish the affection between the members of the family. Maybe the pontiff had something to do with that too, he thought. Having a pope who thought the family was the be all and end all of society couldn't hurt this family unit. Luca had never met Daniel's parents, but that didn't stop the professor from saying, "You've got to be Luca. Daniel's told me everything about you, but I guess I expected your Swiss Guard flamboyant uniform. Stupid me."

Luca laughed, "We're not all pantaloons and pikes. Only for ceremonial events, sir. I'm incognito now. The better to lop the heads off anyone who threatens the Holy See."

"Speaking of which," said Markoz, "Liam—the Holy Father I mean—gave me a call this morning and told me what happened last night. It's good you were there for my son. I'm glad he has a good friend, but I'm even happier that his friend can actually protect him. These are strange times." He shook Luca's hand. "Come on into the Center and meet my wife. She had the staff cook you guys a great welcome dinner."

As they entered, Daniel continued to be impressed. The Center was modern, clean, and most importantly, air conditioned. Even though he was still young, Daniel had developed a taste for some of the finer things in life. A cool room in the midst of the Fertile Crescent fit his comfort level just fine. It was at that moment that his mother came bursting out of the mess hall, stopped and beamed at all of them. Her brunette hair flowed in the breeze she had created, and her eyes crinkled in concern and welcome. Coming up to Daniel she gave him a warm hug, looked him over and said, "I am so glad you are ok. And this must be Luca. Thanks for taking care of my son yesterday." Luca beamed in pleasant embarrassment, lost for words at the moment.

Markoz and Frances Azar made a dynamic couple. They were fit and weathered from the Babylonian climate. Clearly, Frances, or Frannie as she told everyone she liked to be called, was the one with the sense of humor. Laugh lines creased her face, making her welcome anyone she met with a warm and inviting smile. Obviously, she was the best public relations rep Markoz could have for his excavation.

Rebecca looked at both professors. "No trouble at the airport and no trouble on the trip. We didn't seem to be followed, and I can see that things are peaceful here. Did Brian fortify the perimeter while I was gone?"

Markoz said to Daniel and Luca, "As you probably now know, Rebecca and Isaac came as a team from America. The Smithsonian thought we needed better security so these were the two we got and I have to say I am really pleased. Brian Jeffries was tasked with security, and though he no longer holds the title, he was happy to relinquish it in order to have two extra minds and sets of hands to beef up our defenses. Nothing's really happened yet. It's what we expect will happen when word of our discovery gets out that worries us."

He continued, glancing over at Rebecca, "So to answer your question, yes, Brian hired a few of the locals we trust to stand watch each night. He started training today and will continue that all next week. And he supervised the setting up of the electronic perimeter. At least we will know who's coming to wipe us off the face of the earth."

"Don't worry sir," said Luca. "In talking to Isaac on the way here, he shared with me some of his ideas. We think we can keep all of you safe, unless an army comes after us."

"Let's pray that doesn't happen," said Frannie. "Rebecca, please show them our new accommodations, and let them clean up. Dinner—that would be rack of lamb—will be ready in an hour. Here are the keys for their quarters." With that, she disappeared back into the mess hall, her husband following.

Isaac and Rebecca showed them to their dwellings, two homes close together, not 500 meters from the Center. Rebecca said, "You two guys get the two middle homes here in the cul-de-sac. Isaac and I each have the two homes on either side of you. Brian is off in the other area with the student archeologists—archs we call them. See you in sixty." With that, both she and Isaac went back to the center.

Like two collegians, Daniel and Luca had to check out each other's places. Exactly identical, they had a living room, a small bedroom, a bathroom and a kitchen. Tight but comfortable.

"What's that?" said Luca, looking in the corner of the shower. "It's huge, and it's alive!"

Daniel sneaked a look and smiled. "Meet the giant centipede, Luca."

"It's a foot long! And it's mouth—the pincers!"

"Here," laughed Daniel. "Let me get this one for you." Just outside the door was an old palm frond. Snagging it, he walked over to the shower and coaxed the beast onto the leaf. It twirled itself around the frond and seemed content. Daniel tossed it back outside.

"I forgot to tell you," he said to Luca. "Iraq is full of wretched and dangerous wildlife, and the centipede is the least of your worries. If it bites, it will hurt you but certainly won't kill you. Wait till you meet the death-stalker scorpions."

"Death-stalker?" balked Luca. "Scorpions?"

Daniel was having too much fun with this. "And of course, the saw-scaled vipers. Both can kill you in extremely unpleasant ways. My Mom's the medic here on site and has to treat the bites and stings frequently. She can give you the gory details. Lesson one: don't touch anything that moves unless you know what it is and how much it hates you."

Luca wiped the sweat off his face. "Good to know." Then he tossed Daniel out of his place so he could take a shower.

BEHOLD, THE DREAMER COMETH!

Thursday Evening, 2/24, Babylon

THE 'RACK OF Lamb Welcome Home, Dani!' dinner was a great success. Frannie had managed to convince the Iraqi cooks to whip up a Middle-Eastern feast. Daniel was amazed, but Luca and the rest of the archeological crew cared less for the finer details as their eyes bulged with delight at the amount and variety of things to eat. Along with the lamb was a Tahini Mustard, Sweet Potato, Lentil and Arugula Salad. Civilization had definitely arrived back in Babylon. "Might be a little too heavy," said Frannie, "but I figure all of you had a busy day traveling or excavating." She was right.

"Gotta tell you, Mom, I haven't had *mujaddara* in ages." Daniel dug into the rice and lentil dish topped with caramelized onions while Luca helped himself to the pomegranate roasted carrots with feta and brown butter.

"Beats pasta any day," he said. Good wine and bread were served and all was topped off with *baklava* for dessert.

All the while they ate, the guests were regaled by Markoz telling tales of the Babylonian Empire, particularly from the time of Nebuchadnezzar. "Tomorrow, when you see what we have found, Dani, these stories will come to life." Markoz stood and toasted the company with a flourish. The dinner had taken two hours, and Daniel was exhausted. As the party broke up, he was happy he was headed straight to bed.

As he walked to his quarters with Luca, he looked up at the Bright Road, his name for the Milky Way. He always loved the desert at night. On this cool evening, the air was clear enough for there to be a faint star shadow outlining their figures. Even the Hand of God Nebula seemed to have risen just for the occasion, the new heavenly phenomenon shining high in the night sky.

Saying goodnight, Daniel laid his clothes aside and fell into bed. He quickly said his breviary, praying the psalms as prayerfully as he could, but sleep rapidly overcame him, and he dreamed.

Unlike his namesake, the Old Testament prophet Daniel, the Catholic priest was neither a believer in the power of dreams nor the recipient of any but the most common types of imaginings that populated humanity in the darkness of sleep.

That's why in this dream, he felt astounded. There were no murky or vague figures as was normally usual for him. All was clarity.

He was on a small tell, a hill that covered archeological ruins, very close to where the remains of the Esagila—the Temple of Marduk— were. Suddenly, the hill receded, and he saw himself standing on the walls of the Temple. Beneath him on the plain were hundreds of pagan priests, Babylonian he assumed, swinging censors full of incense and shaking small tambourine-like instruments, making the air vibrate with a noteworthy sound like shattering crystal. While not exactly beautiful, it was mysterious and not unpleasant. Acolytes, standing by their sides, carried torches in the night.

Fear gripped his heart, however, when he heard the whispering from the robed priests. Only one word, and it was very clear to him. "Numinous," they said. He remembered his studies of the old texts, particularly the dreams of the patriarchs and prophets. Sometimes they saw visions of what was to come. At other times they simply dreamed dreams and had to consult with the Jewish priests as to what they might mean. But once in a great while, they received what was known as the 'numinous experience', a dream and vision so 'other' that the dreamer knew instinctively it came from outside his consciousness, given as a gift. Always momentous, the faces of those who received such things were briefly transformed into a vision of glory, for they looked upon what was divine, and truth was imparted into their hearts. He knew this was that kind of dream.

The priests kept repeating the word "numinous", and then, through the double column of censor bearing ministers, enveloped in the smoke of incense, walked an exalted personage, a king of ancient days. Immediately, Daniel knew he was looking at Nebuchadnezzar, King of Babylon, as he once was. The man carried himself as a ruler and was of impressive size. Wearing a fez-like conical headgear as a crown, with hair coiled and beard oiled, he stopped at the foot of the temple walls and looked up at Daniel. His golden armor shone in the torch-light, and the red tunic he wore underneath gave him a magnificent appearance.

The King spoke, and Daniel understood him perfectly. "Behold, the Dreamer comes again! Long have we waited for your return. There is not much time. As in my day, so in yours, evil has come upon the land and seeks to devour all that is good, true, and beautiful. Your path is woven through the Bright Way, in the stars above you. Do you carry the ring you were given, the ring I once wore when I ruled the world?"

Daniel found himself speaking, "I do. Here on my right hand." He raised his fist, and suddenly, the ring burst into a fiery blue flame. Daniel could see its shape as the Star Sapphire within the crystal cerulean flames. Suddenly from four of the six diamonds on the outer points of the star, light shot forth into the sky. The priests whispered a collective "Ahhhh" as the points of light arranged themselves in the heavens.

As Daniel watched, it was as if they began to form independent constellations, and, for him, it was easy to see what they were. Three standing individuals soon were outlined in the vault of heaven. Another lay prone at their feet. For a moment, their forms took further shape, and Daniel could swear they too were robed Babylonian priests or royal courtiers stretching their hands out to him. Except for the one lying prostrate. He looked like desiccated flesh; a corpse almost skeletonized. And there was wailing from those heavens.

Fear gripped Daniel, and he didn't know what it all meant, but in a moment the points of light winked out. Glancing at his ring, he saw only one diamond remained luminescent. The others were extinguished, and he could not comprehend. He lifted up his head to the King who had stood silent through all of this.

Nebuchadnezzar, if that who he indeed was, held a scepter in his right hand and pointed it at Daniel. From his mouth came a voice at once strong but compassionate.

"By the rivers of Babylon
Where we walk until this age ends,
You shall now sleep softly
And dream no more this night.
Your mind is troubled,
So, rest and see.
When all becomes clear,
Then you shall know,
That your heart, your mind, your soul
Are fused to this land.
You shall know its secrets,
And the dreams of many peoples.
Your friends shall be with you again,
And you will breathe with new life.
And in time,

Two shall seek you out,
One before me, and one after,
And tell you the story of the star you wear,
So that the world may be saved."

And when the King spoke the words, "your heart, your mind, your
soul," he touched first his own heart with his free hand, palm on his
chest, and then placed the back of his palm on his forehead. Lastly, he
crossed his arms with the scepter so that his embrace signified the soul.
A simple gesture, but all the priests in unison followed his lead. Then
the King, whose face was painted with ochre and colors from a myriad
of dyes, smiled at him.

The emotions of the King broke through the mask of color, and
Daniel felt a genuine appreciation of the man whom the ancient world
thought a god king. Then, as if they turned to the mist that often rises
from that dry, flat land in the dark hours of the early morn, all the
figures lifted up and vanished into the heavens. But their whispers con-
tinued to susurrate over the sands, "Remember Babylon. Walk with us
by the rivers of Babylon."

Daniel groaned in his sleep as the visions of the night fled, but it
was a soft cry of wonder, and in his dream state, he idly questioned
whether he would remember any of it in the morning. And for the
rest of the evening, he fell into a dreamless sleep. Little did he know,
that the One who sent the dream was preparing him, giving him the
strength to face tomorrow and the task he really didn't know he had
accepted.

THE DIRECTOR INTERVENES

Thursday Evening, 2/24, Washington, D.C.—Babylon

WHILE DANIEL WAS wrestling with his visions, Rebecca was talking on her satellite phone.

"Yes, Director, we made it here safely with no incident. Fr. Daniel and Luca seem quite competent in their respective positions."

Leslie Richardson, tucking a loose blond hair behind her ear, said, "We were able to help the Italians tamp down word of the terrorist confrontation with Daniel and Luca the other night."

"Good," said Rebecca. "Luca filled in both Isaac and myself. Fr. Daniel took this near-death experience rather well."

"Remember, he's often trained with the Swiss Guard. The pontiff, as well, prepared him over the years by having him taught a variety of martial arts and even Irish stick fighting. It only takes one bullet to snuff out any martial arts advantage, but the practice of it gives great confidence to its practitioners. The fact that he and Luca are unafraid in the face of danger will allow you and Isaac to keep your eyes to the horizon for possible trouble."

"Speaking of which," said Rebecca, "are you giving us permission to let anyone know of our government ties? I mean, we can't be walking around with sophisticated equipment without questions eventually being asked."

"Neither the American military nor the Iraqis are aware of who you are," said the Director. "I enlisted your aid after the altercation at our compound beneath the Lincoln Memorial, and when I did, I decided no government can be trusted right now—even ours."

"So, I take it, that my genie-in-the-bottle stays secret as well."

"Of course," said Leslie. "The Ranbir Singh avatar can advise you and Isaac all it wants, but the hologram stays with you two alone. Only absolute necessity can lead you to break your covers."

"Any idea who attacked you?"

Leslie sighed, "The pseudo-cop remains unidentifiable. No criminal record, no spy record, nada. I suspect Iran is behind this, but how they would ever have found out about the Antiquities Department is a mystery. And this chief spy can't figure it out. Doesn't bode well for any pay raise."

Rebecca laughed, "You blew that when you enlisted me and Isaac's services. The Mossad trained us well and were willing to part with us as long as we share intelligence with them."

"I didn't care much for the deal, myself," said the Director, "but your own archeological experience and Isaac's weapons expertise are tailor made for the AD. I don't expect you to have to engage militarily, but I think we have to have the option in case things get dangerous. More professors have been murdered for less than a tomb in this business. I know it's not 'Indiana Jones', but the danger is there, and I want us to be prepared. Just remember, you are American citizens now, and your first loyalty is to us. We do the sharing with the Israelis, not you."

"Understood, Director," said Rebecca.

"I want an immediate report when the tomb is opened tomorrow," said Leslie.

"As soon as I can, but we are a small group. Dr. Markoz is not allowing the student archs in for the preliminary opening. We are recording everything, but he wants it low key, unlike the famous King Tut reveal."

"Any government officials expected?"

"No, he didn't want them either. If he has to restage the opening, he will, but because this find was unexpected and because the tomb is so large, we don't know what we will actually discover. So, he decided to go ahead on his own without informing the Iraqi government."

"Dangerous," said Leslie.

"Not really," replied Rebecca. "As you know, he's held in high esteem in the corridors of the government, and he's positively revered here among the locals. Though some people will be annoyed, they see him as one of their own and not in the clutches of the foreigners, especially the despised Americans."

"And after all we've done for them," remarked Leslie, drily.

"They don't see it that way, and frankly, after the destruction we drove through on our way out of the city today, I'm not surprised. Even Fr. Daniel had tears in his eyes."

"Did he recognize much of his old neighborhood?"

"Not at all," said Rebecca. "He said he felt like he was driving through the Martian landscape."

"I'll let you go, Rebecca, but remember to keep a close guard over the priest. We'll have an international incident if anything happens to him."

"I take it the pope was pretty insistent on that."

"You take it well, and believe me, I didn't know he had such blunt words in his vocabulary that demonstrated how terrible it would be if anything happened to his adopted nephew."

After Rebecca signed off, she lay, eyes wide open, in her bed thinking about what was to come on the morrow. A talented archeologist, she let the Mossad recruit her when she was only sixteen. She did most of her operations in digs around Israel and Jordan, making sure that antiquity smugglers were not attached to enemy combatants. She could stop their smuggling, but her real task was to make sure they weren't spying for some Arab nation.

It was actually Isaac who first approached her for recruitment. She liked him and though he was tall and chiseled like a long-distance runner, she wasn't physically attracted to him. Always smiling, his freckled face and red hair just didn't match up with his Jewish heritage. Somewhere, there was a northern European experience for one of his ancestors. She, on the other hand, was darker skinned with straight, raven hair, and though her figure was attractive, she was powerfully muscled. She needed to be on the digs. They made a strange pair, but their friendship was very strong. The Mossad let them partner together quite often.

When Leslie Richardson informed the Director of the Mossad what was going on in Babylon and made her proposal, she was surprised that Moshe Finder agreed immediately. Such cooperation would expand the Mossad's reach into Arab territory and give them an inside look on Dr. Markoz's discovery. He made some feeble protestations about Leslie's demands that the two spies become American citizens and transfer their major allegiance to the CIA, but he felt he still got the better of the deal. Once Israeli, always Israeli, and besides he attached some strings to the two that he had no intention of letting go.

Those strings were not on Rebecca's mind this evening. Her thoughts lay in puzzling out any problems that might waylay them tomorrow, and how long it would be before enemies would tip their hand and try to steal what the Azars had found. Keeping the priest and parents alive while protecting the treasure could be a hard task.

The director had made it clear that, despite the pope's insistence, their lives were secondary to the relics. Rebecca might have a difficult decision to make, and before she slept, she murmured that lives were more important than things, even if her bosses disagreed.

ISIS REDIVIVUS

Thursday Afternoon and Evening, 2/24, Fallujah

ABU SHADID WATCHED from the corner of a bombed out building in Fallujah. Just as a bus drew up to the mosque across the street, he saw the van trundling toward it the opposite way. Crossing his arms and putting his hands over his ears, he blew out his breath as the bomb went off. Far enough away not to be injured or rupture any internal organs, he still was knocked down from the shock wave and just missed a brick smacking his head as the concrete was jarred off the building he sheltered behind.

The screams told him he was successful. He didn't particularly like bombing near a mosque, but even in Fallujah, once an ISIS city just starting to crawl out of hell, this was the place to get the highest body count.

ISIS had been cleansed from the landscape during the Trumpian Desolation of the area. The U.S.A. was good at what it did best in enemy territory—killing and destroying. But Abu was laughing at the memory. He had done two years at Iowa State University in an Iraqi student exchange program before he had been recruited by ISIS. He stayed one summer in the States, and he remembered Americans trying to keep their oh so manicured lawns neat and tidy. Dandelions.

That's what the Americans called the weed that broke up the clear green carpet. They religiously pulled them up, but never eradicated them because they were too impatient. To kill a weed, you had to get the roots.

America never got to the roots of ISIS. Abu had this crazy thought of ISIS as the dandelions of the desert. True, they did great damage, but the Americans always left a little bit of the terrorist group behind. Abu was new growth. Slowly but surely, ISIS was infiltrating Fallujah again. He had been recruited a year ago and was now seen as a veteran since ISIS fighters tended to come from the villages and go to Paradise with great frequency. He was one of the long-lived ones. In a rather short time, he had become both a sniper and a bomb maker—steady hands were happy hands.

He was acting on the orders of the commander of the area— Farid Tahan. Farid had turned out to be a good tactician and was now trying his hand in strategic operations. He wanted to extend ISIS' influence south from Fallujah into the Babylon arena, and he had been given the blessing of the head of the Islamic State, Hasan Naziri.

This escapade in Fallujah would go a long way toward making Abu Farid's righthand man. Symbolically kicking the dust off his sandals, Abu walked silently away from the bloody site as sirens wailed in the distance. With all the violence still present in Iraq, he doubted whether this would get much notice from the press, but the one he wanted to impress would insist on all the details. He sent a text to Farid indicating success and knew he would be debriefed that evening.

When Farid heard that the bombing went off without a hitch, he was pleased. Abu was good at keeping his commander informed. And Farid was impressed. Abu had not failed in any undertaking he had been assigned. Successful in practice, he was also excelling in longevity. Farid was happy to have a soldier who had a brain for once instead of the drones he often got, who were always too ready to martyr themselves for Allah.

For the past several days, Farid had heard rumors about activity down in Babylon. Like most people in Iraq, he had heard of the famous archeologists, the Doctors Azar. They were an international treasure and because they were not overtly political, almost all sides revered them. Almost. Farid did not. They were westernized scholars whose commitment to the Islamic cause was gravely suspect. Markoz was a Christian and his wife was obviously Jewish. In the Islamic State they would not be permitted to live, but as for now, his superiors told him to hold off on any assassination attempts. Because of the rumors.

Word had come to Farid of a discovery in the sands of the ruins of Babylon. A big discovery. One which could enhance the reputation of ISIS if it possessed it, or which could enrich its coffers if it decided to sell it.

Later that evening, Farid called Abu to his quarters. Abu expected to be debriefed, but the ISIS commander disposed of that matter swiftly.

"You did an excellent job today, Abu. The body count has risen to 53 and is expected to go higher. The Iraqi sycophants in Fallujah will sleep troubled tonight as their grip on power begins again to wane."

"Allow me to tell you what happened," said Abu.

"Not necessary this time. I have another assignment for you. Word has come that a major archeological discovery has been found in Babylon. In the days to come, this will make international news. We need to know what the discovery is and what it means for the Islamic State. Take fifteen men and travel there tomorrow and investigate the situation. If you feel it necessary, you may engage the archeological team. I want them only threatened, not harmed, but they need to give us information on their find."

"What if they resist?"

"Then you may cause discomfort but not death. Start with the local help, then the students and if necessary, the professional team as well. But do not harm the professors. I understand their son has come for a visit. He is a Chaldean priest and under Vatican protection. It is not in our interest to make an enemy of the pope, so tread lightly there. Then bring back the information to me, and I will decide what our next step is."

"As you wish," said Abu, excited to be given a command of his own. "I shall pick the best men and be gone by morning."

"Travel swiftly. Keep them silent, and keep them from shooting guns in the air. You do not want to advertise your presence. Word will leak out anyway once you get there, but be mice in the desert rather than lions in the dunes. Do you understand?"

"Yes, commander, I do, and I will not fail."

"See that you don't. I have become quite impressed by you, Abu. Great things await you if you are successful."

With that, Abu was dismissed. He went to the barracks on the base that was not more than four kilometers from Fallujah and began to put together his team. The bright-eyed idealists, he crossed off his list. He wanted the killers, even though he didn't plan on any killing. They made the most patient soldiers, however, and would resist doing anything stupid. Within an hour, he had his quota filled and his team preparing to leave in the morning.

ESAGILA—THE TEMPLE COMPLEX

Friday Morning, 11/25, Babylon

SEVERAL THINGS HAPPENED simultaneously early Friday morning, Babylon time. An ISIS patrol, made up of three vehicles, set out from Fallujah towards Babylon. An Air France passenger jet landed in Baghdad with one of its passengers being the noted Islamic scholar and charismatic imam, Nabil Kasser. Finally, a very excited archeological team met for breakfast at Babylon Center.

Markoz and Frannie could barely contain their excitement. Over a breakfast of scrambled eggs and leftover lamb done shish ka bob style, Markoz laid out the morning's activities.

"There are now twelve main members of our team as of this morning: Myself and Frannie, my son Fr. Daniel and his friend Luca, Brian, Rebecca and Isaac and, of course our five, resident student archeologists."

Daniel looked them over as the student archs were introduced. All of them were from Yale and in their early twenties. He hoped they didn't think that working on a famous dig would bring them riches. He couldn't imagine a worse paying job than archeology, except, like he told Luca, anthropology. Yet, the chance to work with the great Professors Azar would bring them prestige, should his

father and mother find anything substantial and the students go on to
be professors themselves. Over time, he expected to get to know
them, but right now, their names just flew over his head.

They did not, however, escape Luca's notice. He knew this was a
small team, and he had spoken with Isaac, Rebecca and Brian last
night about the possibility of trouble. He had wanted to know if the
students would be of any help should problems come their way.

Brian, who knew them best, was non-committal. "Greg Bowman
is the biggest of the lot, and I've picked up that he's a hunter back
home in the forests of Vermont. Lacy Michels is a cyclist when she's
not digging, so—probably useless in a fight, excellent in an escape.
Roger Trake is getting his fine hands dirty for the first time in his life.
I'll be surprised if he makes it another two weeks. Again, useless for
our needs. But the twins, Albert and Fred Brummel are a different
story. They are a little older, having served time in the Navy. They
were Navy Seals and involved in removing several terrorist groups
from our area around here. Smart as can be, they may not look like
Schwarzenegger or The Rock, but they've killed, and I think would
do so again if necessary."

"What in the world are they doing here?" asked Luca.

"What are you doing here?" rejoined Brian. "I mean, you are
here to make sure the Doc's son doesn't get killed, and these guys are
here to give back a little life to the people since they had brought so
much death. I'm just glad they are here. They are worth a company of
men."

"None the less," said Rebecca, "we can't hold off an army, only
impress a little fear on small bands of troublemakers that come our
way."

"What about ISIS?" said Luca.

"I don't think they'll be a problem," said Brian. "They haven't
really bothered us for the twenty years this excavation has been going
on. The professors are very popular in the country and they are not

political, so they have a lot of support. Nothing they do threatens ISIS."

"Except now," said Luca. "Somebody wants my friend dead and tried very hard to kill him the other day. I don't know if it's ISIS or someone else. All I know is they tried once, and I suspect they will do so again, particularly if they hear we have found anything they can use to enhance their Islamic state."

Rebecca laid her hand on his shoulder. "We'll do our best. We are well-armed and you've brought some special goodies with you that will be helpful."

Luca laughed at this. He had brought plenty of weapons but was particularly proud of the two shoulder rocket launchers he had managed to pack with all the other "stuff." They would certainly not be defenseless. Rebecca, Isaac and Brian had a good relationship with the Iraqi Army command in Baghdad, and they would only have to hold out a couple of hours before reinforcements came to their rescue. At least that was the plan.

Luca took a quick look at the support staff that Markoz was introducing. They were locals but not simply peasants. Many were skilled construction workers—obviously they got a lot of work putting back up what terrorists bombed down. The engineers were from Baghdad and had worked on digs before. They were excellent at building the scaffolding, steps and anything else needed to reach the places Markoz, Frannie and the team wanted to go. They would not be going down into the site this morning. There was simply no room. Luca did not trust them one bit, but he had no real evidence to suspect any of them of trying to harm his friend. But he would keep close watch.

Markoz was done with the pep talk, and Daniel and Luca both looked at each other, excitement peaking on Daniel's face.

"Wait till you see this, Luca. The ancient Temple of Marduk, is within the Esagila and it's cool enough. I should know. I worked excavating it for enough summers. But when Dad suspected there was even a lower level beneath Marduk's Temple—well, that was what made this extraordinary site, spectacular. Dad and Mom have been here for twenty years, off and on, and know the basic plan of the Esagila. It had been excavated before, the last time in-depth around 1920. But Mom and Dad are the ones who really gave it focus. It's such a mess down there because everything is made of clay. The pyramids and the tombs of the kings of Egypt are much easier to deal with because they are made of stone. Over time, mud brick collapses. We can still excavate it and find stuff, but it's just more difficult."

"What's so special about the space underneath the Marduk Temple?" asked Luca.

"Well, here's the thing," said Daniel. "Dad hasn't told me everything, but last night he said that the chamber is not made of mud brick, but instead stone that had been brought in. Do you realize how impossible that sounds? Whatever was down there was meant to stay down there, nice and dry, and perfectly preserved. Nebuchadnezzar had the power, the people and the riches to make this happen, but it is still extraordinary. Truly on the level of the pyramids.

"Sure enough, Dad breaks into the chamber and there, right in the middle of this stone room sits a huge sarcophagus, big enough for a giant, or several giants. And on its lid is all this Akkadian cuneiform script with that one English line. How freaked is that? Dad says the cuneiform is hard to decipher. It's in a dialect unfamiliar to him and he's hoping I can translate some of it. We'll see."

"Ah, the boy wonder," said Luca laughing. Turning serious he said, "Hope you can work fast. With the trouble in Rome, I have a hunch we will be facing the same here as soon as our enemies know we are present. So, ooh and ahh this morning, and get your butt working this afternoon to make sense out of what your father has found."

It wasn't long before the twelve were tromping through a dirt-packed path towards the Esagila, which, from the surface, basically looked like nothing but a mound of dirt. Afterall, it was covered by seventy feet of debris, so the construction workers had devised an elaborate elevator system to go directly down to the middle of the Esagila complex. For years, the two archeologists had been excavating underground. Daniel thought it was reminiscent of the Scavi excavations underneath St. Peter's Basilica. Archeologists, there, had unearthed an entire city of the dead complete with streets and avenues and houses. Since the Basilica couldn't be torn down, they simply excavated the necropolis seventy feet under the church and reconstructed it underground. Same thing here thought Daniel. Good thing he wasn't claustrophobic.

It was rather anti-climactic when they all assembled underground. Well-lighted with artificial torches in wall sconces, the Welcoming Chamber was mostly bare except for exceptional wall carvings and beast images on enamel overlaid walls.

"There's a lot more here than you think," said Markoz, "but you need the right skills to see it. This is not what I have brought you here to behold. Come with me and let's walk over to the Temple of Marduk, and I think you will be more impressed."

They were not. The Temple was similar to the gathering area they had just left, only smaller. Again, there were hints of its former greatness. King Nebuchadnezzar was said to have coated the walls of this Temple with gold and endowed it with precious objects laid before a solid gold ten-foot-tall statue of Marduk. The pedestal was still present, the statue and the gold were not.

"Someone like Frannie and me," said Markoz, "and I hope my son and the student archs, will find such an ancient room impressive, but it will not stun the world. What I found several months ago will.

Beneath this Temple is another chamber, made of solid stone—the work that it must have taken to get that stone here, well it just amazes me. It is exactly the size of the Temple Marduk. In fact, I think it is the real Temple of Marduk and when you see it, I think you will understand."

He walked over to the pedestal that once held the statue of the god. "Notice this is made of stone. For the life of me, I can't figure out how this remained undiscovered for so many centuries. The stone is not simply affixed to the floor. It is a pillar that goes below the floor. Every relic hunter, king and seeker of treasure made the wrong assumption that the pillar was buried into the clay and mud, because that's all there is around here. But they were wrong. Technology is wonderful, and our instruments picked up that there was a lower chamber here. We thought it would be full of water because even though the Euphrates has moved much further west since ancient times, the water table is still high. We were fools to think this."

He walked over to a door in the floor and lifted it open. Dry air issued forth, and Daniel could see a narrow stairway descending.

Markoz looked at the other eleven rapt listeners. "We dug a bit and dug some more till we figured out that under ten feet of clay, there was a roof of stone beneath us. Then we were very careful to open up a hole and descend into the lower chamber. Come see what we have found."

Markoz made Daniel go first, and as he descended the stairs, he was treated to his father's flair for the dramatic. All around him was gold light and he could hardly make out a single detail beneath him. Walking carefully down the stairs, he noticed a huge block of something dark in front of him. Everyone traipsing behind made not a sound.

"My God," said Daniel as his eyes grew used to the sight. "This is incredible!"

Before him lay a huge chamber, forty by sixty feet, completely covered in gold. There were wall sconces which originally would have held real flaming torches, but his father had fitted flickering artificial flame torches in the receptacles, similar to the ones in the above temple complex. Markoz had put protective transparent covering on the floor so that there was a path upon which they could walk. Daniel immediately discerned that this temple would have gotten very little foot traffic. Gold was not particularly fragile, but you certainly didn't want to tromp all over it, even in bare feet. Inlaid within the gold were fabulous enameled tiles the color of lapis lazuli in the form of the creatures of the sea. On the walls, the same was done for creatures on the land, and, on the ceiling, were the most fantastic birds Daniel had ever seen, especially the peacocks, their flared tails full of precious stones, exploding with color. The gold around them sparkled with brilliance.

He saw, too, the pillar of stone from above, and it came down, resting on the floor in the shape of another pedestal. But it was not empty. Instead, a golden, ten-foot-tall statue of Marduk stood there with its hands outstretched. Daniel knew this had to be the statue that every Babylonian king since time immemorial had to have present at his coronation. In fact, he could not be king, authority was not transferred to him, until he grasped the hands of the god and received the god's assent. The statue was supposed to have been stolen by the Persian King Xerxes when he vandalized Babylon in the fifth century B.C.E., but that apparently was a myth, for here it was. Yet, even the beautiful golden statue was not the room's centerpiece.

That was taken by the huge tomb in the middle of the temple. It was seven feet high, fourteen feet wide, and fourteen feet long, and it was not gold. It was black.

"Just like the *Kaaba* in Mecca," said Daniel referring to the rock sacred to Moslems all over the world.

"Indeed," said Frannie. "It's a meteorite, but not just any kind of falling star. It's been hollowed out, and there is something inside. Our instruments cannot penetrate it very well, but it registers as mostly hollow—mostly. We are pretty sure it's a tomb, though we do not know whose it is."

That's when Daniel used a step stool and took a look at the top of the rock and saw the inlaid gold Marduk Tablet covering most of the horizontal space. Engraved with large Akkadian cuneiform script, it shone warmly in the torchlight.

Sure enough, at the end of the cuneiform text was a last Akkadian line of figures and the English words, *November 1, the year the Beast traverses the heavens.*

"Mom, Dad," said Daniel in a shaky voice. "We've got a problem. This is going to change the world."

THE REVEAL

Friday Morning, 2/25, Babylon

"I KNOW IT is going to change the world, son. I just don't know how," said Markoz. "My Akkadian is pretty good, but this is a different, very strange dialect. I know the gist of what this says, but the details are beyond me. Thought you might be able to shed some light."

"What do you think it's about?" said Daniel, looking down from his perch on top of the tomb.

"Best as I can make out, it is a prophecy using a lot of Gilgamesh imagery. That's the Babylonian hero who made it his task to be the Middle East monster hunter. The tablet talks about a monster who consumes the people of the world, and some struggle with evil that takes place on this extraordinary date of November 1."

"What makes you think the date is this year?" asked Daniel.

"Just a hunch and a guess at what the cuneiform really says."

"Well, if you're correct, that's why this tablet is going to change the world," said Daniel. "That battle hasn't happened yet. But you are right. I can get you a more exact translation. This is a dialect spoken around King Nebuchadnezzar's time right here in this area, but it was used, we think, by temple priests only. They made some changes in grammar and inserted a few Persian and Medean words just to mix it all up. Give me a moment."

Everyone maintained their silence, but Markoz's eyes fixed on the ring Daniel wore. His right hand grasped the edge of the tomb. Markoz swore that in the flickering torchlight, the ring shone a faint blue. He looked toward Frannie, his wife, who was obviously seeing the same thing. It was so faint, no one else noticed. She glanced at him with a slight smile. They never knew exactly what the ring could do, but at other times when Daniel worked the site through the years, the ring had suffused a soft sapphire light whenever he was concentrating. It was often, then, that Daniel came up with ideas and insights far beyond what he should have been able to do, as if the ring was augmenting his already fearsome intelligence.

They heard him gasp several times, and then he jumped down off the step stool and faced the small crowd.

Luca knew his friend well and said, "I haven't seen you look this pale since the other day when we had that problem in Rome."

"What problem?" squeaked Roger Trake, the rather fragile student arch, who was clearly overawed by what he was seeing. He, like the other student archs, had not entered this room before. "No one said anything about you having a problem."

Markoz could be harsh at times. "Really, Luca? Did you have to bring that up?"

Frannie said, "I told you it's best they all know. What happened to our son could happen here. Could happen to all of us. Go on, Luca, tell them."

Luca grimaced, angry at himself for raising the anxiety of those present, and said, "There was an attempt on Fr. Daniel's life before we left for Baghdad. Obviously, somebody knew he had the ability to shed some light on what the professors have found. Problems could come here, and depending on what Daniel has just found out, we all might have to take a quick vacay back to Rome."

"Look," said Markoz, particularly focused on the students, "I've given this a lot of thought, and I'm willing to put anyone who wants to leave in a van straight back to Baghdad and on a flight home."

The twins just laughed and Albert Brummel said, "Fred and I would have to feel a lot more threatened before we left a place like this. Besides, this is the find of the century."

"Agreed," said Lacy. "I'm not about to miss this opportunity just because something might go wrong. I knew what I was getting into when I came to Iraq. I admit I had a hard time convincing the nervous parents."

"Don't worry, Roger," said a patronizing Greg Bowman. "I'll make sure the lions, tigers and bears won't get you."

Roger sneered, "Thanks, but I can take care of myself."

"Right. Sure," laughed Greg. "Yet, I'm here, if you need me."

Markoz looked them over once again. "If you change your minds before noon, let me know, and I'll get the transportation you need. Now, tell us what you think, Dani."

"I'll tell you what the tablet says," said Daniel. "I mean this is a rough translation but here goes:"

By the rivers of Babylon
We dreamed the dream—
The night visions of terrible power.
A Beast from shadows between the stars,
Whose mouth is fire,
Whose breath is death,
Has risen in our minds,
And devoured our hearts.
So, we sleep,
In the arms of the nether world,
But our brother from long ago walks again.
He walks beyond the veil.

He has seen the Beast,
Whose mouth is fire,
Whose breath is death.
He tells us to wait,
To wait the passing of the years,
For a time to come,
When the dreamer returns.

Daniel paused a moment, and Rebecca said, "That's just the usual apocalyptic claptrap. You can find it on any tablet all over the Middle East."

"But there's more," said Daniel. "The language intensifies. Here, let me get it right." He jumped back up on the stool and bent over the bottom half of the inscription. "It goes on,"

The earth shall shake;
The tomb shall open;
Blood shall flow;
Darkness shall seep
Into the land between the rivers,
Where war has waged
From age to age.
Armies ride the Beast,
Whose mouth is fire,
Whose breath is death.
The dreamer and the guided one
Shall unite against it.
War and bloodshed break out—
The fire from its mouth.
Pestilence and famine descend—
The death from its breath.

The pillars of the earth shake,
In the year of the Lord, November First,
When the mark of the Beast
Traverses the heavens.

"You are right, Rebecca," said Daniel, "that this all sounds re-markably familiar. Most of it is in the familiar cant of apocalyptic prophecy. Except for two things—two things that will change the world. First is a reference to the dreamer and the guided one. Any Moslem, not just a Shiite, will lift their heads high at that knowledge. The guided one is the Mahdi, the spiritual deliverer of the Moslem people who will lead them into the New Age. He will team up with Issa, an Arabic name for Jesus, and together they will usher in this new heavens and new earth. It's puzzling that the tablet refers to a dreamer and not Issa, but that could mean anything. The Islamic people will not split hairs on that.

"The second thing is this sentence in English and this date, *the Year of the Lord, November First, when the mark of the Beast traverses the heavens.* Before I left Rome, the pontiff told me that the Jesuit astronomers at the Vatican Observatory at Castel Gandolfo had discovered a new comet in the solar system. They think it will be especially bright, brighter than Halley's Comet was in 1987. The pope impressed upon me that the fragmented and violent nature of the world today would most likely inspire a lot of superstitious muttering among people. He told the President of the United States that he believes this comet will be the celestial Mark of the Beast the plaque refers to."

"The Marduk End Times Tablet says nothing like that," said Brian Jeffries.

"Correct," said Daniel, "and, by the way, I like the name, but the pope intimated that the people themselves, once they learn of the tablet will think the comet has something to do with the Beast."

Isaac turned to Dr. Markoz and said, "Any idea as to the identity of this Beast?"

"Not a clue," said Markoz. "Other purported Babylonian prophecies, including those in the Book of Daniel, were written in the centuries leading up to the birth or just after the time of Christ. Usually, they meant anyone from King Antiochus of the Seleucid Empire in Syria to Emperor Nero in Rome—no modern person is ever referenced by name."

"We've got some time," said Daniel. "Spring and summer actually. The more we study this, the closer we'll get to an identity of this so-called Beast. We can then figure out whether we have to worry or not. My guess is not, because usually these figures remain symbolic, even if there are visible events in the heavens. Besides, we might get a few more hints when we open this tomb."

"First thing we want to do," said Frannie to the group, "is get this tablet free of the sarcophagus. I want it taken to the center and put in the study room where Fr. Daniel can do his magic."

SPIES ARE US

Friday, Late Morning, 2/25, Babylon

BRIAN JEFFRIES TURNED the video off as the workmen gently lifted the gold tablet up the narrow stairs on its way to the Center. He had been surprised how easily it detached from the sarcophagus. Now, the tomb looked like a roughhewn block of stone, all alone in the center of the subterranean Marduk Temple.

Like everyone else, he wondered what was in the crypt. It looked solid, but he knew there was a seam about one foot down from the top that wound its way completely around the rectangular stone. Dr. Markoz and he had discovered it when they subjected the rock to many tests. It was, however, invisible to the eye.

What the tests could not show was what was actually inside. Both he and the two professors had determined that it was hollow and something was in there, but an opaque fog seemed to cloud all the types of visualizing they had at their disposal. Dr. Markoz had yet to determine the best way to lift the lid off without damaging anything inside. He and Markoz would meet this afternoon to figure that out.

Then, he'd kill the doctor. At least that was his plan. Once the contents of the tomb were revealed, Brian had no more use for the archeologists. First Markoz, then his wife, then the students. He planned for Rebecca and Isaac to be outside the camp when this happened. His commander, Farid Tahan wasn't wild about the coming executions—he had, after all, forbidden the new ISIS team that was being sent to harm the team. But Brian argued that the ensuing chaos would benefit them, and Farid had reluctantly agreed.

Markoz's son and the Swiss Guard would be a little tougher to handle, so he expected to enlist one of the contractors, who was an ISIS sympathizer, to do the deed.

Brian laughed to himself. He had to be the whitest ISIS member in the entire world. He had been recruited years ago, when ISIS had its Caliphate. He had taken a dangerous trip to Damascus to pick up some artifact for Markoz and been approached in the bazaar by none other than Farid who now had risen far up the chain of command since those days. Farid was charming and talked about how much the cause needed Brian, the fair-haired thirty-something from the U. S. A. He had no religious convictions, and that did not seem to bother Farid much. The money lure was persuasive as was the chance to be something more than an archeologist's security guard. Thus began, what Brian called, a 'beautiful relationship.' He really hadn't had to do much over the years, just keep Farid apprised of what the Babylon dig was all about. He must have done a good job because, not more than a year ago, he had been taken to see the great Hasan Naziri, leader of the new nascent Caliphate.

That meeting was pivotal. Brian had told him that Dr. Markoz and his wife were close to new discoveries. Unlike Brian, Hasan had deep religious convictions and saw the Caliphate as a continuation of all the Babylonian kingdoms before, only doubly blessed by Allah, because it walked in the path of the Prophet Mohammed. Brian remembered Hasan's eyes boring into him. They were black as the night and totally empty. He asked for an oath from Brian of total loyalty and willingness to kill in the name of the Prophet. So, this is where my lust for gold has led, he thought. But he thought that for only a moment. He looked straight back into those bottomless eyes and swore that loyalty oath and pledged to kill in the Prophet's name if necessary. After all, in for a penny, in for a pound.

And that was that, until just a few weeks ago. Word had reached Hasan that a grand discovery had been made. It was the biggest find in the history of the dig. Once again, Brian had to meet Hasan, only this time, Farid attended the meeting as well. They told him that ISIS wanted the contents of the tomb, that he would be the caretaker of whatever relics were present, and that he would be responsible for their well-being.

He was surprised his conscience, such as it was, wasn't troubled. Markoz and Frannie had been nothing but good to him through the years, and yet, getting his hands on the greatest archeological find of the century seemed to wipe the guilt away. He had killed before.

There was that one time, in high school, when he had pushed his friend off the cliff they were hiking at Wyalusing State Park in southern Wisconsin. He really didn't know why he did it. But he didn't feel particularly bad about it.

His parents, thinking that he would be scarred for life at what investigators said was a tragic accident, took him to a counselor who warned his mother and father that their son definitely had some sociopathic tendencies. They and he refused to listen and 'accidents' continued to happen to those around him. Violent to his wife, that marriage soon ended in divorce. He had gone into the security business, which proved to be a release valve for his anger. Those who crossed him paid dearly. His employers never kept him long, and when the chance came to join Dr. Markoz's team, he jumped at the opportunity. A forged resume smoothed his way. He found he liked the job, and for a while, the exotic locale and the interesting work kept his needs at bay, till Farid Tahan called him with a better offer.

He had decided to arrange an accident right here in the chamber to take care of Dr. Markoz. His grieving wife could be a suicide in the evening. He chose to put off the student archs' demise thinking that many deaths would draw the authorities from Baghdad. They'd probably come anyway, but an accident and a suicide were much easier to explain than blatant murder.

He was parsing the details in his mind when he heard someone shouting his name in the upper chamber. It was Rebecca calling for him. Something about an unexpected visitor.

A MEETING OF MINDS

Friday, Late Morning, 2/25, Babylon

MEETING BRIAN IN the upper chamber, Rebecca said, "We've got a visitor, a VIP, I believe, from the limo and the two government SUVs that shadowed it."

"Who is it?" said Brian, thinking his best laid plans were already delayed.

"I have no idea," she said. "He's tall, fairly young, Arab descent. That's all I know."

"Well," said Brian, "that ought to bring everyone out to gawk. Let's go join the scrum."

By the time they arrived at the Center, most of the people on the dig had come to see the new visitor. It appeared that both Markoz and Frannie knew him.

"Ladies and Gentlemen," said Markoz, "I want you to meet a very important man, one who I had the chance to meet last year in Damascus at the conference on Ancient Archeological Ruins of the Levant. This is Dr. Nabil Kasser of the IWSI, the Islamic Worldwide Studies Initiative. Dr. Kasser has heard of our work and has come to get an up close and personal tour. Accord him every courtesy. As you were."

Most everyone went back to work except for Daniel, Luca, Brian and Rebecca. Markoz said, "I didn't want to tell the others, but Dr. Kasser has heard the rumors of our find, and I could not think of anyone better than him with whom we should share our knowledge."

Frannie made the introductions, and when she got to Daniel, she said to Kasser, "This is our son, Fr. Daniel. He's been with us for years on our summer digs ever since he was a child. Now that he's grown up and a busy priest at the Vatican, we're lucky to have him with us." She gave a dramatic sigh. "The pope is his godfather and adoptive uncle. Daniel, I'm afraid, is always occupied with the secret affairs of the Vatican."

"Mom!" said Daniel blushing. "Really!"

Luca couldn't resist. "Oh, it's true, Dr. Kasser. Daniel is the Sherlock of Vatican. He knows the Vatican Archives almost as well as the pope."

"And who might you be?" laughed Kasser.

"Why," said Luca, "I'm Watson, of course. Seriously though, I'm Luca and I'm pleased to meet you. Will you be staying with us long?"

"At least overnight, if I can impose upon Markoz and Frannie's hospitality." He raised a quizzical eyebrow in their direction.

"Stay as long as you wish," said Markoz with a smile. "Daniel and Luca can show you to your quarters."

"Sir," said Luca, "if it's okay with you, Rebecca and I have a perimeter check to do."

"Dad, I'd be happy to show Dr. Kasser around."

"As you wish. Nabil, I'll see you and Daniel in an hour at the Center. I want you to take a look at the tablet we found."

As the little group broke up, Luca said to Rebecca, "There's more to our good doctor than meets the eye."

"That's a Sherlock thing, Luca," said Rebecca. "You're just the obtuse Watson." She laughed at her own joke, but Luca turned solemn.

"Seriously, there's an air of mystery around him. Famous imam popping in for a visit on this day of all days. I wonder what he really wants."

"Probably what all academics want—a little bit of fame and media attention. My hunch is that this is the place to get it. After seeing the tablet, I'd say we've got just a few days before the news media descends upon us. The team will keep quiet, but the staff will eventually talk. Then, of course, there's the contents of the tomb. Markoz mentioned that he and Brian were going to have to strategize how to open it."

"You've been here longer than me," said Luca. "Any worries about the people here? I have to tell you that the attempt on Daniel's life was so sophisticated and coordinated that I can't believe whoever is behind it will give up easily. By now, they will have figured out where we have gone."

"I did the usual security check on everybody when I got here," said Rebecca, "even though Brian said he had vetted everyone. Dr. Markoz is pretty lax when it comes to doing that himself, so he delegated Brian to do the heavy lifting. As far as I could see, Brian did a good job. I rechecked everyone on the team—they seem to be fine. The staff is more difficult. They are locals without a lot of written history behind them. Other than name, education and work record, we don't know much about them. They're the weakest link. I have Isaac talking more in-depth with the foremen to see if anything troublesome pokes up its ugly head."

Luca stopped their perimeter check for a moment. His face grew hard as he said, "You don't know me well, at least not yet, but you need to understand something. For some reason that even I do not know, the pope has placed enormous trust in his nephew. Before we left, he told me to protect him at all costs. For the Swiss Guard, that means at the expense of our lives. If something should happen to me …"

A chill of fear ran up Rebecca's spine. The down-home country boy affect that Luca liked to put on was only a mask. She recognized a fellow professional. Swallowing hard, she said, "I hear you. Nothing is going to happen, but ..." she put her finger on his lips as he was about to object, "should anything like that occur, I will defend him with my life."

Luca exhaled, "Thank you." He looked over the empty desert and said, "We can see for miles. I know it looks like sand and dirt here, but this land is old, very old. And as much sand and dirt as there is, there is more blood here, blood spilt through the centuries. I can smell it. When I was in grade school, they called this place the Fertile Crescent, but really, it's the Valley of the Shadow of Death, and blood fills its rivers. Be on guard, Rebecca. I feel that all is not as it seems."

A TALK WITH THE MAHDI

Friday, Late Morning, 2/25, Babylon

DANIEL TOOK THE professor around the camp, proudly showing what his father and mother had accomplished. Nabil seemed duly impressed, but he plied Daniel with questions.

"Your parents love you very much. You must be an only child."

"Yes," said Daniel, "I was born in troubled times, and Dad was just starting out with the excavation here in Babylon. Mom hadn't joined him yet. She was busy with me." He smiled. "I was a handful, so they say."

"Is that why they named you Daniel?" said Nabil. "Because of this place?"

"Yes. It was a compromise, I think. Mom is Jewish and my father is Christian. 'Daniel' sort of split the difference."

"Ah," said Nabil, "Daniel the Prophet of Israel and Daniel the Jewish Prince of Babylon."

"Maybe, but I think they just liked the name."

"Daniel was a great dreamer and interpreter of dreams," said Nabil. "Are you like your ancestor?"

Daniel looked at him sharply remembering his dream of the night before. "Sometimes I dream. I got a degree in archeology, and I run across a lot of ancient stuff on dreams. The old ones put much more stock in them than we do today. Here in Babylon, we have unearthed hundreds of tablets dealing with dream interpretation. I've translated a few, but no other scholar has touched them yet. It's kind of sad really. I think the ancient Babylonians, and those that came before them, put so much emphasis on dreams that to ignore what they said about them is to miss much of who they were and what they believed."

They were quiet for a moment and then Nabil said, "I agree with you. I have dreams, and they sometimes puzzle me. I search the Quran for an explanation but seldom find any answers. Perhaps you might try your hand at interpretation?" Nabil smiled.

Daniel shook his head, laughing. "I'd be a poor one to try and figure out anyone's dreams. I'm a researcher. If it exists in clay and if it is in one of the ancient languages I know, then I can give an answer, but modern dreams, I think not."

"Don't sell yourself short, Fr. Daniel. Names mean something and being around this dig for so many years—well, let's just say that the ambience of the place has to rub off on you. You might be better than you think."

They had arrived back at the Center, and Markoz was waiting for them.

"Dr. Kasser," he said. "Come and see what we did this morning. This tablet will be a surprise to you, as will my son's ability to translate it."

THE END TIMES TABLET

Friday, Late Morning, 2/25, Babylon

IT WAS JUST the three of them that went in to the conference room. "We call it the 'End Times Tablet,'" said Markoz pointing at the object set on sturdy tables. Nabil stopped in the doorway gasping, "I thought I was going to see some broken clay remnant, not something carved in gold to last through the centuries." He moved slowly towards it and gently touched its smooth surface nobbled throughout by cuneiform writing. He brushed a shock of brown hair off his glasses as he bent over to examine the tablet in depth.

"Akkadian. It's written in Akkadian," he said.

"Kind of," said Daniel. "It's a dialect rarely preserved on ancient tablets. That's what makes it so difficult to decipher."

"How do you know it?"

"The major degree in Archeology from Sapienza University in Rome requires each candidate to excel in at least one dominant ancient language. I chose Akkadian and was good at it. I even had time to study the dialect you see before you. It's the only thing in archeology that I know better than my father and mother."

Markoz laughed and ruffled his son's hair. "You know more than you think."

"What does it say?" asked Nabil.

"It's a vision and a prophecy," said Daniel. "It talks of dreams," and here Daniel glanced over at Nabil, "and in those dreams a dreaded Beast from the heavens comes to ravage the world. Whatever the 'Beast' is, the tablet does not say. It could be something represented by the comet or the comet itself. But the tablet talks of the dreamer as someone who has died but will come again. He has seen the Beast, whether in reality or in a dream, the tablet doesn't say. Three other things stand out: First, the dreamer appears, then someone called the 'guided one'."

Nabil hissed an intake of breath. He couldn't help himself.

"You have heard of such a person?" asked Daniel.

"Perhaps, but it is a convoluted legend. No matter. Go on."

"Second," said Daniel, "the mark of the Beast will be seen in the heavens and herald the coming of this monster. There will be an alliance between the dreamer and the guided one and together they will fight the war and bloodshed, the famine and pestilence, which the coming Beast shall bring. Third, and most importantly, all this shall happen by November 1, our time. Up until the final sentence, this whole Tablet speaks standard apocalyptic fare, similar to others down through history. What makes it so significant, as you can see, is that the final sentence is in modern English. How can this be?"

"A forgery, perhaps?" queried Nabil. "It's been done before."

"Indeed, it has," said Markoz. "However, for weeks, since it's been discovered, I have proceeded on that premise, putting this tablet through a myriad of tests. My findings are startling. One hand carved the text. The grout used to affix the tablet to the sarcophagus is made of the same material as similar bindings from the Babylonian era. Pollen fragments embedded in the grout also come from the time period relevant to Nebuchadnezzar. All other tests pointed to a provenance of Babylon, circa 600 B.C.E. This is no fake or forgery."

"That's still not enough proof," said Nabil. "Forgers have gone to greater lengths to falsify test results."

"Yes," said Markoz, "but there are supporting arguments. Within this secret Temple of Marduk were a collection of clay tablets, mostly dealing with the reign of the King. But several contained astronomical observations. The astronomers were awaiting the appearance of a heavenly body called 'The Beast.' I don't know what it was."

"What about the Hand of God Nebula that appeared last November?" said Nabil. "Could that have been the sign? It is spectacular and though the date is a year off ... perhaps ..."

"I don't think so," said Markoz. "The Babylonian priests said it was 'like a comet' but larger and somehow different. They expected it to appear in the year King Nebuchadnezzar died. It never did. This was the only mention of the failed prediction in history. My guess, from their own astronomical observations, is that it also appeared in 3200 B.C.E., but we certainly aren't going to find any records on that. We should, however, test out a hypothesis. I have an astronomer friend at NASA, who is a whiz at finding comets. We have the coordinates for the heavenly object that was supposed to appear in the heavens 2600 years ago. We have a prophecy about the 'Mark of the Beast' appearing around November 1. Let's ask my friend to use the Hubble Telescope on those coordinates and see what he finds. If it's there, he should be able to identify it. If he discovers anything, the only thing I will ask is that he name it the 'Marduk Comet', in honor of the Babylonians and their ancestors who first discovered it."

"We can compare it to the object the Vatican astronomers found. It might be the same," said Daniel.

"This is all too much," said Nabil. "I would never have believed your work would reveal such things."

"Well," said Markoz, "as with most discoveries, years of hard work and little acknowledgment always go before the great find. All this has come to a head in just the last several weeks. You couldn't have come at a better time. Come now, we'll have lunch and then back to work on the sarcophagus. We have to find a way to open it safely."

"Could it house the Tomb of Nebuchadnezzar?" asked Nabil.

"I doubt it," said Daniel. "The King's body was supposedly dragged through the streets after Xerxes desecrated his tomb when the Medes conquered Babylon after an uprising. I suppose anything's possible, but I suspect the tomb holds someone else very important. Maybe a high priest."

"Don't get ahead of yourselves," cautioned Markoz. "Keep an open mind and be amazed at whatever we find. It is sure to be stupendous. Nabil, you should know that the sarcophagus is carved from a meteorite, and I have no idea how the Babylonians did that. The alloy is extremely hard, and their tools would not have been strong enough to accomplish the task."

"Another argument for a forgery," said Nabil.

"Perhaps," said Markoz. "But before we make a final determination as to authenticity, let's get the tomb opened."

ENEMIES IN THE MIRAGE

Friday, Noon, 2/25, Babylon

"ALREADY, IT'S HAZY on the horizon. Even my binocs can only get vague images." Luca harrumphed in frustration.

"Any groups of people visible?" said Rebecca.

"Here, take a look yourself. My eyes are crossing."

"Ah," she said, "that's what's wrong. I thought your face was folding in on itself."

Luca laughed. "You know, I've never been in a desert before. Daniel threw a giant centipede out of my quarters yesterday, and today I squashed a scorpion I found in the corner of my bathroom. He was just skittering there in the corner, brandishing his little sword dipped in deadly poison. All the little vermin like humid places."

"Careful with those things. Their sting will make you wish you died."

"So I've heard," he said. "Now, do you see anything?"

"Bedouin off to the west with the ubiquitous camels. They're harmless. Dust cloud due north. Several jeeps or SUVs, I think, if they're kicking up that much dust."

"Problems for us?"

Rebecca put down the binoculars and squinted. "Could be. They're traveling somewhere with purpose. Not much out there. We're the only real item of interest."

She pointed for Luca's sake. "Look. They've stopped."

"How do you know?" he asked.

"The dust cloud went stationary. But there's not even an oasis out there. I estimate they are five to six klicks away. And my guess is they have come for us."

"Sounds ominous," said Luca. "Come for us as in 'come to hurt us' or come for us as in 'scout and see'?"

"The former I would guess. Three jeeps or SUVs are overkill for a looksee."

"That your intuition kicking in or your Mossad training?"

Rebecca looked startled. "How did you know I was in the Mossad?"

"I may look like more brawns than brain, but I can do research too. Besides, I used my sat phone to call back to my commander this morning, and he had a nice little cheat sheet on you. He knew you also left the Mossad recently, both you and Isaac."

"Are you surprised at what you learned?"

"Not really. You are even more competent than what I thought. You've dealt with ISIS before."

"Twice, and they're vicious. I don't know who these guys are, but if they're ISIS, we're in a lot of trouble."

"Did you train with Isaac?"

"No, but I have worked with him. He's a newbie and though in security, he is much more comfortable with munitions and communications."

Luca smiled. "You mean communications then munitions, right?"

"What are you getting at?" she asked, genuinely puzzled.

"Well first he has to tell them he's going to blow them up, and then he has to press the plunger."

She laughed a fresh, clean laugh. Luca was pleased she didn't rattle easily. He grimaced as he realized she probably had much more experience than he did. Fortunately, she didn't ask him about it.

"My training and my gut," she said, "tells me we are going to have a run in with whoever is in those vehicles, sooner or later. It's nearly lunchtime. Team and staff will be in the Center Mess, and we can give a general update on what to do."

They were late for lunch, but that was just as well. They took Markoz, Frannie, Daniel and Brian off to the side and filled them in. With a nod from Markoz, Brian called for quiet in the room. He asked everyone assembled to give the new security team their absolute attention. People nervously shifted in their seats, not knowing what to expect.

Both Luca and Rebecca made rather light of the situation but said this was a great time to practice security protocols. If an alarm sounded from the Center siren, all staff except those assigned to security were to assemble in the Center as was the team. They were to prepare the building for assault. That pretty much consisted of pulling down steel shutters over the windows. The heavy block building was built to withstand small arms fire and light munitions.

Brian had trained staff security in the use of firearms. They were the only locals he trusted with armaments. He didn't think any of the local staff were ISIS, at least Farid had denied it, so he didn't look for any enemy action from within. Except for himself of course. He didn't want some fanatical grunt screwing up his plans. But Farid had cautioned him not to reveal himself under any circumstances. His cover was too important. Brian believed the ISIS group Rebecca and Luca had spotted had no intention of killing any of the team.

Brian said to the assembly, "Most likely, there will be no immediate problem. This still looks like a contingent of men content on watching us. Rebecca and I will let you all know if there is any trouble."

Isaac pulled Rebecca aside, and they had a rather heated conversation. Apparently, from what Luca could overhear, Isaac was miffed he was left out of the planning. Rebecca, however, was good—very good. Somehow, she placated him. As Luca walked over, he heard her say, "Isaac, you're the best munitions person we have. We're going to need the flash bangs, and you'll probably have to make some smoke as well if they approach us. We'll want to show that we can defend ourselves. So, heavier munitions just as a precaution. Regular grenades if the Center is attacked. Check out Luca's bag of toys for anything that might be useful. We won't win a pitched battle, but we might bruise them enough to make them run away for a while till General Farouk gets here with reinforcements." Somewhat mollified, Isaac moped away.

She looked at Luca who shrugged his shoulders. "You men," she said. "Damn egos are so easily hurt."

"I have a very big ego, so just be careful when you step on me," said Luca. "I bruise easily."

TO SLEEP, PERCHANCE TO DREAM

Friday, Afternoon, 2/25, Babylon

"THANKS FOR SCARING the hell out of every person at lunch, Luca," said Daniel with just a little sarcasm in his voice. "We'll get a lot of work out of everyone this afternoon."

"Couldn't be helped, Dani," said Luca. "Three SUVs full of an unknown number of men parked just within eyesight of our camp. Gives me the willies."

Daniel laughed, "The willies?"

"What? Did I say it wrong?"

"No, no, you said it right. It's just fifty years out of date."

Luca blushed, "They say it on the sci-fi show *Babylon 5*. Future enough for me."

"Geez," said Daniel, "It's an ancient sci-fi show—as anachronistic as it seems. I've got to get you something more up to date to watch if you're going to practice your English picking it up through television shows."

Luca plowed on. "Doesn't matter. The point is: they're not the good guys. Let's just hope they don't want to start an international incident, or just do their usual terrorist thing."

Daniel parted with Luca as the Swiss Guard headed for the perimeter again. As much as he liked his friend, the day had already been packed with amazing revelations, and he wanted a chance to think about them.

Casting off his boots and black cargo pants, he threw himself down on his bed and mused over the gold Marduk Tablet. There was no doubt it was authentic, but it was also unique. Nothing like this had ever been found before. Clay tablets were the writing material back in the day of the empire's greatness. Babylonian pagan priests regularly studied the stars, and their astronomical knowledge was extensive, even mixed up as it was with astrological gobbledygook. They had left copious records, but their findings were as dull and scientific as their modern counterparts.

The discovery of this End Times Tablet, however, was momentous. The words themselves were frightening, but the fact they were engraved in gold seemed to give them even more emphasis. What was most intriguing to Daniel was the utter lack of vandalism concerning the tablet or even the entire underground Marduk Temple. The Esagila Compound had been repeatedly ransacked over the years, but not this room, buried underneath the original complex. Daniel was ready to admit that the meteorite tomb, plus the tablet, plus the opulent, secret Marduk Temple was quickly forgotten because of the fear they engendered. The ancients of the time were aware of their power and were loath to disturb the tomb. By the time of King Nebuchadnezzar, Marduk had become the chief god of the Fertile Crescent pantheon, and, indeed, had almost achieved monotheistic status. Messing with his stuff would seem a real bad idea to any ancient.

The heavy lunch made Daniel drowsy as he reflected on the strange and fortuitous arrival of the Syrian professor and his response to the find. Taking his iPad, he did a little research on the scholar, noting his Islamic books and history of the Shiite Twelve Imams.

Not exactly the most riveting stuff. Even his institute, the Islamic Worldwide Initiative, though it did worthwhile things, was not packed with excitement. Yet, he knew about the Mahdi.

Not being able to keep himself awake, Daniel dozed and felt his eyes open onto a dream world similar to the one he had seen the night before.

This time, the modern camp filled in the empty spaces in the landscape of his dream, though the tell, where the Esagila had been built, was still there. The King and priests were gone, and he felt hot in the noonday sun. Walking through the camp, he found it deserted. Not even Luca was up on the perimeter.

The heat lifted off the sandy dirt in shimmery waves as far as his eye could see. Suddenly, he caught sight of a flashing light far out in the distance close to the horizon. He knew immediately it must be the encampment of their unknown visitors. Looking more carefully, he guessed the flashing light was the sun reflecting off a pair of binoculars—binocs Luca called them, a shorthand term, he got from the show 'The A Team', making Daniel smile.

Knowing this was a dream, Daniel wondered if he could stare at the distant wielder of the binoculars and will to see him. In dreams, one could do those things, so he concentrated. For a moment, it was as if two trains were rushing toward one another and heaved to a sudden stop, dust clouds all around. When the dust cleared, a rather nondescript Arab was staring at Daniel wonderingly.

"How did you do that?" said the Arab in perfect English.

"It's a dream," said Daniel. "Don't you know this?"

"I closed my eyes for a second," said the Arab, "and found myself here."

In a moment, the discomfiture of his unexpected guest vanished, and a shrewd look came into the Arab's eyes. "My name is Abu Shadid, and perhaps this ... dream ... of yours which I have had the

*good fortune to enter is a good way to give you a most important mes-
sage. We want the contents of the tomb, and whatever you have discovered today."*

*"You are too far away to know if we have discovered anything,"
said Daniel dismissively.*

*"The desert has ears in the sand and eyes in the sky. We know
about the golden Marduk Tablet. So, tell me, what does it say?" Abu
gave Daniel a shockingly fake smile of encouragement.*

*The priest snorted. "Not a chance. I don't even know who you
represent."*

*"We are ISIS," said Abu with a growl. "And my commander
would like your cooperation so as to avoid unnecessary conflict."*

*"This is my homeland," said Daniel. "You and the Americans
have made it a graveyard. I have no intention of giving up our patrimony to a corrupt and degenerate pseudo state."*

*Abu snarled, "Wrong choice, priest. Not only are you an infidel,
but you are a stupid one at that." He unslung his rifle and pointed it
at Daniel.*

"It's a dream, you fool," said Daniel. "You cannot hurt me here."

*Abu pulled the trigger, and Daniel felt his left shoulder explode in
pain. The terrorist pointed again, but suddenly from around the cliff, a
howl was heard. No mournful wail, the sound was a fierce challenge
and distracted Abu for a moment, allowing Daniel to throw himself
behind a pile of discarded clay bricks.*

*From around the hill came a huge, gray wolf dog, saliva dripping
from his mouth in the heat. It howled again, and then fixed its gaze on
Abu. The Arabs, generally speaking, thought Daniel, hate dogs, but
this was no mongrel that moped around the streets of decaying Arab
towns. This was a fearsome foe.*

"Grigio!" cried Daniel. "To me!"

*The wolf dog bounded over to Daniel and sniffed his wound. Then
he tore after Abu who was already shooting at the animal. He was*

either so nervous that his shots went wide, or he simply missed because of fear. Grigio tackled him to the ground, and as the terrorist screamed, the wolf dog took Abu's left hand into his mouth and squeezed. Thousands of pounds per square inch came down upon fragile fingers, and without puncturing any skin, Grigio crushed Abu's hand.

As the screams went on, Grigio released, and Abu scrambled to escape. The dog let him go and returned to Daniel who was near to passing out.

"How?" he said. "How did you get here in the nick of time?"

It was a wolfish smile that Grigio gave, but Daniel was not afraid. He tried to reach up with his good arm to touch the dog, but the dust from the sand rolled in and took his sight away.

He groaned in agony as his eyes popped open. He had fallen off his bed and smashed his left shoulder into the concrete floor. He looked for blood, but, no, that was in his dream. His shoulder was just bruised and not that badly either. He sat up, rubbing his eyes, amazed the dream had been so clear and felt so real. It warned of danger, and Grigio had even shown up. Daniel laughed at the absurdity of it all, until he looked down on his black clerical shirt and saw a bundle of grey fur sticking to his shirt pocket. In the distance, he thought he heard a howl.

Throwing the door open, he was amazed at how quiet the camp was. He looked at the time and gasped. He was late. His father expected him at three o'clock, and here it was nearly three-thirty. He and the others must be down in the tomb.

Throwing his cargo pants and boots on, he hustled across the camp to the Esagila. Sure enough, he heard his father's voice coming from the underground tomb. Rushing down the stairs, he uttered an apology and stopped. Only his father and Brian were present.

"Where's everyone else?" he asked.

Markoz gave a sad smile, "After you left lunch, the others stayed behind. They were a bit stressed with Luca and Rebecca's warning, so I had them take extra time for a bit of a siesta. That's why I didn't come and get you. I thought you needed the process time as well."

Daniel nodded and said, "Thanks, but what are you guys working on? Have you thought of a way to raise the lid of the sarcophagus?"

Brian looked at the tomb and said, "We know there is a seam here even though it is invisible. One foot down from the top of the tomb, all the way around." He said it like he was speaking poetry. "We also found a seam right down the center of the lid. The gold tablet was laid over it, but the problem is the same as with the other seam. It was sealed with some element that eludes identification. The lid is in two pieces. That's the good news. But, just like the other, it's as if it was welded solid to the rest of the sarcophagus. That's the bad."

"I take it we won't just be lifting it off?"

"Right you are," said Markoz, "and I'm reluctant to put an acetylene torch to it. I have no interest in damaging it. The meteorite has abundant iron in it. It's possible that a large magnet used in some demolitions might be helpful, but that would entail dismantling— gently—a large part of the ceiling to lower the equipment, and I don't want to do that either. But I will if I have to. The gold on the walls and ceiling are panels affixed to stone. They were laid after the mosaics were set. It will be delicate work and should delay us no more than a couple of weeks."

Daniel hissed in impatience, "That long? Surely, there must be another way."

An explosion of far-away gunfire kept the others from answering. All three raced topside to see what had happened. Running through the Esagila, Daniel figured the gunfire was happening in the northern part of the camp. He was faster than Brian and his father, and arrived at the edge of the camp to see Luca and Rebecca pointing SG 552 Commando rifles at an open-air truck holding fifteen Arab fighters each with AR-15s pointing skyward. Fortunately, they hadn't been shooting at anyone, just exercising the stupid practice of firing into the air to gain attention. They just couldn't help themselves. From out of the passenger side of the truck stepped a man who appeared to be the leader.

Daniel bit his tongue and then whispered to Luca, "I know this man."

"How could you possibly know him?" whispered Luca back.

But Daniel didn't answer. He was looking at the left hand of the man, wrapped in a bandage, arm in a sling.

THE MAHDI SPEAKS

Friday Afternoon, 2/25, Babylon

AT THE SAME time Daniel noticed the man's hand, the leader of the fighters picked out Daniel in the group. His eyes grew wide and he said, "You!" And then he laughed. "How is your shoulder, priest?"

Daniel grimaced and said, "Better than your hand, I think."

"You know this man? How?" said his father.

"Later, Dad," said Daniel. "His name is Abu Shadid, and I think he is an ISIS terrorist. He's going to ask you to hand over what you've found."

"Your son is perceptive," said Abu. "Indeed, that is what I have come for."

"Why?" said Markoz. "So you can destroy it, like your soldiers have done to all the ancient ruins and artifacts you've come across?"

"If it takes away from the glory of Allah, of course," said Abu. "However, at this time, my soldiers are here merely to keep the peace as we observe your discovery and seek ways to transport it back to our commander. No one needs to get hurt."

"Sweet Jesus and Mary," said Markoz. "This has got to be the first time you haven't killed and then asked questions later."

Abu seemed to drop his head in shame, but then grinned. "Well, we've learned not to act so hasty. But make no mistake, we never walk far from our roots. Now, lead on good Doctor to the secret Tomb of Marduk."

Luca and Rebecca raised their rifles, and Abu's soldiers did the same. A deadly, silent stalemate swept over the group.

"Enough!" said a voice. Everyone looked to see Dr. Nabil Kasser striding forward, Frannie right behind him. "Stop this insanity this instant," he said, walking past Daniel and towards Abu.

"That's far enough," said Abu, a pistol magically appearing in his good hand. "And who are you?"

"You should know who I am, since you belong to ISIS. I know your leader, and he knows me. You long for the Mahdi do you not? If so, you have heard me speak about him."

He turned back to Markoz. "You have a spy in your midst. That's the only way these men could have known of today's activities."

Focusing his gaze on Abu, he continued, "Your men certainly have heard of me. I spent last summer preaching at the Damascus mosques. Some no doubt heard me personally."

There were mutterings among the soldiers.

"And those who didn't witness have heard the whispers around the campfires. I have come to bring peace and judgment."

The soldiers look wide-eyed at Nabil and said amongst themselves, "Mahdi, Mahdi, Mahdi," until the name became a kind of chant and Abu had to silence them.

"Shut up, all of you!" he said. "You," he said to Nabil, "are not the Mahdi. That person is a myth, and if he did exist, he would be more noble than a simple professor. Yes, I've done my homework. I know who you are. A pretender. A false prophet. I should kill you where you stand."

"You'll not touch him," said Luca. "He is under our protection."

Abu laughed. "You have two guns against my fifteen. I could kill you all in seconds."

"And yet you won't," said Rebecca. "Look up toward the Esagila," she said. "Tell me what you see."

Abu froze in fear and anger. "Where did you get that?" he said.

"'That is Isaac, my munitions expert," she said, "and he happens to be holding a rocket launcher, a gift from the Swiss Guard of Rome." Luca nodded his head to Abu and smiled.

"Rome," spat Abu. "Your pope should not have interfered. You have opened him up to the reach of our hand."

"You already made a move on him when you tried to kill his nephew," said Luca. "Long ago, we made ready to confront you whenever you decided the Vatican was fair game."

Abu paused for a moment. He did not know of the attack on Daniel in Rome, and if this sniveling, worthless excuse for a soldier from the Vatican was correct, some other ISIS cell must be responsible. For a moment, he wondered why Farid hadn't informed him.

"No matter," said Abu. "I only came today to give you a message, to give you time to do the right thing. You cannot hope to win against us, so tread carefully and talk swiftly. We will be back."

Nabil spoke again, "Soldiers of ISIS. The time for war and violence is coming, but it shall pass you by if you embrace the peace of the Mahdi. What shall be is far bigger than you. Join me in keeping the Day at bay. The world does not have to end in blood and death. As Allah says, 'The way of peace is open to us.' Join me."

"Do not listen to him!" shrieked Abu. "He is weak, a tool of the West."

"Join me," said Nabil.

Abu fired four pistol shots in the air to gain the attention of his men who seemed to be hanging on the professor's words. Abu jumped back into the truck and ordered the driver to leave. In seconds only a cloud of dust was left hanging in the air.

"They'll be back," said Markoz, "and I'm not sure what to do. Calling General Farouk might precipitate a crisis and turn the attention of the world on Babylon. It's too early for that."

"Let them be for now," said Nabil. "I gave the soldiers enough to think about that they will be reluctant to do Abu's bidding for a while."

GETTING TO KNOW YOU

Friday Afternoon, 2/25, Babylon

AS PEOPLE RETURNED to their work, Nabil approached
Daniel. "May I walk with you for a while once again?"

Daniel smiled, "Sure you wouldn't prefer the air-conditioning of
the Center?"

"I find it exhilarating to feel the same heat as the ancients felt so
many centuries ago."

"Oh, trust me," said Daniel, "you'll get over that."

"I wanted to know how you recognized Abu." He looked pene-
tratingly through his wire-rimmed glasses at Daniel.

Daniel ran a hand through his black, sweat-drenched hair. "I
dreamt of him. I took a little nap after lunch, and I dreamt of him
just like we saw him now, and he told me what he wanted. He hurt
his hand in my dream, and shot me in the shoulder. When I woke up,
I banged the same shoulder as I fell out of bed, and as you could see,
his hand was bandaged. I've never had a dream that foretold the future before, well, except for the one last night."

"Amazing," said Nabil, "just like your namesake, the prophet
Daniel. He was quite the dreamer as well."

"Actually, I think he mostly interpreted other's dreams."

"Ah," said Nabil, "but we truly don't know for sure, do we?"

He laughed easily and Daniel found himself liking the man. "Why did you really come out here today?"

Nabil's face grew serious. "Babylon has always been a nexus of power. Both Christians and Moslems, and of course the Jews, hold it to be a sign of the world's corruption, but I think it is just because it became so powerful. The Jews who experienced the exile didn't like being away from home, but they were impressed with the life and culture of Babylon and adopted many of its ideas and customs. For instance, the Babylonians didn't invent angels, but the images those spirits wore for the dwellers of the Fertile Crescent certainly helped the Jews put flesh, if I may say that, to their own experience of those spirits."

"Correct," said Daniel. "My namesake was entrusted by King Nebuchadnezzar with the whole province of Babylon once he and his three friends gained the king's confidence."

"The King loved them," said Nabil. "That had to be one of the major reasons he endowed them with such worldly power, that and the fact that their God, blessed be his Name, seemed even more powerful than Marduk."

"It all changed when the Jews got back to their homeland," said Daniel. "Slavery does that to people. Wonderful as Babylon was, the survivors of the exile grew to hate it with all its pagan lusts, ambition, power and pomp. My hunch is that they lost a lot of sons and daughters to that culture which indigenized and worshipped the Dark God. Those survivors didn't have a high opinion of Marduk."

"Always religion," said Nabil. "The most divisive force on earth. Did you know the historians of the late twentieth century said that all the major wars fought in this millennium would be wars of religion?"

"I did know that," answered Daniel. "Sometimes even historians can be prophets. Just look at my homeland. Babylonians, the Medes, the Persians, Greeks, Parthians and all the other conquering peoples have flowed across this fertile plain. It's endured paganism, Zoroastrianism, Judaism, Christianity and Islam. Religion after religion replacing one another in importance. And now it looks like a desert. Do you know why, Nabil?"

"Tell me."

"Because the rains stopped falling, and the land was watered in blood. So many people have died here. Millions upon millions. The only thing that hasn't changed is Babylon's penchant for drawing the whole world into its own problems. Look at today. ISIS has within its power to precipitate an international incident. The innocent people of this camp could die, and whatever is found in the tomb could be used to start a world war."

"Do you think the contents of the sarcophagus are that important? Perhaps it's just Nebuchadnezzar in there, having escaped Xerxes' wish to desecrate his body."

"I don't think so," said Daniel, recalling his first dream. "I feel that whatever that tomb holds also holds the hope and dreams, fears and nightmares of the people on this earth. I don't know which to expect. You still haven't told me why you have come? Have you had dreams too? Are you the Mahdi?"

Nabil smiled ruefully. "I do not dream like you. But I have ideas. I feel Allah, blessed be his Name, is calling me. Distantly, I am related to the Twelfth Imam, so biologically I can claim a link to him. But I am much closer to him in philosophy, religious views and temperament. I know he disappeared twelve hundred years ago, and when he reappears, he is supposed to be the same Imam, but lately, I have felt this call, this purpose, this destiny."

Daniel's eyes had grown wide.

"Don't worry," said Nabil. "I am not a fanatic. I do not seek world domination as the pseudo-Mahdi's of the past have done. The true Mahdi is to be a sign of peace in the midst of turmoil. Daniel, do you know who the Mahdi seeks? He seeks the one called the Dreamer. The Mahdi is the guided one, the messenger of Mohammed and the Dreamer is a Christian, the follower of Issa, Jesus."

"Surely, you don't think …"

"I don't know, but I came here seeking answers. My public life is for all to see. Read my sermons, and you will see that I have planted the seeds of the Mahdi's message. Those men today were ready to believe I was the real deal. I'm not, yet. I need to find the Dreamer. I need a sign." Nabil stopped at Daniel's quarters and took his shoulders in his hands. "Do you know where I may find him?"

Daniel's mouth gaped, and he had no words.

Nabil gave a soft laugh and said, "Let me know if you do."

SKEPTICISM

Friday Afternoon, 2/25, Babylon

LUCA WAS OUT of his quarters the moment Nabil disappeared around the corner.

"What did he want?" he asked.

"He thinks I'm someone who's supposed to help the Mahdi. Because of the dreams I'm having."

"What? You didn't tell me anything about dreams."

"I haven't had the chance." Daniel filled him in on how he knew Abu and how interested Nabil was in that fact.

"I didn't tell him about the first dream I had. It was so weird."

"As weird as Grigio showing up and chomping down on an Islamic terrorist's hand?"

"Yep," smiled Daniel. "Nebuchadnezzar was there."

"Oh great, now you're going to go all Old Testament Daniel on me."

"The thought had occurred." They both laughed.

"Still," said Luca, "Nabil didn't just show up here by chance. That little scene out there could have been just for our benefit."

"I don't know," said Daniel. "He does think there's a spy."

"Well, I'm sure there is. This is post-war Iraq. Everyone spies on everyone else. By the way, while you were chatting it up with the professor, I called back to headquarters again and asked about Abu Shadid. While they were checking, the Colonel said the pope requested a detachment of four guards in addition to me to protect you in whatever adventures you get us all into. They may be sent here if things get worse. The pope is also redoing part of the Vatican Archives where we can set up shop. Looks like you've got yourself a permanent assignment, and I've got to keep your holy backside out of all things bad. Your uncle, though, thinks it will take five of us Swiss Guard to keep you out of trouble."

"It might just," said Daniel.

Luca noticed a little dust cloud out where the locals were excavating part of the Etemenanki, the ziggurat thought to be the biblical Tower of Babel. "A couple of people are taking off somewhere in a jeep," he said as he picked up his binoculars to look. "It's Professor Nabil with one of the locals. I wonder what they're up to?"

"You're too suspicious. We can't go spying on him. He's a guest."

"He's a mystery," said Luca, "famous VIP or not. I'm going to check in with Rebecca. She's up at the Center. I'll see what she thinks about it."

"As for me," said Daniel, "I'm going back to the tomb and see if Dad's there. Maybe we can figure out how to open the thing without damaging it."

AN UNLIKELY ALLIANCE

Friday, Late Afternoon, 2/25, Babylon

THE JEEP SPED across the desert road toward Baghdad until Nabil and his driver were out of site of the dig. Then, it veered west across the desert, picking its way slowly towards the ISIS encampment.

When they arrived, they found the soldiers armed and waiting for them. Abu approached and said, "What are you doing here?"

Nabil sneered. "After your foolish attempt earlier this afternoon to intimidate the archeologists, I had a talk with Azar's son, the priest. Surprisingly, he may prove to be a help to us."

"Are you the one who tried to have him killed?" said Abu.

"I was aware of the attempt."

"Aware, or the one who caused it to happen?"

"That," snapped Nabil, "is none of your business. I mention the priest now because I have re-evaluated his worth to us."

"I was told," said Abu, "that a visitor was coming to the dig to-day that would assist me."

"What? Your spy told you this? Who is the informer?"

"One of the security team. His name is Brian Jeffries, and I assure you, he is faithful to our cause."

"An infidel?"

"No longer," said Abu. "His information for the past several months has never been wrong, yourself being an example of that."

"I have been given access to the site and a front row seat to the tomb opening. Markoz Azar, like all scholars," said Nabil, "trusts another scholar implicitly as long as they don't think he'll steal their research. I saw much today that gives me great excitement. We must see what the tomb holds."

"Didn't I say that today?" said Abu.

"Yes, but you said it with guns pointing, looking like the expected terrorists you are. As you explained to the group, we are a bit more refined now. I'm here to tell you to hold off on doing anything violent. Let me see how much I can learn first."

"I have told Brian to have the professors and the students meet with an accident after the tomb is opened."

Nabil paused in silence, then said, "If necessary, the two professors can be dealt with after the tomb's opening, but leave the others alone. Daniel could fill in for his father. But he would be much more helpful if his parents remain alive. We need someone familiar with the entire excavation. He knows the dig and is better in the translation of the tablet."

"I will explain to Brian."

"He is not to know about our association with each other."

"As you wish. However, I will contact Farid and ask his permission for our plan."

"No, I will contact Farid and bring him up to date," said Nabil tersely.

Abu ground his teeth in frustration. One did not advance up the ladder of ISIS without bringing word of success. "Why should it be you? Farid commands this sector, and I report to him," Abu said.

Nabil reached out and swift as a snake grasped Abu's injured hand. "More is at stake here than you know. I have heard it said that you have served well, but make no mistake. Farid takes his orders from Hasan Naziri, and the leader of ISIS takes his orders from me."

Abu hissed in pain and anger.

"Never forget," said Nabil, "I am the Mahdi." As soon as that word was uttered, the other soldiers fell to their knees and raised their arms, shouting this time, "Mahdi, Mahdi, Mahdi."

Nabil looked more intently at the suffering Abu, "Your soldiers seem to understand. Is there any further difficulty you have with me?"

"No," said Abu.

"'No' what?" said Nabil.

"No ... Mahdi."

"Good," said Nabil and raised Abu back to his feet and embraced him. "Stay here till I send for you, and do not worry. You will have plenty to do in the camp. We just need to let time take its course for events to reveal the secret of the Esagila."

On the way back, Nabil felt his hands trembling. He clutched them together so his driver would not notice, and his mind raced.

He had exaggerated his authority to Abu. It was true that Farid and Hasan listened to him. After all, he was a major source of funds for their activities. He had alluded to the presence of the Mahdi on earth by reminding them that the times seemed ripe for such a revelation, but he had not revealed himself as the One. Why?

His studies, his research into the ring, the success of his preaching throughout the Muslim world—all these things had built his confidence that the still, small voice in his heart was truly real. It whispered to him of destiny and Allah's will. Still, he was not convinced. He was just a man.

True, and the Mahdi was just a man—endowed with special abilities. Other than his intellect and mesmerizing voice, and of course his wealth, Nabil was nothing that special. Except that ordinary people were talking about him as if he was the One. Farid and

Hasan treated him with great respect, and he thought that deference was more than just a lust for his money. But he felt he needed another sign. He just was not sure his calling was a real thing. That's why the ring was so important.

The mystery surrounding Fr. Daniel Azar also puzzled him. Actually, he did not know who tried to murder the young man, or if someone was only trying to capture him. But he had begun to believe today that Daniel might be crucial to his plans. He seemed to know more about the tablet than his father, and, perhaps, he might have some knowledge about the ring.

The young man's dream had surprised him. Nabil was a rational scholar, but he believed that some dreams were numinous—that is, they connected with a higher reality. Daniel seemed to have had one or more of those. He would bear watching.

The jeep rolled into the excavation site, and the driver let Nabil off at the Center where Luca and Rebecca were waiting, seemingly for him. His mind raced for a good cover story as he smiled at them, forcing himself to relax as he extricated himself from the tight passenger's seat.

"I had this kind workman drive me around this whole area where Babylon once was. I wanted to get a sense of what it must have been like. Instructive, really."

"But professor ..." began Luca.

Nabil waved his hand. "Oh, I know what you are going to say. I shouldn't have gone out so far away from camp, but, truly, I didn't feel in any danger. However, it was a dirty and dusty business, all that sightseeing. If you'll excuse me, I'll get myself cleaned up. And perhaps a nap will be in order before dinner. I can't tell you how pleased I am that Markoz and Frannie asked me to stay a few days. I hope I can be of help to the cause." With that he smiled and left them.

"Smooth as silk," said Rebecca.

"Yeah, a real practiced liar. I saw his jeep go up towards Baghdad, not zip around this site. I wonder what he was really doing?"

A GIFT OF WISDOM

Friday, Late Afternoon, 2/25, Babylon

AS LUCA AND Rebecca were talking with Nabil, Daniel was making his way back to the tomb. As he climbed down the stairs, he could hear his father and Brian arguing.

"Look," said Brian, "giving Professor Kasser access to the tomb is a bad idea. What if he publishes before you? What if he takes some of the credit? This is bad, Markoz, and goes against every practice of archeology."

"So says Frannie," said Markoz. "You two plot this out together?" Markoz raised his bushy black eyebrows and then smiled. "You know I'm just joking. But I've never been in this for the notoriety. You know the things we are finding. Nothing in Egypt's Valley of the Kings comes close to the discoveries we've made. I'll get my fame out of this and so will you. Who really cares if he shares a bit of the limelight? I'm just about to publish the results of the finds this dig has made over the past decades, and you know how that will up-end the scholars' views."

Daniel appeared at the end of the stairwell saying, "Really, Dad, you're ready to tell people about what you've found?"

"I am, son," said Markoz. "We've always known the Babylonians were an advanced race of people. We just didn't know how advanced. Most research in the Middle East has veered the West toward Egypt because of the political upheavals of this area in the past two centuries. But Frannie and I, and of course, you, since you were a little boy, and Brian here, have stuck it out these many years. Look what we've discovered.

"For so many decades, historians have seen this area of the world as a series of empires, rising and falling, and they have written history as if those empires were the true story. But they aren't. They are ephemeral, passing things, frosting over substantial cake, the cake being the culture of the area. For most people, for thousands of years, the empires were just an exchange of rulers. The style of living, the way of writing, the curriculum that was taught in the schools, and most importantly the religion that was believed never changed much."

"You're saying," said Daniel, "that the folks in Gilgamesh's era of 2800 B.C.E. would have been pretty comfortable twenty-two hundred years later in Nebuchadnezzar's time."

"Exactly," said Markoz. "Think of how out of place we would feel if we were to go back to the time of Jesus, and that was just two thousand years ago. But Babylonian society was so stable, that it enabled new ideas to grow and develop without the upheavals we have seen in the West."

"Or maybe," said Brian, "they just stagnated and never changed."

"But you know that wasn't so," said Daniel. "Science and technology developed greatly."

"If that was really true," said Brian, "wouldn't a person from those elder days feel out of place in Nebuchadnezzar's new Babylon?"

"Not at all," said Markoz, "because of the continuity in society. The technology would have amazed them, but the language, the stories, the culture of the people would have been a much gentler transition into the future than what was found in the West."

"And that," said Daniel, "sounds to me like someone had a plan, a long-term plan for the development of this area, because it's beginning to look like it was the melting pot for peoples throughout the world. We've always called it the Fertile Crescent, the place where the first civilizations, the first cities developed and so on, but it now looks like the source of so much more knowledge for the world."

"Exactly," said Markoz. "And this tomb will be the culmination of that knowledge, of that I am sure. If we simply look at it as a tomb for a king, it is a mystery. So large and undisturbed. But what if it is more than a tomb here? What if there is unknown knowledge placed in there?

"After the time this crypt was constructed, Babylon virtually disappeared, and the area's culture began to undergo great change. It continued on for hundreds of years, but its death was near. Jews and Christians and Zoroastrians began to populate the area and learned much from the dying civilization, but that all evaporated when Islam came in and rode roughshod over the ancient ways. They were iconoclasts, and though Christians and Jews were enemies of the pagans, they were smart enough to learn what they could from them. Islam could care less and in a very real way, buried this culture."

"So, this tomb," said Daniel, "represents the summit and the last high point of an ascendant Babylonian civilization?"

"Yes, and I know what you are going to say. 'How can a tomb, that may hold the body of one of the most powerful kings who ever lived, or something else even more splendid, tell us so much that we don't already know about Babylon?'"

"The thought had crossed my mind," said Daniel.

"Mine too," said Brian, his skepticism clear in the tone of his voice.

"Hear me out," said Markoz, yanking on his mustache. "Look at the size of this thing. Why so big for one body? Why should it encase a body at all? And why was this room never plundered? In the time of Nebuchadnezzar, surely its presence was known, because clearly it was used in worship. And yet, the conquerors who soon came after the fall of this dynasty never opened it or ransacked this part of the Esagila. It's as if it was hidden. But we found it, buried under one hundred feet of soil. All that dirt wasn't here when Cyrus came, or Xerxes fired the city, or Alexander took over. They should have easily found this place, and yet they did not."

"You're saying it was hidden somehow," said Brian.

Markoz walked over to the tomb, running his hand across its rough exterior. "It was concealed, and whenever its last priests died, it was forgotten, until us. I do not think it was our efforts that discovered it. The tablet on top of this sarcophagus was clear. Whoever placed the tomb here, wanted it to be found at this time. We've been led to it in some way, and our patience and hard work has been a test to see whether we were worthy to find it."

"That's a little superstitious," said Brian.

"Only if your mind is conditioned to a scientific method that allows for no outside interference other than that which the visible sciences provide."

"You think someone or something led you here, Markoz," said Brian, incredulity raising the pitch of his voice.

"I do," said Markoz, looking at Brian and his son intently.

"You know, Brian," said Daniel, "we religious guys have a broader view of the universe. The scientists the Vatican has employed over the years, including its astronomers and archeologists, may not have all been believers, but all of them knew that science could not answer everything. And they knew that intuition was not simply new ideas popping up inside their minds from nowhere. The Vatican scientists and many others besides believe that knowledge must be tempered by wisdom, and wisdom is the gift of the gods, so thought the ancients. We moderns think God has a hand in directing our pursuit of knowledge."

Brian snorted, "What could be better than the tech we have?"

"Dreams," said Markoz.

Daniel looked up at him sharply. "Dreams?"

"I'm not crazy," said Markoz. "I just know from my study here at this site for the past several decades that the Babylonians put great stock in dreams and not in a superstitious, peasant way. They believed the gods communicated to them sometimes through a special kind of dream. Their intuition moved them to new understandings and new inventions. The time of dreams ended with the death of the Babylonian culture. But perhaps it is about to begin again."

Daniel could feel his body shaking. "Dad, have you had those kinds of dreams?"

"Several times," said Markoz with a smile. "In fact, one of them led me to find this tomb. It was the most remarkable dream. It happened about three months ago. Your mother and I had fallen asleep in our quarters after ten p.m. one evening like we usually do. I fell into a deep slumber, and that was unusual for me. I dreamed a dream of great power and wonder."

I dreamt I was on the tell of Esagila and as I looked down, I could see a statue on the desert floor. It was quite large, over ten feet tall, with its hands stretched out. I knew what it was immediately. It was the statue of Marduk that was paraded around the city each time a ruler was to be crowned. The ruler had to take the hands of Marduk for him to be accepted by heaven and by the people. I was curious, so I walked down the hill to see the statue more closely. It was gold, and it shone under the silver stars of the sky. And as I approached it, someone came around from behind it, and I gasped. It was a man, but not like one I had ever seen before. All I could think of was the description in the Book of Daniel of one like a 'Son of Man'—that's how spectacular this person looked.

He was luminescent in the night, tremendously magnificent and beautiful, and he spoke to me. "Markoz Azar, welcome. Your work here is known far and wide and you are to be commended. But much is still required. Put your hand in the hand of the statue and you will know what to do."

I trembled then, and my faith kicked in. "But sir", I said, "this is a pagan statue of a dead people. I fear for my soul to ask it for knowledge or wisdom."

The vision laughed, "You are already wise, Markoz, but you need not fear. This statue never had godly power. At best it was a conduit for what is known throughout the universe, and that is how you shall use it this evening. Be not afraid. Put your hand on the statue."

I did. It was like electricity flowed through my mind. The statue's other hand lifted and pointed. I turned toward the Esagila, and the hill became transparent. I saw the parts of the temple we had excavated, and I saw another temple, this one we stand in now, and, in a flash, I knew where to dig. I was about to look more deeply throughout the hill when the vision ended.

The extraordinary man laughed and said, "I think that is enough for one night. Follow your intuition now and reveal to the world what you are to find."

"That was my dream," said Markoz. "Amazing, don't you think?"

"Dad, why did you never tell me?"

"I didn't tell anyone except your mother. Believe me, she was as surprised as you are now. And I couldn't tell you. It would have to have been by sat phone, and as I mentioned before, we are being watched and listened to. I didn't want to give such information that could be so easily stolen."

"So, you followed your dream," said Brian.

"I did. The next day, we began excavation, and now here we are."

"I always wondered how you knew where to dig," said Brian. "I thought we found this on a whim."

"Not on a whim," said Markoz. "We were directed here. That's how I know this tomb is so important. Whatever we find in it will shatter the complacency of the world. That's why I'm not too worried about what Professor Kasser does with what he knows. All will work out as it should."

Daniel was amazed at his father. The staid archeologist who never had time for flights of fancy or the superstitions of the locals, found a tomb based on a dream, one very much like the one Daniel had. Something was afoot here that made chills run up and down Daniel's spine.

Brian and Markoz made to leave, but Daniel decided he was going to stay for a while. When he was alone, he ran his hands along the sides of the tomb wondering, are we just the current creatures to inhabit this earth, albeit the smartest ones ever to have lived, or are we, even more perhaps, such things that dreams are made of?

THE BLOOD IS LIFE

Friday, Late Afternoon, 2/25, Babylon

AS DANIEL RAN his hands along the sarcophagus, hoping to find the seam that sealed the top of the tomb to the rest of the vault, he felt the ring on his hand begin to vibrate. He heard a buzzing in his ears as well. As he approached the south end of the sarcophagus the vibration and buzzing lessened, but the opposite happened as he wound around the tomb to the north. For a moment, he took his hands off the meteorite, but the vibration and buzzing continued. A thought entered his mind and he turned to look at the golden statue of Marduk, which had been paraded around the streets of Babylon. His gut told him this was the real one, used for centuries. Whatever Xerxes took that fateful day long ago, well, that giant statue was forever gone, ground and melted into gold dust and ferreted off to some king's treasure chamber. And that's why Daniel wondered if this statue still bore a secret.

He walked more closely to it and felt the ring vibrate even harder, shaking his hand. The buzzing in his ears became almost unbearable. He never knew why he did it, but, suddenly, he placed his right hand in Marduk's left. For a moment, nothing happened, and then he screamed in surprise and agony. Out of the palm of the statue's hand, a blade extended and slashed Daniel's palm.

He staggered backward and almost fell, but his right hand shot out and grabbed the corner of the tomb. Immediately, the vibration of the ring and the buzzing in his ears stopped. He was so startled that he ignored the pain in his hand. He noticed the blood dripping down the sarcophagus and he gasped.

The blood flow stopped just a foot beneath the top. Looking more closely, he saw that something was absorbing it right at that spot. Intuitively, he pressed his palm against it and wiped it straight across. A thin red line appeared. Fascinated, he pressed his hand against the sarcophagus again and began to trace the line around the tomb. The red line never faded.

"My blood," he said out loud, "it reveals the seam!" After tracing the line, he got the step stool he had used before, and stretching out over the top of the vault he traced another line of blood, splitting the top of the tomb in a linear half. Again, he gasped as a line appeared, lapping up the blood, revealing a seam. He took a handkerchief out of his pocket and wrapped his bleeding hand tight. Then, he snapped pictures with his phone, muttering, "Dad will never believe this."

Once again, the ring vibrated and the buzzing began in his ears. Without meaning to, he leaned his hand against the vault to look at the ring, and he was seized in great agony as if lightning was coursing through his body. The ring shone bright blue, and Daniel saw it morph into a fantastic blue sapphire with six diamonds at the edges connected to the fiery blue stone by platinum strips forming a six-pointed star. There was a flash of light, and a loud bang, and Daniel was flung backwards, his body coming to rest against the gold statue of Marduk.

"Jesus, Mary and Joseph!" he prayed. "What just happened?"

The vault itself began to groan, and the blood red seams Daniel had traced turned to fire and ran down the corners of the tomb as well.

The tomb separated into four sections and began to draw apart. Once the length wise partitions had moved three feet out, the lid of the sarcophagus split as well and began to separate, revealing the interior of the tomb.

Though he was in shock, Daniel didn't want to miss a thing, so he climbed back up on the stool and peered into the crypt. All he saw was murk and mist. A roiling fog moved inside, and he fully expected some decayed hand and arm to pierce through the vapor and grab him around his neck, muttering in a Boris Karloff voice, "Ankh-se-na-mun!" The 'Mummy' movie reference would have enthralled Luca.

Daniel shook his shoulders to shrug off the fear and laughed to himself. Too many horror movies with Luca, he thought, and he wished his friend was here.

For a moment he watched the moving mist, and, to his surprise, it began to clear. Beneath him a beautiful diorama, a moving tableau, rolled out, and he knew immediately what it was: Babylon at the height of its greatness, and it was beautiful. He saw the eight gates to the city, and Nebuchadnezzar's palaces to the east. The streets were laid out marvelously and green palm trees and flowers filled the avenues. He looked at the closest palace, and the view became closer and clearer. He saw the magnificent Hanging Gardens, one of the seven ancient wonders of the world.

"It's stunning!" he said aloud, and suddenly, the view changed and his sight was drawn to a main avenue where walked many people dressed in fine robes. He could smell the flowers and hear the rumble of many conversations, but he was drawn to four men who were walking purposefully toward the palace. Three of them were tall, wearing the headdress of the courtiers of the time and with them was a fourth man dressed in royal robes.

Daniel didn't know why these men were important. He simply felt them to be. Suddenly, the man dressed differently than the others glanced upward, and Daniel shook with amazement. He felt as if he were looking at himself in a time long ago. The resemblance was remarkable. But what really frightened him was that he felt the man could see him as well. That fear was realized when the man pointed upward and grabbed the sleeve of the friend nearest him. The man was wearing the Star Sapphire ring. Suddenly, all four had their eyes set on Daniel. He stood upright, but the movement made the stool wobble and he soon found himself once again on the floor. Up righting the step stool, he stood and gazed into the mist again, but the vision was gone. Everything was opaque once more.

As the minutes ticked by, no new vision manifested itself and Daniel descended to the floor. As he did so, he braced himself on the vault and the tomb groaned again. As before, the ring on his finger flashed, but there was no vibration and no ringing in the ears. Fortunately, there was no pain either. But the sarcophagus retracted back to its original position, and the flaring red lines that marked its seams and partitions faded, and the entire vault looked solid once more.

Daniel could have sworn none of this was real. He looked at his hand, and the ring had returned to a simple deep blue band, but his hand began to hurt like hell. Blood was still seeping through the cloth he had put around his palm. He walked over to the statue of Marduk and looked in the deity's left hand. No blade and no sign of how it appeared.

"Hell, if I'm shaking hands with you again you ungodly asshat."

SUTURES AND SHARING

Friday, Late Afternoon, 2/25, Babylon

"ARE YOU GOING to tell me how this happened?" said Frannie as she set up the medical items she needed on a tray in the infirmary.

Daniel didn't answer right away as he gently unwrapped his hand over a stainless-steel bowl.

"Well," she said, "however you did it, you managed to snip a few blood vessels. I'll have to cauterize and suture these shut. It's going to cause a bit of pain."

"Like more than I have now?" said Daniel ruefully.

"Probably not much more," said his mother with the first signs of sympathy coming through her voice. "Again, how did you do it?"

"I shook hands with Marduk," said Daniel, grinning a little bit. "Seriously. I don't know why I did it, but I just placed my hand in his. My ring was vibrating, and there was this buzzing in my ears. It seemed the thing to do."

He was amazed that this utterance didn't bring a response from his mother. After a few moments of getting her surgical instruments ready, she said, without looking at him, "We're going to have to tell your father about this."

"You don't know the half of it. I put my hand in Marduk's, and a blade came out and sliced my palm."

"Hmm," said his mother, "tetanus shot then too."

"Mom," he said, "look at me. Don't you think all of this is kind of strange?"

"Yes, as a matter of fact I do. But your hand is bad, and that's the first thing we fix. And because this is going to hurt, why don't you tell me what else happened while I work."

And he did.

She had him sutured and the wound freshly bandaged just as he came to the finish of his tale. She took out a small flashlight and shone it in his eyes. "No concussion and the buzzing in your ears seem to have left no serious repercussions, so I'm guessing you have no subdural hematoma."

"Geez, Mom," said Daniel, "clinical much? Your bedside manner is terrible."

A small smile crept over her lips. "It's how I handle anxiety. Look, what happened is remarkable, and your father will be so excited. But I'm looking at this as a mother and as the mother-figure for everyone here at the camp. You don't know what it's been like the past several months."

"How could I?" said Daniel. "You two never treat me as an equal and you hardly ever fill me in on what you're doing."

"Quiet, dear. Mummy's sharing now and I don't do that often."

"Isn't that the truth," said Daniel under his breath.

His mother gently cuffed him on the side of his head. "I heard that, but you have to understand. All I've felt these past months is increasing danger. When I heard today that there was a spy amongst us, all it did was confirm my worst feeling. There's a pall of fear over these Babylonian ruins. And then of course there is ISIS. Their little visit today has made the camp very jumpy. And I don't know how to fix it."

"I know, Mom," said Daniel. "That's why Uncle Liam sent me. To make sure you weren't in danger."

"I love you, son, but what are you going to do if we are in danger? You're a priest and an archeologist."

"Well," smiled Daniel, "thanks to Uncle Liam, I'm a ninja priest with a great bodyguard. You know Luca, Rebecca and Isaac can keep us safe."

"I don't know any such thing," she said. "Your father has spent decades building up good relations with everyone in the area. But it just seems to me that it is all falling apart. The attempt on your life the other day has ratcheted things up. Wanting to know what we're doing here is one thing; trying to remove my son is another."

"Not to worry, Mom," said Daniel joking. "After all, I have a magic ring."

"Ah yes," said Frannie, "the ring. Other than splatting you on the ground this afternoon, what do you think it's doing for you?"

Daniel turned serious. "It healed you once, and it did have something to do with opening the tomb."

"Hmm," said Frannie, "it didn't do much for your hand today. Look, I know it's important, but I know enough about ancient artifacts to realize that some have their own agendas. The day that devil put it around your finger and it molded to your hand, I worried what was to become of you. Now, it looks like events are moving, and we don't have much control over them."

A tear slipped down her cheek.

"Mom, really, it's ok. You should be excited about the tomb. We've got to tell Dad. He'll be furious that we've waited this long."

"Let's tell him over dinner, just the three of us."

"Like a family?" smiled Daniel.

"Like a family." And a genuine smile rolled over her face.

Then Daniel fell unconscious off the chair.

His father picked that moment to come into the infirmary, and rushed to help his wife lift Daniel onto a bed.

"My God," he said, "what's happened to him?"

Frannie told him, but added, "I've got his blood work almost done, but my guess is that there was an opiate drug smeared on the blade. The Babylonians weren't above using that on their sacred knives to help induce a religious ecstasy or a trance."

"You think that's what's happening here?"

Frannie was scanning the blood work data. "I see opiates present in his blood, so I think I'm right on this. The statue was meant to be used in religious worship, not to kill."

"I hope you're right," said Markoz, "but how did all this happen?"

Frannie explained further and Markoz said, "He got the tomb to open? How can that be possible after all these centuries?"

"You tell me. You're the one that got that monster Saddam Hussein to give the ring to him. But don't get your hopes up just yet. Daniel said that the tomb closed again just as he was staggering up the stairs to come to me."

"Let's hope he can do it again," said Markoz.

Shaking her head with a frown on her face, she said, "Why don't you first hope he recovers from whatever is currently coursing through his veins? Speaking of which, let me give him his tetanus shot and another dose of Narcan to take care of the opioids. We can make him comfortable and see if a little rest will give the drug time to wear off."

Markoz stared at his son with worry in his eyes as his wife took off her son's clothes and tucked him into the hospital bed. They watched him together for a while until the late afternoon sun began to lower toward the horizon. Seeing that he was quickly stabilizing, they shut the door to the infirmary and went down the hall to the cafeteria to bring him back something to eat.

THE *SIRRUSH*

Friday Evening, 2/25, Babylon

THE SECURITY TEAM and Professor Kasser already had their trays of food, and Markoz filled them in on what had happened to Daniel without giving specifics other than that he had found a way to open the tomb. Luca left immediately with a tray for Daniel, anxious to check on him. He didn't like the idea of leaving Daniel alone for any amount of time.

He and the security team had taken another walk through the camp and found everyone on edge and restless. Even the locals who were standing watch on the perimeter were nervous, and Brian made sure they would call in at the first sign of trouble.

As they talked, the security team decided that ISIS wouldn't try anything that evening, but Rebecca and Luca expressed the view that there were other paths that danger could tread.

"If it's not ISIS, then who?" said Isaac.

"We're still not sure that anyone from ISIS was behind the Rome attempt on Daniel's life," said Luca.

Brian said, "I think the locals are spooked by something else. The student archs were telling me that the work they're doing on the Ishtar gate is causing some controversy."

"What do you mean?" asked Isaac.

Brian answered saying, "The archs are revealing more of the tiled walls of the gate's inner passageway. It's beautiful, really. All sorts of animals decorate it, and though it's impressive now, it must have been spectacular in its heyday."

"Why the problem with the locals?" said Luca.

"Well," said Brian, "the animals revealed are the normal ones you would expect. You know, the usual lions, tigers and bears, oh my. But there are some fantastic beasts mixed in with them, and some of the locals have a real superstitious dread about them. Take that fear, mix it with the ISIS threat today, and you've got a camp on edge. Already a few fights have broken out, and tempers are flaring. We'll have to keep a close eye on things tonight."

Quietly opening the infirmary door, Luca found Daniel still asleep. He tried to rouse his friend and got a few moans for his troubles, but Daniel was still unconscious. Luca sat down by his bedside, deciding to wait for a bit before trying to wake him again.

He must have dozed, jerking awake when Frannie came bustling in to check on her son.

"Didn't eat anything yet?" she asked.

"No," said Luca, "but I was just going to try to wake him again."

Frannie checked Daniel's vitals and found them acceptable. Turning to Luca, she said, "I'm going with Markoz to where some of the locals have set up their campsite. A few of them have a fever, and I want to treat them and see if I can not only make them feel better, but keep any contagion from spreading further. Do you mind watching Daniel for a while?"

Luca gave her his most impressive smile, "No problem. It's what I do."

She left, and he managed to wake Daniel enough to get him to take some fluids.

"Quit your grumbling," said Luca. "You're lucky old Marduk didn't slice a major artery or two."

Daniel opened his eyes and looked at his bandaged hand. "Shot, stabbed, wonder what's next?" he muttered.

"Such a whiner," said Luca. Then he gasped, "Dani, the ring!"

A faint blue glow began to pulse through the sterile wrap around Daniel's fingers and palm.

"Oh, oh," said Daniel, "something's up."

He had just finished speaking when Dr. Kasser burst into the infirmary.

"Quickly," he said, "They'll find you here. We have to get to the Iraqi camp."

"Who will find us?" said Luca, suspicion dripping from his voice.

"No time. You must trust me. Let's get him dressed."

Luca certainly didn't trust him but sensed enough urgency to jump to his feet and help a groggy Daniel get back into his clothes.

All the while, he tried to get information out of Nabil. But all Kasser said was, "Things, coming from the desert. The locals are hysterical."

They hurried out of the infirmary and through the doors of the Center. The sun had set some time ago, and twilight cast its murky gloom throughout the base camp. Even though the streets seemed deserted, Luca sensed they were not alone. Shadows, cast by flaming torches twisted around the buildings. Through the silence, a hissing and rustling was heard down the path close to where Luca and Daniel's quarters lay.

Nabil pulled them down behind the waste containers as the noise grew louder, like sand susurrating through the dunes. To Luca's horror, a nightmare came stalking around the corner of a mainte-nance shed. On its back rode a rider, dressed in billowing black Bedouin robes, a scimitar flashing in his hand. That would have been wonder enough, but the beast he mounted was not of this world. Twice as large as the biggest horse, it pushed forward with legs ending in the back claws of an eagle. There was little sound because, instead of hooves, the front legs padded with the paws of a lion. A scaly back, like a dragon, rustled quietly while a short-cropped tail whipped back and forth. Luca and the others ducked further down as a long serpentine neck with the head of a snake rose high. Horns, crest and a seeking, snaking tongue, hissing, rounded out the horrific presentation.

"Allah be merciful!" whispered Nabil.

"It's a *sirrush*," said Daniel, now wide awake, eyes open in horror. "Don't you recognize it?" he said. "The figure is all over the walls of the Ishtar gate and the temple. It was Marduk's favorite servant animal. As for the rider, I don't know who he could be. But the *sirrush* is the deadly one." Words came unbidden to his lips, *"Its mouth is fire; its breath is death."*

Luca snapped open his holster and drew out his Sig Sauer 220. The beast must have heard because it whipped its neck around and stared at the waste containers. Suddenly, urged on by its rider, it leapt forward.

Luca stood and shot a full clip at the monster and the Bedouin. He hit both but it only slowed them.

"Run!" shouted Nabil. And they ran. Nabil had been to the Iraqi camp earlier that day so he ran off in that direction. Daniel and Luca followed, no better choice presenting itself. Daniel, still a little groggy, stumbled often. Clearly, they were going to be overtaken once they got away from the buildings and headed toward the Iraqi encampment. Luca didn't really understand how going there would save them, and he didn't think they would make it anyway.

Stopping suddenly, he turned, jammed a new clip into his pistol, took a stance, and began firing toward the approaching assassin. He aimed better this time, catching the rider in a head shot which knocked him off the *sirrush*. Then, as the beast narrowed the distance to a mere twenty feet, Luca unloaded the rest of his ammo. Every shot struck the chimera in the serpentine head, the last one almost obliterating the fanged mouth. The serpent dragon crumpled into a heap at Luca's feet quivering. Silence suddenly reigned again.

He just stared, shocked at what he had done as Rebecca, Isaac and Brian came running full speed around the center, pistols at the ready.

"What in God's name is that?" said Isaac.

"A *sirrush*," said Daniel, "a beast from Babylonian myth. And what it is doing walking this earth is beyond me. Let's look at the rider."

The rider lay in a crumpled heap, the top of his head and most of his face shot off, but they all could see he was Bedouin.

"The Bedouin are a most superstitious lot," said Brian. "This thing he was riding would have him shaking in fear against a sand dune. Who in the world could have convinced him to ride the beast?"

"Not ISIS," said Daniel. "I don't know where this comes from, but this attack was not political. ISIS wants what is in the tomb. This attack seems geared to keep us from getting into the sarcophagus. I think it was after me." He turned to Nabil, who had doubled back to where Luca and Daniel were. "You knew it was coming. How?"

Nabil Kasser looked surprisingly calm. "Didn't you hear it's cry? I was out walking, and there was a wailing from the desert. I looked to see a rider on a beast from hell coming our way. I, too, feared it was after you, for you are the only one who has succeeded in opening the tomb. I hoped to get you to safety in the Iraqi camp."

"How would that have helped?" said Rebecca. "This thing and its rider could have caused untold damage amongst all those people. Are you that much of a coward that you would lead this beast to innocent people?"

"I am no coward," said Nabil with a furious anger barely kept in check. "But I hazarded a guess that this rider and his mount were for our benefit or doom as it were. If we were chased by a herd of these things, then mayhem would have been the purpose, but just one? No, it was a message for us. Cease and desist, now. And if the Bedouin or beast could have killed Daniel, they would have, but even if they failed, which they did, the message would be clear."

"Agreed," said Luca. "But let's be sure. I want a watch placed on our base camp's perimeter. Anything that moves in the desert tonight needs to be challenged. And let's get some weapons more powerful than the pistols we have. This was a close one. I'm surprised we lived. Thank God for hollow point bullets."

He turned back to the *sirrush*. "I doubt this one and his companions, if he has any, have been roaming the desert these past years. Myths come to reality like this are doubtful. Chimeras, on the other hand … Chimeras, the blending of two different species, have been made in some gentech labs but they never live long. Dani and I were at a presentation to the Swiss Guard on the subject, believe it or not. Chimeras or animal hybrids have been used in some low-level crimes lately, as if someone was experimenting with their effectiveness. Imagine the cost to create such things. There are only a few people in the world with the wealth to do that. The chimeras were smaller than this, mostly variants of dogs and catlike creatures. This dragon thing represents a major advance. The conclusion of our presenter was that chimeras were more for show than power, made to scare not to kill."

"Guess he was wrong in his assumption," said Daniel.

Isaac moved toward the animal. "Good shot, Luca. But there's one fang left in what remains of its mouth and it's dripping a liquid." Finding a stick nearby, he held it out and caught a few drops. It hissed like acid. "Hmm … definitely not just to frighten."

Suddenly, a blue flash seemed to explode from the corpses of the Bedouin and the beast, swiftly consuming them in fire.

Startled, Daniel put his good hand over the ring and looked to see if anyone had noticed that the blue light's source was from it. Only Nabil was looking at him curiously.

Rebecca said, "Where did that come from? Or maybe this thing had a self-destruct mode in it so we couldn't take samples."

"Someone did their homework well," said Dani. "They could not have used a more archetypal monster to instill fear in the locals. The *sirrush,* seldom seen in ancient days, never reported now, still has a place in the stories of the people, particularly the Bedouin. Was anyone else with you, Professor Kasser, when you saw these two coming over the desert?"

"Yes, of course," he said, "I had stopped to talk with a couple of Brian's guards that he had placed around the perimeter. They were horrified and ran. By now, everyone in the Iraqi encampment will know what they saw."

"What were you talking to them about?" said Luca. He still did not trust this interloper.

"Just getting to know them," said Nabil. "They had heard me at one of the Baghdad mosques several years ago."

"I don't like any of this," said Luca as he stomped into the night.

A few moments later, Daniel knocked on Luca's door, opened it and found the Swiss Guard pacing up and down the small living room.

"Too many bad actors here, Dani," he said. "Once again, we don't have a clue as to what's going on. And I don't like that Professor."

Daniel gave a rueful laugh. "That's pretty clear. And that we have enemies is pretty clear too. What we now know for sure is that ISIS is one of them—that was proven this afternoon—but somebody else, more powerful, has a different agenda and is willing to kill even before we open the tomb."

"But why you, Dani?" said Luca. "Your parents are more in-volved in this dig than you. You may be a whiz at languages, but your father and mother know much more about Babylon than you do. Why doesn't our new enemy go after them?"

"It's the ring," said Daniel. "Has to be. You saw it destroy what was left of the *sirrush* and the rider. I caught our Professor looking at me strangely. I think he knows I had something to do with that fire. And look, even my hand is healed." Daniel unwrapped the bandage, showing a hand without a trace of the blade's slash. Impressed as Luca was, he quickly cut to the chase.

"I told you," said Luca bitterly. "Nabil Kasser comes as a friend, but he, too, is after something. I don't think he's allied with this new enemy. He was scared out of his mind tonight like we all were. But we're going to have to watch him."

"I think the attempt on my life in Rome and the one tonight are connected," said Daniel, "maybe even with that chapel hit years ago. ISIS and the professor don't seem out to kill me. At least not yet," he laughed. "But the other three attempts are a different story. What if there's a third player here who has other motives? ISIS and the pro-fessor may have different agendas as well, but they are only curious as to what the tomb holds. They think it may be significant, but they aren't sure. Whoever is behind the attempts to kill me is more certain. They want whatever is in the tomb for themselves, and without any intermediaries to discover it. We're not done with this enemy yet. They created a monster out of legend and out of time. Serious money and skill are behind them, and I think they won't hesitate to create complete chaos to get what they want. Not just my life is in jeopardy."

"We know that now," said Luca. "Good thing I prepared for that eventuality. I'm getting Rebecca, Isaac and Brian together, right away. We have to have a plan. You go get some sleep. You're as pale as a ghost. By the way, I'm glad to see the ring working again. Can't figure out why it didn't take out the *sirrush* and the rider though."

"It has a mind of its own. I don't control it. Maybe it knew you could handle that thing."

"Well," grumbled Luca, "if so, it knew better than me. Now go to sleep, I'll fill you in on our meeting tomorrow. You've got lots to do at the tomb in the morning."

RANBIR

Friday Evening, 2/25, Babylon

WHILE LUCA SPOKE with Daniel, Rebecca went to her quarters and used the sat phone to call the director. She caught her in a meeting, but Leslie had her hold while she dismissed whoever she was talking to.

"Can't be anything good, or you wouldn't have called," said Leslie when she was back on the phone.

"Right you are, Director," said Rebecca, and she filled her boss in on what was happening. "I have to tell you that Fr. Daniel almost packed it in tonight. You should have seen that creature, and that Bedouin looked like one of the Black Riders from *The Lord of the Rings.*"

"Colorful but not helpful," said Leslie. "What's your assessment of future danger?"

"I don't really know. The attack tonight puts a new enemy in the mix, I think, one that poses a threat more dangerous than the usual *modus operandi* of ISIS. That we can handle, and if they throw more troops than the sixteen or so we've seen, we've got General Farouk to back us up. But this chimera thing has me worried. I had not even known of chimeras being used in any ops anywhere in the world. Frankly, I didn't even know they existed."

"I want you to link with Ranbir after we get off the phone," said Leslie. "Have him do a search and assessment of this new danger and who could be behind it. Sync with Luca and make sure that one of you three will stand guard outside Daniel's quarters throughout the night. He seems to be the key to all of this."

"What about Professor Kasser?" said Rebecca. "I thought his appearance today was awfully fortuitous. He doesn't seem like an enemy, but Luca seems very suspicious of him. Know much about him?"

Leslie said, "His office isn't very far from here, and of course we have had him under surveillance for several years. On the surface, he seems the mundane academic, but when he travels and speaks at mosques, he's much more political and apocalyptic. He's no terrorist, but his proclamations that the Mahdi is coming sure have fired up the Middle East. We don't intervene because his is just about the only moderate voice the Moslems hear."

"He basically invited himself for the next couple of days, so he will be involved with the opening of the tomb. Dr. Markoz seems to like him and welcomes his expertise. I can see how Dr. Markoz has been able to operate peacefully here for years. His negotiating skills are rather breathtaking. Everybody, including ISIS seems to really respect him."

"That," said Leslie, "will last only as long as nobody knows who you and Isaac really are. Everything collapses if that is found out. Now, about the possible spy. I checked the staff once again, and three subjects stand out: Brian Jeffries and the twin student archeologists, Fred and Al Brummel. Brian has often gone to Syria, supposedly on business over the years, and the Brummel boys were Navy Seals and had several contacts with Arabs whose reputations are rather murky. You might keep your eye on them."

"Will do, Director. I'll keep you informed." With that she signed off.

Taking off a small pin on her shirt inscribed with *salam*, the Arab word for peace, she popped off the pin itself and inserted the button into what looked like a little charger from her backpack. It had a simple on/off switch which she pressed.

There was a tiny beep, and just to the right of her desk appeared a full-size hologram of a man dressed in Sikh attire. "Ah, Miss Rebecca, Ranbir Singh at your service."

"It's just Rebecca, Ranbir."

"As you wish, Becky," smiled the simulacrum.

"Ranbir …"

"Yes, Becca?"

"Never mind."

Ranbir smiled again, "How may I be of assistance, Miss Rebecca?"

It truly was amazing, she thought. This holographic image connected by satellite with the computer at AD headquarters. She had met the hologram once before and was astounded at its capabilities. The fact that it was working perfectly here in the desert truly exceeded her expectations. She absently chewed on a fingernail as she explained to Ranbir what had happened and focused on the chimera mystery.

"One moment, Rebecca," said Ranbir. Let me tap into the local power supply so I can operate at full capacity. He raised his eyes to the ceiling for a moment and then snapped his fingers. His image seemed to brighten. "Plenty of power for what we need. Luca was right about chimeras becoming part of the underworld's weapons for mischief. Only a few have actually been produced and used. They are unpredictable and rather difficult to keep alive. I must say that I am not sure the chimera you met tonight has any relationship with the rather amateurish attempts known so far."

"Where do you think it could come from?"

"One of the reasons the director continued the work of her pre-decessor is that rather odd things are happening around the world. For instance, in Ireland, last fall, strange creatures were seen galli-vanting all over the landscape causing all sorts of mayhem. It lasted only for days, but, trust me, the memory is seared into the minds of the people who experienced them. Some of those creatures could be tagged as chimeras, but our best possible estimate is that they were not manufactured creatures. Also, similar reports from the heartland of the U.S.A. have convinced the government that something very strange is going on. Let's just say the boys and girls at Area 51 who love to speculate are being given more respect than usual."

"Aliens?" laughed Rebecca.

"No, of course not," said Ranbir. He was silent for a moment but then began flipping his ceremonial Sikh knife back and forth between his hands. "These reports are more on the level of Sasquatch, Moth Man, and ghostly appearances. We tend to discredit these publicly, but there is enough evidence collected over the years to make our own scientists wonder if we know everything that wan-ders this earth. Of course, there is always the possibility of a rift in space/time."

"You've got to be kidding me," said Rebecca, standing up in disbelief.

"Calm yourself," said the hologram. "It's not as if this is impos-sible. Scientists at CERN, the European Organization for Nuclear Research in Switzerland have already created an infinitesimal black hole within its particle accelerator. It was a surprise to them when it appeared, and they were thankful it didn't blow up the universe."

"I'm grateful too," said Rebecca, "but so what? What does that have to do with a *sirrush* waltzing through our base camp tonight?"

"What do you think lies beyond a black hole?" said Ranbir in his most professorial voice. "We're one side. What do you think is on the other?" The hologram paused for dramatic emphasis. "Exactly, a rift. And if the space between is permeable, perhaps things can cross to and from."

"Too sci-fi for me," said Rebecca.

"More unbelievable than a *sirrush* amongst you this evening?" said Ranbir.

Rebecca was quiet for a moment. "What do we do then?"

Ranbir began to pace the room, slapping his knife on the palm of his digital hand. "Bart Finch, my creator—you met him, did you not? You know, the guy who looks like he'd be at home at an Antifa rally. Don't tell him I said this," he whispered conspiratorially. "Bart, my creator, installed a program in me that will search historical records to find similar references to anything that Dr. Markoz or his wife Dr. Frances would find here in Babylon. I will run that program and compare it with persons throughout the world who might have a similar interest in these types of things and see if we can out our potential new enemy. It will take some time."

"Why?" said Rebecca. "It's just data."

"Bart's program also gives me the power to evaluate that data and make decisions on applicability. By morning, I'll have something for you. Now turn out the lights, get some sleep and I'll see you bright and early Becky. Ciao!" And Ranbir blinked off.

In the silence, she was bemused that the hologram ended the meeting. Cheeky and a bit disturbing for a simple digital creation. "Oh, and by the way," she whispered, "it's Rebecca." She said it to no one in particular, but was satisfied that she got the last word.

ISIS AND THE RIFT

Friday Evening, 2/25, Six Miles West Of Babylon

REBECCA WAS NOT the only one on a sat phone that evening. Brian Jeffries put in a call to Abu Shadid who was sitting around a campfire with his terrorist buddies six miles northwest of Babylon, Brian was furious.

"What did you mean to do today, making your appearance like that and threatening Dr. Markoz? Everything was going to plan, and you come along and bluster, letting them know there is a spy in their midst."

"You are not in charge of me, Mr. Jeffries, nor do you give me orders. We each do what we must."

"Well, you nearly blew it. The excitement we've had this evening, at least, has shifted attention away from our leak in security."

"What are you talking about? We took no action at the camp this evening."

"I know that, but someone did, and I'm asking you to look into it. Did you see anything strange out in the desert around twilight?"

"No, not at all."

Brian related what had happened and Abu interrupted.

"Surely someone was smoking hashish and seeing things. This is something from a nightmare, not reality."

"Wrong," said Brian. "I and many others saw it. It was a *sirrush* with some kind of monstrous Bedouin rider mounted on it. He even had a scimitar. You are right that it looked like some drug induced vision, but I assure you, it was real. The Swiss Guard called the beast a chimera. Do you know what that is?"

"I'm not an idiot, Mr. Jeffries. Chimeras are in all of our mythologies here in the Middle East. But they are exactly that—myths."

"Not anymore," said Brian, "and get your head out of your ass. I'm talking manufactured chimeras, something that a bio-geneticist could create. I'm talking gentech here."

"There are no research laboratories left in the area," said Abu. "You Americans saw to that, and it's still too politically unstable to rebuild anything."

"Look," said Brian, "you know the area. This thing and its rider were seen coming from just northeast of where you are camped. Do you think you might take a look around, and see if anything is amiss?"

"I will surely do that in the morning."

"No," said Brian, "now. Morning might be too late. Someone or something will be missing the *sirrush* and its rider. A search might be going on."

Abu whistled an exasperated sigh. "As you wish, but not on your order, but because it makes sense to see what's out there this evening. I still think this is an object of you and your companions' fantasies."

"Think what you will, but arm yourselves. You'll be glad you did."

Abu was tired of listening to his men gossip around the fire about wives and children, so he took a couple of them with him and headed east out of their camp in the one Humvee they brought with them—courtesy of the Americans who had abandoned it a few years previously. It could take the rough country they'd be traveling. He had gotten coordinates from Brian, so he drove a few kilometers east and then turned north onto a small path that led into the hill country. He had no plans to drive on a dirt track all the way to Baghdad. A small hill about ten kilometers from the Babylon ruins attracted his attention. Worth exploring because of the view it provided, he drove up to it and told his companions to accompany him to the top.

The view was a good one on this amazing starlit night. How could he hope to find anything even as large as a *sirrush* in this waste-land? It was hopeless. He lit a cigarette and thought back on his days at university in Damascus. He had forgotten the name of the profes-sor who had taught him the archeology of the area, but he remem-bered the class on myths and monsters. He knew very well what the serpent dragon looked like and what the ancients thought it could do. If such a thing were alive now, it would strike the fear of Allah into every human heart that beheld it.

But that wasn't going to happen. Myths were myths and that was that. He had smoked two cigarettes when he saw it. A ripple in the darkness on a sister hill about a kilometer away. What caught his attention was that the ripple was stationary, not like a heat wave off the desert ground. It was just big enough to see at the base of the hill.

Throwing down the butt of his cigarette he hissed for his com-panions to follow. Reaching the Humvee, they piled in, and Abu drove as fast as he dared cross country with the headlights off to get to the hill before the ripple winked out. He had no clue of what it could be. Once his companions saw it, they uttered superstitious nonsense causing him to berate their lack of faith.

Parking the vehicle, a quarter mile away, the three men crept closer to the anomaly just a few hundred yards before them. Amazing really, thought Abu. There was no light coming from it. It was simply a ripple of darkness, able to be seen because it was blacker than the night around it. It was in the shape of a circle with a radius of about thirty feet, the base of the circle just touching the ground.

Abu had loved science fiction as a child and had watched as many American programs on the subject as possible. This looked to him like some kind of gate, though there was no stable structure around it. It looked deserted, but Abu was a cautious man and picked out a pile of rocks to hide behind with his men. They were there a good thirty minutes, and even he was beginning to get bored.

That was when they heard it. A soft rustling in the dirt, a frisson of sound against the sand. Around the hill it came, with no rider directing it. Looking every bit like the figures on the ruined walls of Babylon, only much larger, the *sirrush* whipped its serpentine neck back and forth, it's snake-like tongue protruding out of its fangs, sampling the night air.

Abu had imagined what the Babylonian version of a dragon might look like, but Jeffries description had done it a great disservice. Terror ran down Abu's leg as his bladder let loose in fear. He couldn't move, and he was grateful they were hidden from its sight. He could see it was no stupid beast as it tested the air around it, scenting for prey. It looked to step through the rift, but then it stopped, turning back its head again toward the hidden Arabs. That was all it took for one of Abu's companions to lose his nerve and dart out from around the rocks and start running back towards the vehicle. Abu watched his last man make to stand up and catch the runner, but Abu jerked him back down.

The *sirrush* had smelled the humans, but its eyes captured the movement of the fleeing man. Suddenly, it pounced forward moving gracefully as a cat, its sinewy neck close to the ground with its snake head pointing directly ahead, dragon eyes focused on its prey.

The man never had a chance. The beast was upon him immediately and simply beheaded him on the spot. Then it ate him in three bites. It was horrific. Abu felt his gorge rise, but had to swallow it down as he held on to his companion to keep him from fleeing as well.

The monster looked like it would search the area, but a cry from around the hill caught its attention. A dark-robed Bedouin appeared, with a whip, cracking it in the air, and calling for the *sirrush* to return to him. Surprisingly to Abu, the creature meekly turned and went back to its master. The Bedouin mounted the beast and without any fanfare, walked it directly into the rippling darkness. They vanished into that black hole. A slight buzzing reached Abu's ears and he heard a soft pop as the rift blinked out of existence.

There was nothing left but blood streaks on the desert floor where their companion had been attacked. Abu forced his one sur-viving man, a dribbling, weeping mess, to follow him back to where the rift was. Nothing remained there either, no sign that anything had been there before. Kicking a rock to where the rift had been, Abu turned in disgust and led his man back to the vehicle. He had seen PTSD before in combatants. His man hadn't even fought, but he was ruined. He would be of no use to Abu anymore. So, he shot him, there on the desert track, and left his body for the morning vultures. Fear was nothing to be ashamed of, but cowardice would not be tolerated.

THE BEDOUIN

Friday Evening, 2/25, six miles West of Babylon

AS ABU DROVE off, the rift shimmered into existence again. The Bedouin stepped out alone and watched the lights disappear into the distance. He thought of destroying the vehicle, but he restrained himself. Needless death was definitely unnecessary. There had been enough tonight.

His brother was dead. Of that he was sure. As was the *sirrush* he was riding. They had never returned from the Babylon dig. They were to retrieve the priest who wore the ring, but something untoward must have happened. How the priest continued to escape was beyond him. The Bedouin's other brother had failed in the attempt in Rome. Now, he was on the run, somewhere in Europe.

The three had been very close. They had grown up in several of the Bedouin settlements started by Saddam Hussein to wean the nomads from their desert life. The brothers barely remembered their traveling days, for they were young when their parents were doomed to the putrid and poor permanent housing Hussein had thrown up for their tribe. They moved from one shantytown to the next over several years. Hardship bound the brothers together. It made the Bedouin strong, but his brothers barely thrived. Though he was the second son, his brothers were weak and depended on him for strength and purpose. They followed him into the machinery trade—driving and repairing trucks used for Saddam's army. It was a life, a poor one, but at least they survived. None of them had married. And so, they slogged through the days and the wars, until last year.

The Bedouin had been driving from village to village, delivering supplies to the auto repair shops along the way. He stopped for a moment by a hill where he noticed a darkness shimmering in the noon of the day. What it was, he did not know, but he had to investigate. It should have frightened him but it did not. In fact, he welcomed something new to lift the drudgery of his dull existence.

Walking up to the rift, he stuck his hand through the blackness, and nothing happened. Screwing up his courage, he plunged through. The darkness vanished as he pressed through the shimmering energy. He felt as if he was stepping aside normal reality. Before him was not darkness, but light and a completely different world. Oh, it was still a desert landscape, but a fertile one, as if in the middle of an oasis. Much cooler and quite verdant with a running stream and a small lagoon, palm trees providing shade.

Beautiful, thought the Bedouin, beautiful beyond measure. Surely this was a vision of Allah's paradise. But that was shattered as he stubbed his sandal against a rock. Sucking in the pain, he looked forward and saw something on the ground not far away.

It was a carpet, and upon it sat a silver tray of figs, pomegranates and wine along with bread. Seeing no one, and feeling very hungry, he sat down on the carpet to enjoy his unknown provider's hospitality. Anyone from the West would not have touched it, for they would have seen it as a *fae* place, an Otherworldly land. They knew that to eat food in a place such as this was to be ensorcelled, enchanted—at least that's what some said. But for the Bedouin, who knew not such western things, it was normal to partake, for food was the sign of welcome. Usually, the benefactor was visible, but perhaps he had just vanished somewhere for a moment.

The Bedouin had to admit, it was a welcome noonday feast. The fruit could not have been sweeter, the bread more filling, the wine more refreshing. After he ate, he felt sleepy and closed his eyes for what he thought was just a moment, but when he woke, the afternoon shadows were long and the evening breeze was beginning to blow.

Then he saw and gasped in horror. How he could have missed them, he did not know. White bones, poking up through the ferns by the pond, human bones. Scattered among them were silver trays and dishes, obviously from meals long past. Those that had eaten before him had died. For a moment he felt ill, but the feeling passed. He was strong and not fearful. He had not stolen hospitality, and he could not believe that the one who gave it would be so evil as to try to kill him for eating the feast. This was not heard of in Bedouin life, not even in the settlement camps where his tribe languished.

No, something else was happening here. He did feel different. Not sick, or weak, or fearful. Instead, strength flowed through him. He stood up straighter as power made him feel taller. He felt he could grasp the world if he was given a moment to do so. He believed he had passed a test that these other dead men had failed. They had eaten and they had died. He ate and lived, and had been transformed. Perhaps in this other world, food was poisonous to those who were weak. He, however, had passed a test. Tears of gratitude fell down his face as his mind opened to new possibilities. That was when he saw the *sirrush* and her two offspring.

They were on the other side of the pond, looking at him. She was huge. The two little ones were twice the size of a horse, but she was bigger than the largest elephant. No sound came from them; they only stared.

Of course, the Bedouin knew what they were, and he should have been afraid. But there were words on the evening breeze. *"Master them,"* the words whispered to him, and without a moment's thought, he called to them as if they were camels, and they plunged through the pond towards him.

Again, he was not afraid. The mother sniffed him, and younger ones nudged him, but they seemed respectful of his presence. He could hardly believe it as he mounted the female, easily leaping upon her back, a clear ten feet above him. More amazingly, she let him mount and ride her. Throughout the oasis they went, followed by the younglings. Truly this was a marvelous world, but, though the Bedouin kept his eyes out for his absent host, he saw no one else.

Dismounting back at the carpet, he stroked the necks of all three *sirrusha*. They purred back at him, seemingly delighted by human touch. That was when the evening breeze whispered to him again, *"The ring. Find the ring."*

"Yes, Master," he found himself saying, for he knew this could not be Allah, for Allah would have no need to find anything. This had to be someone else.

He looked around for the ring, but did not find it amongst the bones by the pond. Perhaps the ring was not in this world. The moment he thought that, the atmosphere shimmered, and he could have sworn he stepped forward, but when he did, he stepped back onto Iraqi soil.

All this had happened last autumn. That's when the Bedouin had been reborn. He returned to the settlement, and his brothers knew he was different. He looked taller and stronger. He had presence. All the tribe kept their distance from him, so other did he seem. All except for his brothers.

He loved them and wanted to share his new found world with them. He took them to the little hill, showing them the rift. He stepped sideways into the oasis, and they followed, even though he had to take their hands to banish their fear. Once they saw, they believed everything he said.

The Bedouin told them of the *sirrusha,* how they were the ancient god Marduk's servants. His brothers worried their own souls would be damned for consorting with demon beasts, but the Bedouin assured them that Marduk and these beasts had to be like *djinn,* in-between creatures, part good, part evil, and that if the three brothers kept their wits about them, their souls should be safe.

He led the two young beasts to meet the brothers. Of course, the brothers were frightened to death, but he showed them how tame they were and obedient not only to the Bedouin's voice but to the brothers as well. They learned to ride. Only later, did the Bedouin let them see the mother of those beasts. Her, he did not let his brothers ride.

They questioned him why Allah would have allowed them to see a piece of paradise and introduce them to the *djinn,* these supernatural creatures. That was when the Bedouin told them about the ring and the voice that told him to acquire it.

During the days that had passed, while his brothers grew as strong as he and learned to ride the *sirrusha,* the Bedouin had walked at close of day alone in the oasis garden and listened again to the evening breeze. He was taught what kind of ring to find, and who might have it. He learned that some secret rested deep in the ruins of Babylon, a secret that was about to be discovered, a secret that the Bedouin had to possess and bring back to the oasis.

But then, his elder brother got tasked to go to Rome.

"Why must you go?" said the Bedouin, and the elder brother told him that whispers on the wind hinted the ring might be on the hand of a young man, one of the priestly caste in Rome. The voice on the wind thought it might be just a rumor, but had to make sure.

The elder brother, always deferential to his younger sibling, said, "Do not worry. The voice sends me as a fail-safe. It should not be that dangerous, and I shall return unharmed."

The Bedouin acquiesced and decided to take a job of repairing vehicles on the site of the Babylon dig with his youngest brother where they watched and waited to see what the archeologists would find. The time came for his one brother to kill the nephew of the pope and take the ring on the young priest's finger. But that attempt failed miserably. Hope sprang again in the heart of the Bedouin when he found out the priest was coming to Babylon to see his parents. He tasked his remaining brother to kill the young man and take the ring, but alas, it was clear that attempt had failed as well.

And now, shortly after his brother had been struck down in the camp along with the *sirrush*, the Bedouin sat on the carpet in the Otherworld under a night of shining stars, the two *sirrusha* sleeping beside him. Once again, the breeze kicked up, and he heard words of pain on the wind. "*Prepare yourself for power,*" it said. Barely had he risen up on his knees when agony filled his body and he screamed out his suffering. The mother *sirrush* merely raised her head. The Bedouin felt as if his bones were being riven from his body. Through the pain, he thought some of those who had died before him may have gotten this far with the *djinn* before their useless corpses were thrown into the weeds. But then, the pain was gone as if it had never been.

Yet, he felt something new within him. He didn't know what he should call it, so he called it magic. He just knew that he could do things he could not before. The voice spoke again though the wind, *"Find the ring, and bring it to me. Find also the secret buried deep in Babylon."*

And the Bedouin sat down on the carpet, and planned till the sun rose in that garden of the dead.

AT THE TOMB

Saturday Morning, 2/26, Babylon

DANIEL WAS THE only one who really slept that night. He was worried his dreams would be nightmares, what with his encounter with the *sirrush* and the Bedouin who wished to kill him.

But his sleep was dreamless, and he woke refreshed. He felt rather guilty as he strode into the cafeteria only to find a very sleepy staff picking listlessly at their breakfast.

"Did I miss a party last night?" he said, trying to lighten the atmosphere. They just blankly stared at him.

"Guess not," he mumbled as he went to get something to eat.

"We're going to try the tomb again at 10 o'clock, Dani, after you say Mass for us," said his father. "We hope you can open it again like you did yesterday."

"Well, let's hope I don't have to punch a hole in my other hand," said Daniel.

"Wouldn't be bad if the time ever comes to make you a saint. You'd have a good start on the stigmata."

Daniel smiled at Luca, "See, food really does wake you up."

The mood darkened when Rebecca said, "I was able to do a little research on our chimera theory, and I think I can safely say that the research and development that has gone on throughout the world concerning that is just not at the level to cause us problems. In other words, no mad scientist is creating the kind of monster we saw last evening. Its existence remains a mystery."

Disturbed, they all ate in uneasy silence.

Afterwards, they had a bit of time to waste, and Daniel pulled Luca aside, "Come with me. I want to call my uncle."

"Hey, man, even a pope has to sleep. It's barely morning in Rome."

"All the better. We know we'll have him to ourselves."

Luca and Daniel shared a sat phone together, and Luca had offered to keep it, so it was to his quarters they went. The call went through directly, and Pope Patrick answered on the first ring.

"Finally!" he said, no trace of sleep in his voice. "I've been hoping you would call. I have news."

"So do we," said Daniel and he filled the pontiff in on yesterday's happenings.

"A *sirrush*?" said the pope. "You've got to be kidding, and with a Bedouin riding it to boot! This confirms that there's a third entity wanting your ring and the contents of that tomb. You're sure Rebecca couldn't find a link with someone who meddles in cryptozoology? Regardless, what that says to me is that whatever is in the tomb is far more important than we once thought. ISIS will continue to be a problem and isn't the only one interested."

"Uncle Liam," said Daniel, "I think ISIS will be after you now."

"Let them, Dani," said the pope. I'm well protected, and with the information you've given us about Abu Shadid, Farid Tahan, and Hasan Naziri, we will be able to keep tabs on them here. My reach doesn't make it to Babylon, so you will have to be extra careful."

"Do you know anything about this Professor Kasser?" said Luke, loud enough for the pope to hear him.

"Luke thinks he's the devil incarnate," joked Daniel.

"Luke's right to take him seriously," said the pope. "I met him once several years ago at a conference, and though his words are moderate, his dreams are like those of most imams—a worldwide Caliphate, except that he sees it as a much more beneficent government than his peers. Whether these are his true feelings or not are immaterial. He is to be watched. Still, he is only one person. His moderate ideas will not sit well with ISIS or the other radicals."

"What's your news, Holy Father?" asked Luca.

"The head of the CIA lands here this afternoon. Ostensibly, she is coming for a personal visit before she continues her trip in Europe. She is Catholic, you know. However, she contacted me yesterday and wants to meet privately this evening concerning the Babylon matter.

"News of the tablet's message is beginning to seep out. World leaders are beginning to whisper about its effect on the populace. I'm afraid you boys have found yourself in the midst of a growing global crisis. I trust you both to take care of each other and to watch out for Vatican interests. Foremost, however, is your safety. I do not believe that ring will let you give it up, even if someone tries to take it, Dani. Just make sure their attempt to do so doesn't result in your demise. Luca, protect him at all costs."

"Yes, Holy Father," said Luca as they signed off.

"This is going to be just great," said Daniel. "Three enemies opposed to one another, after me and the treasure of the tomb, and here we are all going to gather around it in a few minutes. What could possibly go wrong?"

Daniel celebrated Mass for the staff at the Center. Couldn't hurt to start the day off with prayer. The Iraqis from the camp came as well, seeing Daniel as a kind of religious celebrity. Daniel couldn't help but notice the look of pride on his mother's face. He loved her, but he could never understand why she didn't convert. She told him once, "I have to do this for myself. There are so few of the Jewish people left, and here in the Middle East, I need to walk these sands my ancestors trod as a Jew. Do you understand my son?" He didn't really, but he loved her just the same. Many of the locals were Chaldean Christians, and they too were proud to have one of their own celebrate the Eucharist. Amazingly, Luca served the Mass with a piety and a humility he seldom exhibited anywhere else. Daniel never ceased to admire the need of humanity to reach out to the Infinite.

Later, when he and Luca arrived at the tomb, the student archs, the security team, Daniel's mother and father, Professor Kasser along with Walid, the dig's vehicle maintenance man, had already descended into the temple. The Bedouin was there to scope out the measures necessary to raise the lid should Daniel not be able to succeed a second time.

Daniel looked around the nervous group, excited for the moment, and said, "Well, let's try it again and see. I'm going to first guess that my blood won't have to be used again—and here he glanced back at the Marduk statue with its outstretched hand. This sarcophagus is a pretty sophisticated device, and I doubt it was just blood it needed to open, or that would have happened before through all these centuries. It needed a specific type of blood, something peculiar to me. Let's hope it kept a record of it and can sense my DNA as I place my palm along the upper seam."

Which he did, and there was a flash of blue light for just a moment, quickly forgotten as a groaning commenced. The four corners separated again, and the lid split in the middle as the two halves slid in opposite directions.

Daniel said, "Step up here and take a look." Markoz's Iraqi carpenters had built a riser around the bottom of the sarcophagus, encompassing the four sides with the tomb's expanded width, so people would be able to see into the crypt itself. Just like before, a swirling mist could be seen roiling below the separated lid.

"This is what I saw yesterday," said Daniel. "Now watch closely." Daniel waved his hand through the mist, and the fog began to clear. Once again, a diorama showed a moving tableau before them. Clearly it was the area now being excavated, but pictured millennia earlier. The scene it showed was three dimensional, and though, in scale much smaller than reality, the detail was magnificent. Men and women and even animals moved. Birds could be seen flying. The Etemenanki, the famous Tower of Babel, was almost complete, and business was brisk at the nearby Marduk Temple.

Brian was fascinated by all this. He leaned far over the edge, dropping his head toward the scene. Suddenly, one of the guards on the temple walls must have seen him, for he stretched back a bow and let fly an arrow. All the spectators in the tomb were amused until the arrow struck Brian in the cheek, causing copious blood to run off his face.

"Son of a bitch," he said, reaching for his sidearm.

"Brian, no!" shouted Daniel, and reached for Brian's arm as he began to sweep his gun over that tableau seeking the tiny soldier who shot him.

"Don't be a fool, Brian!" said Markoz, grabbing Brian's shoulders and pulling him backwards off the riser. In a rage, Brian turned toward Markoz and wrestled with him briefly, before a shot rang out.

Like a sack of rice, Markoz collapsed to the floor, bleeding from a wound to his chest.

The brothers Brummel, Navy Seals that they were, were closest to Brian and wrestled the gun out of his hands without further incident. Brian sank to the floor, hands up to his bleeding face.

"It wasn't supposed to be like this," he wailed. Disarmed, he was quickly forgotten as the tomb closed automatically, and the other student archs began to panic.

Rebecca stepped up to Lacy Michels and slapped her face, "Get a grip, girl. Frannie brought you out here because she thought you could handle the stress. This is stress, now go get her first aid kit."

She hurried up the ladder, while Albert and Fred tried to make Markoz comfortable. Greg Bowman's superior attitude was broken by the violence, and Roger Trake simply fell to his knees weeping tears.

Luca held Daniel back as his mother examined Markoz who seemed to be conscious, eyes wide open.

"You have a sucking chest wound, dear," said Frannie mechanically. "Bullet punctured a lung. It's gone in and out though, so let's see what I can do for you." Lacy was gone but a few moments and returned with the first aid kit.

Markoz gasped, "You'll do fine, but let Dani and Luca help you. Send the others away."

"You heard him," said Luca, "Greg, Lacy, Roger, and you Brummel guys, go topside and make sure the specifics don't get much farther than this tomb. I don't want the locals to know much about it. Professor Kasser, that's your job, to keep the locals calm. Tell them that Dr. Azar will be okay. Rebecca and Isaac, take Brian to the Center and lock him in the storage room. Set a guard there."

They exited without complaint, glad to have something useful to do. Brian didn't even put up a fight as he allowed Rebecca and Isaac to drag him up the stairs and out towards the Center. None seemed to notice Walid hover almost unseen by the Marduk statue.

Markoz motioned for Daniel to come closer. "Just like that evening long ago when you were a child, lay your ring hand where I am hurt."

"What are you talking about, Markoz?" said Frannie. "Boys, he's delusional already."

"No, he's not, Mom," said Daniel. "The day Saddam Hussein lost power and I came here, you had a terrible fever. I laid my hand on you and you got better. Dad never told you?"

"He did not," said Frannie, her lips firmly pinched like if Markoz lived he would certainly hear about this misstep.

Daniel came closer to his father, knelt down and saw the blood pumping from the chest.

"Whatever you're going to do," said Luca, "you're going to have to do it now. This is really serious. He doesn't have much time."

"I know, I know," said Daniel and he placed his hand over the wound.

He felt the hole in his father's chest sucking at his palm and the blood running through his fingers. But he also felt a strange warmness that was not coming from arterial blood and a vibration that was located on his ring. Suddenly, the ring flashed brightly, but this time stayed blue, suffusing the room in a sapphire glow.

Frannie gasped in wonder, and Luca tightened his grip around Daniel's shoulders. Daniel's head was thrown back and Luca gasped as his friend's eyes flashed a silvery gray. A sigh came from Daniel's mouth and he returned to the present, looking normal once again. Blood was all over the professor's chest, but Frannie bent down and quickly examined the wound.

She looked at Daniel, tears in her eyes, "The bullet wound, it's gone!"

She lifted him higher and checked his back. That wound was also sealed. Markoz was not bleeding anymore.

Luca broke the silence. "Ah, Dani, you could have told me you have a first aid kit on your ring finger."

Daniel smiled and said, "Yeah, but if you knew I could do this, you'd get yourself into far more trouble. C'mon, Dad," said Daniel, "let's get you to the infirmary for a real check-up."

A CONFRONTATION

Saturday Morning, 2/26, Babylon

WHEN THEY ALL got into the Temple proper above the secret Marduk complex, they found Nabil Kasser waiting for them.

"Daniel, please, I must speak to you," he said.

"Kind of a difficult time don't you think, Professor?" said Luca.

"Could we do it later, Nabil?" said Daniel.

"Really, it must be now."

Daniel sighed and said, "Mom, Dad's ok, but check him anyway. Send word to the others around the camp that it was just a grazing flesh wound that bled a lot. Luca, could you help my mother get him to the infirmary?"

Luca shifted his gaze back and forth from Nabil to Daniel. "I'd rather wait here with you, for your safety."

"Seriously," smiled Daniel, "I'll be fine, and I'll come as soon as I can."

Luca grimaced but complied, easily supporting Markoz in his arms.

"Now what can I do for you, Professor?" Daniel felt so tired.

The confines of the Esagila were dead quiet, and though it was brilliant daylight outside, the gloom in the room was only sparingly scattered by the burning torches. After all, they were still seventy feet underground.

Nabil had a look of great compassion on his face. "I'm sure he will be fine, Daniel. So many unexpected threats and violence surrounding this dig. I'm sorry to add to it."

"What do you mean?" asked Daniel.

"I could not help but notice the blue flash that instigated the opening of the tomb. I was not seeing things, was I?"

"No," said Daniel reluctantly. "It will show up on video, so you may as well know that my ring activated the tomb's mechanism. Somehow, the ring used my blood from my wounded hand to record my DNA and used it as a kind of passkey to open the tomb."

"You mean the wound that is no longer there. How is that possible?" said Nabil, looking at Daniel's hand. "The blue flash was so subtle; I doubt anyone noticed it."

"Luca and my parents did. They know that my ring has an affinity with this temple complex."

"You mean your Star Sapphire Ring, don't you?" said Nabil smiling.

Daniel involuntarily stepped back. "How do you know it's called that?"

"I know about the ring. I've known about it for several years. I am a student of the ancient King Nebuchadnezzar as well as an observer of Iraqi politics as practiced for over a century. The ancient king had a talisman of great power. It enabled him to build the Esagila Temple and Etemenanki, the legendary Tower of Babel. Some said it was a ring or a jewel on his scepter. Then sometime near his death, he lost it or it was taken from him. At first, I wasn't sure it was the ring I was seeking, but Cyrus the Great wore a sapphire taken from the Temple Treasury, and Xerxes later wore the same. It didn't seem to have any power in their hands.

"It disappears for a while but ends up with Alexander the Great who uses it to great efficacy, putting all the peoples in this area under his thumb. Gone again, it does not reappear until Crusader times in King Baldwin's hand. It has power then, for how else could an up-start noble set up the great Latin Kingdom of Jerusalem?

"The ring travels again through time, appearing now and then but never with power. It is just a curious bauble. King Faisal II of Iraq wore it till his death. Women swooned over it, but most thought in the hands of that corrupt king it was just costume jewelry. And then ... and then, Saddam Hussein took it off the decaying hands of Faisal in his grave. How and why the ring worked for that madman I will never know, but it did. He used it to build his power and to stay in power despite the myriads of men willing to assassinate him.

"But a curious thing happened. On the night of Shock and Awe, Tariq Aziz, the Foreign Minister of Iraq, wrote, in his seldom seen memoirs, of a talisman being given to someone by Saddam Hussein. I have done much research, Daniel. Saddam saw few that evening. But rumors persist that Tariq brought a boy to see him. I think that boy was you, and that he gave you the ring. How am I doing?"

"Quite well," said Daniel, surprised he was this calm over what was becoming a looming threat. How stupid he was to let Luca go.

"You are correct. Saddam did indeed give me this ring, but as you see it is not a Star Sapphire. It's just a simple band carved out of meteorite rock. What makes it so important to you?"

"I cannot lead my people without the ability to give them signs and wonders. The Bedouin and even the modern Arab are a supersti-tious lot. They need miracles to believe in the power of one man to lead them."

"The Mahdi, you mean."

"Yes, I have spoken to you of that before."

"Yet, you seem much surer now that the Mahdi is you."

"It is possible," said the professor. "You must understand, the Mahdi is to partner with Issa, your Jesus, as a companion of his to usher in the end times."

"What Jesus calls the new heavens and the new earth?"

"Exactly, I knew you would see what I mean."

"But how," said Daniel, "do you know you can work the ring? You said yourself, it has gone through most of its history as a piece of jewelry, not as a ring of power."

Nabil's face fell. "You are right. Clearly, you can make it work, or it could not have opened the tomb. But me? I do not know. Star Sapphire or not, that is why I must try it on to see if signs and wonders will come because I wear it."

"Sorry to disappoint," said Daniel, a terseness present in his voice. "But the ring has never been removed from my finger since the day Saddam Hussein put it on me. In fact, it cannot be removed."

A ripple of emotions washed over Nabil's face. "Impossible," he said. "The ring has come off and on people all the time through the years."

"Maybe," said Daniel. "But it has not come off my hand. And I will not let it come off."

Pure hatred and need suddenly sparked in Nabil's eyes. "I could take it from you," he said, pulling out a small Ruger pistol. "I don't want to do it violently. In fact, I want to share it with you. The prophecies say we must share power."

"Listen to yourself," said Daniel. "You talk like a madman, not like the Mahdi. Besides, I'm not Issa. I'm just Daniel. For some reason, the ring has come to me, and I don't even know what it means. But I'm not lying when I say I can't give it up, nor am I lying when I say I wouldn't if I could."

Nabil gave a cry of despair and extended the gun towards Daniel. Daniel moved fast and wrapped his hand around the barrel.

Again, there was a flash of blue. Nabil yelled as he let go of the melting gun, and clutched his burned hand.

Crouching, cradling his arm, Nabil said, "I won't kill you. I'm not that type of a person. But I must have that ring, even if I have to cut it off of your finger."

Nabil lunged, this time with a knife in his good hand. Daniel kicked him in the chest and settled in a crouch to fight this assailant who never seemed to give up. That was when he heard the growling.

It was around the corner in the next room of the temple.

"What is this?" said Nabil. "You have dog filth protecting these ruins?"

"Didn't think so," said Daniel, not sure what was happening. "Maybe you ought to get out of here."

"Maybe you ought to give me the ring before I cut it off you." With that, Nabil lunged again.

In the middle of his thrust, a grey ghost grabbed his arm and held him fast.

"Grigio!" said Daniel. "Couldn't come at a better time!"

"Get him off my arm!" said Nabil, fear and pain coursing through his voice.

"You're lucky you have an arm. The Arab guy who tried this yesterday ended up with a broken hand. If you'll behave, he'll let you go."

Nabil slumped to the floor, weeping, the dog standing guard over him.

"Can you tell me why you were willing to go all Gollum on me?" said Daniel.

"I have the chance to make the Middle East into something better than it is."

"Yeah," said Daniel, "your precious Caliphate. I know all about how wonderful that is."

"Not the one I propose. Not the one the true Mahdi is supposed to inaugurate."

"And you really think you are him?"

"I don't know. Just now, I didn't do a very good job convincing you did I?"

"You were going to shoot me and stab me! Of course, you didn't do a very good job!"

"The gun wasn't loaded, and the knife was just a letter opener. Neither could have done you much harm. I just wanted to scare you."

"Well," said Daniel, "that makes me feel so much better, and it so much easier to trust you. Luca has a saying for guys like you. He got it from his trips to America. He'd say you are being a momentous prick. Me, I say you're just a thug. Don't ever try anything like that again, or I swear, Grigio here will have you for lunch."

The dog yipped in agreement.

"Now come on, let's get you to the infirmary and get you cleaned up. I have no intention of mentioning this, not even to Luca. We will say you fell in surprise when Grigio came around the corner. That good enough?"

Daniel extended his hand, and Nabil took it, gingerly, saying simply, "Thank-you."

JUST A FLESH WOUND

Saturday Afternoon, 2/26, Babylon

"WAS THERE A problem?" asked Luca, looking at Nabil's wounded arm when Daniel and the professor came into the infirmary.

"No," said Daniel, "The professor fell coming up the ladder and has some scrapes on his arm. I can fix it for him. Dad, how are you doing?" said Daniel to the prone figure on the hospital bed.

"Not bad at all, son," glancing at Nabil. "Just a flesh wound from that bullet, hardly a scratch—though it sure hurt like hell."

"Good to hear," said Daniel, giving his father a quick hug, whispering, "I've got this covered. No one except Mom and Luca will know the truth."

He also decided not to tell anyone, even Luca, of Grigio's intervention with Nabil. As usual, the dog had disappeared once the crisis had passed.

He stood up and said to the room, "What could have possessed Brian to do such a thing?"

"Well," said Isaac, who came in with Rebecca at that moment, "Abu said there was a spy. Maybe it's Brian."

"I can't believe that," said Frannie. "He's been with us for years."

"Mom," said Daniel, "people change."

"Offers change too," said Rebecca. "Maybe someone promised him something that he couldn't refuse. I checked up on him a couple of nights ago. Markoz, he's been your major intermediary between yourself and whoever you needed to contact in Damascus. He spent a lot of time there, and it's a hotbed for the ISIS underground. Maybe someone got to him."

"Even I don't accept that," said Markoz. "He's always been loyal. In fact, we couldn't have done this dig without him."

"Exactly," said Luca. "He knew everything about what you had found, and, I'm sorry to say, Doctor, that there are others who would like to know what is sealed in that tomb."

"Bring him here. Luca, take Isaac, and let's have it out now."

The two left the room as Rebecca said, "Markoz, you have at least three major enemies trying to relieve you of the burden of the tomb—ISIS, the spy, and whoever sent that monster from Jurassic Park. They are not going to stop. In fact, once word of today's attempt makes the rounds, chances are the timetable will be moved up. I think we should request General Farouk's presence as well as a small contingent of Iraqi troops."

"That bad, huh?" said Daniel. "If they come, the world will soon know what we have yet to open. Sure you want to take that risk, Dad?"

"We have to. The safety of everyone on the dig requires it. I do think it best that we arrange to have the student archs fly home, at least till this mess gets sorted out. Let them know, Frannie, and let's get the earliest flight out for them."

The door to the infirmary slammed opened. Isaac barreled in with Luca just behind.

"He's dead!" said Isaac.

"What?" said Frannie. "How? Why?"

"His throat was slit," said Luca. "Someone came in the back window without him knowing, crept up behind him and killed him. There was no struggle. He bled out immediately."

"Dammit all to hell," swore Markoz. "He was a valued colleague."

"Who tried to kill you!" said Daniel.

"I'm not so sure," said Markoz.

"You wrestled with him for the gun. That would never have happened if he truly cared for you," said Luca, and the grimness of his statement plus the unexpected death quieted them.

"More than ever, we need to call General Farouk," said Rebecca. "We have an assassin loose in camp."

And perhaps another enemy thought Daniel, glancing at the silent Nabil Kasser.

AN AUDIENCE AT THE VATICAN

Saturday Afternoon, 2/26, Rome

SHE CAME TO him in the late afternoon. The pontiff decided the public part of her visit could be then, even though it was almost unheard of to do a formal diplomatic meeting on a weekend.

Leslie Richardson came to see Pope Patrick with all the decorum that marked a high-level U. S. representative of the government. She looked stunning in her all black executive dress with a black mantilla covering her blond hair. Pictures were taken; gifts were exchanged; official statements were read; the press was dismissed.

Then the pope took her to a room with far more comfortable chairs overlooking the late winter Vatican gardens.

"Leslie," he said, "take off that veil and relax. You are among friends here. Can I get you tea or coffee, or something stronger?"

My God, she thought, he actually winked at me. Two can play that game. "Scotch, neat please."

"Glenfiddich or Dalwhinnie?—my favorite actually."

He was smooth; everything her briefers told her he would be. But she was charmed, so she said, "Haven't ever tried Dalwhinnie, so let's be adventurous."

"Ah, now, you won't be disappointed," he said in his best Irish brogue.

A monsignor brought the drinks and when he had left, the Pope lifted his glass, saying, "*Slainte!* Leslie, Cheers! You are truly welcome here."

"Delicious," she said, after tasting the Scotch. "I think President Putnam would like this."

"You can get it in America, but I'll be sure to send both him and you the special thirty-year vintage with you on your return, as long as you hang up the icon of the Blessed Virgin, I gave you, in your office. It won't hurt to have the most powerful woman in heaven and earth looking after the most powerful woman in the administration."

"So full of charm," said Leslie, laughing.

"Remember I was a Vatican functionary for many years—diplomacy is second nature to us."

"You lay it on thick, Your Holiness, so I take it this private meeting is the important one."

"Indeed," said the pontiff, turning serious. "I am so glad you could make this trip on such short notice, but as you guessed it has to do with the Antiquities Department of the CIA and the worrisome situation that your President and I have concerning Babylon."

"We know your godson, your nephew that is, arrived safely the other day, and my contact with the archeological team ..."

"Ah, I figured you had an agent squirreled away somewhere in that group," said the pope with a smile.

"She's head of security and has filled me in on some of what has been happening, but you are surely more up to date than I am."

"There's been an attempt on the life of Dr. Markoz, I'm afraid."

Leslie blanched and said, "I had not heard."

"It happened while you were inflight, but Markoz is unharmed." The pontiff explained. He told her about Brian Jeffries being the shooter.

"But how could Markoz survive a gunshot at point blank range?" she asked.

"It's one of the things I wanted to talk to you about. I sent Fr. Daniel to the dig because he's quite familiar with what's been going on there. He also possesses several gifts, one of them being an expert in the Akkadian language, the ancient speech of the Chaldean peoples, indeed of the whole Fertile Crescent for thousands of years.

"His translation of the End Times Tablet is disconcerting at best. When it is published, as it certainly will be in the press once Markoz makes it public in a few days or a few weeks, it will cause apocalyptic hysteria."

"Surely," said Leslie, "the academic community will subject it to severe skeptical scrutiny."

"Yes, but the more they talk, the more the average person is going to pay attention, and one thing we learn from history is that apocalyptic messages are extraordinarily powerful and can change the shape of world history. Particularly when the apocalyptic message is very old but references a very current date."

"November First of this year," said Leslie.

"Indeed. And the events of the past few days in Babylon have upped that concern, at least in my mind. Too many enemies with different agendas are in play here. And you do not know the most important element in all of this."

"Please enlighten me," she said.

"It's why I asked you to come. It has to be told in person, for you would never believe me otherwise. There is an ancient ring, parts of which appear to be made out of the meteorite rock of the tomb. It was given to my nephew when he was eight years old by Saddam Hussein."

"You're kidding, right?" said Leslie. She could hardly comprehend what she was hearing.

"He was the giver, but Daniel's father was the manipulator of all the events that led to the gift. Based on what he had discovered of the ring and the fact that it seemed to have been once in the possession of King Nebuchadnezzar, Markoz wanted it back under his control. Maybe, it was a foolish wish. Perhaps Saddam knew what would happen, but he gave it to Fr. Daniel and the ring accepted him."

"Accepted him? I don't understand."

"The ring molded itself to his ring finger. It cannot come off."

"That's unusual, but I still don't see the problem."

"The ring," said the pontiff, "is a ring of power. It ... can do things."

"What do you mean? Frodo stuff and all that?"

"Not quite, but Saddam found it just as his reign began so many years ago, and he gave it up on the night of Shock and Awe. It kept him in power all those years."

"How could you possibly know that?"

"It's a hunch," said the pope, "but a good one based on what Fr. Daniel told me long ago the night he received it. A bomb went off in the room of the palace next to where they were meeting. It blew glass and shrapnel throughout the room hitting Hussein, my nephew, and Tariq Aziz who had brought my nephew to that murderous thug. They were shrapnel proof. None of them was injured. And in case you are thinking that was just a fluke, the ring opened the tomb yesterday and today, and healed Dr. Markoz of a fatal gunshot wound. You would never know he had been harmed."

"That's amazing! But what does it have to do with the tablet and its message?"

The pope sighed. "Because it's made of the same material as the tomb, we think they go together. Whatever is in the tomb is going to deepen this mystery not debunk it. We have only hours to figure out a plan to deal with this. After that, word is sure to leak out about what has been discovered. My Swiss Guard, your agents and the Iraqi military should be able to handle threats on the ground, but world leaders are going to have to figure out how to handle whatever earth-shattering news the Tomb opening will cause."

"You said that Brian Jeffries was murdered?"

"Yes, and it seems he was the unnamed spy that ISIS mentioned. His murder was caused by an enemy we do not know, presumably the one that has twice tried to kill my nephew, once with bullets, once with a monster."

"And you think our people can handle that situation on the ground?"

"Yes," said the pope. "I am sure all are well-trained, and Fr. Daniel has the ring. Already, it has shown the power to heal, the power to open the tomb, and I'll bet it has even more secrets. Sounds like a good start to me."

"You are not what I thought you would be," said Leslie.

"What do you mean?"

"When I met you a few weeks ago, you seemed the typical religious leader, albeit a younger and more charismatic one than usual. You're awfully worldly for a pontiff."

"I'm the head of one point five billion people. Whatever happens at that tomb in the next few days is going to affect millions of people I'm responsible for. You represent the last remaining super-power; you'll have no choice in the matter. It will concern you no matter what. Don't you think we ought to use what little time we have left to do some planning? Refill?"

THE ARCHS WORRY

Early Saturday Evening, 2/26, Babylon

THE STUDENT ARCHEOLOGISTS were out in the cul-de-sac around which their tiny homes had been placed. Taking advantage of the cooler evening breeze, they were discussing the events of the day.

"I don't get it," said Greg Bowman. "I thought for sure Dr. Markoz was a goner when the gun went off. There seemed to be a lot of blood for just a flesh wound."

"I didn't sign up for this," said Roger, refusing to sit, trying to pace his nervousness away. "I mean it's dangerous enough here, but then with Brian turning out to be a spy …"

"Maybe a spy," said the Brummel boys. They were the oldest of the archs, having been Navy Seals before going to the university, but they didn't seem to mind their label. As twins, they had undergone all sorts of nicknames. Comfortable in their ability to handle nearly anything, they tried to soothe the group's worry. Al said, "Look, I think Rebecca and Isaac will be able to break down Brian and figure out who he spies for. Who knows? Dr. Markoz may just let him leave. It will cause fewer problems."

Just then, Isaac appeared from around the corner. His face looked so solemn that Lacy stood up and said, "What's wrong? What's happened?"

"Bad news, I'm afraid. Have to tell you that Brian's dead."

Gathering around Isaac, the group broke out talking, questioning why and how all this had happened.

"Shut up will you, guys!" When everyone quieted down, Isaac continued. "He was murdered in the storage room. His throat was slit, and we don't know who did it."

Roger took that moment to vomit in the middle of the road. Fred grimaced and told Roger to take a seat. "Seriously," he said, "we have no ideas, no suspects?"

"None," said Isaac. "I'm only here to tell you that Frannie wants you all gone on the earliest plane possible for your own safety."

Everyone heard the truck coming. With all that had been happening, it wasn't surprising that the horror of a car bomb flitted briefly through their minds. But then, they saw it was just Walid, the vehicle maintenance man, returning with the archs' SUV. He had been repairing it the past few days. Parking it in the cul-de-sac, he got out and said in broken English to Al, "Everything is fixed. Is all okay? You look like you are going to a funeral." Walid had tried hard to fit in with the students, and they had been teaching him how to make jokes in English, all except Fred. He couldn't stand Walid. Saw him as a simpering, untrustworthy Bedouin. So, he took this opportunity to show his true feelings.

"You're such an idiot, Wally. Can't you see we're discussing serious things? Things that are none of your business, by the way. Now get out of here."

A look of hate rippled across Walid's face as he said, "Please do not call me Wally. It is disrespectful. My name is Walid. In Arabic, it means 'first born son'."

Fred spat on the ground at the feet of Walid. "I don't care if it means 'bastard baby', just get yourself gone and don't go gossiping about all this to your friends."

Walid scuffed the spit into the ground and glared at Fred.

"Enough," said Isaac and then looked at the Bedouin and said with a kinder tone, "Walid, we have a lot to do. Thanks for fixing the vehicle, now if you'll excuse us …"

"So sorry," said Walid and handed the keys to Isaac as he left.

Al cuffed his brother on the side of his head, "Do you have to be such a jerk to that guy? What pisses you off about him?"

"I don't know," said Fred, watching the Bedouin depart. "He just bothers me. The wheels spin round his mind, and I can't see what he's thinking, and he doesn't tell us much by what he says. I don't trust him."

"Back to the subject at hand," said Isaac.

Al looked at his brother, and then said, "Fred and I want to stay. We can be of help to you."

"I'm not sure that's possible," said Isaac, "liability and all that."

"I sure as hell don't want to stay," said Roger. "The sooner away from this dirt pile, the happier I'll be. Things are getting too chaotic."

"When would we leave? I mean, I would still like to see the opening of the tomb," said Lacy.

"Tomorrow probably," said Isaac. "Frannie and Rebecca are checking flights right now."

Greg looked at Lacy and said, "Hey, maybe we can still get to see it before we leave."

"I'll pass," said Roger. "I'll look at the pics in the *National Geographic.*"

"You're such a pissant, Rog," said Fred. "Isaac, check with Markoz and see if we can stay. I'm ready to kick some Bedouin or ISIS ass if they're behind Brian's death."

WALID ACTS

Early Saturday Evening, 2/26, Babylon Wilderness

WALID WAS FURIOUS at the insult. Disrespectful words were bad enough, but spitting at his feet? That was an affront worthy of death. He could have killed Fred right then and there, but that would have blown his cover. He still had the knife that he had used to dispatch Brian taped to his calf, out of sight of Isaac and the archs. He had been watching the team for weeks, and thought Brian's action was pure stupidity. He had figured Brian as an ISIS operative, but the spy moved too early. It put his own plans in jeopardy.

Walid was the only one of the locals allowed down in the tomb that morning, and he was mightily impressed by what he saw. Clearly, the tomb held wonders. The diorama, that moving tableau that he witnessed, was proof enough of that, and then when the archer had attacked Brian, he was shocked. The Bedouin was sure that the miniature arrow strike had hurt—after all, it had drawn blood—but Brian seemed to lose self-control. When Markoz wrestled with him for the gun, Brian's eyes were full of rage, as if he truly hated the professor. Walid knew a betrayer. This man wanted Markoz dead. Walid wanted Markoz alive to open the tomb and was just about to intervene, when the gun went off.

He saw the hole in Markoz's chest. This was no glancing flesh wound like they tried to make it out to be later. This was a fatal shot. Brian was blubbering on the floor, but Walid knew fakery too when he saw it. A ghost of a smile crept across Brian's lips as he continued to wail.

Then the most amazing thing happened. The priest lowered his father to the ground, ripped off his shirt and began to probe the wound. Frannie was there and together they blocked off Markoz, but Walid was in the right position to still see.

Fr. Daniel's right hand hovered over Markoz's chest and then pressed on the wound. That was when a blue light flashed from his hand into Markoz. Walid saw it clearly, just as he believed he had seen the same light before the tomb was opened. He had been told the priest had the ring. He even sent his brother after it last night, but Walid had not noticed a ring around the priest's finger before. Now, he clearly saw it on his hand as it faintly glowed. He remembered the voice on the wind in the Otherworld—*Find the ring.*

Could this be the one? he thought. And then he knew. Because when Fr. Daniel took his hand away from the wound, the wound was gone, as if it had never been. Not even a red pucker where a healed bullet wound would have shown. Markoz's chest was smooth and clear. No one else had witnessed this; Walid was sure. He was the only one in the underground temple who could clearly see, besides the priest, Frannie, and Luca. A quick glance around the temple chamber confirmed that until he looked again at Brian. Walid remembered the man had stopped his blubbering and was staring in wonder, not at Markoz, but at the priest instead.

This betrayer, thought Walid, had seen the ring as well, and the covetous look on his face told the Bedouin that as soon as he could, Brian would make a play to snatch that ring. It was at that moment that Walid decided the spy had to die. No doubt Brian had been tasked to take out Markoz by someone else, and the ring would make an additional prize for whoever was his master. Walid just could not let the man live.

Coming out of his reverie, Walid looked over at the tomb. The Swiss Guard, priest and Markoz's wife were still bent over the professor. Walid crept up the stairs and quickly followed Brian and his jailors.

It was a simple matter to trail Rebecca and Isaac as they took Brian to the Center. Walid knew the layout of the place and figured the only room secure enough to hold the assassin was the storage room. He knew he had to act fast, so as soon as he saw them leave the building, he crept out around back and gently knocked on the window. Brian came to investigate but raised his hands in frustration as he pointed out that the window was unable to be opened.

A few gestures, some mouthed words, convinced Brian to find a cloth and hold it over the window as Walid broke it with a rock. Walid smiled. The Iraqis who built the place were so predictable. Tasked with putting bulletproof glass in the Center, they had skipped this window since it was just the storage room.

"Thank you, Walid," said Brian, obviously relieved. "I will reward you, but first I must get to the ISIS camp."

Walid said, "I saw what happened. You tried to kill him."

"Tried?" said Brian. "He should be dead by now. It was a fatal shot."

Walid nodded. "I saw. You acted too soon."

Brian looked at him. "Killing Markoz wasn't my first choice. I want the ring. ISIS wants the ring."

"You are the spy?"

Brian grimaced. "I hate that word. I converted to Islam over a year ago. I believe what you profess and fight for the Caliphate. I had intended to dispatch Markoz later, but when he touched me and tried to take away my gun, I lost it."

"You converted to Islam?" said Walid.

"Indeed," said Brian proudly.

"Then that will make what I have to do so much easier. Go with God." Moving like lightning, he put his arm around Brian's neck and with the other hand withdrew a knife from his pocket and sliced open the carotid artery. He darted back to keep away from the blood, but Brian just stood there in disbelief. He tried to talk, but no words came through the second mouth that opened up. He collapsed on the floor and swiftly bled out, dead before he hit the ground.

Walid wiped his hands and knife on Brian's shirt, pleased his own clothes were stain free. Climbing out the window, he saw no one and sauntered casually back to the Iraqi encampment. He still was furious at the insult he had received from Fred. Something would have to be done about that. Once back at the camp, he signed out a jeep and headed into the desert, to the most important hill in the world.

He wasn't sure how he was going to activate the rift, but he needn't have worried. It was shimmering in the evening twilight, and so, he walked right through. Everything was as he expected it to be. The *sirrusha* were not around, but a cool breeze was blowing through the garden-like oasis.

There was a voice on the wind saying, *'Why have you come?'*

"I have found the ring, my Master," said the Bedouin. "You were right. It is full of power, and it is on the hand of the priest son of Dr. Markoz Azar."

"I care not whose hand it is on," said the voice, no longer a whisper, but a palpable presence. "You are to bring me the ring."

"It will not be that easy," said the Bedouin. "There has been a murder, and the camp will be on edge all evening. I am swift and stealthy, but even I cannot do the impossible."

"You are asking for power, then?" said the voice.

"I am asking for a way to accomplish the deed. I wish to be your servant. I have never even seen you. I do not know who it is whose will I do."

"Prepare yourself," said the voice. Suddenly, there was another sound in the air, of footsteps pounding, with massive legs trodding. Through the palm trees came a figure at least ten feet tall.

It walked like a god, but was dressed as a warrior king. Its face was covered by an iron mask, carved curls of hair on its head. One eye socket had been punched out as if a grievous wound had once been delivered there. A long, carved beard of chain link graced the face and poured down the chest. The arms had greaves and leather boots reached up the calves toward the crimson scalloped cloth tunic worn under all that metal. The tunic was belted with thick leather from which hung a knife and short sword. In the figure's hand was a scepter, and though the Bedouin could not see the eyes, he had no doubt this warrior god was looking straight at him.

"I am Marduk," it said, "who once ruled the earth with an iron hand. No one stood against me, and though other powers came and dethroned me, my time has come again. You will assure that this happens."

"Yes, my lord," said the Bedouin grimacing at how easily he pushed Allah to the side as he embraced allegiance to this, this thing. *What was it?* he thought.

"You are my servant," said Marduk. "You have met my other servants, the *sirrusha.*"

"I have," said the Bedouin.

"Watch and be amazed," said the warrior god. The figure whistled, and from the depths of the pond rose the dragon mother. She had been watching everything, quick to come to the aid of her Master should he need anything.

"Once she was my enemy," said Marduk, "but I tamed her long ago. Her name is *Mushussu,* Mother of Dragons. Now she is my most faithful servant as you shall be. But I agree, you cannot go against my foes without power. I see much that I like in you, but true power you do not have, so it must be given to you. Hold out your hands."

To the Bedouin's embarrassment, they shook, as the dragon mother approached.

Marduk said, "you must let her bite your hands and breathe in your face. Remember, her mouth is fire; her breath is death, but for you, it is life and strength. You shall be changed and worthy of being my servant. It will be the greatest pain you have ever felt. It will last but a moment, but the effect is permanent. Then you will truly be able to serve me."

The Bedouin didn't even have a chance to prepare. The *sirrush* was upon him in a flash and had pierced both his hands before he could even move. The pain was instantaneous. He felt the venom move up his arms as he collapsed on the ground, his body exploding in sweat. He felt his heart seize and stop and his breathing cease, but before he passed out, trying to choke out a scream, he felt the dragon's breath on his face. The sensation of intense pain ran through his torso, down his legs, into his feet and then into the ground. Suddenly, he was no longer in agony.

He gasped in breathless wonder as a huge hand reached down to grasp his own. "Take my hand, worthy servant, and let me tell you what you can now do to your enemies."

DEATH STALKS THE DIG

Saturday Evening, 2/26, Babylon

"YOU CAN STAY," she said to the Brummel boys. Frannie found the archs much as Isaac had left them a couple of hours earlier, sitting around a makeshift camp fire in the cul de sac.

"Thanks," said Al. "My brother and I know our way around weapons. We can be of help to the security team. How's Dr. Markoz?"

"Recovering," sighed Frannie. "He was very lucky the bullet didn't hit anything vital. Actually, it just grazed a vein; that's why there was so much blood. He's up and around already."

"Good to know," said Greg. "I'm not happy to be leaving in the midst of all this chaos. Sort of feels like we're running away."

"Look," said Frannie, compassion creasing her brow, "I'm worried for all of you. If it had been solely my decision, Al and Fred would be traveling back with you as well. Isaac spoke for you on your behalf," she said to the Brummels.

"I for one am glad to be going," said Roger. "I signed up to do a dig not fight a war."

"You've made that plenty clear," said Lacy. Giving a hug to Frannie, she said, "Thank Dr. Azar for making this one of the high points of my life. I just hope you got us a plane that doesn't leave till after the tomb is opened."

"You're in luck," smiled Frannie. "The plane doesn't depart till late afternoon tomorrow. But get your sleep now. We're going to get that thing open in the morning no matter what."

Frannie asked the Brummel boys to set up watch that night over the other students, just in case. She left them there around the fire, casting its shadows into the darkness.

And the darkness was not alone. The Bedouin had come back, taken the time to dress in his new black robes and black balaclava with its black kaffiyeh. The balaclava meant only his eyes were visible, and they too were black. Though he felt larger and more powerful, he was indistinguishable from the night, watching silently in the shadows until the group began to retire for the evening.

"I'll take first watch," said Fred. Isaac had come back not long ago with a couple of pistols and asked if the two were comfortable with those weapons. They said they were, pointing also to the ka-bar knives each carried strapped to their thighs.

As everyone left for their quarters, Fred built up the fire once again and settled into a seat before the flames. Truth to tell, he would have preferred to go home. He had gotten tired of the work, though the thought of the opening of the tomb did excite him a little bit. Al thought experience on this dig would help their fledgling security company when they got back to the states. He had agreed, but now he was basically bored and more than put off by the local residents. He had fought them for years, and they still pissed him off just like they always had—lazy, good for nothing Arabs.

Fred heard a rustling in the darkness beyond the fire's light. It seemed to be coming from the side of his quarters. He pulled the pistol and slowly walked in a crouch towards the corner of the tiny house. Then he saw it. Something darker, clinging to the wall like a cockroach. Definitely someone. He almost fired, but then he heard another noise—the plop, plop of things that were soft and wriggling hitting the ground. Whatever they were, they started sizzling as they hit the sand.

The first one was on him before he could move. It was past the top of his boot in an instant, biting him and then falling off. It hurt more like a sting than a bite, and Fred naturally shook his leg and stomped on whatever it was. That's when the others struck as well. Dozens of saw-scaled vipers with bites loaded with death. They climbed on him, biting him everywhere. Because they were small, Fred didn't worry as much, but he should have. The venom of the snake was deadly, causing the blood to fail to coagulate. Bitten dozens of times, the pain was escalating, and he felt as if his body was blowing up inside itself. It was just the interior bleeding, and in less than two minutes, it was over. The intercranial hemorrhage did him in permanently.

The Bedouin's open mouth disgorged the last of the vipers to deliver one more bite, just to make sure the racist pig was dead. He felt full of power and decided to knock on the twin brother's door.

"What is it now?" said a voice. Al flung the door open, dressed in his boxers, staring open mouthed at the Bedouin in front of him. A scimitar flashed, and Brummel's head tumbled backwards into the room, arterial blood spraying the doorway like some obscene invitation to the Angel of Death rather than a protection from that specter. His body collapsed without a sound.

The Bedouin left the door open, Kanye West playing on the speakers behind him.

"Come out!" he hissed into the darkness. "Come out, children, and meet the walkers of the night."

"What are you Brummel assholes trying to do, scare us to death?" Greg Bowen stuck his head out the door and was promptly pulled forward by the Bedouin and tossed before the fire.

"What the fuck?" he said, starting to stand up. He found himself looking at the Bedouin who opened the folds of his robe like some creepy Middle East flasher, but that's not what Greg saw. He saw … things … hanging off the interior of the Bedouin's robes, things that detached themselves from the cloth and came skittering toward him.

He screamed when he recognized they were scorpions, death-stalker scorpions, tails raised, ready to sting. He remembered they were the ones that stung twice—it was the second sting that got you. Greg never got a chance to scream again. He was spending all his energy pounding the things off his body, but his skin was punctured again and again. Really, he tried to call for help, but his breath seized. Trying to gasp, he fell backward into the fire, the snap, crackle, pop of blistering flesh bringing a faint smile to the Bedouin.

That's when Roger made an appearance, flinging open the door and squeaking, "Cut it out you guys, everyone's on edge as it is." Then he, too, was speechless as he caught sight of the Bedouin lurking over the burning body of his friend. The Bedouin suddenly turned and flung out both hands toward Roger. Seeing what came from the Bedouin's fingertips nearly caused him to faint. Giant centipedes seemed to make up the fingers on his hands, and the Bedouin snapped his wrists toward the young man, flinging the centipedes on him. A face full of biting, foot long arthropods would do anyone in, and they sent Roger backpedaling into his room followed by the Bedouin flinging more of the horrid creatures upon the man's body, venomous bites stinging him to death.

Lacy had heard the uproar and knew immediately it was a death sentence if she went out the front door, so she raised the back window and fled. Down the streets of the camp she ran, shrieking for help. She glanced backwards and saw the Bedouin coming. Her college days as a Tolkien cosplayer bloomed in her memory, and she could swear a Black Rider was after her, dark robes billowing, folds of night and shadow reaching to embrace her. And then they did.

She felt the cloth wrap around her, stuffing her mouth so thoroughly that it cut off her screams. She flailed and struggled, but could not get free. She felt the steel slide into her kidney, sharp and piercing pain. She felt the arm around her throat and the knife pierce her vitals again. And then, she knew no more.

CARNAGE AND QUESTIONS

Saturday Evening, 2/26, Babylon

HE HAD BEEN out for a walk, praying his Rosary, when he heard the screams. Daniel was by the Center, and he took off running toward the arch's cul de sac. At least that's where he thought the screams were coming from. It turned out, the last cries for help were much closer to him.

He saw Lacy come racing around a corner, her face terrified, her arms reaching forward for any aid near her. For a moment, he flashed back to another time when he was helpless, when arms were reaching out to him, when an automobile took the love of his life. He could hear himself screaming, but Daniel didn't think Lacy had time to see or hear him because a cloud of darkness raised up behind her, enveloping her in the night. There was another muffled shout, and then the shadows released her. She collapsed on the ground, unmoving.

Daniel ran to her, trying to get a pulse. Seeing the pool of blood, he vomited on the ground. She was dead. Looking around wildly, he tried to see what had harmed her. He heard skittering on the roof of the service shed. Glancing up, he saw a shadowy figure looking down at him.

Fear gripped his gut, but he didn't run. He stood up and shouted, "What did you do to her? Who the hell are you?"

A hiss came from the outline of the shadow's face, "Bedouin. I am the Bedouin."

"We already killed one of you sons of bitches before," said Daniel barely realizing his vocabulary was descending to Roman street talk.

"My brother," it whispered.

"Why?" said Daniel. "Why bother us?"

"You have the ring. My master wants it."

"And who's that?" said Daniel defiantly. "ISIS, the Iraqis, who?"

"Marduk wishes it, and he shall have it." The Bedouin coughed out serpents from his mouth again, and angry scorpions descended from his robes. His hands held high, he flicked his wrists at Daniel, sending centipedes flying through the air to land on the sand writhing toward him.

Daniel didn't even think. Falling backwards over Lacy's body, his right hand shot out and blazed in cerulean blue light. Like some exotic weapon in a video game, the ring picked off each vermin as it approached Daniel. It was over in seconds. Unhurt, Daniel looked up at the Bedouin. For a moment, neither said anything.

Daniel finally said in a whisper, "You'll never have the ring." And then, to his surprise, he made the ring blast the evil thing off the roof. He heard the body hit, but when he ran to see it, nothing was behind the shed. The phantom had vanished.

By that time, the camp was in an uproar. Frannie and Markoz came running from the Center where their quarters were. Stopping in horror at Lacy's body, they saw Daniel come around the corner, his face pale, his eyes terror-stricken.

"What happened here?" said Markoz.

"The Bedouin, a Bedouin, is back and did this. My ring protected me." All three stared in mute shock at the crisped bodies of scorpions, snakes and centipedes lying all around. Daniel came to his senses and gave Lacy the Sacrament of the Anointing. He thought he was too late, but just possibly there was a flicker of life left. Then they heard the screams from the archs' camp.

Some of the staff from the Iraqi compound had heard the commotion, and, as the arch's cul de sac was closest to them, came to investigate. That scene of slaughter caused them to cry out, and it was a weeping group of Iraqis that met the three as they came running.

"My God," said Daniel, "they're all dead!" He knelt down beside each of the bodies absolving them as swiftly as he could, but he knew they were gone. There was nothing that either Frannie or Markoz could do to help them.

Luca showed up then, taking charge. Staring at the carnage was only going to increase the terror in the camp, so he had the Iraqis find sheets and other cloths to cover the bodies. He wanted to make sure that Rebecca and Isaac could see this before the students were removed.

He got Daniel's story and sent a couple of the staff to take care of Lacy, and then said, "C'mon, let's get your parents and get out of here." He called Rebecca on his cell phone, told her to get Isaac and come stat, filling her in on what happened. He figured they could handle this tragedy while he took care of the Azars.

Luca always could make a mean cup of *espresso,* and he figured that's what they all needed in the moment. He took them to the cafeteria where he brewed the cups. The bitter taste and jolt of caffeine steadied them all as he tried to make sense out of what happened.

"What do you mean it was the Bedouin?" said Luca. "I killed that guy the other night, right?"

"Dead as a doornail. You saw his body," said Daniel.

"Then who was this?"

"He said the guy you killed was his brother. Younger one I think, because this Bedouin was huge. I swear to you, he looked like a Ringwraith, just a long way from the Shire."

"You said you knocked him off the roof," said Luca.

"I did, but I didn't kill him. He hit the ground, but when I went back to the service shed, he was gone."

Daniel went silent for a moment, and then he gasped, "Lacy, she stretched out her arms to me, like she was reaching for me to save her. He gutted her right in front of me. What kind of a monster does something like that? And all for this stupid ring." Again, Maria's arms, from a time long ago, reached out for him through the years of memory. Tears ran down his face.

"The ring is not stupid, Daniel," said Markoz.

"It is, Dad. It only activates when there's trouble, and I don't seem to be in control of it."

"But you were son," said Markoz. "That thing threw everything it had at you. Each vermin was precisely killed. The ring has no eyes or ears. It senses your body responding to danger. In fact, I think it can sense physical harm coming your way and reacts. But it could not have hit those targets without your eyes. And the Bedouin, well, you struck him without even having to give it a thought before he did anything else."

"But I didn't kill him."

"And there's a mystery," said Frannie.

"Not so much, Mom," said Daniel.

"What do you mean?" said Luca.

"I asked him who sent him, and he told me."

"Who sent him, son?" said Markoz.

"Marduk," said Daniel. "He told me the pagan god, Marduk, sent him."

Frannie's hand went to her mouth, "Oh, my God," she said.

"What?" said Luca. "What's wrong? How can some ancient demon be here now?"

"Marduk was the chief god of the Babylonians," said Markoz. "In Nebuchadnezzar's time, he had achieved almost monotheistic status. That's why it was so amazing when the King ended up honoring Israel's God, back in the time of the Prophet Daniel."

"In the biblical Book of Daniel," said Frannie, "Marduk is a huge statue that is fed copious amounts of food each day. The priests, by using a secret passage, come at night and take that food and distribute it to their families, but make no mistake, they thought the statue represented the real presence of the god who was quite able to act in their lives. Daniel, do you think Marduk protected this Bedouin tonight from the ring?"

"Mom," said Daniel, "the ring has always protected me. The only other time lethal force was leveled against me, it killed five men years ago. It should have been easily able to kill this thing."

"Unless he was protected," said Markoz.

"Unless he was protected," said Daniel. "Whatever or whoever this Marduk thing is must have learned from the other night. It learned that it's servants could be killed, so maybe it protects them now in some way. Besides, this Bedouin was different. I didn't imagine what came from his mouth and his fingers or what was hidden in his cloak. He has been altered somehow."

Luca looked at Daniel skeptically. "You mean scientifically or supernaturally?"

"Look," said Daniel. "I do religion as my vocation, but I'm also a scientist. We talked about that beast the other night being a chimera made by a lab. I suppose one could alter a human too. But seriously, this is Iraq not the National Institutes for Health. There just are no labs here, at least nothing that could master this level of sophistication. Rebecca already killed that option as a likelihood."

"So, you're saying you prefer the supernatural explanation?" said Luca.

"Not necessarily," said Markoz, "but we should keep open the possibility."

"And the possibility," said a voice, "that it might just be a part of our reality." Nabil drifted into the cafeteria. "I just came from the archs' cul-de-sac. What a horrible tragedy."

"Indeed," said Markoz, "but what did you mean this all might be real?"

"'Supernatural' makes it seem like this horrific act tonight had its source outside our existence. But what if it didn't? What if the Bedouin and all he represents has always existed here in some way? My faith, Islam, has an entire tradition of beings that seem supernatural in other religions but are simply other creations in this universe of Allah's."

"You mean the *djinn*," said Daniel.

"Precisely," said Nabil.

"What in the world is a *djinn*?" asked Luca.

"Just another creature of Allah's, albeit a strange one," said Nabil. "The beast of the other night, for instance, could be of this earth. We believe that *djinn* are born, some good, some bad, and that they live lives parallel to us humans. Sometimes our paths intersect."

"So, you don't think the Bedouin is a demon?" asked Daniel.

"I do not know," said Nabil. "It would be easier if he were not, but he has obviously been changed from a simple human. What do you think he wants?"

"Could be anything," said Daniel, trying desperately to think of a way to change the subject. "My hunch is that he wants what is in the tomb."

"All the more reason for us to open it tomorrow," said Markoz. "Rebecca has informed me that she got in touch with General Farouk. He will be out here in the morning with a detachment of men to provide more protection. As yet he knows nothing of to-night's slaughter. He'll get here late morning."

"Operating on Iraqi time?" said Luca.

"Yes," said Markoz with a twisted grin. "That will give us time to get a head start down in the secret temple."

Frannie had stepped away during this conversation with her phone. "I've told Isaac to get a detail of the staff together and move the bodies into the storage room with Brian's. If you'll excuse me, I have phone calls to make back to the states … to let them know of the work-related tragedy that caused scaffolding to fall on our students, killing them in a terrible accident."

"We can't cover this up!" said Daniel.

"We can and we will," said Markoz. "As terrible as these deaths are, this is not the end of the danger we are in. We, as yet, do not know exactly what we are dealing with here. Murder is an appalling thing, but what is worse is to tell them the truth that will sound like we have lost our minds. Even Nabil's explanation would not be believed. We must claim it was an accident. It must be perceived as an accident, and I'll make sure General Farouk certifies it as such. We have terrible enemies who want whatever is in that tomb. Until we know its secret, we cannot let this situation descend into a media circus, which it will, if word of a supernatural murderer pricks their imaginations."

"I don't like it," said Daniel.

"But your father is right," said Nabil. "What's happening here is too important to descend into a farce. We need a few days before the media takes over the story."

"Rest assured, Daniel," said Markoz, "I honor these students. We will not forget them, nor forget to do something about their murders. You have my word as a father and as the director of this project."

Daniel turned on his heel and stalked out of the cafeteria, Luca right behind.

"They're right, you know," said Luca.

"I know, I know," said Daniel, "but I don't have to like it. It was better when we thought ISIS was behind this."

"They still may have a part to play. They haven't gone anywhere."

"Too many enemies," said Daniel, "not enough good guys."

"What about this General Farouk?" said Luca. "Any help there?"

"I don't know. I've known him all my life. He was in Saddam's army. In fact, on the night of Shock and Awe, he was the soldier who drove me out to Babylon to the safety of my parents. We became close over the years, but his first allegiance is going to be to his country. He was never a Saddam lover, but he is a patriot. Help? I'm not sure. Let's hope so."

They arrived at Daniel's quarters, but before Daniel had the door open, Luca pushed ahead. "Let me check the place first. No more surprises tonight."

He opened the door; his pistol drawn; and went inside. Luca was gone for only moment when Daniel heard a crashing and banging and then the sound of laughter. "Get off of me, you huge oaf!" said Luca.

Daniel rushed in and found Grigio on top of the Swiss Guard licking his face. A small table had been tipped over, but Luca did not look harmed.

"How do you do it, dog?" said Daniel. "This place was locked tight and here you are."

"You know," said Luca to the huge animal. "You would have been handy to have about an hour ago. Things got a little dicey."

Grigio just looked at the two of them with a solemn wolf look on his face.

"He runs on his own schedule, that's for sure," said Daniel, "yet, I'm glad to see him here."

"Me too," said Luca. "At least I can get some sleep now and won't have to babysit you from unknown thugs and supernatural warriors."

Grigio chuffed in agreement.

Daniel laughed again but suddenly felt lightheaded.

"What's wrong?" said Luca, suddenly concerned.

"I don't know," he said, "but I think I'm about to …"

"Pass out," said Luca, catching his friend before he hit the floor. He picked him up and laid him on the bed, Grigio looking anxiously at Daniel's moving lips.

Luca couldn't figure out what Daniel was saying, but he found himself speaking to the dog. "He's dreaming or hallucinating. Watch him, Grey One, while I get a wet cloth from the bathroom."

Daniel felt himself falling, but he didn't think he lost consciousness.

Instead, he found himself lying in some oasis with brilliant stars overhead. It was cooler than in Babylon, and, for a moment, Daniel drank in the silence and peace, until he heard a voice.

"You!" whispered the voice. "I hear you breathe little human. Why are you here?"

Daniel sat up and looked around in fear, "Who's talking? Where are you?"

"Here," said a voice, the sound coming from all sides of him. "And nowhere. You are lucky little human, for though you walk in my world you do not do so completely. This is my world of dreams."

A huge head with a mask, one eyehole punched out and ravaged, suddenly loomed in front of Daniel. If he could have, he would have screamed, but the thing was so monstrous that he could barely breathe.

"How I long to crush you with these two hands and spill your blood here in my domain. But as I said, this is my world of dreams which makes you safe from me—mostly. But hear me well. You cannot escape me. My time has come. Look to the heavens. Tell me what you see."

Daniel looked, and he found his vision could expand beyond the moon, beyond the planets, out amongst the stars. He looked deep into the night sky and he saw, the Thing, what his father called a comet, but what Daniel could see was actually something much more solid. For a moment, he remembered the tablet and its words about the Beast in the sky heralding doom. He watched the object flame, its tail stretching across the heavens, and in the pit of his stomach he felt a hopeless fear.

"You see it do you not?" said the giant in his dreams. "It tears the heavens apart with news of my return. Look at me. Now! Good. Show me your hand, your hand with the ring."

Against his will, Daniel felt his right hand rising. The blue band around his ring finger luminesced briefly.

"It is a small thing," said the giant. "But I desire it. Give it to me, and you might live to be my servant when I walk the earth again."

Daniel didn't say anything. He felt his jaws grind, and a little bit of courage slipped into his soul. He clenched his right hand into a fist and shook it at the ghastly vision.

He saw the giant's hand come towards his face.

Then his eyes popped open, staring wildly at a very concerned Luca and dog.

"What happened?" said Luca. "You were out for just a bit there."

"Dream or vision—something like that. He's out there."

"Who?" said Luca. Grigio yipped and licked his canine lips—his own way of asking the same thing.

Daniel looked at both of them and said, "Now, I know our real enemy is for sure a being named Marduk. See if you can find Nabil and bring him here."

Luca was back in minutes with Nabil in tow. The Arab professor nearly ran back out of Daniel's quarters when he saw Grigio, but the dog didn't even snarl at him. Daniel pretended not to notice.

"Look, Nabil, we need your help. Does Islam have an Otherworld? I mean like the West has in its mythology?"

"You mean like a place for Otherworldly beings like elves, dwarves, things like that? Not really, but we do have a higher dimension, caught up in the air, where *djinn* live."

"*Djinn* again" said Luca skeptically. "I keep thinking of the genie in *The Arabian Nights* or in that television show, *I Dream of Jeannie.*"

"Don't be childish," said Nabil, a faint smile on his face. "Like I tried to say before, *djinn* are powerful beings created by Allah. They are not angels, but they are much more powerful than humans. They can be good or evil, though it's almost always bad news to mess with them."

"I was talking with Rebecca earlier," said Daniel. "The *sirrush* and the Bedouin that we saw last evening, and the huge supernatural Bedouin tonight, just can't be from some scientific laboratory. But Rebecca said she had access to some info that spoke about a rift in space and time where things from this side can pass through to the other side and vice versa. In the West, we call them Thin Places. I don't know what you call them here."

"We have no such word," said Nabil, "but what you say is not that much different then what I just said. I'm afraid very few scientists would give any credence to this theory."

"Yeah, I know," said Daniel, "but they are not here in Babylon on a dig that promises to reveal something about the end of the world."

A CALCULATED RETREAT

Saturday Evening, 2/26, Babylon and the Desert

AFTER HE WAS knocked off the roof, the Bedouin got up and ran as fast as his legs could move. He darted in and out of the shadows of buildings until he got to the last outlying shack. There in the darkness, he shed his robes, stuffing them in the small backpack he carried. Once again, he was Walid, the mechanic. His chest hurt from the ring blast, and he checked to see if he was bleeding. He was not, but he suspected the bruise would be immense. He sucked in a painful breath in relief. He should have been killed, but here he was. He crept carefully back to the Iraqi compound, steering clear of curious onlookers rushing to see what all the cacophony of sound was about in the main camp.

Finding his truck just where it should be, Walid drove out of camp into the desert where the hill was. Marduk had told him how to find the rift. It was a spinning, golf ball size black hole just to the right of one of the boulders at the base of the hill. He touched it with his hand and it expanded to fit his form. Stepping through, he found himself alone in the garden oasis. It was evening there too, only a bright one under shining stars. He could see quite clearly, and he went to the lagoon to clean himself up. He had caused the chaos

Marduk had demanded but failed to possess the ring. Idly as he floated in the lagoon, he wondered what his punishment would be. Somehow, he had disgorged vipers, flung centipedes, and carried scorpions without harm. Perhaps he would be killed, perhaps not. He dressed in his clothes again and sat against a palm tree. He did not know how long he dozed.

Jerking upright, suddenly, he heard the stolid pacing through the garden that had heralded Marduk's appearance last time. He stood respectfully and waited until the giant appeared. The metal rings of curly hair on Marduk's head and beard glistened in the starlight.

"You have failed," it said.

"Partially," said Walid, bowing his head.

"There is never partial success. You have not obtained the ring."

Rather than apologize, Walid recounted what had happened. When he got to the part where Daniel had zapped him with the power of the ring, the giant sighed.

"You are injured," it said.

"It is nothing," said Walid.

"Let me see," said Marduk.

Walid opened his shirt and the giant approached and touched his chest. A healing warmth went through his body, and Walid knew he would not die that night.

"The *sirrush's* breath and venom kept you from certain death," said Marduk. "The ring is powerful, but the one who wields it does not know its true ability. That is also why you lived. Let it be a lesson for you not to underestimate what it can do."

"I will obtain it for you, Master," said Walid.

"I know you will, but these foreigners shall attempt once again to open the tomb. You must be there as my shadow, haunting them to get the truth. I must know what is inside. The ring is not the only thing important to me. Your eyes shall act as the thief tomorrow.

Let your sight get me the information I need, and then we shall decide on a plan to obtain the ring."

The giant turned without another word, but raised his hand in a strange sort of farewell. Immediately, Walid felt a terrible tiredness and falling onto to the ground, went into a deep sleep.

DREAMS OF TERROR, DAWN OF DESTINY

Sunday Night to Sunday Morning, 2/27, Babylon

THE BEDOUIN MAY have slept soundly, but Daniel did not. Instead, he dreamed again.

> *Sorrow, sadness, and woe. Like harpies of old, they clung to his heart, tearing the flesh to bits. He thought sleep would take the terror away, but the slaughter in the night invaded his slumber like the green mist of the gaseous marsh that swept the outer banks of Charon's river. He dreamt in images of myth until the symbols resolved themselves out in the desert wasteland.*
>
> *He was running, pursuing, chasing after the Bedouin, fleeing into the night on a* sirrush. *So close, he could almost touch the murdering bastard, but the thing turned on his mount and glared at him with coal black eyes, letting out a shriek of howling laughter and urging his steed to double its speed.*
>
> *He could not catch them. Watching, yet running, he saw them speed toward a hill, an old tell faintly on archeologist's maps of past centuries. And then they were gone. Breathless, he ran forward.*

Staggering, he came to a darkness there on the sand. Raging from his losses, he came closer and beheld a bottomless pit, the only place the beast and rider could have disappeared into.

He leaned over the abyss, and saw cold, steel-gray eyes staring up from deep within. "Behold, again the Dreamer comes! Step closer, O wise one. Join me here where all will be made clear. Stretch out your hand; let me grasp your palm in friendship."

His fingers traced lightly over the chasm, and the ring flared. A gauntleted claw reached upward, snatching the Dreamer's hand as he screamed in the darkness.

Pale light stroked his face as he sat up in terror. No rest in the night, thought Daniel. He wondered if his ancient namesake wrestled with demons like this in the palace of Nebuchadnezzar so long ago.

His brow furrowed in determination, as he jumped out of bed and dressed in his cassock. By God, he was a Chaldean Catholic priest and his ancestors had fought evil for centuries in this land, and he would be damned if he would let the Bedouin slaughter his friends and seed his terror throughout the ancient ruins.

He called them all, waking them from sleep and telling them his plans. Groggily, they all agreed. He found one of the Iraqi groundskeepers, sweeping the night's detritus from around the Center and had him send word to the Iraqi camp.

He set up for Mass under a palm tree between the Center and the Arab compound. No one had arrived yet when he heard the crunching of sand and dirt behind him.

"Dani, my friend, my sorrowful friend, I have come." Daniel turned and saw him there and breathed a sigh of relief.

"General Farouk," he said, "I didn't know if we would see you. You have no idea …"

"Rebecca filled me in last night, and I have gathered my men, twenty soldiers strong. No evil thing will bother you now."

Daniel hugged the older man. The years had not been kind to the general. The taciturn soldier of Daniel's childhood had grown into a good friend over time, but war and terrorism had gravened the line of care and concern on his face. An old scar etched its crevice from his cheekbone down to his jawline. Yet, even the worries and responsibilities he had to his country could not temper the warmth with which he greeted Daniel.

"I have to do this," said Daniel as he continued to set up for the liturgy. "They deserve to be remembered now, not simply carried off to be put on a transport to America. What kind of a thing would do this? Terrorism, bad as it is, I understand, but this … craven evil is too much. No one deserves to die like this."

"You haven't opened the tomb, yet?" said the General.

"Not completely, and that's what this has all been about. Something and several someones want whatever it holds. We thought you should be here. Whatever is in there belongs to our country. Enough of Iraq's patrimony has gone to thieves, collectors and the plundering rich. But I have to tell you, this is not simply about grave items. Something deeper is going on. The prophecy on the tablet portends harm to the world, not just to the troublesome Middle East. Ah, here they come!"

Markoz and Frannie Azar were at the head of the small group of staff. They greeted the general warmly. And as the welcomes faded, the Iraqis, Christian and Muslim, came from the Arabic compound. To Daniel, it looked like everyone else thought the memorial service was a good idea too.

When all had arrived, he said, "Thanks for coming this morning. I couldn't let last night's evil have the last word, and Mass on Sunday is a good thing to drive the terror away and remember our brothers and sister who lost their lives last evening. I know it appears that evil haunts this site, but my father has said to you many times, and I say to you now that what has been found here will change the world. It is no surprise that there are some things and people on this earth that seek to destroy what has been discovered. This morning, after we are done here, the team members will open the tomb, and the world will discover the secrets of Babylon. But whatever we find, the light in our hearts will dispel any darkness that comes our way."

He thought it strange as he celebrated the ancient liturgy, that so many religions and belief systems had come and gone on the very soil where the makeshift altar rested. As he raised the host and then the chalice, the crowd fell to its knees, all those who were Catholic acknowledging the Presence of God before them and those of the Muslim faith simply giving honor to a similar religion of the Bible.

As Mass came to a close, they all said a fervent "Amen" to that, even Walid, who had slipped in with his fellow countrymen to begin his secret watching for Marduk. He knew Markoz would need him, and he smiled as those around him prayed, knowing that he had a front row seat to the greatest archeological discovery since King Tut. The blood red rising sun shone on his face, and had anyone looked at him, they would have sworn they could have seen the smile of Judas on his lips.

THE TOMB OPENS

Sunday Morning, 2/27, Babylon

THEY TOOK BREAKFAST standing up. The team chosen for this morning's attempt at the opening of the tomb was made up of only necessary personnel.

As they trooped to the Esagila, Daniel had a chance to talk to Luca. "That's not your usual rifle you're carrying." It looked like Luca had broken out submachine guns. Rebecca and Isaac also each had one.

"Just being careful," said Luca. "This is the HK MP7. The rifles we carry would be too big and clumsy in the secret Marduk Temple. Small as these are, the rounds will pierce body armor—or a *sirrush's* skin."

Daniel shuddered. "Hopefully our modern velociraptors won't make another appearance, and maybe, just maybe, our Arab version of Dracula will be scared away from the temple during the sunlight hours."

He was amazed at the change that had come over Luca, Rebecca and Isaac. They appeared quite fearsome. He was the last down the stairway, and when he walked into the subterranean Temple of Marduk, he found the three already positioned around the walls so they could see everyone. Everyone, of course, was made up of Markoz and Frannie, Nabil, General Farouk, and Walid, though Daniel couldn't quite figure out what his father intended Walid's job to be, and, of course, himself. Farouk was dressed in camo and had informed them that his men were just outside the Esagila should they be needed. He too was armed, though only with a pistol.

"So many missing" said Markoz, almost to himself. Looking at all of them, his eyes wet, he said, "This is not how I imagined all this happening. This most momentous event should have been one of high enthusiasm and joy, but all this death … I can't even conceive why it all happened."

Frannie put her arm around her husband, "We will do this in memory of them. They may be gone, but their contribution was important. We will find some way to remember them."

Walid stood stone faced, though a trickle of sweat had begun tracing a path down his left cheek. He hoped they would think it a tear, but he was confident that, no matter what, his secret would remain sacrosanct. He needed to see what was in the tomb and report back to his Master.

Daniel held his hand over the sarcophagus and touched the center seam. Just like the day before, the panels both at the top and on the sides began to separate.

"I can't get used to this," said Nabil. "How they could have constructed this is beyond me."

"As I told my wife this morning," said Markoz, "no Babylonian technology could have done this. This is not simply a set of wheels and pulleys like the Egyptians sometimes had. There has to be a power source within the Tomb itself. Daniel only needs to touch his hand to the meteorite."

"You mean," said Nabil, "he only has to touch his ring finger to the crypt. That ring he wears does the rest."

"That simple thing?" said Farouk, and laughed.

"It's not that simple, General," said Nabil. "It's the Star Sapphire worn by Saddam Hussein."

Farouk blanched and said, "I remember that ring. We all wondered what had happened to it."

Daniel shifted his feet and said, "He gave it to me the night you drove me out here to meet my parents."

"Saddam gave it to you?" said Farouk.

"Indeed, but it has this property of disguising itself so that all you would have seen on my finger is a simple blue band, like it is now."

"But the Star Sapphire is worth millions," said Farouk.

"Its worth is not in currency," said Markoz. "As we have seen, it has a power, one that even I did not know. I'm not sure why Saddam agreed to give it to Dani. The ring has a tendency to find its wearer, so I took the chance and convinced the President that it was a good idea, at least until the American threat had gone away. I was shocked that he actually gave it to my son."

"It should be in the Iraqi Museum of Antiquities," said Farouk, squinting at the band on Daniel's finger.

"No, it should not," said Frannie. "In some mysterious way, it has an active part to play in what we are doing. And we are going to let that part play out."

Farouk was instantly mollified. "Of course, of course. It's just that I'm stunned to find it here."

"Well," said Markoz, "that's not the only thing that's going to shock you. Step up on the riser and look into the tomb again."

The mist was moving, twisting and curling over the top of the sarcophagus as the general leaned closer. Daniel waved his hand through the mist, and it gradually dissipated once again. He was curious as to what scene they would all see this time.

"As before, this is some kind of a holographic diorama," said Markoz, "only much more sophisticated. Whatever we shall see interacts with us on a physical plane—once again, technology the Babylonians never had."

The hologram was resolving itself into the part of Babylon that contained the Esagila and the nearby Etemenanki—the Tower of Babel, only this time the streets were full of people running in different directions, chaotically.

Luca had moved up more closely as had Rebecca and Isaac. "Look at the Tower of Babel. It's not finished, just like the Scriptures say."

"Not finished," said Rebecca, "or partially destroyed."

She was right. There were people on the tower, but they seemed to be swiftly descending. Priests in their flowing robes were at the top, and the King was there. Clearly it was the King, but he was wearing a ceremonial mask and armor and he was throwing down clay bricks assisted by the priests.

"What is going on?" said Frannie. "This isn't exactly the biblical story."

Daniel couldn't help himself. It was like his head was weighed down. He found himself breaking the plane of the hologram, and the moment he did so, all activity at the top of Etemenanki ceased. The King looked up, saw him and pointed right at him, howling as he did so. He tried to speak, but it was obvious he was having difficulty doing so.

That explained the chaos on the streets below. No one could seem to understand one another. Chaos everywhere except at the base of the Temple where four figures stood—three of them dressed as courtiers of the King and one of them in the flowing robes of a royal priest. They seemed calm and at peace, but they, too, turned and looked upward, their serene faces contemplating Daniel.

"They see me," whispered Daniel.

"I don't believe this," said Farouk. "It is a miracle."

Walid had crept closer as well, standing up on the riser, looking in at the diorama, but fear was making his heart pound. Marduk had not told him anything about this. This was sorcery. He wondered if it would make it any more difficult to snatch the ring off Daniel's finger, for that is what he intended to do.

Daniel, meanwhile, was still engrossed in the four figures at the base of the Tower, looking up at him while Nebuchadnezzar raged. The one dressed as a priest lifted his right hand slowly and pointed at Daniel. Clearly, he could see him. Then, the figure did the strangest thing. He opened his palm and turned it inward, and, immediately, Daniel saw that he too was wearing a similar ring. Blue light flashed between them, electricity filling the air. A loud sound, like a fire-cracker going off, snapped in the temple as a spark ignited on Daniel's finger. The minor explosion knocked Daniel off his feet.

"Dani!" shouted Frannie, "Your hand!"

Daniel looked at his hand expecting to see his ring finger gone, but there was no damage, no harm at all. He jumped back up on the riser and looked at the hologram, but the figure was gone. Only the three remained staring up at him. Nebuchadnezzar still raged.

Daniel remembered an odd thing. There was a time, so said the mythical story, when Nebuchadnezzar went mad. He wondered if this was the onset of that terrible malady.

Like clouds in an overcast sky, the mist was beginning again to obscure the scene. Daniel cried out, "No, we must see what happens!" His hands began scrabbling at the fog, trying to cup it out of the crypt, but to no avail. By the time the mist cleared again, all the observers could see was a polished piece of metal on which the tableau had appeared.

"What have we now?" said Markoz. "This we haven't seen before."

"We need to get under that piece of metal," said Daniel.

"Perhaps you need to touch it again with the ring," said Nabil.

"Pardon, Doctor," said Walid to Markoz, "I could get the magnet and see if we can pull it up."

"Good idea, Walid," said Markoz. "See to it, while we think of more options."

"Nabil's option is as good as any," said Daniel, and he leaned over the side of the tomb and placed his right hand solidly on the burnished metal. And … nothing. Nothing happened. No grinding of gears, or smoothly sliding panels this time. The tomb gave up nothing.

"Perhaps, blood?" said Nabil.

"Again?" said Frannie. "Absolutely not!" And she was chorused by everyone else looking down on the metal panel.

"It's not that I'm opposed to giving more blood to the cause," said Daniel, "it's just that we're thinking about this all wrong. We thought the initial blood I spilled was meant by the tomb builders to be accepted as a sacrifice, like to Marduk or something. But I don't believe so. I only had to do it once and then it recognized my touch. I think it took my blood and analyzed it and was able to match the DNA to what it sensed in my hand."

"Amazing!" said Nabil.

"Good insight, Dani," said Markoz. "As I said before, this is not Babylonian technology. Obviously, it is one that far surpasses ours."

"Uncovered any spaceships near here?" said Luca in a lame attempt at a joke.

"No," smiled Markoz, "but if Dani is right, the handprint he just put on that piece of metal plate might handle the problem for us."

There was no sound of grinding. The moment Markoz ceased speaking, the metal plate grew translucent and dissolved in a breath of mist. Fresh, oxygenated air followed upward from the tomb and wafted across the faces of all of the observers.

"Stasis," said Frannie. "Someone or something has been placed in stasis."

"Three somethings, I think," said Daniel. At least, that's what he thought he saw. But not human. Humanoid maybe. Too big and tall to be simply human. Daniel quickly estimated each body to be about seven feet long. But he couldn't see them clearly. At first, he thought that more vapor was obscuring his vision, but then he saw, in the dim flickering light from the temple sconces, that the figures were sheathed in an opaque microfiber type of cloth. Not dust covered, but off white in color.

Just in case, Luca, Isaac and Rebecca raised their rifles.

"They're dead," said Farouk, "no need to get trigger happy."

"They should be dead," said Markoz. "They've been here for 2600 years."

"But what are they?" said Daniel. "And look, at the base of what must be their feet, some kind of jar."

The jar was large, about four feet high, and was not covered by any kind of cloth.

"It's a bone jar," said Frannie, "a container for human remains. It's not unheard of for Babylonians to encase their deceased loved ones in bone jars and bury them later."

For a moment, everyone was silent, and then, Daniel said, "It's the end of their story."

"What?" said Markoz. "What do you mean, 'the end of their story?'"

"Look at what we just saw in the tableau."

"Yeah," said Luca. "Nebuchadnezzar going all bat shit crazy at the top of the Tower of Babel, throwing down bricks."

"But more than that," said Daniel. "We saw four men looking up at us, and one of them disappears."

"Was he struck by a brick?" said Farouk, puzzlement on his brow.

"Maybe," said Daniel. "But it's curious that the holographic image ended there, and the contents of the tomb are then revealed with three humanoid shapes and a bone jar. Maybe what we saw in the hologram was the final part of their lives."

"The guy who showed you his ring," said Luca. "He disappeared. Does that mean he died? Is his body in the bone jar? And why aren't these other mummies in bone jars too?"

"They're not mummies," said Frannie. "The Babylonians either didn't know the procedure, or they felt the climate and ground too wet to preserve them whole and entire."

"If these three are not mummies, Mom," said Daniel, with a smile on his lips, "then what are they?"

"Remember the fresh oxygen you all smelled?"

"Yeah," said Daniel, "and you said, 'stasis'. What did you mean?"

"Why fresh oxygen?" said Frannie. "If they were dead, they certainly wouldn't need it."

"But they can't be alive," said Markoz. "Not after all this time."

"Maybe not," said Frannie. "Maybe, instead, this is part of the method to keep them preserved. That would make more sense."

"Look," said Isaac, "this time the mist is coming back for sure."

The figures were already vanishing under the fog, and as much as Daniel would like to have leaned down and touched them, he felt a great reluctance now to stick hands into the vapor and touch— whatever.

They climbed off the riser and gathered next to the Marduk statue. Walid chose to make his appearance, saying as he came down the steps, "Dr. Markoz, I have two magnets, one portable and one hooked on the truck if you want to lift the tomb."

Markoz absently said, "Thanks, Walid. We may need it later, but come over here and join the discussion. Perhaps you can help us to a solution."

"Dad," said Daniel, "we can't leave here now, not with the tomb open like this."

They all glanced toward the crypt with the mist beginning to flow down the sides of the sarcophagus.

"I'm not saying we should," said Markoz. "But Dani, you know the protocols. We can't just empty the tomb like we're emptying a suitcase. Each step has to be documented; each movement we make has to be videoed."

Daniel coughed as he said, "I know, Dad, but we're so close. If the tomb remains open like this, we should take what opportunity presents to us. Let's at least see what the figures are. They may be just terracotta statues like those Chinese warriors were from the Qin Dynasty tombs."

"Or they may be real bodies," said Frannie.

Rebecca was the only one looking at the tomb when she gasped out, "I think we can forget about terracotta warriors."

The mist had run down onto the floor, and was beginning to cling to the sides of the walls. As she spoke, the others began coughing as they, too, turned toward the sarcophagus.

Daniel didn't know what the others were feeling, but he was struck with awe. Rising out of the crypt were three figures, clothed in the microfiber like cloth Daniel had noticed earlier. Even standing up, only their heads should have been visible, but they towered over the tomb and in the arms of the middle figure was carried the bone jar.

Daniel expected Luca to be ready to shoot them dead again if he had too, but when he looked at his friend, he saw no surprise, just a similar look of awe. None of the rifle carriers pointed their weapons. In fact, thought Daniel, none of us is afraid.

The light from the torches seemed to brighten behind the figures, and Daniel thought he saw someone else, someone whose immense arms appeared to embrace the three. A larger figure, golden in color, great in form, shaped to perfection, just barely able to be perceived, but Daniel thought it beautiful. "One like a Son of Man!" he said in muttered wonder. But the momentary vision was gone. Only the three, titanic as they were, remained.

"It's the mist," said Frannie looking at the others. "At first, I thought it was hallucinogenic, but it's not. It's some sort of anxiety diffusor. Notice none of us are showing any fear or any corruption of our thinking processes."

"Wasn't noticing that," said Nabil. "I'm just awestruck at what I see."

The three figures towered over them, as they stood above the tomb. For several minutes, no one spoke. The torches in the wall sconces did a marvelous job of taking the creepy out of the scene. Their warm, flickering glow cast a light that seemed to fluoresce the shrouds the figures were wearing. And though the observers backed closer to the Marduk statue and the east wall, they did so not out of fear but because the three figures were gliding off the sarcophagus and down to the temple floor.

They moved so silently that Daniel couldn't be sure if they were levitating or just walking softly. The cloth they wore shielded their movements from sight.

He thought, for a moment, that they wished to make obeisance to the statue of Marduk, for they moved in that direction, but the moment Daniel shifted his position, the middle figure moved to intercept him.

"Thanks for protecting me, Luca," whispered Daniel sarcastically as he looked over at a still smitten Swiss Guard. Yet, Daniel wasn't really afraid.

The three figures stopped in front of him, and the middle figure went down to its knees, setting the bone jar just off to the side. Then, the figure made a deep bow, with its head touching the floor.

"What does this mean?" said Walid, but no one answered him.

The figure stood up and moved closer to Daniel. It reached out a shroud covered arm and Daniel could see there were fingers and a hand. Cold and parchment like, the fingers grasped his chin and flowed upward, touching his cheek, his head, and his hair. The arm dropped to the figure's side.

Throughout the Temple, a rasping voice like autumn leaves whisking away on dry ground rose up to touch their ears. "It is him, my brothers. Without a doubt, it is him." And all three huge figures fell to their knees and prostrated themselves on the floor of the ancient Temple.

No one moved. Where would they go? And despite the fact that no one was feeling any fear, Luca, Rebecca and Isaac were beginning to process the fact that they still weren't sure whether these strangers were friend or foe.

With a whispering sigh, the figures rose again, and the middle one spoke once more. "You are he. The Dreamer. Come again. We have not waited in vain."

And with that, the three simply rose up in the following mist, hovered again over their crypt, and descended once again into the tomb, leaving the bone jar behind. But before the tomb closed, the voice was heard once more, "We must confer. At sunset, we shall meet again."

WEBS WOVEN TO CATCH A PRIZE

Sunday, Late Morning, 2/27, Babylon

AFTER THE TOMB closed, they all stood standing in silence. It was Markoz that got them moving.

"Walid, take the magnets back; I'll call for you when I need you again." He waited until Walid was gone and said, "General Farouk, would you be so kind as to check our perimeter with your troops? What happened here will soon be rumors in the valleys and hills, sooner still in the ears of ISIS. They will want what's here immediately." Farouk nodded and left.

"Now, as for the rest of you," said Markoz, "I'd like your opinions on what just happened."

Nabil said, "Never have I seen anything so remarkable. Living beings holed up in a tomb for millennia. I was hoping for a scroll, another artifact, something to explain the tablet, but living beings …?"

Daniel hung his head and said nothing, a slight movement instantly noted by Luca. "You know," he said. "You know who they are."

Daniel lifted his eyes to the gold-scrolled ceiling and said, "I know who they are, just not what they are."

"And," Frannie whispered, "you know who is buried in the bone jar."

"Yes," he answered.

"Please," said Nabil, "don't be silent. Don't keep us in suspense. Tell us what you know."

"First," said Daniel, "did any of you see anything else, someone else?" Each shook their heads no.

"I did," he said. "Just as they rose out of the tomb when they were towering above us, someone was behind them. I could barely make him out, but he was golden, the most magnificent being I have ever seen."

"Who was 'golden,' Dani?" said his mother.

"'One like a Son of Man, coming on the clouds of heaven'. At least that's how the Bible describes him, accurately, I might add. That's how I knew for sure, who they were."

"And they are …" Luca was feeling he had to drag the words out of his friend.

"They are," said Daniel, "whatever remains of the original Shadrach, Meshach, and Abednego, the three young men who survived the burning, fiery, furnace of King Nebuchadnezzar. He cast them in there for refusing to worship Marduk. They lived through that hell when a mysterious individual, one like a Son of Man, appeared in the flames and gave them the strength to survive. Then, Nebuchadnezzar befriended them and made them high officials in his empire."

"Then who is in the bone jar?" asked Rebecca. "They called him the 'Dreamer'."

There was a silence, and, then, Luca took hold of Daniel's shoulders. "Who is in the bone jar?" he said.

"I am," said Daniel, tears on his face. "Or at least they think I am."

There were gasps of wonder from the others.

"The 'Dreamer' is what they called their best friend and leader," said the priest. "He's known better to us as Daniel the Prophet."

"But why did he die, and they live?" asked Isaac. "I know the story well. They disappear long before Prophet does."

"In the book, maybe;" said Daniel, "maybe not in reality. He was the only one who died, or maybe he died years later in whatever stasis was preserving the others. Never the less, he was their leader, and they could not part from him."

"Not just that," said Luca. "They think their dead friend lives again in our Daniel."

"Mom, Dad," said Daniel. "You've said nothing. Did you know?"

"No, Dani, we did not," said Markoz, shaking his head. "But we are not completely surprised. You see, I found this secret temple many months ago. Just a few Iraqi workers, Brian, your mother and I did the excavation—not that there was much to do. The temple was in pristine condition. I had walked above it countless times and then, on a cold winter's day, I kicked a stone and it struck metal. That should not have happened.

"I thought it was some stray pipe from one of Saddam's useless forays into his amateur excavations. He had started many digs before appointing me Chief Archeologist on the site. Anyway, curious, I went to find the piece of metal and found the beginnings of an ancient—old, but not primitive—air circulation apparatus. It's the very one that brings fresh air down here now. I had it repaired and extended it through all the detritus up to the surface.

"There was no way," he continued, "this could ever have been missed by the countless digs that have gone on here for the past two hundred years. Yet everyone missed it but me. It was as if someone had decided that it was to be found. Then, I had a dream, that this magnificent temple lay underneath the Esagila. It was all the evidence I needed to begin the excavation.

"Curiouser things happened after that. Somehow, the few of us that knew kept the secret. Such a temple find should have sent the world's press scurrying here as fast as they could travel. But word never got out. The tomb was the *piece de 'resistance* which made the temple even more priceless, and still no one talked. For a while. I guess, eventually, Brian tipped off ISIS. Now that I know, I'm even more amazed that they never thought to interfere until now.

"The long story short, Dani, is that though I am just as shocked as all of you with what has been discovered, I'm not so surprised to find an intelligence, maybe three intelligences, behind all this."

"Doctor," said Luca, "how do we know those ... things aren't dangerous?"

"We don't know," said Markoz. "We don't even know if they're human, cyborg, or something else."

"His hand was dry and papery when he touched me," said Daniel. "It wasn't metal. It was like it was dehydrated or something. I'm guessing human or alien, not robotic, but, skeptic that I am, I'm saying they are some kind of human, tall and big though they be."

"I think we should open the bone jar," said Frannie. "They identified its contents with Dani. So, let's see what's in there."

She had a box cutter in her pocket. Walking over to the bone jar, her boots tapping softly on the golden floor, she bent down and looked at the seal. "It's a clay seal overlaid by a wax covering. Unorthodox as this is, let's see what's in there."

It took her less than three minutes to carve through the wax. The clay was impossibly soft and she was able to strip it from the jar as easily as a child unrolls a piece of poster putty. Frannie looked at her son, her eyes saying, "Prepare yourself." He nodded once and she unscrewed the top of the jar and pulled off the top.

A sigh as of long ages past was heard as new air filled up the empty spaces in the jar. Putting white gloves on, Frannie then gently tipped the jar, reached in and pulled out a femur bone. It was human.

"The bones are loose in here, and I believe the skull is in three pieces. No doubt about it, this is their friend, Dani, and now they think he's you."

Daniel didn't touch the femur. In fact, his mother quickly placed it back in the jar and screwed the top back on. He thought about the skull being in three pieces and remembered the mad King throwing bricks from the Tower of Babel. He wondered if that was how the Prophet met his demise.

"DNA," he said. "We have to check its DNA and see how it compares to mine. Maybe they think I'm the original Daniel's long lost relative. You've got the technology in the lab to test it, right?"

"We do," said Frannie, "and I'll get on it. A more detailed test will take weeks but we can have a workable sample comparison ready quite swiftly, enough to tell us something."

"I don't mean to be a killjoy here," said Rebecca, "but how is this earthshattering? We can never tell the world that we found three live humans from the sixth century B.C.E. No one would believe us; they'd just think Dr. Markoz was starting his own Middle-Eastern version of the Barnum and Bailey Circus with a new curious oddity to go with the Bearded Woman or the Lizard Man. And what about the tablet and the threat it entails? How is it connected with any of this?"

"All good points," said Markoz. "We've been summoned to a conference with our new guests this evening. Perhaps we will get more answers then, if we are not disturbed by other interested parties."

"Exactly," said Luca, "It seems that the strangers have loosened their control over this site, and it and all the contents are becoming more and more widely known to our enemies. ISIS will make an attempt to possess this excavation, at least long enough to empty the tomb and strip the temple of its gold. Whatever or whoever that mysterious Bedouin is, and the beasts he might control, it will be back as well. I recommend sending the surplus Iraqis home, keep the

Iraqi security guards, if they'll stay, and Walid and his employees to keep our vehicles running."

"We need to harden the Center," said Rebecca. "With General Farouk and troops here to take the brunt of any full force attack, that leaves us to secure the Center and keep the rest of the staff safe. Brian mentioned before that you have steel shutters to blockade the windows. We'll have to get those ready now."

"Indeed," said Markoz. "As I said before, the building was built to withstand small arms fire and even a grenade or two. We expected to find priceless things here and knew we would be an easy target for thugs, thieves and even terrorists. But General Farouk is a friend, and I have always laid plans that kept us alive till he and his troops could come. We are doubly lucky to have him here already."

"And what about our newly discovered neighbors?" said Nabil. "Will those three be friend or foe?"

"Better hope they are friends," said Daniel. "I shudder to think what they would look like riding *sirrusha*. Who knows how much more room they have in that Tomb to hide things?"

LAST STAND OF
A DYING CALIPHATE

Sunday Late Morning, 2/27, Fallujah

ONCE FARID TAHAN had confirmed the death of Brian Jeffries, he moved swiftly with his contingency plan. Using his sat phone, he contacted the head of ISIS, Hasan Naziri, and informed him of Babylon's status.

"Jeffries is dead," he said to Hasan, news that was met with silence on the phone. "But I have everything well in hand. He was a great source of information, but once an infidel, always an infidel. I knew he could not be trusted in the end, so I had other plans also developed."

"How did he die?" questioned Naziri in a voice that droned like lazy bees on a summer's day.

"He was murdered. They put him in the storage room in the Center once he made the attempt on Markoz's life and discovered he was a spy. He was killed there."

"Do we know who killed him?"

"That's just it. The more we know the stranger it gets. My information comes from Nabil Kasser. He called me this morning before he went to the tomb. They were going to try to open it again. The imam is not exactly our friend, but he is also not our enemy. I think he seeks something from the tomb or from Markoz Azar. He hasn't told me what that is, but he will by the time I am finished with him. Mahdi, indeed." His words dripped with contempt.

Naziri said, "What did he say about Jeffries' death?"

"A strange story. Unbelievable, actually. Only his reputation kept me from disconnecting the phone. He claims a lone Bedouin, riding some mythical Babylonian beast, has been terrorizing the site. 'More than human,' he says. He believes that this Bedouin is responsible for the death of Jeffries as well as the five student archeologists. They, too, were murdered last night."

"The Bedouin did our work for us," said Naziri. "But I know of no Bedouin tribe who has the intelligence, interest, or ability to pull something like this off. Do you think the reports of a beast are true?"

"Maybe it's a lion. There are a few here about sneaking into the area from Iran, but Nabil stressed its Otherworld nature."

"Pay no mind to that," said Naziri. "I am troubled that we have someone else who wants the contents of the tomb. That can be the only reason the Bedouin is making his presence known. What are your plans?"

"I've recalled Abu for a conference this afternoon. I'll triple his men and give him extra fire power, and tonight they will assault the camp. We will try to keep one of the Azars alive, perhaps their son, just so we can make sure we miss nothing in the tomb. The temple itself is plated in gold, so it will enrich our treasury, but if we have any trouble opening the tomb, we will simply use explosives. We don't need another U. N. Heritage Site. Like ants in the desert, the foreigners continue to meddle in our lives. I will have Abu dispose of the others who do not die in the fire fight. It could be fierce, however. Nabil says that an Iraqi general and a handful of troops showed up this morning to steady the nerves of the archeological team."

"That will be Farouk," said Naziri. "He's a fool. You should have enough men to take care of him and his soldiers."

"Already planned for," said Farid.

"We have a reputation to maintain, but we also must plan our next step. The West does not foresee another rise for the Caliphate, but I do. Do not underestimate Nabil Kasser. He, of course, is not to be harmed. He may indeed be the Mahdi, and if so, we can use him as an ally. His reputation would give us status."

"Excuse me, Hasan," said Farid. "We're going to massacre the camp tonight. They'll just see us as regular terrorists."

"No, they won't. You've put together an armed force that is going to go up against Farouk and his men, made up of standard army personnel. We will look deadly, not anarchic. You have prepared well, changing our tactics just enough to make us look respectable. Our strategy, however, is markedly evolving. Nabil needs support from this area's Muslims. We can get him that. And we need legitimacy. He gives that to us. For a while, our Caliphate *redivivus* will have to be an idea, a movement, under the guise of the Mahdi, but make no mistake, if he is successful, so shall we be. We will be conquering lands again soon. Already, I have directed our foreign actions to be less terroristic in nature."

"Meaning what, exactly?" said Farid.

"Meaning," said Hasan, "we shall start legitimizing our status in the world, ready to take our place as cooperators with the world's nations. The contents of the tomb may prove to be a gift we can give to the world as a show of our willingness to leave behind barbarity and embrace a more civilized status.

"Nabil's previous contact with us reflects his immense interest in the tablet they found over the sarcophagus. It's apocalyptic, talks of a coming war, and worries about who shall win. That sounds to me like something ISIS might be very interested in. Don't you think?"

"Yes," said Farid, laughing, "and our new strategy starts tonight."

"Don't fail me, Farid," said Naziri in his soft voice. "ISIS cannot afford another defeat at the hands of the West."

ANOTHER BETRAYER PONDERS

Sunday Noon, 2/27, Babylon

HE SIMPLY WASN'T hungry. That's why he skipped lunch and took a walk, instead, down toward the Iraqi tents. The workers and their families were treating this as a holiday so it didn't seem like an evacuation. Of course, they were worried about impending violence, but the Azars had effectively given them three days off and sent them to Baghdad, work payment cash in hand. The Iraqis were so war weary that the strange circumstances they found themselves in seemed just like another normal part of life.

Nabil was not feeling normal. In fact, anxiety gripped his heart. He couldn't believe that Daniel had not told Markoz about his attempt to grab the ring. And then, he treated him as an ally with questions about the *djinn*. What an enigma the priest was. Nabil knew the young man despised ISIS, respected Farouk, was loyal to the Vatican and fiercely devoted to his Swiss Guard friend. Nabil couldn't stand Luca. The feelings were mutual. Luca looked at him like he was some Judas in hiding. Perhaps he was.

He, himself, didn't know where he actually stood. He was pleased that Daniel had been asking his advice. And the suppositions they had talked about were interesting, but he just didn't have time to go down that rabbit hole.

He wanted the ring. He must have the ring. The fact that it might not work for him didn't even enter his mind. He had told Daniel the truth. He needed its power to establish his legitimacy as the Mahdi. It was one of the last pieces of a chain needed to link so many of his ideas together. He felt he was doing it for the Islamic people, at least those who were Arabs. The Mahdi transcended the divisions in the religion. Acting as one faith, Islam could do so much in the world that would be good and constructive. Perhaps he could help it shed its image of a destructive, iconoclastic force.

The problem was Fr. Daniel Azar. Nabil knew the prophecies, never written down in the Quran, but copied in other texts and certainly passed down through oral tradition. The Mahdi was to have a Christian collaborator. Yet, if Nabil forcibly took the ring, could he still count on Daniel's help? Probably not. Hence, the dilemma.

His thoughts were disrupted by children coming up to him. "Mahdi, Mahdi!" they said, smiling and laughing. He smiled and laughed with them. Apparently, their parents had been talking. Some of the older ones peppered him with questions. "Are you him? Are you the one who is to come? Or do we have to wait for somebody else?"

"Would you like me to be the Mahdi?" he said with a smile.

"Of course!" they shouted. "You could come to Baghdad with us. We're leaving in an hour. We could go to the mosques."

A solemn child of about ten years old broke out from the group and stood before him. "We could be your army. We could be your soldiers."

He placed a hand on the boy's head and said solemnly, "I need an army of believers, not soldiers. The world I want to live in is one of peace, so you will not always have to fight. You could be safe, and go to school, and no one would harm you."

"Can we be the first recruits in your army of believers?" said the child.

"Of course," laughed Nabil, "if your parents will allow it. Now I cannot join you in Baghdad, but here—here is money for you to buy sweets for yourselves and your family."

They were ecstatic with the gifts and ran to tell their parents. But still he was troubled. The Mahdi was not supposed to act alone. Issa was supposed to be with him, some sort of Jesus figure. Some of the texts said it would be Jesus himself; others claimed it would be someone appointed by the long dead Prophet.

Again, Nabil thought of Daniel. He had already been chosen because of the ring. Not by Saddam surely; he was just a pawn in a much bigger plan. But the ring had chosen Daniel for some reason, and that reason was tied into what he had seen this morning. He knew he was right not to call Farid or Hasan Naziri back again with what he had witnessed. They would muck up his decision making. No, Daniel and the three undead somethings had more to reveal, and Nabil's intuition told him that perhaps Daniel could be the representative of the two other monotheistic religions that would help the Mahdi ascend to power. Of course, Daniel would never be chosen by either Jewish or Christian authorities. He was too young and insignificant. But he had the ring, and to Nabil's mind, the ring conferred legitimacy. Besides, the ring could do things.

Nabil found himself making another decision. He could wait for the ring. If it was near him, that might be all he needed. An alliance with Daniel might be just the ticket. He felt less bad about his lust for that piece of jewelry. Could he convince Daniel that he was sincere? He thought so. Necessity often brought people together, and Nabil certainly thought trouble was coming down fast and hard upon the Azars, perhaps as early as tonight.

He thought of ISIS's offer of cooperation. He didn't trust them, but they needed him perhaps more than he needed them. Still, their offer of support was important, but it made the bile rise up in Nabil's throat. It wasn't exactly 30 pieces of silver, but he knew if he stayed with ISIS, he would eventually have to give them Daniel. It was the way of things, here in the Middle East.

His stomach clenched in anxiety again until he was distracted by a truck coming his way. It was Walid.

"Imam, can I give you a ride to the Center?" The man smiled obsequiously at him. Such a simple person, thought Nabil. He, too, was caught up in this web of plots and counter plots.

"Of course, you can, if you wouldn't mind," said Nabil, and climbed into the cab with the Bedouin.

TWO MEETINGS DECIDE FATES

Sunday Afternoon, 2/27, Fallujah and the Desert

IT WAS FORTUITOUS, and neither recognized it. At a cross-roads not far outside the ruins of Babylon, two trucks met briefly. Abu Shadid and his driver barely glanced at the man in the other vehicle. Abu waved him on to wherever he was going, and after the man had driven away, they proceeded on the road towards Fallujah.

It was Walid Badawi who Abu had waved on. Abu didn't even give him a second thought, so consumed was he about his upcoming meeting with Farid. The commander had told Abu that plans had changed and wanted to update him personally. It wasn't a long trip to Fallujah, but the day had turned quite warm, and Abu hoped to be back to his camp in time for dinner and a quick bit of training for his soldiers.

He was surprised when Farid met him outside his camp with open arms and armed men shooting off rifles in the air, yelling ISIS victory slogans.

Abu got out of the truck, embraced Farid and said, "Who did we kill? What victory have we won?"

"None yet," smiled Farid. "This is all in preparation of the victory you shall win for us this evening."

Abu looked at him quizzically, and Farid said, "It should not come as a surprise to you that Hasan Naziri has been very pleased with your work and wishes you to command more men. In fact, he wishes you to take Babylon tonight and take the tomb along with whatever is in it. This is to be a military operation, not simply a seize and grab. We want to possess the ruins for as long as it takes to find whatever the Azars have deemed valuable. At least one of them must be taken hostage, but we prefer it be the priest. The others can be disposed of. I'm sending you back with twice the number of men you have now. Your force of fifty should be more than enough to take the ruins."

"Hasan Naziri honors me and my men. You do know that General Farouk arrived there this morning," said Abu, as he swallowed nervously.

"Indeed," said Farid. "But his men number only twenty. You will be equipped with extra ordnance which should be enough to easily overpower them. Our victory over a regular army unit from Baghdad will let the world know that ISIS is back, even if in a slightly different form."

"Prisoners?" queried Abu.

"None," said Farid, "except for the one hostage and Nabil Kasser, who must be treated as the Mahdi and as our honored guest. He, too, is exceptionally valuable. Keep him and the priest safe and guard the tablet from any harm. One thing the Azars are absolutely correct on is that the inscription on that tablet is earth shattering and will convulse the world. That can only benefit us."

Farid invited Abu inside his tent and they had tea together, discussing the details of the evening's upcoming battle. As the tea settled Abu's stomach, he reflected that this should really be what the American's called a 'cake walk'. Farouk, his troops, and the minimal security staff should pose no real problem.

Now, as Abu and driver were approaching Fallujah, Walid was driving up to the hill. He expected the rift to still be there and it was, though no one would notice. It was very small and from even a short distance simply looked like heat haze rising from the sand.

Walid walked up to the rift, placed his hand inside and watched the rift grow large enough to admit him. Stepping through, he found himself face to face with the adult *sirrush*, looking hungrily at him.

"Do not be afraid," rumbled the now familiar voice. "She shall not hurt you."

The *sirrush* moved forward and snaked out a tongue, touching Walid's forehead.

"However, you must learn her name if you are to ride her," said the *djinn* as the giant moved into view around a large palm tree. "Her name is *Mushussu,* and she is the mother of all the *sirrusha* in this land. Call her by name."

And Walid did. The enormous beast immediately folded her legs like a camel and allowed the Bedouin to mount her back. Marduk spoke, "She will carry you without saddle, reins or bridle and you shall never fall. She shall be faithful to you unto death. I have given her to you to defeat my enemies. Now tell her to stand. I have glamoured her with the ability to understand any language and she will obey."

Walid did as he was instructed, and the beast stood.

"What do you see?" said Marduk.

"Just the oasis, Master," said Walid.

"Tell her to call her children," said Marduk.

Walid did so, and as he looked over the lake, the rushes and the palm trees, he noticed several heads popping up above the grass to the hooting sounds of the mother *sirrush*. They were the normal sized *sirrusha* he was familiar with, and there were many.

Marduk was so tall that the standing *Mushussu* allowed the mounted Walid simply to look the *djinn* in the eye.

"Tell me what you have discovered," said Marduk.

Walid did so, informing his master that the ring could not be separated from Fr. Daniel Azar's hand. He would have to be killed and the finger amputated. Then, he spoke of the beings he had seen, three in number, all majestic.

There was a rumbling in the chest of the *djinn* who said, "I did not know they were still alive."

"Who are they, Master?" asked Walid.

"Old enemies; very old foes. I had thought they perished millennia ago, but they were only hiding. Strong sorcerers, they could cause us problems." And here, Marduk, smiled, white teeth shining through the mask he wore. "That is, had we not known of their presence. Still, they must be taken seriously."

For a moment he was silent, and Walid was becoming increasingly nervous. "I have decided," said Marduk. "Your first priority is still the ring. You may kill the priest and take his finger. Do not separate the ring from it. Bring it directly to me. You may destroy anyone who stands in your way."

"There is an army general there, Master," said Walid. "He has many soldiers. How can I overcome them?"

"Ah, little Bedouin," said Marduk. "You underestimate the power I gave you before. Fear and stealth shall also be your weapons, and you will be equipped with additional power to achieve your goal. First, you shall ride *Mushussu,* and lead her children into battle. The sight of the *sirrusha* will strike fear into those who see them. And should they go to war, they shall take the battlefield.

"Once again, I shall give you my aura to protect you and to keep you from normal sight. Human eyes shall simply pass over you. It is possible that, if you are still and someone looks directly at you, they may see your shadow, but they will question their vision, giving you time to kill them and move on."

"Yes," said Walid, "it shall be done as you say."

"Rest now," said the *djinn*, "and when evening comes you shall ride and give me the victory I need to walk the world again."

RENDEZVOUS AT THE TOMB

Sunday Evening, 2/27, Babylon

THEY MET AS the sun was setting, just Daniel and Luca, Rebecca and Isaac, Markoz and Frannie, Nabil and General Farouk. It had been a quiet afternoon which allayed some of their fears. Most of the Iraqi help and their families had gone to Baghdad. The troops relaxed and kept an eye out for the absent ISIS militants in case they should return.

They met in the Esagila above the secret temple. A solemn lot they were, but there was an undercurrent of excitement. All the deaths they had experienced couldn't take away from the anticipation of what was to come.

Markoz had set up the cameras and insisted they be filmed as all descended the steps into the secret Temple of Marduk. Their surprise was manifest when they found they were not the first to arrive. The grey wolf-dog, Grigio, was already there, lounging placidly next to the tomb.

"Get that beast out of here," snapped Nabil. "He could disrupt everything."

"I don't think so," said Daniel firmly. "He has been by my side whenever danger was present. He comes and goes as he pleases, and

I think sending him away would be a bad idea. Let him be and let's get on with this."

"Get on with what?" asked Rebecca. "They said they would appear here. Aren't we at their mercy?" Nervously, she flexed her submachine gun in her hands.

"I don't think we'll need the weapons," said Daniel, "and I'm not sure how much good they would do against whatever we are about to meet here."

Markoz ran his hand over the sarcophagus somewhat distractedly. "There are two things that must be accomplished when all this begins. First, we listen to what they say. Second, we find out what happens next. I don't mean to be a smart ass, but are they planning to live here, go somewhere else, reveal what's in the tomb—what's their plan? The reason I say this is because we have about forty-eight hours before the press starts trickling in. That's how long it will take the rumors the Iraqis will spread to take hold. Don't you agree, General?"

"I do," he said, "and I have no intention of withdrawing and leaving you to face ISIS, the press, or your strange guests alone. It will be chaos here in a few days."

"That's why I'm concerned about the life forms we have encountered. They must not be harmed or exploited. They must ..."

Markoz stopped in the middle of his sentence as the tomb began to open again but on its own this time. Everyone instinctively stepped back, and even Grigio went to join Daniel.

The tomb duplicated its previous status when it opened. A flowing vapor, like dry ice would produce, wafted over the opening and drifted down the sides. Only the diorama did not appear again.

For several minutes nothing happened, and in an exasperated voice, Luca cried out, "We're here. What do you want of us?"

A voice rumbled out of the tomb, "We know you are present, and we have come."

As it spoke, the three figures seen before, swathed in their burial shrouds, rose out of the tomb appearing to float on the cloud of mist. For a moment, they stood there beholding the archeological team, and then, their hands lifted up and the shrouds fell from their bodies.

Everyone gasped as before them stood three large males, dressed in the Babylonian clothing of imperial courtiers. A long white short sleeved tunic stretched down their bodies, with a golden girdle wrapped around their waist, descending in scallops of overlapping cloth to their knees. Around their torso, they wore a robe, brilliant as the colors of a tropical bird, red for one, blue for another, gold for the third. Their heads, with dyed black hair curled and oiled, were covered with a fez like cloth lifting about a foot above their forehead. Their long beards, dyed black, were curled and oiled as well, squared off in the middle of their chests. Each held a short staff, and, while young, they looked like they came from ancient times. But all this was hardly noticed by the observers. Their gaze was riveted on the visitors' eyes. They were a solid silver grey, with both pupil and sclera merging together with the same color. Those eyes made them look positively alien.

As one they moved forward and seemed to float down to the golden flooring. Each was about seven feet tall and towered over everyone else in the temple. Again, the observers involuntarily took a step back, except for Grigio who stood there, tail wagging.

Daniel heard a rumble in the room, and it was a moment before he realized it was the three strangers laughing at the dog.

The one in the blue robe, he that was in the middle, said in perfect English, "Ah, companion to our friend, it is good to see you again. Well met." The dog yipped in what appeared to be happiness.

"Thank you for coming," continued the speaker to the humans present. "You will have many questions, and may I say we have waited millennia to answer them. But before you ask, allow us to explain."

As before, all three knelt on the floor, bowing in obeisance to Daniel. Then they stood again. The middle one continued to speak, "Long has it been since we have seen our beloved friend," he said to Daniel.

"I do not know you," stuttered Daniel. "I have never met you."

"Yet, you are our friend. Perhaps you have had time to find out how this may be."

"Daniel," said his mother, "I was able to begin the process of comparing your DNA with the remains in the bone jar. It is early, but already some results are in. If the trajectory stays the same, the DNA—yours and the sample in the bone jar—will be identical. I'm not sure how that is possible."

"It has been prophesied by the Daniel we knew," said the speaker. "We are not backward country peasants," he continued. "The Daniel we knew and loved died as you saw him die, killed by the bricks thrown by the insane King Nebuchadnezzar from the top the Etemenanki—what you call the Tower of Babel. There is only one life for us in this existence, and, yet, you, Daniel, are our friend from of old. Perhaps we can speak of this later and explain further."

Daniel was speechless, as were the others, so the speaker continued. "We see your faces. You wonder whether we are human. The answer is—we are. But you have greatly underestimated what you would call Babylonian technology. The stasis chamber, the clay tablets within this tomb, other objects buried with us, all represent the height of Babylonian scientific achievements. When our King recovered his senses, we convinced him of the importance of constructing this temple and its tomb, and we asked to be encased within."

"But why?" asked Daniel. "Why risk death like that?"

"As you can see," said the speaker, "we did not risk death. We prolonged our life so that we could bring you a message and offer our assistance. To alleviate your curiosity, let me tell you what happened when we were entombed. The how of it will have to wait till this time of crisis is passed.

"The stasis chamber suspended our anatomical activity—slowed it down actually to an almost imperceptible level. Simply put, we did not age. Secondly, our minds, though comatose, were still active. Among other things, we were able to learn the languages and cultures of the peoples throughout the ages we existed in stasis."

"Impossible!" said Markoz. "How could you hear? How could you see what happened?"

"Yet we did, and I must ask you to trust what you see and hear now. How we did it is not a secret, but it is complicated, and we have no time to discuss it now."

"The gold tablet on top of the sarcophagus," said Daniel, "we've translated it, but obviously you must be the ones that put the English sentence in at the very last."

"Yes," said the speaker, "but when we were entombed that last line was not inscribed. As the time currents coalesced around the pernicious doom facing this planet, it became evident to us that our warning would best be heeded if it was written in the language most acceptable to this time period. We had a way of inscribing that tablet, placed when we were entombed, with that English sentence and date, when we were convinced the time was now to call you all here."

"But you can't be human," said Luca. "Your eyes ..."

"Will return to their natural color when the effects of stasis wear off."

"But your size," continued Luca.

"Ah, that will stay the same. We were the best, the brightest, the strongest of men when we were chosen."

"But Daniel, here, your supposed friend, is not like you at all. He's like a little hobbit to you," said Luca.

Again, the rumble went through the room as the three started laughing.

"He was always such," said the speaker, "and yet he was one of the best, brightest, strongest and most perfect of men, chosen by the King."

"I know who you are," said Daniel, "and I can't believe it. It seems impossible."

"And yet," said the speaker, "we are who you see. Speak our names so that our otherness may disappear. You know us in your heart."

"Shadrach, Meshach and Abednego, the three holy youth who were thrown in the burning, fiery furnace by the King because they would not worship Marduk as god—that is who you are. You were protected as you walked in the flames by one who looked like a Son of Man, burning bright gold with wings in that terrible blaze." Daniel said to the three. "I saw him when you first appeared. It was like he was lifting you out of this tomb."

"He has never deserted us," said the speaker. "He is always with us."

"But how did you know, Daniel?" said Frannie.

"We did not meet him until after our trial by fire," said the speaker. "But he had his own trial with Nebuchadnezzar who threw him into a lions' den for not worshipping the false god. Daniel was guarded by the same Bright One. But we know him now, O mother of our friend, by what he wears on his hand. When he perished long ago, the ring slipped off his finger, and found its way to the King. When the King died, it wandered through the ages back to the hand of Daniel, himself."

The three held up their right hands, and on each of their ring fingers a Star Sapphire gleamed. Like blue lasers, beams struck out to find Daniel's ring, and for a moment the temple was brilliantly lit with coruscating blue light.

"My name is, indeed, Shadrach," said the speaker, "and we have come to warn you of and help you defeat the terrible evil come to doom your world. Shortly before Daniel lost his life back in our time, our astronomers had re-discovered this strange comet that invaded the heavens. It was foretold, and so it was found, for it had visited at least once before, causing all sorts of catastrophic maladies. Yet, as our astronomers observed the phenomena, it went dark and disappeared. It never made its predicted appearance above the earth. But we were not fooled. Heavenly bodies simply do not disappear. We knew it would come again. And we knew from its appearance so many thousands of years before, that it brought only evil to earth. It is a harbinger. We call it the Beast for it heralds the coming of evil such as the world has seldom known. Parts of it fell to earth the last time it appeared and the world was ravaged. It may be the Beast itself or simply its herald, we do not know."

"Then what is this evil?" said Luca.

"To call it the Beast is not wrong, for it has many shadows. Wherever it appears, its mouth is fire; its breath is death. However it falls to earth, however it comes to ravage us, we must deal with its incarnation. Already, I fear it is here and the flaming dragon in the sky will simply announce its revelation."

"There have been strange things happening on earth," said Daniel. "There has been plague, there have been strange rifts in what we call the space/time continuum. Some of us believe that there is another dimension or an Otherworld that is spitting out its inhabitants onto our existential plane. My uncle, the pope, Irish that he is, calls it an excess of Thin Places that we are plagued with, and the evil has appeared from them. People are touched by this even if they don't know it. Riots and even wars seem more prevalent."

"It is as we fear," said Shadrach. "This time, this place, this coalescing of probabilities is revealing the coming time of doom."

Shadrach, nor the others, said anything more.

"That's it?" said Daniel. "We're going to sound like deranged and crazy scientists, telling people their doom is at hand. It's bad enough that the End Times Tablet will get millions of people to believe that the end of the world has come."

"As I said," replied Shadrach, "we are here to help, but we cannot solve this problem on our own. Otherwise, we already would have done that from our stasis container, from our tomb."

"Great, just great," said Daniel, as gunfire began to erupt outside the Esagila.

Farouk checked his radio and heard the news that ISIS had appeared with many more men than before, and that a battle was beginning outside the perimeter.

"And so, it begins," muttered Luca, as the dog howled its rage.

THE BATTLE UNFOLDS

Sunday Evening, 2/27, Babylon

THE BEDOUIN CHARGED through the rift mounted on *Mushussu* with many *sirrusha* following. As they swiftly passed through the narrow gorge leading from the hill, he chanced to look west as the sun dipped below the horizon. He saw a dust cloud far in the distance, paralleling his own direction.

He knew it was the ISIS militants, charging toward Babylon. No matter. It would end up fitting his plans well. He veered somewhat to the southeast, intending to enter the ruins through the Iraqi encampment. In that way, he would be far enough from the ISIS forces as to remain unseen. Yet, he doubted that General Farouk would be expecting a pincer movement from his foes. It was bound to be an interesting evening.

Abu Shadid, for his part, had given a resounding speech to his men when he arrived back at his own camp with the reinforcements. He had said to them, "My brothers, we are going to war against the infidel this evening. They have something we want, namely the tomb of the long dead pagan infidels who once lived in Babylon. Farid Tahan, my superior, and Hasan Naziri, commander of all ISIS forces, have forged a new path for us. We shall rebuild our Caliphate and legitimize ourselves to the rest of the world. Therefore, no cultural destruction. Discipline yourselves. We are a fighting machine. Kill those who oppose us, take no prisoners, destroy no artifacts. An exception: the archeological team should not be harmed unless they resist, and, if possible, the priest should be captured alive. General Farouk and his troops are expendable. Annihilate them."

The militants cheered, but a whisper began among them and grew to a low roar as they uttered the words, "Mahdi, Mahdi, Mahdi."

Abu signaled to them to be silent. "As for the Mahdi, I have received from Hasan Naziri the command that should the Mahdi reveal himself to us, we are to honor him, keep him safe, and obey him in all commands. An alliance exists between us and him."

The men cheered at this and fired guns in the air as the convoy set out for Babylon. Abu was less confident as he rode in silence at the head of the convoy. He was unsure of Nabil Kasser, the purported Mahdi, and damn sure that no command of his would be followed unless Abu agreed with it as well. Niggling in the back of his mind was another nagging problem. The events of the other night at the hill not far away from their encampment continued to bother him. The fearsome creature as well as the Bedouin had not made another appearance, but Abu couldn't help but think he had not seen the last of that strangeness.

The journey was not long, and before the moon rose, they found themselves on the outskirts of Babylon. They were armed with rifles, grenades and even a few rocket launchers, but Farid had refused them heavier weapons because of the importance of the ruins. Even now, on the outside of the archeological dig's perimeter, Abu and his men found themselves surrounded by important ancient remains. After ISIS's destruction of Palmyra and the Taliban's demolition of the ancient Buddhas in Afghanistan, ISIS had decided to forgo such cultural atrocities in order to signify its wish to be seen as a stable government entity fighting for its freedom and independence.

The convoy pulled up about a hundred yards from the perimeter and found it had the time to place the trucks and SUVs behind the shells of ancient remains. They could see Farouk's men already threaded throughout the perimeter. Abu estimated that the size of the general's force was considerably less than his own. He was not worried about Markoz's security team. There were not enough of them to pose a threat.

Abu allowed his men to shoot off several rounds in the air, hoping to provoke the presence of the general. He was not disappointed. Five minutes later, Farouk appeared with his adjutant, a lieutenant who signaled to Abu a wish to parley.

Abu clearly was uncomfortable with this new type of army discipline. He'd just as soon shoot the bastard and begin the slaughter, but Farid had told him to stick strictly to the conventions of normal armed conflict. However, no one was going to talk to the lieutenant but himself. He wanted to clearly understand Farouk's intentions.

"What do you want here?" said the lieutenant in a crisp, unyielding voice. He had walked forward to meet with Abu.

"We wish no trouble," said Abu, a smile on his face. "We only wish to observe the results of the tomb's opening today."

"Impossible," said the lieutenant. "The contents of the tomb belong to the Iraqi government, and General Farouk is here to make sure that the particular provenance of these treasures remains with the Iraqi people."

"Babylon is an old city," said Abu, "older than any government now in the Middle East. Perhaps whatever lies here belongs to all the people."

"That is for governments to discuss," said the lieutenant. "The general wishes for you to depart in peace. You will not be permitted to enter the confines of the dig."

"You know who we are," said Abu. "Are you sure an armed conflict would be in the best interest of your feeble government?"

"The General wishes to inform you that ISIS has been destroyed before, and the same can be done again. Babylon would be as good a place as any to see a repeat of the devastation that has been visited upon you in times past."

"Ah," said Abu with a smile, "I see that our negotiations have broken down." Then he shot the lieutenant in the face. Before the unfortunate soldier's body had even hit the ground, Abu was running back to his men screaming, "Fire, fire!" That was when all hell broke loose as both sides began shooting.

General Farouk immediately noticed this was not the chaotic firing pattern ISIS had been known for. The militants were disciplined and fanning out around the perimeter. He could see that they would soon begin offensively pressing his troops. Barking orders to his officers, he set up his men to resist the advance and marched himself back to the Center to make sure the archeological team was taking refuge.

Farouk seldom lost his temper, but he felt his blood pressure rising when he arrived there. The building was prepared with the defensive shielding on the windows fully deployed. He checked inside and found Markoz and Frannie, as well as Isaac and Rebecca present, but was infuriated when they told him that Nabil had just left. Farouk was aware of Nabil's wish to be accepted as the Middle Eastern Mahdi. He thought it was nonsense, but as usual, the Iraqi government could not make up its mind on Nabil's importance and so had left Farouk the only order it could get all the representatives to agree upon—leave him alone. But Farouk sensed mischief. However, there was no time to go after him.

Farouk looked at Markoz and said, "Where is your son and that Swiss Guard of his?"

Markoz looked worried and said, "He didn't follow from the tomb so Luca has gone back to look for him." Surprisingly, Farouk did not feel the sense of worry he expected to experience. He had been pleasantly surprised at the competence of the Swiss Guard. He'd have to leave the safety of Daniel in his best friend's hands at least for the moment.

Farouk looked at the little band and then said, "Gather round. Here's what we're going to do."

GODS IN THE RUINS

Sunday Evening, 2/27, Babylon

DANIEL HAD NOT moved, even when the gunfire began. He was in awe of the three figures standing before him, and now that he was alone with them, he spoke, "What do you want with me? Why do you think I am some reincarnation of your friend?"

The figure on the left moved forward slightly. Daniel was not sure there was much difference between any of the figures. Their headdress, hair and beards all looked the same. Their faces were marked with some kind of ochre which accentuated their completely grey eyes. Their rich clothing shimmered in the light of the flickering torches. To Daniel, it appeared all too surreal. Frankly, the only thing keeping him from fear was the dog, Grigio, who sat beside him, his tail slowly swooshing on the floor.

The figure that had moved spoke, "I am Meshach, perhaps the closest of the three to the Daniel we knew. Your mother was nearest to the truth," he said. "Babylonian science had a much different nomenclature for genetics than you do, but our comparison of your knowledge with ours shows enough compatibility to make this assessment: First of all, your DNA shows a pattern that reveals a linear link to the original Daniel. Simply put, you have his DNA.

Second, there is much more of his DNA in you than should be present if you are simply his ancestor. You have had dreams, young Daniel?"

"Yes, recently," he said.

"They have been of the past?"

"And the future as well," said Daniel. "And they have been very confusing."

"And were they like other dreams you have had during your lifetime?"

"No," said Daniel. "I am a scientist, an archeologist and a priest, and I know enough of dreams to be able to distinguish their types. The new ones are numinous—they have a quality of otherness as if my imagination is not producing them, but they are, instead, being given to me."

"Exactly what I thought you would say," said Meshach. "There is a richness in your DNA which your science cannot yet understand, but—simply put—there is so much of our Daniel's DNA in you that you are now beginning to access his memories and abilities. In many ways you are our old friend."

"I am me," snapped Daniel. "I'm not some replicant of some long dead prophet."

"Indeed, you are not," said Meshach. "I have misspoken and upset you. You are yourself, an individual born in this time and place. And yet, you are not. There is the genetic presence of the ancient Daniel, so rich and prevalent that we will have to guide you as it begins to reveal itself to you. It can be ... disconcerting, for one who is not yet ready."

"Why?" asked Daniel. "Why is this happening to me?"

"It was prophesied by Daniel himself. Before the King, lost in his madness, killed our friend, even as the brick which struck Daniel was falling like a stone from the top of Etemenanki, he looked at us with compassion and sorrow and held up his right hand upon which rested the ring. When he was struck, the damage was terrible and we forgot the ring for a moment. When we went to take it off his hand, it was gone. Nebuchadnezzar had it next. How he got it, we do not know. But the rings choose their owners. Who were we to question it choosing the king? Thus, began its journey through the ages to its time now where it rests on your finger once again. It is the source of power that will enable you to come into your destiny."

"Mumbo-jumbo," muttered Daniel, and even Grigio yipped in confusion. The third figure stepped forward and spoke.

"I am Abednego," it said, "and the rings have always been the focus of my study. Those who wear them form a bond, a band of brothers if you will."

"For what purpose?" said Daniel.

"To fight the Beast, the enemy of humanity."

"Nonsense! The last one to have this ring before me was Saddam Hussein, hardly a servant of the Light."

"And yet, if he possessed this ring, he served the Light in some ways, even against his will."

"What is your purpose; why do you come now?" asked Daniel, somewhat overwhelmed by all this news.

"Perhaps it would be better to ask, 'Who comes now?'" said Abednego. "You will notice on your ring, when it is in its Star Sapphire mode, that there are six diamonds, forming a star, surrounding the sapphire. Those represent the six ring bearers."

Daniel looked at the ring on his finger and noticed something. "There are only four diamonds shining; the other two are dark."

"Indeed," said Abednego. "That is because only four of us are in contact with one another. There are two other ringbearers. One of them we know, but he is lost to us in the past. The other is unknown, but we think he inhabits your time period as well."

"Why are you here, then?" said Daniel. "What made you appear now?"

"You did," said Abednego. "Twenty-eight years ago, we were awakened from our stasis at your birth. Only our minds functioned, the rest of our bodies remained inoperative. We could communicate with each other, and we quickly discerned that you were the one we had waited for—perhaps. We only became sure when you came into possession of the ring, when it accepted you and molded itself to your hand."

"Like magic," said Daniel.

The rumble of ancient laughter filled the Temple of Marduk again. "Not magic," said Abednego with what looked like a small smile on his face. "Science—the ring recognized your genetic compatibility."

"But it had rested on the hands of others through the centuries."

"You are not the only one descended from Daniel," said Abednego. "That particular genetic line has popped up through the ages with varying strengths. Depending on the strength of the genetic code, the ring would acclimate some of its powers to the one who wore it."

"You are kidding me," said Daniel. "Now you are telling me Saddam Hussein was related to the prophet Daniel. He was a monster!"

"Who in the end was not the one we sought, merely a carrier of the ring, a placeholder, if you will, for a while."

The sound of gunfire intruded again into the tomb. There was a pounding above the temple and Luca came rushing down the stairs. "We have to go," he said. "ISIS has come."

Shadrach spoke, "The militants are not the only ones who have arrived. An ancient enemy has stretched forth his hand this evening and let loose an abomination upon the earth. It is almost here. We will help you fight it and the other ... things it brings."

"What is almost here?" asked Luca.

"*Mushussu*," said Shadrach, "the mother of all *sirrusha*. She comes, an ancient horror permitted to roam the earth again." He bent down to look in Luca's eyes and said, "Her mouth is fire; her breath is death, and he who rides her possesses the dark power of the enemy. You cannot confront them alone."

For a moment, Daniel could swear the images of the three blurred, but then he was sure because they transformed into something like elemental spirits, their figures vague and transparent. They ascended upward through the ceiling to the battleground above. To Daniel's surprise, Grigio followed them, right through the ceiling, as transparent as they were.

"That's how he's done that all these years," said Daniel.

"Whoa!" said Luca, "wish I could do that."

"Come on," said Daniel. "Let's see where they are going."

THE BATTLE FOR THE CAMP

Sunday Evening, 2/27, Babylon

ABU LET HIS men get used to the battle. Their firing brought little damage to Farouk's forces, but he wanted them to drive off their excess energy before he moved forward. He was astounded that Farouk's troops stayed stationary. As far as Abu was concerned, the weakest part of the plan he had formulated was the beginning thrust forward. His men would have to cross open ground. His men were sitting ducks, and yet Farouk's forces did not come forward and wipe them out.

Of course, Abu couldn't know that Farouk was not immediately present. He was taking care of defensive positions around the Center and his officers opted for this holding pattern.

It was only a minute or two, and then, Abu decided to move his men inside the perimeter. He had already informed them that territory was not their goal. The camp was too small to worry about that. What he wanted was the death of Farouk's men. His militants were to target individual soldiers and eliminate them. Abu had trained them well, and he could feel the surprise of the opposition to face an ISIS force that was not spraying ammunition everywhere but, instead, was initiating focused fighting.

Battles such as these never lasted long, though it could seem an eternity for those who fought. Abu's men had sudden success against the soldiers nearest the perimeter. They were able to pick off the individuals of the first defensive line quite easily and move into the labyrinth of modern storage sheds and ancient ruins.

Farouk's troops quickly learned that the storage sheds made the worst defensive positions. Abu had given the okay to blow them up with the rocket grenade launchers. He was less eager to hurt any of the ruins, but by the time Farouk's men figured that out, many of them lay dead or dying.

General Farouk was soon on the scene, saw what was happening, swore, and ordered his men forward. The sudden onrush of troops surprised Abu's men, and for a moment they faltered. Abu saw an opening, however, and with a shout split his men into groups of six, sending them down the alleyways to engage the army much more closely.

The lines bent back and forth for a few minutes, like sound waves through water, and then, to Farouk's consternation, the ISIS forces broke through. Farouk knew his men were prepared for hand-to-hand combat, but he honestly had not thought that would be necessary. ISIS had never before shown much talent at focused individual combat. But they did now.

Abu had equipped his men with ka-bar knives. In their training, he had focused on close quarters combat which he knew would work well within the confines of the archeological dig. It was a bet that paid off.

His group of soldiers engaged the enemy and swiftly dispatched them. Abu wanted Farouk, and though he imagined the general would be surrounded by his men, Abu sent his own force through the maze of buildings toward where he thought the general would be. He took a more roundabout way, hoping to engage Farouk from the rear.

He circled around to some sort of ancient courtyard with flattened clay huts looking like the remains of some dwarven race. The years had not been kind to Babylonian ruins. But there, just as he suspected was the general, looking northeast toward where Abu's other militant groups were approaching.

That distraction was what Abu needed. He rushed forward just as his men engaged the soldiers defending the general. He leaped off one of the low-lying huts and smashed into Farouk, trying to hook his arm around the military man's throat.

General Farouk was a big man. Abu should have flattened him to the ground with his leap, but the general retained his balance. However, he was unable to keep Abu from getting a hold around his neck. He bucked and turned, trying to get the smaller man off him, but Abu was tenacious and began to squeeze with one arm as he pulled his other, the one with the knife, back to prepare for a strike.

Abu loved films and all the trivia that went with them. One of his favorites was *The Lord of the Rings*, and one of his beloved actors was Christopher Lee. As Abu pulled the knife back to strike, a memory flashed through his mind. Lee had been a spy in World War II, and Abu remembered an interview Lee had given. The esteemed actor recalled that his character was supposed to be stabbed in the back in the scene about to be filmed. The director wanted Lee to scream, but in his best British sarcastic voice Lee said, "Do you know the sound a man makes when he is stabbed in the back?" The director shook his head. Lee said, "He makes no sound. There is only the soft sighing of escaping air."

And that's exactly what happened to the general. He did not scream or yell when Abu plunged the knife into his back, piercing a lung. He simply went stiff for a moment and then relaxed, falling to the ground, Abu on top of him.

He couldn't believe it. He had killed the great General Farouk. Wiping the knife off on the general's uniform, he looked up and saw that his men had dispatched the general's protective force. He and they screamed loudly in Arabic that General Farouk was dead. Throughout the labyrinthine ways of the ruins, the cry was taken up and shattered the morale of the Iraqi troops.

Abu had driven into his men that their penchant of celebrating victory prematurely had lost them battles in the past, and so the cries of Farouk's death did not bring a pause in the battle. Instead, Abu's men pressed even harder to eliminate those who survived. He had no intention of taking prisoners.

BLOCKADE AT THE CENTER

Sunday Evening, 2/27, Babylon

REBECCA AND ISAAC clearly heard the sounds of battle, even behind the walls of the Center. There was no doubt that the fighting was coming closer to them. They would be under siege in moments. Farouk's plans to defend the Center simply by hunkering down and resisting would not work.

"Come on," they both said to Markoz and Frannie. "We've got to plan a distraction. They hurried to the infirmary, and Rebecca ordered the archeologists into beds and covered them up."

"What good is this going to do?" said Markoz, his anger growing.

"Really," said Isaac, "I've got to agree with him. What good is this going to do?"

"I have a secret friend I've been keeping from everyone, just in case a situation like this ever happened. I want you to meet Ranbir Singh."

She pressed a button on her camo lapel, and, immediately, six feet ahead of her, appeared the hologram of Ranbir Singh. She had gotten used to his appearance, but others gasped in wonder as the hologram solidified into what seemed a solid human presence.

"Good evening, Miss Rebecca," said the Sikh, bowing deeply. "And good evening to Miss Rebecca's friends."

"Miss Rebecca?" said Isaac, an eyebrow raising up.

"Don't get me started," snarled Rebecca. "He never learns."

"And may I say," said the hologram, "that it is quite the honor to meet the distinguished Doctors Azar. However, I see you are bed-ridden. Is it something serious?"

"No, you pompous ass," said Rebecca. "They are there to cause a distraction, and you are their doctor attending them. Your presence will give us precious seconds to take care of anyone who breaks into the building."

Already, they could hear the thumping on the outside door and expected explosives to be set shortly.

"Ah," said Ranbir, "our expected guests have arrived early."

Without another word, Rebecca placed the pin on the night stand, and she and Isaac rushed out to cover the entrance just as an explosion rocked the building.

"So, Rebecca and Isaac," said Markoz drily, "are not independent security consultants."

"Of course not, Dr. Azar," laughed Ranbir. "Both are CIA, just like myself."

The hologram was still laughing when rifle fire began outside the infirmary. Isaac and Rebecca cut down the first six men that came rushing into the Center, but a fresh contingent poured in right after them. They held their fire from their defensive positions and let the militants come forward. The infirmary was just behind them, and the sound of the reception area glass breaking led the two to open fire again. They were outnumbered and were forced from the hallway into the kitchen. To give themselves time, they slammed the steel door shut.

"Oh dear," said a voice from inside the infirmary.

The soldiers kept their heads, realizing that the priest or his parents might be on the other side. They kicked in the door and saw before them two people in hospital beds and some kind of foreign doctor with a turban holding a broken beaker.

"Now see what you did," he said crossly. "This was medicine for my sick patients, and I dropped it amid all the chaos you are causing."

"Stand away from them," said one of the militants.

"I'm their doctor," said Ranbir. "I'll not let you harm them."

"We have no intention of harming them, but we might make an exception with you."

"Oh my," he said, "I was afraid it would come to that. Just a moment please." He looked up to the ceiling, causing all of them to follow his gaze. The lights dimmed momentarily, and he said, "This will only hurt a moment."

The lights in the room dimmed as Ranbir sucked power from the lines. He dropped the broken beaker, and lasers, like daggers, shot from all ten of his fingertips, burning into the soldiers, killing them instantly. They fell in a heap onto the floor. Markoz and Frannie leapt out of their beds and ran to the soldiers.

"How?" said Markoz.

"Never mind that. Obviously, I've been upgraded," said Ranbir crisply. "They were a danger and had to be eliminated. Let's find Miss Rebecca and Isaac and get out of here."

HERE THERE BE DRAGONS

Sunday Evening, 2/27, Babylon

DANIEL AND LUCA burst out of the Esagila and into chaos. Rocket propelled grenades were going off everywhere, and gunfire riddled the air. A loud cheer went up from the western perimeter.

"That can't be good," said Luca. "Sounds like Arabs claiming victory."

Daniel's stomach clenched, and he wondered if Farouk was still alive. He turned to Luca and said, "We ought to try to contact ...", and then a huge concussion encompassed his head and he heard and saw no more.

"Dani, Dani!" cried Luca, bending down and cradling his friend's body. He had seen where the rifle fire had come from, and after gently laying Daniel on the ground, he picked up his sub-machine gun and returned fire, silencing whoever had taken the shot. Looking down at his friend again, he noticed that the head wound was a superficial one, bleeding heavily but not penetrating the skull. He breathed a sigh of relief and began administering first aid.

Daniel neither felt nor heard any of this.

His eyes opened to a blood red full moon hanging low in the western sky. The Hand of God Nebula soared high in the northern heavens while in the east spun the strangest comet that Daniel had ever seen. It was as if someone had thrown a flaming cylinder that flipped end over end in the heavens, dragging a fiery tail behind. It was huge, and it was descending to earth. It was not simply a sight to see; it was an evil to behold. It just felt wrong to him. And when it smashed to the earth, there in the dark of night, it kicked up a blood red soil that polluted the seas and land. The stench was awful and Daniel began to shake. The Beast had come, and death now stalked the earth.

He opened his eyes to see Luca bandaging his head.

"What happened?"

Luca smiled and said, "You are the most God-blessed person I know. To have escaped death three times in a week is just amazing. A bullet crease is all. Concussion maybe; headache surely. Never let go of that ring."

Before he had finished speaking a huge fireball exploded ahead of them, near the Iraqi camp. A grenade had found the fuel dump. As Daniel looked, he saw something thundering through the flames, something huge and out of this world. To him, it looked like a dragon, golden-green scales shining in the firelight, long sinuous head bobbing and weaving, its eyes seeking, its horns sparkling in the flames and its crest shining in the light. There were no wings, but on its back rode a demon in black, and though Daniel's eyes were spinning he knew they were in grave danger.

"Run," he said to Luca. "Get out of here now. Leave me!"

"Crap to that," said Luca. "I'll not be leaving you." He lifted up his submachine gun, taking aim at the creature. The thing shivered to a stop not ten feet from them and blew a mist out of its nostrils, the fullness of which enveloped Luca's face. He fell without a word onto to the desert floor.

The dragon moved slowly forward and lowered its head to Daniel's level.

"Are you the Beast who is to come?" asked Daniel. "Are you the one prophesied in my dreams?"

A voice spoke in his head, whispering like sand susurrating on the dunes of the desert. *"There are many shadows, and I am but one. My mouth is fire; my breath is death."*

Daniel could see licks of blue flame around the beast's fanged teeth and he felt the reptilian tongue touch his cheek.

"There are many shadows," said a voice. As Daniel's head cleared, he could see it was the Bedouin, his black robes flowing in the wind, as he rode this monstrous dragon. The Bedouin stretched out a gloved hand and said, "Give me the ring. It's all you have to do. It's all I want. It's all he wants."

"Who wants it?" said Daniel. "And why? There are others. How will one help your Master?"

The voice in Daniel's mind spoke again, *"Do not question he who guides me. My mouth is fire; my breath is death."* A jet of flame shot from the dragon's mouth toward Daniel.

Instinctively, Daniel threw up his right hand, already fluorescing blue, and blocked the flame.

"Cease!" cried the Bedouin to his mount. "I do not want him harmed. Not yet."

He made to dismount, but at that moment, a submachine gun opened fire and blew him off into the sand. Daniel saw Luca trying to get to his feet and the dragon lunging to make short work of his friend. He made a fist with his hand and drove a blue force shield into the animal, throwing it backwards several yards.

"Come on," said Daniel, lurching to his feet and grabbing Luca's arm. "We've got to go. Let's head for the Iraqi camp. Maybe, there's some place to hide."

"Couldn't agree with you more, little buddy," said Luca.

"What? Gilligan's Island?" laughed Daniel crazily, "At a time like this?"

"It could be the last time I pay homage to one of the best shows ever on television."

"Maybe, I should have let the dragon have you," said Daniel.

"Speaking of which," said Luca as they ran, "what was that thing? It was three times the size of that animal the night before."

"Believe it or not," said Daniel, already out of breath running beside Luca, "I think it was Mom—I mean the mother of the *sirrusha*. And it has a name—*Mushussu*. It's the main dragon Marduk tamed to be his servant. It is a seriously badass dragon. You're not going to just be able to blow its head off."

"I have no illusions that I killed our Bedouin either," said Luca. "My hunch is that he is protected somehow. He looked jacked up, on steroids or something, all Arnold Schwarzenegger Terminator type."

"I don't have a clue what we're dealing with," said Daniel, "except while I was unconscious, I had a dream about that comet coming down to earth and bringing death and woe everywhere."

"Do you think the Bedouin and the dragon are it?"

"I don't know. I asked them, but all they said was 'There are many shadows.' I don't even know what the hell that means."

"There's a place," said Luca, pointing ahead. "Maybe we can hide there."

They looked behind but were not followed, yet they knew, without a doubt, that the Bedouin and the dragon would not give up so easily. There was a store slapped together with metal siding and clay walls in the middle of the Iraqi compound. Peering in, they heard a noise, and Luca nearly got his head knocked off by a rifle butt, but Daniel recognized Isaac immediately.

Markoz and Frannie along with Rebecca and someone else could be seen in the gloom. After a brief reunion, Daniel looked at the stranger and said, "I don't think I can deal with anything else new tonight. Who are you?"

"Ranbir Singh," said the voice, "at your service."

"He's a hologram from the computer based at the CIA Antiquities Division," said Rebecca. "We're not quite who we said we were."

"Clearly," said Daniel.

"And that's okay with me. CIA are my kind of people," said Luca. "And look, our very own Obi Wan Kenobi," he said, smiling and hesitantly offering his hand. He was surprised with the firm grip in return.

"More than a hologram," said Luca.

"Indeed," said Ranbir. "I must bid you farewell now. My power source is about to be severely limited, and I want to be at least able to function as an information source. My guess is that the ISIS militants will soon blow all the power to the ruins. I won't be able to siphon any to help you other than in an advisory capacity."

"That's all right, Ranbir," said Rebecca, "your help has been invaluable already."

"We wouldn't be here without you," said Markoz.

Ranbir had already blinked out of existence.

"Geez, I think he was blushing. Just about as useful as Obi Wan Kenobi," muttered Luca.

"We've got very little time," said Rebecca. "I think Farouk's men have been defeated or are in retreat. Abu and his ISIS goons will find us here for sure."

"They'll want Daniel," said Luca. "He's the one with the ring, and it seems that everyone wants that tonight. But they'll have to fight to get it. The Bedouin is back, mounted on the Babylon version of a dragon so big that it makes the *sirrush* we saw the other night look like a puppy dog. And this is the spooky Bedouin by the way, with all his little bag of tricks and creepy crawly things."

"We're not alone," said Daniel. "I left the Temple of Marduk, because our three visitors left it as well. They say they're human, but they can do things most humans can't, probably because they wear rings similar to what I have. They kind of evaporated on me and zipped through the ceiling to reconnoiter what's going on throughout the ruins. My guess is that they will care less about ISIS and concentrate on the Bedouin. If he comes back, we're going to need their help."

MYTH AND TERROR WAGE WAR

Sunday Evening, 2/27, Babylon

AS THEY WERE talking, screams broke out in the distance.

"Maybe ISIS didn't win the battle," said Isaac.

"Or," said Luca, "something else came for them, a something else out of their worst nightmares." Just then the lights went out.

All of them left the Iraqi store and crept out to get a view of what was happening. The brilliant stars shone down upon them. Few of the ISIS fighters had been killed by the Iraqis. It was clear they were all making their way to the Iraqi compound. But out of the desert, weaving and sliding came the *sirrusha*. Lots of them.

They gave not a thought to Daniel and his friends but headed straight for the militants who knelt and started firing immediately. Some of the reptilian things went down, mortally wounded, but there were many, and they quickly overwhelmed the fighters. It was a slaughterhouse. The *sirrusha* made no noise. Daniel saw puffs of mist and blue flame around their nostrils and mouths and knew some deadly poison was taking down the soldiers before they were dispatched by tooth and claw. He was so entranced watching the massacre that he didn't hear the man approach him who stuck the point of his knife in his kidney, whispering, "Move, and you'll die."

All of Daniel's companions were similarly accosted and Abu Shadid allowed himself a quiet laugh. "The brave security force. How stupid, allowing itself to be distracted."

Luca berated himself bitterly, but said to Abu, "Of course you're right, but having a front seat to the new Jurassic Park in Babylon is quite the distraction. You really can't blame us."

That's when Abu, who with his five men had come the long way around from the northwest, chanced to look out at the battlefield to watch the rest of his men get slaughtered by the *sirrusha*.

It was the moment Rebecca needed. She pressed her little lapel button and Ranbir blinked into existence. One of Abu's men shot him twice in the chest.

"Ow! Damn that hurts!" said Ranbir as the bullets dropped harmlessly to the ground. "I'll need to talk to Bart to get my programming to make that just a tingling next time." He moved forward and jerked the rifle out of the militant's hands, and punched the man in the face with a rifle butt, knocking him out.

"What is this thing?" said Abu moving to intercept Ranbir.

"Oh dear, Miss Rebecca," said Ranbir flickering, I've exceeded my auxiliary power supply. The avatar winked out.

Luca, Isaac, and Rebecca didn't waste a moment. They turned on their captors. They, too, were armed with ka-bar knives but they had the offensive and killed them immediately.

Daniel was not so lucky. He heard a whisper in his ear, "I told you not to resist," and felt the knife enter his body, piercing his kidney. He screamed. Abu reached down to hack off his ring finger as Luca flew into him, tackling him away from his friend.

The militants holding Markoz and Frannie backed up with their knives at their captives' throats. Abu was no fool. He knew a stacked deck when he saw it. He rolled with Luca's tackle, got up and fled into the darkness. Luca drew his pistol, but rather than shoot the fleeing Abu, turned swiftly and fired, punching two holes in the fore-heads of the fighters holding the archeologists captive.

Markoz and Frannie fell to their knees gasping, but otherwise unharmed. They heard their son moaning and crawled to him. Frannie immediately saw the problem.

"He's grievously wounded. We've got to get him to the infirmary."

Luca looked at her and said, tears streaming down his face, "There's a few things blocking our way."

From out of the skies came a howling wail.

"What else can happen this night?" said Markoz, wiping the sweat off his son's head.

They all looked up and saw three white trails of stardust, and a fourth following—that's how they explained it later—shining in the sky as they dropped toward the earth. Daniel could see that too and wheezed, "Shadrach, Meshach and Abednego—they've come, and so has Grigio."

They stood on the plain between the Center and the Iraqi compound, and they were luminescent in the night. The *sirrusha* who were mauling the bodies of the dead fighters, ripping and tearing with their burning teeth, turned and charged the three. It was not even a close battle. The *sirrusha* were large and their pestilential breath horrible, but to their surprise, the appearance of Grigio shook their concentration. Like an Aussie Shepherd let loose among the cattle, Grigio herded the lizardly things into packs and would neither let them attack or flee. It was a slaughter as the energy from the rings on the three stranger's hands blasted the *sirrusha* apart as Grigio herded them in circles. It was over in minutes.

The three tomb survivors turned toward the compound and seemed to float over the sand.

"Let me see him," said Shadrach and he bent down to lift up Daniel.

"I'm afraid according to the story," said Daniel, "that I'm about to leave you guys again. So sorry about that." He coughed as blood dribbled from his mouth.

"Do not believe that, young friend," said Shadrach. "We have learned the power to heal in our long stasis. You have only recently accepted the reality of what your ring can do. As time goes on, it will mesh with your body and provide even more protection and healing ability. But, for now, you need our help." The three pressed their ring hands into his bleeding wound, and a pulsing blue stopped the hemorrhage. "There," said Shadrach, "already, you should be feeling better."

Daniel felt power stirring within him, and the terrible pain in his back lessening. He heard his mother cry out as he climbed to his feet.

"This is not done yet," said Daniel. "Something else is out there."

Just then, a black knife flew out of the darkness, striking Meshach in the chest. He gave a gasp and fell to the ground as everyone looked out on the plain and saw *Mushussu* moving swiftly toward them, the Bedouin standing on its back readying another knife.

Meshach had already pulled the knife from his chest. Everyone saw the wound close up, almost immediately. He held out his arm and fire burst from his hand. It should have destroyed *Mushussu*, but it simply went around the beast without harming it. "It is warded," cried Meshach. "We will need to get next to her to do her harm."

"Give me the ring!" screamed the Bedouin. *Mushussu* belched blue flame out toward the group, but Abednego and Shadrach blocked it with a shield of their own.

Everyone's eyes were on the hideous sight out on the plain, and the monsters ahead of them, so they didn't see Daniel at first. He was ten feet out in front of them before they noticed, and at the first cry from his father, Daniel waved them silent.

"You want me?" he said to the Bedouin and the beast. "You want my ring? Are you so sure you can touch it, possess it, even carry it to your Master?"

"I think it is more ancient than you, made from the star fire of heaven and given to us for just such a time. You, *Mushussu*, you with the mouth of fire, the breath of death, can you take the ring?"

Daniel approached the huge *sirrush* and watched as it stood up on its hind legs. As it reached the apex of its height, Grigio flew out of the night and tackled the Bedouin, knocking him off his mount. *Mushussu* didn't even notice. It looked to smash the small human into the dust of the earth, but Daniel simply waited. And as the *sirrush* came down to crush him, Daniel held up his arm, ducking under the fanged mouth and sliced the beast's neck with a thin line of blue flame. The head rolled away in the dirt while the body flung itself into the air in its death throws, blood and viscera cast into the night.

The Bedouin screamed his hatred, shook off the dog and was upon Daniel in a second. Daniel immediately knew he was out-matched. He managed a punch in the Bedouin's face, and he dodged away from another knife.

"How many knives does this freak have?" said Daniel to no one in particular. But before he could get stabbed again, he felt the cool-ness of mist in the air, and he was surrounded by lights that envel-oped and protected him. A hand shot out in the dark and grasped the throat of the Bedouin. It pushed him back and away from Daniel. Then Daniel saw one of the strangers—he later figured out it must be Abednego—simply lift the Bedouin into the air and slam him re-peatedly on the ground till he moved and screamed no more.

Daniel ran over to the unmoving body and pulled off his balaclava.

"It's Walid!" he cried.

"I can't believe it," said Markoz running up to the body. "He was with us when we entered the tomb. Why didn't he act then?"

"Because" said Abednego, "he was without his Master's direction; he was without the *sirrusha's* protection; he was a vessel only, and as you can see, alone, he was nothing."

Random fires started by the grenades crackled throughout the archeological camp and the Iraqi compound. Other than that, silence reigned over the grotesque battle field.

All of them looked up at the strangers towering over them.

"Who was the Bedouin's Master?" asked Rebecca.

"An ancient one," said Meshach, "what the people around here might call a *djinn*, a being of incredible, almost godlike power."

"It was Marduk," said Daniel.

"Perhaps," said Abednego, "or something like him. There are many shadows of the Beast."

"You know," said Daniel, "in just a few hours' time, this place is going to be overrun by authorities. You guys can't really hide. What are we going to do with you?"

"We were called to this time and place," said Shadrach, "and here we will stay with you. We have ways of fitting into your culture. We will return to the tomb to prepare, but may I suggest that we leave before authorities arrive. We will still be hard to explain."

"Neither Frannie or I can go," said Markoz. "We have to protect the site and whatever you choose to leave within the tomb itself. Plus, we have to explain the End Times Tablet. The Iraqis were babbling about it before they left, and news of it must be all over Baghdad by now. The press will be coming, a foe more powerful even that ISIS."

Daniel opened his mouth, but Luca said first, "You have to go, Daniel. The pope needs a first-hand report on this."

"Besides," said Rebecca looking at Isaac, "Our boss is in Rome as well. In just a few hours we can all be there to give a report to the two that most need to hear it."

"But Dad," said Daniel, "when you reveal the tablet it's going to shake the entire earth."

"Maybe," said Markoz, "but even bad news can be dealt with. Besides, we really don't know what kind of catastrophe it portends, and we've got time to prepare for it, and we have some new friends to help us."

The three strangers smiled and then rose into the air and made their way across the desert back to the Tomb.

"Yeah," said Luca, "just ordinary 2600-year-old humans."

"We have an hour or so," said Daniel. "We've got to call Tony and Franco and have them get the plane ready. Rebecca and Isaac, you'll fly with us if you can drive us to the Baghdad airport."

"What about all the bodies?" said Isaac.

"Look," said Daniel, "the *sirrusha* are already melting away, just like that one did the other night, same way with *Mama Sirrush*. If I could make a suggestion. Dad, you should call Farouk's superior. They'll have troops here in hours to take away the bodies of combatants. But I would also invite the press, a lot of them, so that you can have this news conference while the Iraqi forces are here. Keep your enemies close."

"I know General Habib," said Markoz, "and he is a friend. I'll call now and see what he can do. Maybe we can make some sense out of all this hell."

"Ok," said Daniel, "a plan then. Let's regroup in an hour at the tomb and see what our strangers have planned."

SLIP-SLIDING AWAY

Sunday Evening, 2/27, Babylon

"I SAW IT all," said Nabil. Abu hurried him past the Center and towards the eastern perimeter of the camp. "Those beasts, that huge one, the Bedouin, and those three whatever they were, shining in the night sky, plus that cursed dog."

Abu said nothing, but his brain was working furiously. Nabil had slipped out of the Iraqi shop and hidden in a nearby shack. Now, thought Abu, the only way to salvage anything from this terrible night was to take the Mahdi back to Farid. The ruins would be crawling with Iraqi soldiers by morning. Maybe Farid could pull a rabbit out of his hat and make the total slaughter of both sides look like a victory for ISIS. Somehow, he doubted it. He knew he should have told Farid of the beasts; he just didn't believe that the terrorist commander would believe him. Nabil might help with that.

"Did you get any video of the battle?" said Abu.

"Not your part," said Nabil, "but I did get video of the *sirrusha* attack on your men."

"Excellent!" said Abu, his voice brightening. He might be able to redeem something from this night.

"I still want that ring that priest has," said Nabil. "It is part of my destiny."

"Apparently," said Abu, "others feel the same as you. We have much to think about, you and I, and some little time to put our story together before we face Farid."

"I am the Mahdi," said Nabil. "He will believe what I tell him."

"You don't know Farid," laughed Abu. "But you will. You will."

SECRETS OF THE TOMB

Sunday Evening, 2/27, Babylon

WHEN THEY WENT back past the Center to get their things from their quarters, they found General Farouk lying in the dust. Despite his terrible wound, when they turned him over, he had a look of peace on his face.

"He was my friend," said Daniel. "I've known him all my life."

"And he died protecting you," said Luca, "as he has always done. Come on, let's get some clean clothes and hop it back to the Esagila. We can't do anything else for him now."

They all reconnoitered at the Esagila at the appointed time and waited till everyone was there to descend into the subterranean Temple of Marduk.

They weren't the first, and it wasn't three spectral giants that they saw. It was the wolf dog, lying on his back, his legs waggling in the air as one of three tall but ordinary men rubbed his belly, laughing.

"You've morphed!" said Daniel. "You're ... you're normal."

"In a manner of speaking," said a man, scholarly looking with wire-rimmed glasses, black hair and beard closely cropped. In fact, all their beards and hair looked stylishly modern.

"Shadrach?" said Daniel.

"In person," smiled the fit-looking professor.

A tall but heavily muscled man with wavy black hair, smiled warmly and said, "Meshach, at your service."

The third just smiled, but he had a runner's build, and they all figured it was Abednego. Daniel noticed that the eyes of their guests were no longer alien-looking, but they were a curious dark grey, though they were normally structured eyes. On each of their ring fingers was a dark blue band.

"How?" asked Daniel. "There's no way you can be simply human."

"Your time," said Shadrach, "is curiously preoccupied with aliens, cryptids, and other mysterious creatures. Humans are the most mysterious, and the mistake that even your modern scientists make is presuming that the humans who came before you were more primitive than you. Each of you should know from your own experience of history that the acquisition of knowledge is not a linear thing, nor is humanity on a straight diagonal line towards perfection."

Turning to Markoz, Shadrach continued, "Within this tomb you will find amazing astronomical discoveries that will keep your scientists busy for years. We have also included the clay tablets containing the entirety of our medical knowledge. And lastly, you will have the historical records of the empire and what came before. There are discoveries there that will surprise you. There are also three small boxes, one belonging to each of us. We shall take those with us, for the knowledge contained therein is not ready for the human race of this time period to discover. Soon, but not yet."

"What of the gold tablet that topped this tomb?" said Markoz.

"Ah, yes," said Abednego, "as you call it, The End Times Tablet. It is an enigma, is it not? Yet, it tells of a terrible evil fast approaching us. We will help you decipher its exact meaning and assist you in protecting your civilization. Make no mistake. It tells of the single most pressing problem facing humanity. What you have experienced here in these past hours is only a thread of its poisonous web."

"You should get moving," said Markoz. "Isaac has agreed to stay on here as bodyguard in case there is more mischief coming our way."

"What about the *sirrusha*?" said Daniel. "Will there be more where they came from?"

Meshach nodded, "A commendable concern, but we have dealt the dark foe a terrible defeat this evening. He will not soon send his creatures into this reality again."

Abednego added, "The *djinn*, Marduk, is still simply testing his power. This was a major setback, and he will have to rethink his strategy."

"Do not be that optimistic," said Shadrach. "The loss of the Bedouin was terrible for him, but he had lost another just two days before. Daniel told me that the Bedouin was a fixer of vehicles, and that he had two brothers. Now he and one brother are dead. We must assume the third is aware of the rift, of Marduk, and the *djinn's* plan. As we do not know of this brother's whereabouts, we must assume that Marduk has a fallback option, though we know not what it is."

Daniel and Luca looked at each other. Daniel swallowed nervously and spoke. "We might have some idea. We still don't know who tried to kill me last week in Rome. Perhaps ..."

"Perhaps," said Luca, "we ought to get home as soon as possible. We'll call the pontiff on the road and caution him of the danger."

GOING HOME

Monday, Early Morning, 2/28, On the Road to Baghdad and Into the Air Towards Rome

THE JOURNEY WAS swift but uneventful. Rebecca drove, exceeding the speed limit every chance she could get. They took the largest SUV they had, but the three strangers, morphed down to size as they were, still were huge. And then, there was the dog. It made for a cramped ride.

Luca was able to connect with the pope and Daniel explained to his uncle in roundabout terms what had happened.

"You might be in danger," he said to Pope Patrick.

"Noted," said the pope, "but I have with me even now four of Luca's friends from the Swiss Guard, guarding me personally. I'll inform them of the danger that seems to have supernatural overtones. Also, tell Rebecca that I foresaw something like this and asked her boss to stay an extra two days. She is still here now and joining me later this morning for a little tour of the Vatican Gardens. She has two Secret Service men with her as well. We will await your arrival and make plans after you arrive."

"Also, Uncle Liam," said Daniel, "my father is going to make public word of the tomb later today. Literally, expect all hell to break loose."

"I'm not surprised," he said, "that tablet is going to cause us many months of pain, particularly if any of the prophecies are true."

"Uncle Liam," said Daniel, looking back at the three strangers, "they think I'm their Daniel, come to life again, and Mom kind of confirmed it in a weird sort of way."

"You've always been a dreamer, Daniel," said the pontiff. "Maybe this is part of your destiny. Get yourself home safely. We'll talk about it then. See you in a few hours."

They drove into the airport without any incident and found their plane, *Sky Pontiff*, ready, fueled and waiting. It took only moments for Luca and Rebecca to stow the weapons and other gear, and for Daniel to make his guests comfortable. He knew the three men couldn't go around with those strange names so he brought up the subject.

"Ooh, Ooh," cried Luca in his best Three Stooges imitation. "We could call them Moe, Larry, and Curly."

It wasn't just the three men that looked at him in silence. Rebecca, Isaac and Daniel just glared at him.

"Or maybe not," said Luca. "Just trying to be helpful."

"It's a topic for another time, then," said Daniel.

"Not bad to wait," said Luca, more seriously. "Normal names for guys who look extraordinary aren't going to make them fit into society any easier."

"True," said Daniel. Turning to the men, he asked them, "Do you understand what we are talking about? We want you to fit in with this culture, but you still look amazingly out of place."

"We do understand," said Shadrach, "and we will endeavor to find a solution."

Just then, Franco popped back into the passenger cabin to let them know they were almost ready to leave. "I still can't believe it, Daniel. Where did you find these guys? I want them for my winter basketball team."

Daniel flashed his most brilliant smile—so did the three men. "I think they might be ready to play in a couple of weeks. Right guys?" The three just kept smiling. It was awkward for a moment, until Daniel remembered to include Grigio. "Got room for a ball boy on the team?" Franco ruffled the dog's ears and said, "Absolutely, but first, let's get you all home."

And without missing a beat, Franco shook the hands of the human guests, patted the dog once again, and officially welcomed them all aboard, going through all the safety checks. Amazingly, though the new guests seemed quite taken with the technology, they showed no surprise at flying.

Apparently, thought Daniel, whatever they had chatted about entombed inside their sarcophagus for millennia, must have included the possibility of flight. Nothing much surprised them. These guys were like sponges, soaking up every new thing they saw.

The flight was smooth, and Daniel even dozed for a while. However, when they were over the Adriatic Sea, not far from the east coast of Italy, an alarm went off in the plane.

Tony, the co-pilot, came over the speaker saying, "We're being painted by some kind of radar. Could be lining us up for a missile shot."

"Missile fired!" shouted Franco.

"Chaff deployed," said Tony more calmly.

They heard what sounded like ripping plastic, presumably the deployed chaff, and seconds later heard a distant explosion. The plane plunged about a hundred feet, leaving all the passengers but the three young men and the dog looking rather pale.

"Ah," said Luca, "this might be the time for your 'advanced human science' to take a hand in our defense."

Shadrach looked at Luca benignly. "Your pilots seem to have things well in hand."

"Fr. Daniel," said Franco on the speaker, "that was indeed a missile, but we evaded it easily. The fact that another hasn't been fired yet tells me that whoever it was simply was testing us. I don't think they expected to knock us down."

"No," said Daniel, "they just wanted us to know that they know we are back home. They'll come for us again, but after we land."

"What have you gotten yourselves into, Fr. Daniel?" asked Tony.

"Trouble," said Daniel. "Lots of it I'm afraid, and I think you're going to have to get used to it. My uncle has more of these jaunts planned."

"Then it will be no problem," said Franco over the loudspeaker. "We are happy to serve, and don't mind danger. Keeps us awake on long trips."

They wasted no time at Fiumicino Airport. The pope had a limo waiting for them, and they made the twenty-minute trip in fifteen. It was still early in the morning, and traffic wasn't heavy.

Arriving at the Vatican, Luca ushered them swiftly onto the palace grounds, and had a contingent of Swiss Guard lead them to the papal quarters.

Daniel was happy they had made it without further incident, but he had a feeling the Swiss Guard were going to be more than pleased that there were ancient walls around the place.

A MEETING OF WORLDS

Monday Morning, 2/28, On a Yacht in the Adriatic Sea

HE HAD LAUNCHED the missile from his fortified yacht off the east coast of Italy. He knew when the plane took off from Baghdad. The transponder one of the corrupt airline officials placed on the plane worked beautifully, so he could track it with ease.

Truly, he didn't want to shoot it down, though if the pilots were stupid enough not to use the plane's defenses then so be it. He would rather take them all, pope, CIA Director, and passengers in one fell swoop.

The blinds on his study's windows were drawn against the rising sun, and the peculiar light it caused in the room kept his face in the dark. Before him sat the Bedouin, the last of his family, really the last of his kind.

"Your brother failed," he said to the Arab. The Bedouin was dressed entirely in black including the balaclava that covered his face.

"I realize that," said the Bedouin in a heavy accent, "but as the oldest, it falls to me to complete the task. Who gave the order that led to my brother's death?"

"Why the one who is in charge," said the man, the humor in his voice revealing that there must have been at least a small smile on his face.

"And who is the one in charge?" said the Bedouin.

"Ah," said the man, "there are many shadows. A shadow is hard to place. It flits here and there, and oftentimes we do not know who it belongs to. Sometimes it belongs to one, and then, by the light of sun, moon or star, it switches places and belongs to another. For you today, the shadow you see before you is the one who is in charge."

"As you wish," said the Bedouin.

"Our mission has changed. The ring is no longer the priority."

"Why is that?" asked the Bedouin.

"We know of four ring bearers," said the man. "They will all be gathered together in the papal apartments later today. It has been determined that killing those who wear the rings and destroying that wretched jewelry would aid our task most precisely."

"But you wanted the power of the ring."

"Yes," said the man, "when we thought there was only one, but now there are as many as six. We need to destroy as many as we can".

He continued, "The rings must be destroyed with those who possess them. Each is a Star Sapphire representing a six-pointed star, but the ring can mask its identity. Destroy any ring you find. As I said, four bearers mean there remain two outstanding. You will be needed for another action to clean up the mess your brother has caused. Now, do you have what you need to accomplish your goal?"

"Just one thing is needed," said the Bedouin.

"Yes," said the man behind the desk. "Let me get it."

He turned in his swivel chair to a credenza on which sat a large terrarium. He thrust his hand down through its top entrance and plucked a wriggling reptile from its comfy home.

He placed it on his desk, and as he released and stroked its long, sinuous neck, the Bedouin saw and sucked in his breath. "It's a *sirrush!*"

"Ah, you know your mythical beasts. Just a baby, I'm afraid, but it is a cute little chimera. I must make more. Yet, small as it is; it is powerful enough for our purposes. You know what they say about a *sirrush* don't you?"

The Bedouin nodded. He had seen the pictures on various re-productions of the Ishtar Gate of Babylon, both in the museum of Baghdad and in museums throughout the world.

"They say," said the Bedouin, "its mouth is fire, its breath is death."

"You want power, hold out your hand," said the man.

The Bedouin did as he was told and the tiny beast puffed out a little mist from its nose as a tiny stream of blue fire ran around its mouth. Then, it bit the hand of the Bedouin.

To his credit, he did not scream. He was, after all, the Bedouin, the last one, the Chosen. But it hurt. As the venom shot up his arm, he felt himself expanding, a feeling of power pervading his being. His awareness was no longer confined to his body. His mind opened and other realities whispered to him, offered him power, agreed to assist him in this task. He looked at his benefactor and sucked in a breath. Even the Bedouin was stunned in horror. He could not see the man's face but behind him, around him, above him and presumably below, writhed shadows that had purpose and power. They whispered to him as well and urged him onward.

"I shall go," said the Bedouin.

"Contact me when you have accomplished what you must do," said the man.

Without another word, the Bedouin left. The man watched him go, then gently lifted the infant *sirrush* up to eye level. "I must make more of you," he said. "You and your kind are extremely helpful." He placed the dragon in the terrarium, tightened his yellow tie and put on his black sport coat. John Nance had many things to do today.

THE VATICAN ATTACK

Monday Noon, 2/28, The Vatican

THE BEDOUIN HEARD the Angelus Bells ring at noon even though he had not a clue what they stood for. There was no rift here in Rome to help him nor adult *sirrush* to accompany him. There was no sadness within him either over the news of the death of his brothers, just a simmering rage that longed for revenge. When the three of them had discovered the rift a year ago, they were smitten by the beauty it revealed and the horror it concealed.

Why the *sirrusha* present at the oasis did not kill them outright, he did not know. He knew some other being walked amid the oasis as well. He could sense it presence, even divine its will, but he did not meet it. He could not believe it when his brother contacted him the week before saying he had met the *djinn* of the oasis and its name was Marduk. Why should the second oldest be given this gift? Yet, the Bedouin did not reveal his true feelings to Walid, his brother, and now he was glad he withheld his anger. For he was the last, the one chosen to complete the task given by the man who perhaps was the *djinn* itself. The Bedouin did not know.

What he did know was that he could walk in the daylight in his outlandish costume without anyone aware that he was present. It was the gift of the *sirrush* and the other realities that enveloped him in their embrace. He drove himself to Rome, which took several hours, parked his auto, and walked the few blocks down the *Via della Conciliazione* towards the Vatican. All the way, he was invisible to the pedestrians around him, his black cloak floating in the wind, merging with the shadows the sun splayed on the ancient stone.

When he reached the Vatican, he felt as if a shadow came over him, a diminishment in his power. He decided it was his superstitious Bedouin imagination playing tricks on him. He knew where the entrance to the palace grounds was, and he strode confidently between Bernini's pillars on the right side of the piazza. He meant for all practical purposes to simply walk past the Swiss Guard on duty at the *Portone di Bronzo*, the Bronze Door.

Such was not to be. The Swiss Guard somehow heard him or saw a shimmer that gave him concern and immediately cried for him to halt. The man was poking his halberd into every crack and corner he could find.

The Bedouin processed this information in seconds. The other realities that enveloped him, shrouded him, hid him from others had slipped and failed him so it seemed, or were testing him. For the moment, all he had was his enhanced strength and size, and the ka-bar knife he brought with him, which he used to immediately slice the neck of the Guard who collapsed without a sound.

He had to hurry. This was not a secret entrance, though few tourists ever traveled through it. He threw open the door with new found strength and killed the Swiss Guard in the interior corridor. He swept past the ticket office and proceeded into the Vatican proper. He needed a place to plan, so he mounted the side of the ancient observatory housing the Tower of Winds and impossibly climbed the vertical wall. Ah, he thought, the powers that be were simply testing before. A small clear window met his gaze and he smashed it without

anyone hearing or seeing him and he was in. Apparently, he was able
to glamor the window enough so no one would notice it was broken.

He went to the Meridian Room where the frescoes showed the
same Calming of the Sea by Christ and the Shipwreck of St. Paul that
the pope and Daniel had talked beneath the week before. He had
never seen these paintings and stopped for a minute to look. The
shadows on the water and the dark waves stood for the chaos of the
world that threatened to overwhelm the disciples with Christ and had
nearly cost St. Paul his life. The Bedouin, obviously, was not of the
Christian faith, but he felt touched by the chaos he saw in the scenes.
He wondered if the one standing in the boat managed to quell the
waves, or the man being cast overboard in the other painting ever
reached the land. He doubted it, for chaos and the night held sway, as
this bastion of the infidel faith was soon to find out.

He sat on the floor to catch his bearings and plotted how he
would get to the papal apartments, which admittedly were not far
away. He decided on the direct approach.

He climbed out the window he had entered before, sure that he
was high enough that he would disappear into the landscape once
again. No Swiss Guard were near. On the roof, on the exterior wall, it
did not matter to him. He made his way patiently to the papal apartments, a shadow in the sun, flitting over ancient walls and roofs.

THE VICAR OF CHRIST

Monday Noon, 2/28, Papal Apartments, Vatican City

LESLIE RICHARDSON, HEAD of the CIA, had received two phone calls of import in the past twenty-four hours. The first was from the pope suggesting she stay on a few days. He wanted to give her a private tour of the Vatican Gardens while they waited for news from Babylon. The pope was sure that Markoz would go public with the news of the End Times Tablet soon. Next, she got a call from Rebecca just a few hours ago, apprising her of all that had happened in what her contact called the Battle of Babylon. She could hardly process the implications, but when she arrived and was escorted into the papal apartments, the pope immediately confirmed what she had heard from Rebecca.

"I'm sorry we have to meet here," said the pope.

Leslie smiled. She had been easily lulled the day before by the homespun familiarity the pontiff had. She said, "I'll behave myself. There won't be a breath of scandal."

The pope laughed loudly and said, "No, I mean these apartments are so uncomfortable. No wonder Pope Francis moved into Santa Marta—that's the Vatican hotel just inside the walls where the clergy stay when they come and visit."

"Why did you move back here?" she asked. "Missed the pomp and ceremony?"

"Not really," he said candidly. "I knew I would embark on brand new activities for the See of Peter, and I needed more isolation, more secrecy as it were. The hermit of the Vatican needs his privacy.

"I really do want to give you the grand tour of my garden and the rest of my little nation, but that's not really why I asked you to delay your return. Your country and my Church will soon face a restive world—an explosive situation which will cause great upheaval."

He continued, "Have you had the chance to study the contents of the tablet?"

"I've read it, and your nephew's new translation," said Leslie, "and of course I forwarded a copy to Bart Finch, my computer genius. He's run it through the computer and had the document compared to others like it down through the years. Obviously, it is unique. The English date makes it so. It is standard apocalyptic language, he said, just way more precise than most of the end of the world prophecies are. He finds no hidden messages or symbolic clues. That's the other unique thing. He tells me apocalypses are often so symbolic that they become confusing because they can be matched to any date or historical event. This tablet is different. It refers to a very specific event."

"That's my assessment, too," said the pontiff. "We've got a date for the end of the world, and everybody is going to want to know what to do about it."

There was a formal knock on the door of the apartments. The double doors opened and two Swiss Guard led in the archeological team along with Grigio. Daniel walked over to his uncle and hugged the pope tightly. He whispered, "It was truly terrible. We are in deep trouble."

The Swiss Guard left and shut the doors, but Luca stepped forward, saluted the pope with the three fingered Trinitarian salute and said, "I have returned your nephew safe and sound, as you asked. His activities were beyond reproach and his heroism must be mentioned. We have faced what no one has faced before."

The pope smiled, "Well done, Luca. My nephew told me of your actions in this matter, and I have already discussed with Colonel Minitti that you deserve a promotion. He agrees, so I raise you to the rank of Captain."

"Thank you, Your Holiness," said Luca saluting once again. "I do not deserve the honor."

"Well, you will certainly earn it because the Vatican is putting together a group similar to the one the CIA has formed, and someone has to be in charge of security. It's as good a time as any for me to introduce to you Leslie Richardson, Director of the CIA. And you must be Rebecca Perez," said the pope. "From what I've heard, you were spectacular these past few days, and if I were you, I'd ask for a raise." The pope's eyes twinkled and Rebecca couldn't help but beam.

"Now," said the pontiff, "let us have a look at our guests of honor." Dressed in his white cassock with the matching zucchetto on his head, he was as imposing as the three men. He grasped their hands warmly and said, "I am Pope Patrick, which most likely means nothing to you, but we will discuss that later. Much more importantly, out of myth, out of history, out of time, into our present you come. You bear ancient names of great power and dignity and you claim my nephew as one of your own.

"Much needs to be revealed, but all that can wait. Both Leslie and I are current with the information you have given my nephew, so the paramount factor operating now is dealing with what will be a certain attack on the Vatican and upon us. Even our meeting here is fraught with danger. We should not be together, not while this *djinn* or whatever is looking for us."

At that moment, the double palatial window, used by the Pope for some of his blessings over St. Peter Square burst inward, showering them with glass, and the Bedouin swept in, landing in front of the three strangers.

"We killed you," said Daniel, amazed that the black-robed specter was among them once again.

"Was it you who killed my brother?" said the Bedouin leveling his piercing black-eyed gaze upon Daniel. "Was it you priest?"

"Yes, I had a hand in the killing, and I'd do it again. He was evil and murdered so many. I have friends that lie dead in the sands of Babylon because of what he did."

The hands of the three men from the tomb began to luminesce blue around their rings, but before they could activate them, the Bedouin had taken out three black knives and thrown them at the hearts of each of them. He was deadly accurate, but though they gasped, they ripped the knives from their chests and surged forward. They never reached the Bedouin. They suddenly stopped with a rictus of pain on their faces and collapsed.

Leslie was already on her feet, and had pulled her Ruger out and was firing at the Bedouin to no effect, but Daniel had time to use his ring to blast a force field at the Bedouin sending him back out the window—almost. His hand caught the sill, and in a feat of superhuman strength, he lifted himself up and hurled himself back into the room.

Rebecca and Luca were firing their sidearms as well, but like some macabre imitation of Superman, the Bedouin just stood there absorbing the ammo. For a moment, all became silent, and then the Bedouin started laughing. He pulled out a Mark 21 stackable offensive grenade, pulled the pin and dropped the shell onto the floor, vaulting out the window and up onto the roof. Three smaller grenades were stacked together. Within the ornate room, the explosion would pulverize everything to marble dust.

It was then that Grigio roared into action. He ran to the grenade, grabbed it in his mouth and leapt out the window. In just moments a terrible explosion occurred outside, shattering the rest of the window, sending glass and shrapnel from the marble window sill over the pope and the rest of his guests. Daniel ran to the window and looked for the dog, but nothing could be seen of him. He screamed his rage into the square. The explosion, and the fact that the papal apartments seemed to be occupied, turned the visitors in the Square into a roiling mob as they incorrectly assumed the pope had been slain.

The pontiff pulled Daniel back inside and said, "Listen, your three friends are grievously hurt and we must save them."

"How can that be?" said Daniel. "They should be able to easily heal themselves. They've done it before."

The Pope said, "The Bedouin and our enemy have learned from last night. The knives that struck them down are most likely poisoned, and your friends are having difficulty diffusing the toxin. You will have to use your ring to help heal them as you once healed your own mother. We need them in perfect health in case this is just the first phase of the attack."

"I don't know how," said Daniel. "That was so long ago, and their wounds are so great." He looked at all the blood running from their ruined chests. The Bedouin must have indeed used a special poison on them to further incapacitate the three men. They were not moving.

"I will help you, Dani," said the pope.

"How? We have only one ring and theirs won't come off their hands."

"How do you think we all weren't killed by the force of the blast and the shrapnel that followed?" The pope held up his right hand. The usual papal ring was gone, and on his ring finger was a Star Sapphire. "I found it in the archives after I was elected. It must have been there for ages. It just fell out of an ancient wood box next to a book I was looking at. I think it wanted to be found. The book I was looking at was some of the lost sermons of St. Anthony of Padua, the Wonder Worker. I think he possessed this ring at one time, for he was known as a great healer. There's a sermon in the book that tells how to heal, so let's try it shall we. The ring worked fine to protect us all from the blast. Shadrach, Meshach and Abednego, deserve to live in our time. They have waited so long."

"How do we do it?" said Daniel.

"Empower your ring, as I will mine," said the Pope. That Daniel knew how to do. He only had to think of the Star Sapphire in its original form.

"Now, take your hand, and with mine, press on the wounds. We both must empty our minds of all that is dark and shadowed and fill it with the light of Christ. The rings will respond."

And they did. But it was not pleasant. Mixed in with the incredible amount of blood was the taint of *sirrush* venom. Daniel paled as he willed himself to be one with the ring. Here, in the holiest place on earth, the Beast still managed to extend its killing hand.

As the pope and Daniel pressed on the wounds, each of the three young men's rings linked with the pope's and Daniel's. The flow of blood stopped, the wounds sealed, and each of the men sucked in a deep breath. It was a mess, but they were alive.

Leslie Richardson and the others had never seen such a thing and though she wasn't a believer, there was a little more room in her heart for wonder than before.

Luca and Rebecca ran to the pontiff. Luca said, "We have to get you out of here. No telling what might be coming next."

"I think it's over," said the pope, "but I understand."

The doors slammed open again, and several Swiss Guard as well as Leslie's bodyguards rushed in. The room was in ruins, and with the amount of blood, they thought surely the Pontiff or his guests were dead. Seeing that everyone was alright, they hustled all of them out of papal apartments and down to a more secure part of the building. The sounds of ambulances and fire sirens pierced the Roman traffic as word began to spread of the terrorist attack on the Vatican and the attempt on the life of Pope Patrick.

EPILOGUE

Monday Late Afternoon, 2/28, Babylon and Rome

MARKOZ AND FRANNIE were ready. The Iraqi army had come in the morning and cleared away the bodies of ISIS and Iraqi troops. General Habib, also a friend of Markoz, restored order almost immediately. The returning Iraqi workers soon followed and with them came the curious press. Markoz had put out word that he was holding a press conference concerning a new find in Babylon.

He thought it best to give a call to the pope, since what he was going to say would require the pope to address the Church. He'd leave it up to the pontiff to inform other governments. He placed the call and smiled when he heard the voice of his friend.

"Your Holiness, Liam my friend, you wouldn't believe what we've gone through here, although if Daniel has told you anything, remember he exaggerates."

The pope laughed and filled him in on everything that had gone down in the Vatican. The terrorist attack and the attempt on his life hadn't fazed him much. Markoz had toughened him up over the years when they were on digs together.

"I think my news will put you as the second story," said Markoz. "Frannie and I have been talking and I think we will just present the

End Times Tablet as is with a little historical background and leave the astronomers and world leaders like yourself to puzzle the rest out. I want to tell everyone of what else we found in the tomb. I was able just to glance at some of the clay tablets, and the amount of new information, astronomical, medical, and historical is astounding. It will rewrite the importance of the Fertile Crescent and push our knowledge of humanity back thousands of years. I will mention that, too, today, but no one will remember it. The world will go crazy, but people have to know about this. There will be a catastrophe of some kind on November 1, and we must be prepared,"

"I agree," said the pope, "and that's why I'm taking your son and making him the head of group that will operate out of the Vatican Archives. The group will be called *VERITAS*—Truth. It will deal with these types of occurrences, find out what they mean, and see what else we can learn in the limited time we have. The President of the United States has empowered the Antiquities Division of the CIA to help in this endeavor. Together, we will try to make sure that the Light prevails, not the dark. We have won a major strategic battle in the past few days. The rings are weapons of wonder, and the three young men you found alive in that tomb have come specially to help us. That gives me great hope. So, let's get to work Markoz. Make your discovery known, and let's do what we can to save humanity."

***

After the CIA contingent had left for the airport and the three young men had been given quarters recently built in the Vatican Archives for the new group *VERITAS,* Daniel and Luca walked down the *Via della Conciliazione* in a terribly dispirited mood.

"I couldn't find any evidence of his body," said Daniel. "Of course, we couldn't find the body of the Bedouin either. But why do I think that evil bastard is alive and faithful Grigio is dead?"

"I miss him, too," said Luca. "I know I kidded both you and him incessantly, but he was the best."

They had reached the Tiber River and sat on a bench watching the river placidly move through the city as it had done for thousands of years. Daniel's left arm was draped behind his shoulder when, suddenly, he felt something cold and wet.

"Luca," he whispered, "we've got company."

Both turned at the same time and laughed. There was Grigio, smiling at them as always.

"Oops," said Daniel, putting his face on the neck of the dog, "my eyes are springing water."

"Ah, I'm thinking that's okay at this point," said Luca.

All three were silent for a few moments, and then Daniel said, "What, nothing profound to say at a time like this?"

"Well, yes," said Luca, "as a matter of fact I do. Remember that show about the Canadian Mountie and his dog?" And then, in his best Sergeant Preston of the Yukon voice, he put his arm around Grigio and said, "Well, Grigio, this case is closed."

The End

FROM THE AUTHOR

My friends,

I hope you enjoyed this first novel in the new series called THE VATICAN ARCHIVES. You'll be hearing about more adventures that involve Fr. Daniel Azar and his best friend, the Swiss Guard Luca Rohner. These new stories take place in the Conorverse—that world inhabited by Conor Archer and his friends. Conor Archer is the protagonist of two, soon to be three, urban fantasy novels. Someday, these stories will intersect. And now, you are a part of that family as well. We are a tight knit group of people looking for adventures that ennoble and celebrate humanity.

THE TALES OF CONOR ARCHER
by E. R. Barr
ROAN

SKELLIG
(both available from Internet bookstores)

DRIFTLESS
(coming 2022)

Series, like THE VATICAN ARCHIVES and THE TALES OF CONOR ARCHER, depend on the support of readers like you. One of the ways to guarantee more stories like these is to leave a book review on the Amazon or Barnes and Noble websites. If you enjoyed *GODS IN THE RUINS*, please take a moment and write a review. It's the best way you can thank an author.

E. R. Barr

ABOUT THE AUTHOR

E. R. Barr spent his youth wandering around "Conor Country" known better as the "Driftless Area" of the southwest corner of the state of Wisconsin. The Mississippi and Wisconsin Rivers and the lands around them, dotted with Indian mounds and filled with stories and legends, fueled his imagination. Not till he started traveling world-wide did he truly begin to see connections between Ireland, Scotland, Wales and the lands where he was born. His forebears came from those ancient nations and settled there in Wisconsin. Always wondering why, he kept searching for answers. A Catholic Priest, a university professor, high school teacher and administrator, a popular speaker on all things Celtic and Tolkienesque, E. R. Barr makes his home in northwest Illinois. He is the author of the urban fantasy series, THE TALES OF CONOR ARCHER including the novels *ROAN* and *SKELLIG*. This is his third novel. Find out more about him and Conor's world by checking out the following website:

www.talesofconorarcher.com

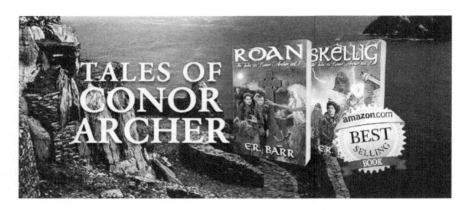

Coming Early 2022
A VATICAN ARCHIVES THRILLER
BENEATH BISHOP'S BONES
by E. R. Barr

What could rest in Canterbury Cathedral that might save or doom the world? Join Fr. Daniel Azar, his friend, Captain Luca Rohner, and the Vatican Group VERITAS as they race against an international foe to discover a treasure that could prevent a world catastrophe.

Printed in Great Britain
by Amazon

26727151R00199